Praise for the n

"Well-developed characte
this gripping novel. This lat
should not be missing from your reading pile."
　　　—*Library Journal* (starred review) on *Missing Daughter*

"Rick Mofina's books are edge-of-your-seat thrilling.
Page turners that don't let up."
　　　—Louise Penny, #1 *New York Times* bestselling author

"A pulse-pounding nail-biter."
　　　　　　　　　　　—*The Big Thrill* on *Last Seen*

"*Six Seconds* should be Rick Mofina's breakout thriller. It
moves like a tornado."
　　　—James Patterson, *New York Times* bestselling author

"*Six Seconds* is a great read. Rening Ludlum and
Forsythe, author Mofina has penned a big, solid
international thriller that grabs your gut—and your heart—
in the opening scenes and never lets go."
　　　—Jeffery Deaver, *New York Times* bestselling author

"*The Panic Zone* is a headlong rush toward Armageddon.
Its brisk pace and tight focus remind me of early
Michael Crichton."
　　　—Dean Koontz, #1 *New York Times* bestselling author

"Rick Mofina's tense, taut writing makes every thriller he
writes an adrenaline-packed ride."
　　　—*New York Times* bestselling author Tess Gerritsen

"Mofina's clipped prose reads like short bursts of gunfire."
　　　　　　　　　—*Publishers Weekly* on *No Way Back*

"Mofina is one of the best thriller writers in the business."
　　　—*Library Journal* (starred review) on *They Disappeared*

"*Vengeance Road* is a thriller with no speed limit! It's a great
read!"
　　　—Michael Connelly, *New York Times* bestselling author

RICK
MOFINA

THE
LYING
HOUSE

mira

mira

ISBN-13: 978-0-7783-0888-1

Recycling programs for this product may not exist in your area.

The Lying House

Copyright © 2019 by Highway Nine, Inc.

This book is for Barbara

THE
LYING
HOUSE

Can there be such a thing as a white lie, a little lie?
The lie is absolute evil. There can be no small lie;
who lies, lies wholly.
—*Les Misérables*,
Victor Hugo

1

Lisa Taylor clawed through the torpid fog between sleep and consciousness, unease pinging in a corner of her mind.

What was that noise? Is someone in the house?

But by the time she'd blinked awake, she heard nothing in the stillness of her bedroom but soft, rhythmic snoring. She turned to her husband, Jeff, the obvious culprit.

She nudged him.

He shifted, grunted into silence but was still out.

Lisa closed her eyes and tried floating back to sleep, but it was futile. Jeff had resumed snoring. She fought the impulse to take a sleeping pill—a bad habit she was trying to break. The digital clock on her night table displayed 2:13 a.m.

She could wake Jeff, but he was exhausted. Sometimes he got up in the night to work in his office while she slept. So much had changed for them in the past weeks: Jeff's big promotion and its accompanying pressure to perform, their whirlwind move, leaving her job and everyone in Cleveland. The company had wasted no time getting him rolling on a major project that involved leading a big presentation tomorrow.

Let him sleep.

Lisa propped against two pillows, reached for her book, clipped on her book light and returned to Raskolnikov's psychological torment in *Crime and Punishment*. After a few pages her concentration shifted back to her own life.

Was this sudden move to Florida going to work out? She'd given up a great position and people she loved back in Ohio.

"Florida is where we'll start the next chapter, *the best chapter*, of our lives," Jeff had told her, implying that they would start a family here, something he, being ambitious and so driven to succeed, had always put off whenever she'd raised it. Still, Lisa had always envisioned that they would have children in Cleveland.

So much for the best-laid plans.

But now that she was thirty-four with her clock ticking, and having sacrificed her career for his, she expected motherhood as promised. She looked at Jeff, her hardworking snore machine.

You'd better be on board to make some babies, buddy.

Through the dim light, Lisa saw the unpacked boxes in the corner and sighed. It had been a little over three weeks since they'd taken possession of their house and they were still settling in. She was awed at the price of their huge new Spanish-style home, way more than what they'd paid for their little brick colonial in Shaker Heights. It was such a financial stretch for them.

And their new neighborhood of Palm Mirage Creek, slivered between Coral Gables and Coral Terrace, had to be one of the most beautiful in the entire country. Great weather, little crime, close to top-ranked schools—a good place to raise a family.

Now wide-awake, Lisa put her book down to get a drink of water from the fridge downstairs.

Her phone and Jeff's were charging on their night tables. Lisa took hers, pulled on her robe over her wispy nightgown, stepped from the bedroom and switched on the hall light. She checked her phone. No new messages.

Downstairs she turned on more lights and for a moment stood in disbelief that this house was really theirs. She was thankful that Jeff's corporation had covered most of the moving expenses—rare in his profession these days—to transfer them from the Cleveland office to the larger Miami office. His higher salary had picked up the rest of the costs.

But they still carried a lot of debt, and it made Jeff nervous that she was now earning less, even though she believed that with his increase in pay they could get it down in a few years.

On the main floor, she moved through the living room with its vaulted ceiling, the oak coffee table and the lamps. The sofa looked so old here; they really needed a new one. She paused for a moment, then walked across the tiled floor of the grand foyer and, to be safe, tested the front door.

It was locked.

All the front windows were secure.

Lisa switched on more lights, went through the kitchen with its granite countertops, gleaming stainless-steel appliances, the oversize island and walk-in pantry. The kitchen door to the side entrance and double garage was secure, too.

So were all the rear windows.

For good measure, she checked the pantry—nothing but unopened boxes from the move.

She got a glass of cold water from the fridge, feeling its icy tentacles soothing her dry throat, cooling her stomach. Satisfied, she started back to bed when she heard a faint noise and stopped.

What was that?

Holding her breath, she strained to listen. Feeling vulnerable, she considered a weapon—a bat, a cleaver, something. No guns were in the house; she and Jeff had an aversion to them.

She heard nothing more.

Lisa wished their system were in place. The company Jeff had hired was booked up and coming to install it next week. Maybe she'd ask him to call them in the morning, request they speed things up.

Calm down. All the doors and windows are locked.

She reasoned that she was still getting acquainted with their new home. The sounds could be the air-conditioning system, the hot-water tank, or even coming from outside—something to do with the pool, or a passing plane. How far were they from Miami Airport?

It could be a million things.

I'm sure it's nothing.

On her way from the kitchen, she checked the main-floor bathroom. No one was there. Walking along the hall, she heard a sound again. It was coming from the air duct.

That's it. The air-conditioning system likely needs a tune-up.

She sighed with relief.

Before returning to bed, she took in the great room, her favorite. She loved how it offered indoor–outdoor living space divided by a sliding glass, floor-to-ceiling door. It opened to their covered porch and in-ground pool in the backyard. The pool's underwater night-lights made it look so serene, tranquil, inviting. On a whim, she wanted to dip her hand in the water. Maybe to confirm the pool was really theirs. She reached for the sliding door's handle and caught her breath.

A tiny seam separated the door from the frame.

The door was unlocked.

I know I checked this door before I went to bed, and it was locked.

When she tried to lock it, it wouldn't click shut, and something rattled. She pushed it open, stepped outside. The locking mechanism had been eviscerated. Nothing remained but torn and twisted metal.

Someone's broken into our house!

Heart pounding, Lisa rushed back inside, heading for the stairs.

"Jeff!"

Hands shaking, she raised her phone, her fingers trembling as she trotted, pressing nine, then one, before a shadow swept over her.

Jeff Taylor's mind swam in a semidream state, taking him back through time to one of his first days in a new grade school. He wore donated clothes: pants that were too big, a shirt still bearing a faded mustard stain. He'd come so far since those days. He'd battled shame, then pulled himself up, working nonstop and getting loans to put himself through college, vowing to do whatever it took so he would never, ever go back to having nothing again.

Never.

That's how he'd earned his way in the world, how he got his job, won the promotion and the move to Miami. Tomorrow morning he would lead the presentation to the South American group. So much was riding on it, the pressure so intense—

Jeff stirred awake.

Wait, was that Lisa?

He opened his eyes, sitting up. She wasn't in bed. The bathroom lights were off, the bedroom door was open, the hall light—

Lisa called for him.

He shot from bed, flew down the stairs to the main floor and stopped dead in his tracks.

Lisa's phone, its screen fractured, lay on the floor.

Jeff moved into the next room, not believing his eyes.

A man held Lisa, her back locked to his chest, his gloved hand grappling her mouth. Jeff charged at them before a glint of steel flashed—a knife pressed against Lisa's throat.

"Don't move! I will cut her!"

Dressed in black, his face covered with a balaclava, the man's eyes burned through him. Jeff stopped, held up his palms.

"Please, don't hurt her."

The man kept one arm pressed against Lisa's chest and began moving, lifting her, her toes brushing the floor as he hauled her toward the open sliding-glass door. Lisa's eyes ballooned with terror, struggling in vain as he got closer to the door.

In an instant Jeff saw the doors of the hallway storage closet yawning open to a landslide of unpacked boxes, deducing the intruder had hidden there. He eyed Lisa's phone some distance away on the floor. So did the intruder, who was now at the door with Lisa.

"Don't even think about it—I will stick her so fast!"

"Let her go, please!"

The intruder halted at the door, then ran his free hand over Lisa's breasts, squeezing, and forced his masked face against hers while glaring at Jeff. Lisa fought, but he pushed the blade harder to her neck, his hand slithering down past her belly and grabbing her.

Then he dragged her into the darkness, leaving Jeff paralyzed as her screams escaped, echoing in the night.

2

The world stood still.

A lifetime passed in a heartbeat before Jeff rushed through the open door.

"Lisa!"

The blood rush hammered in his ears as he searched the blackness, scouring the pool, the shrubs, the fencing. He switched on the exterior lights. He couldn't find his wife.

"Lisa!"

"H-here, I'm here."

Crouched against a pool chair, she was hugging herself and shaking. Jeff flew to her, held her to keep her from coming apart. As she sobbed in his arms, he scanned their yard.

The intruder had vanished.

Breathing hard, Jeff battled to comprehend what had just happened, praying to God that it was over.

Sirens wailed.

Within ten minutes of Jeff's call to 9-1-1, the first police units arrived. Others followed. Emergency lights splashed red and blue on the homes nearby as events unfolded in a surreal haze.

Adrenaline continued coursing through Jeff's body. Clutching her robe, Lisa couldn't stop trembling as the sky thudded. A Miami-Dade PD helicopter was circling overhead hunting for the suspect, its blinding searchlight probing the surrounding rooftops, yards and streets.

The first responding officers separated them. Hawkins, a woman, talked to Lisa in the living room, asking if there were firearms in the house and if Lisa was injured.

"Not physically, but he—" Lisa, her voice wavering, brushed at tears and touched parts of her body to describe the attack.

Ramon, a male officer, took Jeff into the kitchen, taking down his description of the suspect and details of the incident in his notebook. Ramon paused to speak into the shoulder microphone of his portable radio. It crackled with cross talk. A moment later, a dog barked, and another cop, this one named Brenner, arrived with a German shepherd on a leash.

Brenner huddled with Ramon and Hawkins before they approached Lisa.

"Mrs. Taylor," Brenner started, "I hate to ask this, but my partner, Sable, needs the suspect's scent. It would help us if you could allow her to get it from you."

"I don't understand," Lisa said. "I told the officer where he climbed over the fence and the direction he ran."

"Yes, but it would help if Sable could smell where the suspect's body touched yours."

"Mrs. Taylor," Hawkins said gently, "we need you to remove your robe for the dog."

Lisa looked at the officers and then at Jeff whose expression urged her to cooperate. She swallowed, her face reddened, then she removed her robe, allowing the dog to smell the front and back of her nightgown. The dog then led Brenner outside and over the fence on the attacker's trail. Lisa put her robe back on and pulled it closed.

The officers resumed working with Jeff and Lisa on their preliminary statements. Then they walked them through the house for a quick check to see if anything was missing, all while more emergency units arrived. When Hawkins finished, she wanted the medical team that had arrived to examine Lisa.

"We need to be sure about what he did to you."

"He didn't rape me," she said. "I already told you what happened."

"I know, but we need to check for any trace evidence to use if we arrest him."

"I told you what he said after he took me outside. Please, you have to arrest him."

"We will."

Two paramedics with a trauma kit took Lisa to her bedroom and closed the door. They made a careful assessment of her before concluding that, while she'd sustained no visible physical injuries, she was experiencing mild shock.

Jeff went with Ramon who, along with other investigators, examined the damaged locking mechanism on the sliding door where the intruder had entered their home.

"You don't have a security system?" Ramon said to Jeff.

"We just moved in. They're coming next week to install it."

"Did you have a system for your previous home? Some companies will let you relocate your service."

"No, we had no system there."

"Place like this, I would think you'd make security a priority."

"Yeah, well." Embarrassed, Jeff watched the chopper probing the area. "We were told that this neighborhood has a low crime rate, so I didn't rush it."

"Low crime is not *no crime*. Just about everybody in Palm Mirage has a home system," Ramon said. "Do you or your wife possess any firearms?"

"No. We don't like guns," Jeff said. "When I was a boy, my father was—" he swallowed "—killed in a hunting accident with his friend."

Jeff and Ramon moved to the living room, where the officer responded to calls on his radio, then continued speaking with Jeff. "We're putting out a description of the suspect and details of the incident on the neighborhood-watch alert network. It'll go out in texts, calls, emails, online alerts to get extra eyes in the surrounding area looking for the guy."

"Good."

When the paramedics were done, Ramon and Hawkins then had Lisa and Jeff conduct a quick re-enactment of what happened, with Hawkins making a video recording. Lisa couldn't stop her tears. Every step was excruciating, but they forced their way through it.

Afterward, they returned to the living room, and Jeff's attention went to the front window. Amid the flashing lights outside, another cop unreeled yellow police tape, cordoning off his property. Beyond the tape, Jeff saw people on the sidewalk, some wearing T-shirts and sweatpants, others in housecoats. Some were taking pictures with their phones or cupping hands to their faces. The tape bowed upward as a man and a woman ducked under it and approached the door.

"The detectives are here," Ramon said. "They'll take over."

Jeff dragged both hands over his face.

And to think, he'd just been marveling at how far he'd come in life, how hard he'd worked and how fortunate he was. Now his wife had been assaulted, his home was a crime scene and, in some part of his gut, he felt the dawning of a distant fear.

Could this be my fault?

3

"Mr. and Mrs. Taylor, I'm Detective Camila Cruz. This is Detective Joe Reddick."

Cruz was in her midthirties. Her brown hair, parted on the side, touched the shoulders of her blazer, which was open to provide a glimpse of the badge clipped to her belt and her holstered side-arm. She shifted the small zippered binder she held to shake hands with Jeff and Lisa.

A firm, confident grip signaled that Cruz was alert and primed.

Reddick was taller, about six feet of solid build under his polo shirt and khakis. He looked haggard, his stubbled face creased from seeing too much of what a case-hardened cop sees. His thinning dark hair was tousled, his goatee flecked with gray. Intense eyes, strong handshake.

"Before we get started, you'll have to excuse us." Cruz nodded to the investigators at the sliding door in the great room and unzipped her binder. "We need to consult with the officers who first responded."

The detectives huddled where the crime-scene tech was examining the damage. Talking in soft tones, taking notes and pictures, they occasionally glanced at Jeff and Lisa, who, out of earshot, watched from the living room. Desperate to restore order, Lisa found a degree of composure in the sudden need to be a hostess. She went to them, offering to make coffee.

"No thank you, ma'am. That won't be necessary." Reddick smiled. "We don't want you to disturb or touch anything. If you'll just wait where you were, we won't be long."

Jeff slid his arm around Lisa's waist. He could feel her trembling as more crime-scene people arrived. Taking direction from the others, they started working throughout the house, concentrating on the path of the attack. They took photographs, video recordings and brushed fingerprint powder everywhere.

Cruz took a moment to explain. "Our techs are going to focus on the areas where you saw the suspect," she said. "They'll look for prints, for anything he may have touched or left behind. We'll also collect your fingerprints, for a set of elimination prints."

Some fifteen minutes later, Cruz and Reddick finished their consultations, and one of the crime techs, a guy who looked to be in his early twenties, used a device resembling a laptop to laser-scan Jeff's and Lisa's fingerprints into their system. Then, like the officers had earlier, the detectives separated Jeff and Lisa. While the crime techs processed the house, Reddick interviewed Jeff in the living room. Cruz took Lisa upstairs to one of the empty bedrooms, directing her to a comfortable chair. Cruz sat across from her on a wooden chair, listening, taking notes and checking her recorder while Lisa detailed the incident.

"Before he let me go and ran off, he said, 'I know everything about you. I'll be watching you. I'm going to come back and'—" Lisa put both hands over her mouth, stifling a sob "—'and fuck you.'"

Cruz touched her shoulder. "I'm not trying to diminish any part of what you're going through, or suggest you let your guard down," the detective said, "but often these guys are cowards, more frightened than you, and say things to torment and scare you."

"You have to find him."

"Did you get a look at his face or his eyes?"

"No, he wore one of those black ski masks and was mostly behind me."

"Did you recognize his voice? Did he have any kind of an accent?"

Lisa shook her head. "It all happened so fast."

"Did you notice any distinguishing marks, tattoos, scars, jewelry, or details on his clothes?"

"He wore black gloves, leather maybe."

"Any distinct smells, cologne, body odor, shampoo, anything like that?"

"No."

"Can you describe the knife?"

"I never saw it, but it felt like it had teeth, serrated."

"Do you have any clue as to who he might have been?"

"No."

"Did you post anything online about your move, pictures of the house, the location, the time frame—that sort of thing?"

"Only to family and friends in closed groups, nothing public."

Cruz nodded reflectively and made notes. "Do you have any idea as to why someone would select your home?"

"No, we just moved here from Cleveland."

"Why did you move?"

"Jeff got a promotion with the advertising company he works for. It was a once-in-a-lifetime opportunity."

"And you? What did you do in Cleveland? What do you do now?"

"I was a senior manager with a data-analysis company—statistical research for nonprofit groups. I still work for them, but I gave up my manager's position, and now I telecommute as a data specialist, doing projects from home." She blinked several times, glanced at the ceiling. "Jeff and I had planned to start a family here."

"Do you or Jeff gamble?"

"What? No."

"Do you have any outstanding debts to anyone?"

"Cars, personal and college loans, the mortgage—we're carrying a pretty big debt load."

"Any other kinds of debts?"

"I don't know what you mean…"

"Do either of you use illicit drugs?"

"No."

"Do you have any items of great value that you might have mentioned online?"

"Not really. Maybe some of my grandmother's jewelry, but that's more sentimental than valuable."

"Do you know if anything's missing?"

"We only did a quick check, but nothing seems to be missing. We haven't even unpacked everything."

"Since you moved in, have you received any strange phone calls, wrong numbers, people at your door soliciting or claiming to be lost, strange cars in the area, anything like that?"

Lisa thought for a moment before she shook her head. "I don't think so, no."

"Would you volunteer your phone and computer records so we can see who's been communicating with you?"

"I guess so. I'll talk to Jeff."

"Can you provide us with a list of movers, contractors or services you've used since you've moved in?"

"Yes."

"One more thing, and this is important, Lisa. We're going to need your nightgown and robe."

"Why?"

"For evidence. He pressed up against you, so we may get some trace. I need to be there with

Officer Hawkins when you change and we collect it, okay?"

A moment passed before Lisa nodded.

"I think that's it for now." Cruz touched Lisa's hand. "Do you have any family or friends in Miami?"

Tears rolled down Lisa's face as she shook her head.

"I can put you in touch with counseling and community services, if you need to talk to someone."

"Thank you. I don't know what I'm going to do."

"Please don't take this the wrong way, Lisa, but you're lucky."

"Lucky?"

"This could've been worse."

4

"The knife?" Jeff repeated.

"Yes, describe the knife again." Detective Reddick barely blinked as Jeff answered his questions in the living room.

"It was about six to eight inches, serrated. A fixed blade."

"And the intruder's approximate height and weight?"

"He was about my height, six feet, and he was maybe one seventy."

"And you said he had dark jeans, a dark long-sleeved shirt, gloves and a small backpack?"

"Yes."

"Likely had his tools in the backpack," Reddick said. "And he was wearing a balaclava?"

"Yes, but I could see his eyes and mouth."

Reddick made notes in his pad. "And from what you could see, he appeared to be Caucasian?"

"Yes, he was a white guy."

"Was there anything familiar about him? His voice, his build, anything that maybe reminded you of someone you'd passed on the street, at the mall, a restaurant or gas station?"

"No, we've only been here about three or four weeks."

"Let's go back a bit. I need you to really think. Were there any distinguishing characteristics about him? His voice, any marks on his skin, anything you can remember about the way he moved or spoke, or about his clothing?"

Jeff's hands gripped his legs as he thought for a moment, shook his head slowly before stopping. "His shoe."

"What about it?" Reddick checked his notes. "You said he had sneakers, dark blue."

"Yes, but the left one… I glanced down when he lifted Lisa—" Jeff looked into space as if the scene were replaying in front of him. "It was fast, but I remember the fabric near a left eyelet was frayed, about an inch, exposing white lining."

"Really?" Reddick stared at him. "With everything going on, you saw that?"

"It's weird, but I did see it, because when he lifted her, my attention went there for an instant, maybe because Lisa's toes barely touched the floor."

"Okay, that's specific." Reddick noted the detail. "Now, you say that it appears as though none of your belongings are missing."

"That's how it appears, yes."

"You still have credit cards, bank cards, ID, keys, phones, computers, prescription drugs, that sort of stuff?"

"Yes, it doesn't look like he got anything, but we'll check again."

"It's possible that you interrupted him before he got to whatever it was he wanted. Is there any chance you might know this guy? Is there anyone you might suspect?"

"No. I just wish—" He shook his head, biting his bottom lip, and his knuckles whitened as he dug his fingers into his legs, wrestling with a growing fury.

Jeff's reaction was not lost on Reddick. "What do you wish?"

"That I could've stopped him from doing what he did to Lisa. If I could do it over, I'd find some way to kill that piece of sh—"

"Take it easy."

"I just stood there, frozen, doing absolutely nothing."

"He had a knife to her throat, Jeff. Your response likely kept her from being hurt."

"I should've done something to protect her."

"No one knows how they'll react when something like this happens, believe me. Now, can you think of any reason why someone would target you?"

Jeff leaned his elbows on his knees and thought.

"No. Like I said, we just moved here." Jeff looked at Reddick. "Why do you think he picked us?"

The detective let out a long, slow breath.

"He may have targeted the house because of the for-sale sign, then waited, watched the house be sold and you move in, saw that there was no security system."

Jeff shook his head. "The real estate agent told us that crime was *virtually nonexistent* in this neighborhood. Those were her words. So I didn't rush to get a system installed. They're scheduled to come next week."

"We've had some burglaries and break-ins in Palm Mirage Creek, Coral Terrace, Coral Gables," Reddick said. "Not many, but we get them. We've had others across the county. We'll check their details against yours for any links."

"I feel stupid for not pushing to get security installed sooner."

"Yeah, well, hindsight. You should move on it. At least change the locks today. Call a twenty-four-hour service. Maybe you're covered through insurance. Then call the security company to do their installation as soon as possible."

"I will."

"The locking mechanism on the sliding door is easy to bypass with a crowbar, and it's a distance from the bedrooms." Reddick took a moment to flip back over his notes. "I'm almost done here. I know we've hit on this—bear with me—but given that you've recently moved, can you think of any other incidents, occurrences or situations that happened here, or in Ohio, that could be connected to this crime in any way?"

Jeff blinked several times, and his Adam's apple rose and fell before he shook his head. "No, I can't."

Reddick searched his eyes for a long moment before returning to his notes. "And you're employed with the Asgaard-T-Chace Group? What's that, again?"

"It's an advertising agency. We handle major brands with campaigns that run worldwide, especially during global events, on television, online, billboards, stadiums, traditional media, you name it."

"Commercials, ads, that sort of thing?"

"Yes."

"And what do you do there, with your new promotion, as it were?"

"My title is Senior Executive Strategist for Global Business Development and Marketing. Oh, damn." Jeff raked his hands through his hair, noticing the sunrise and the time. "I'm leading a presentation today for clients who've flown in from Argentina."

"None of my business," Reddick indicated upstairs where Lisa was, then the broken sliding door, "but I think you've got some other things that need your attention today."

Jeff exhaled. "You're right. Would it be okay if I called my boss now, to alert him?"

"Go ahead. We're almost done."

Jeff left the sofa and went to an alcove that provided some privacy. He scrolled through the new contacts in his phone, pressing the one for Leland Slaughter, his director. Slaughter had said he was always up before the sun, so he should be awake by now, Jeff hoped, as it rang.

"Hello?"

"Mr. Slaughter, sorry to disturb you. It's Jeff Taylor."

"It's fine, I was up. What is it?"

"I'm afraid I won't be able to make it in today."

"But you're presenting to the Buenos Aires group today. This is a twenty-million-dollar account for all of South America. The approach is your baby, the one you started in Cleveland."

"I know, sir, but we've had a…an attack. A guy broke into our home last night, I mean early this morning, he had a knife, and he assaulted my wife, and—"

"My God, Jeff, is she hurt? Is she all right?"

"She's okay but terribly shaken, and right now our home is full of detectives and police officers. They're trying to track him with a helicopter, dogs—"

"Okay, okay, I understand. I'm going to make some calls."

"I'm very sorry about this, Mr. Slaughter. I'm aware of the significance of today's presentation. Believe me, I know what's on the line with the Buenos Aires account."

"Don't worry about the presentation. We'll make some—" Slaughter paused, and Jeff thought he heard him curse under his breath. "We'll make adjustments. I'm going to alert our human resources with an order that they're to give you any support you need. If you need crisis help, need to go to a hotel, anything at all that the company can help you with."

"Thank you, sir. I know you were instrumental in my promotion and in moving us here. I don't want to let you down."

"Nonsense. This is terrible. A damned fine welcome to Florida! Take the time you need to get things back on track, and keep me posted."

"Thank you, Mr. Slaughter."

After he hung up, Jeff considered Mr. Slaughter's voice on the call, convinced it betrayed an undertone of disappointment, which gave rise to a new concern. Jeff had developed the concept they were using for the South American presentation while still in Cleveland working on another campaign. It had been a factor in his promotion, the chief reason Slaughter had headhunted him and expedited and underwritten his move to the Miami office. Feeling obligated, Jeff now feared his no-show for the Buenos Aires group endangered his relationship with Slaughter before it had really gotten off the ground.

Jeff rubbed the knot in the back of his neck, returning to the living room at the same time as Lisa, Cruz and Hawkins were descending the stairs. Reddick was across the room in a corner talking on his phone. Jeff saw that Lisa had changed into a T-shirt and sweatpants. He went to her. Hawkins held a paper bag and made notes in her book while talking with Cruz.

"Air support and the K-9 unit didn't pick up his trail," Reddick said after ending his call.

"So he's still out there?" Lisa said.

"Yes, but we'll keep a police presence here

much of today," Reddick said. "We'll be canvassing, talking to the neighborhood crime-watch people, checking surveillance video. We've got a lot to
do." He indicated the crime-scene techs. Aluminum equipment cases closed and latches snapped
shut as they finished packing. "But we're done
here for now, and I'm sure you'll want to get back
to normal."

"Normal?" Lisa cast around. "Cleveland is normal. I don't know what this is."

"Lisa," Jeff took her in his arms. "We'll get
through this."

"We'll catch this guy—we're just getting started,"
Cruz said. "What happened was horrible. I know
how this may sound, but you can't let it consume
you. You've got so much going for you—a beautiful home, a great community." Cruz touched Lisa's
shoulder. "A good place for families."

Absorbing her words, Lisa managed a weak
smile before they all exchanged parting handshakes. The detectives left, and for the first time
in what seemed like forever, Jeff and Lisa were
alone amid the aftermath.

For a moment they stood in their foyer, holding
each other until Lisa's shaking had subsided, and
Jeff's adrenaline had waned. In the quiet, Jeff processed their ordeal with a sliver of fear streaking
across a private region of his mind.

*This can't be linked to what happened in
Cleveland—it can't be.*

5

Needles of hot water stung Lisa's skin in the shower.

She scrubbed herself aw as if the creep's attack had stained her. But as the steam clouds rose, the ice-cold truth coiled like a cobra in her gut. The man who assaulted her had eluded police.

And he'd vowed to return.

Why did this have to happen?

She was really starting to love Palm Mirage Creek, had been greeted warmly by a few neighbors who'd made her feel welcome, but now everything had changed. Leaning back against the shower wall, holding herself, she slid to the floor, sobbing, grieving all she had left behind in Cleveland. She couldn't call anyone: her phone was broken. Even if she used Jeff's, she was unsure she could form the words to say what had happened.

Angry, exhausted and scared, she was stabbed with the need to be with her sister, Joy, a nurse in Cleveland. Lisa envisioned how her sweet nephew and niece, Carter and Charlotte, would be playing in the yard while she and Joy talked over coffee in the kitchen. Lisa would tell her everything because Joy always knew the right thing to say.

And there was Heather, her friend, neighbor and jogging partner back home. She was the best listener, a bighearted woman raised in Atlanta and grounded in common sense. Jogging without Heather was not the same. If anything it made her homesick.

Lisa yearned for her mom and dad. Even though they weren't in Cleveland, she still thought of them as being there, being home. Since her dad had retired and they'd sold the carpentry business, they had joined a program through their church and had been in El Salvador helping build homes for the poorest people in the region.

And she missed her friends in her book club. She was still part of the group, reading *Crime and Punishment* along with them now—*how ironic*—but video chatting with them and drinking wine alone was not the same. On the surface it was fun, but deep down it underscored her isolation. And, no, she wouldn't dare reveal online what had happened to her, not to anyone anywhere…

She couldn't help wrestling with a sense of shame.

And what about Jeff? He just stood there and let that creep molest me, drag me out of the house where he could've—could've…

No, she couldn't blame Jeff for this.

Lisa's thoughts reached for someone else, instead—Morgan. Her friend from college, now a psychologist in Philadelphia. She could see Morgan's warm, intense face, radiating intelligence. Hear her soft, strong voice: *Get up, girl. Are you going to just fold like a paper princess? Get your butt out there, go meet those Florida neighbors, make friends. Don't let that lowlife control your life. He's the one who ran away. He's the coward.*

Morgan would then likely quote somebody like Nietzsche, telling her to remember an adage like *That which does not kill us makes us stronger.*

That might be true for most people most of the time, but Lisa found Nietzsche's line hard to believe, given the tragedy she'd faced when she was nine years old. It certainly had not made her stronger.

It was not my fault, they told me. But every day I live with the truth. It was *my fault. Maybe what happened today is some kind of karmic payback for what happened to Stacey...*

Lisa pushed the thought away and got to her feet in the shower, motivated by a surge of remembering the reasons they'd moved: Jeff's promotion and to have babies. She'd given up her job, a job she loved, to start a family, to realize their dream. That was the plan.

But their move had happened so fast.

Almost as if we were fleeing Ohio.

Jeff had said they were breaking out of a city where snow and slush were a way of life, trading it for palm trees, ocean breezes and their dream. But you've got to add sinkholes, alligators and hur-

ricanes, she'd joked right back. Turning off the
water, she told herself to get a grip.

Don't let the creep win.

But he's out there.

She wiped the fog from the mirror, revealing the
face of a frightened woman fighting tears.

I don't know if I can do this.

Still reeling, Jeff went from room to room assessing the fallout, phone to his ear, on hold with
the home-security company.

David Bowie's *Space Oddity* played in Jeff's ear
as he looked at the black and gray clouds of fingerprint powder lacing the door handles, walls, coun-
ters, tables, appliances. It was everywhere. The
intruder had worn gloves, but the investigators said
he may have removed them to touch something.

Jeff shook his head at the mess, his stomach
churning with rage.

At one point, a crime-scene tech had cautioned,
apologetically, that the graphite powder smudged
like ink when wet and had advised them to hire
professional cleaners. Just another insult to the vi-
olation, Jeff thought, while taking inventory once
more.

With the exception of Lisa's phone, which they'd
have to repair or replace, nothing appeared to be
disturbed. Their tablets, wallets, cash, credit and
bank cards seemed to be fine; nothing taken on
that front. Lisa would have to inspect her jewelry
and her office again after her shower.

In his study, Jeff took stock of the file cabinet

holding all their important records like tax returns, contracts, the deed to the house and passports. The contents appeared untouched. Sitting at his desk before his computer, he looked in an unlocked drawer, the one with a false bottom.

He'd had it custom-made.

Underneath the drawer was a hidden spring-release latch, nearly invisible. You had to know where to look to find it—and nobody did. He released it, slid open the top of the secret compartment. Among the items he'd kept there were his data-storage devices, his memory cards and flash drives, some two dozen in all.

His pulse sped up, and he swallowed.

He'd stored a lot of critical stuff in this drawer and on these devices. It was all well hidden, but after what had happened, he wondered if it was still safe. He didn't have time to check further, but everything looked to be there, he assured himself. But suddenly his mind went back to Cleveland, to the matter he'd left behind and the remote chance the invasion was related.

No way, not possible. It's thirteen hundred miles away. I was very careful. I'm just being paranoid.

Jeff leaned back in his chair, listening to Bowie. If nothing was missing, then everything was okay.

No.

It's not okay.

The images of the attack tormented him: the knife at Lisa's throat, the intruder's hands all over her, brazenly assaulting her, terrifying her while glaring at him, making a twisted show of it, knowing Jeff could do nothing.

And that's what he'd done.

Nothing.

The rational Jeff played the calm, powerless, suburban male, accepting that the only way to save Lisa was by standing there helpless, watching her be assaulted. But inside, deep in the darkest region of his soul, he seethed with mounting fury, a feral frenzied force he had battled all his life to keep caged.

There'd been instances over the years where he hadn't been able to contain it, times it had broken loose from his control. Memory hauled him back, beyond Cleveland, back to Chicago and an incident after his father's death and his mom's downward spiral. He'd been the new kid at another new school, living with his mother in a van, then a homeless shelter, then an apartment with rats. Somehow, the other kids found out. They always found out.

During a ball game on the playground, they began taunting him. "Hey, that shirt you're wearing is the one my mother donated!"

"I bet he's wearing my underwear, too!"

"Get your welfare ass off the field!"

Then the leader, the biggest one, the kid named Marshall, got in his face while the others circled around. "Know what I hear?" he said. "I hear your mother's a drug-addict whore, and you don't even know who your father is." Marshall's eyes glinted, and he smiled. "That makes you a real son of a—"

The cage broke.

Jeff saw nothing but white and blanked out.

The next thing he remembered, he was in the principal's office listening to Marshall, practically in tears, recounting how Jeff had found a bat and with red-hot wrath had swung it at Marshall's face.

"He said he'd make my head explode like a pumpkin."

Marshall related how Jeff had swung the bat at him with all of his might and how he'd ducked with only a fraction of a second to spare, feeling Jeff's swing brushing his scalp, catching a few hairs as it sliced the air.

Marshall said Jeff then walked away, leaving him and the others standing there dumbstruck.

"I don't remember doing that," Jeff told the principal. "I don't remember anything like that."

But the principal had spoken to the other boys and each one had supported Marshall's account. Jeff was suspended for two days. The principal had said he'd call Jeff's mother. Walking home, Jeff had thought she'd be too drunk or high, or with some man, to care or do anything about it. What could she do? She'd always said that doctors attributed his anger and other problems to his father's tragedy. Since that time, all he could do was fight to keep his rage in a cage.

Now, years and miles away, as Jeff sat at his desk processing what the intruder had done to Lisa, what he'd taken from them, how he'd violated their lives, the cage rattled again.

6

Growing impatient on hold, Jeff was walking out of his office when *Space Oddity* cut off and the line came to life.

"Mr. Taylor, thank you for waiting. Sir, the soonest our locksmith can be there is eight tomorrow morning."

"Tomorrow? Your site says emergency same-day service."

"I'm sorry. We have staff who've taken ill and staff on vacation. We're backed up. We can advance installation of your system to this week, the day after tomorrow. We've already done the assessment, so we'll have it completely installed in one visit."

"Can't you make it sooner? I told you we had a break-in."

"I'm know, and I'm very sorry, sir. I'll try to move things up, but for now that's the best we can do. Want us to book?"

Jeff cursed under his breath. "Yes. Book it."

After hanging up, he inspected the sliding door

to the pool. The crime-scene techs had done him a favor when they'd finished. They'd rigged a makeshift lock. But Jeff needed all the locks changed and a good security system installed today. He resolved to call other companies and his insurer, but first, he needed a shower, coffee and food.

He headed upstairs to the bedroom where Lisa had finished dressing. Jeff embraced her, but she remained stiff and edgy.

"Are they coming to install a system today?" she asked.

"I'm working on it."

She blinked back tears without speaking.

"Hey." Jeff took her shoulders. "We'll get through this. I'm going to take a shower, then I'll make us some breakfast."

The aroma of coffee filled their home with the suggestion of normalcy.

Jeff had showered, shaved and dressed. He now sat at the counter eating scrambled eggs and toast, pretending everything was fine, while Lisa stood holding her coffee cup with both hands.

"While I was upstairs, I got through to our insurance company," he said. "They'll send a cleaning company, and they'll try to get a security company today. Once the system's in, they'll give us a discount on our insurance. That will help alleviate the cost."

Lisa said nothing.

"And if all that gets started before noon, I'll go to the office—"

"You'd go to the office? After what happened to us? To me?"

Jeff met Lisa's gaze, disbelief written on her face.

"No, no. I mean—" Jeff looked away. "I mean, once we get things straightened out here."

"I think we should move back to Cleveland."

"What?" Jeff placed his fork on the counter, choosing his words before speaking. "What happened was horrible, but we'll get it behind us. Thank God you weren't hurt."

Lisa's eyes grew fierce with disagreement.

"That was stupid. You know what I mean. I'm sorry," Jeff said.

"That creep is still out there! It's simple. We sell the house, and we move back to Cleveland."

"Lisa, you know we can't do that."

"Why not?"

"Why not?" Jeff searched the walls for the answer. "Honey, it's just not an option with our situation. Look, I know you love this house, you said yourself it's beautiful here, you love this neighborhood. This is where we'll have kids, live our dream."

Lisa hugged herself, fighting tears.

"Lisa, seriously. If I told the company we're moving back, they'd fire me. I'd be abandoning the South American job, a twenty-million-dollar account. They wouldn't pay a cent for another move. We'd be drowning in moving costs and all of our other debt. I'd have no job in Cleveland.

We'd be starting down a slippery slope toward losing everything. Everything!"

"Jeff, that's not true."

"Believe me, I know what it's like to live on the street."

"I know the horrible things what you went through as a kid, but this is different—that won't happen to us."

"It happens to people like us all the time, Lisa. And I swear, I'll never go through that again. Ever. I've worked too hard, come too far. We can't move back. It's just not going to happen."

She covered her face with her hands. After a moment, he heard her muffled voice. "When he had me out by the pool, he said, 'I know everything about you. I'll be watching you. I'm going to come back and fuck you.'"

Jeff's face whitened, anger rippling through him.

He pulled Lisa to him, holding her as she sobbed.

"I'm here," he said. "I'm not going anywhere. We'll fight this thing together. You're brave and you're strong."

"No, I'm not. I'm so— I feel like this is some kind of bad karmic payback for what happened with Stacey all those years ago."

"You're just shaken up. We both are."

"Jeff, I'm scared."

"I know. But we can get through this."

He held her head against his chest for some time before the doorbell rang.

Through the window, they could see that Detective Reddick had returned.

And he wasn't alone.

7

With Lisa behind him, Jeff opened the door to the detective and three other people.

"Hi again," Reddick said. "We'd like to introduce you to some people who want to help."

The first was a tall woman in her forties with blond shoulder-length hair, wearing hoop earrings and a heart necklace. She stood smiling next to a stocky man, affable-looking, in his fifties. Lisa recognized the third man, Jeff's height—six foot, midfifties, rugged face, piercing eyes. He was their neighbor, from the house across their backyard. She'd met him briefly on the street a couple of days after they'd moved in; he'd been walking by and had welcomed them to the neighborhood.

"This is Michelle Judson," Reddick said, "a former sergeant in the Marine Corps." Reddick put his hand on the shorter man's shoulder. "This is Ned Tripp, retired firefighter. And this is Roland Dillard, retired detective. Rollie's your closest neighbor. They're all with the watch group, and Michelle's also with the community association. I have to go, but it'd be good for you to talk to these folks."

After shaking hands, Jeff pushed the door open and invited them into the living room.

"The place is still a mess." Lisa touched her fingertips to the corners of her eyes. "But I've got some fresh coffee."

"Please, don't worry about it." Tripp had a deep voice. "We appreciate what you're dealing with here."

Jeff summarized events as he poured their guests coffee, then led them to the sliding door to show them the assailant's point of entry.

"We want you to know that we feel awful about this burglary, especially with you being new to the neighborhood and everything," Judson said. "We don't get much crime in Palm Mirage Creek, and we want to keep it that way. We're here to help in any way we can."

Tripp tasted his coffee, then nodded to Lisa. "We understand the suspect briefly took you hostage with a knife."

Lisa's face flushed. She hesitated with embarrassment before nodding.

Tripp gave an awkward glance to the others.

"Oh. Sorry," he said. "Being with the watch, we get notifications. We work with police. We had people on patrol last night, but they were south of here. As soon as police alerted us, we mobilized our call-out list, getting maybe fifty or sixty people searching all night for him."

Lisa and Jeff looked at each other.

"Really?" Lisa said, heartened. "That many people were out helping?"

"You bet," Tripp said. "This is a tight community with good people who help each other. That's why we're adding extra patrols around your block."

Lisa didn't know what to say about the unexpected support.

"How are you holding up?" Judson asked her.

Lisa took a moment. "To be honest, I'm still shaky."

"Well, that's one of the reasons we're here," Judson said. "We have professional crisis experts who live near you, if you want to talk to anyone."

"Thanks," Lisa nodded.

Judson put her coffee down, withdrew her phone from her pocket and began scrolling. "Lisa, can you give me your email or number? I'll send you a list of names and numbers. I also have contacts for the community-watch captains, doctors, pharmacies, churches, jogging trails, lawyers, shops, all organized and in some cases rated with comments."

"Thank you, but I think my phone's broken," Lisa said.

"Send it to me," Jeff offered and gave Judson his personal email.

"You don't have a home-security system, do you?" Dillard said.

"No, the installers are behind schedule and will come in a couple of days," Jeff said.

"Couple of days? What's the company?"

"Zolpatz Security."

"Zolpatz?" Dillard stuck out his bottom lip. "They're not the best. Forgive me for imposing, but if you like, I can see about getting a topflight installer here in two hours to take care of everything today."

"Two hours?" Lisa said.

"I can make some calls, if you would like."

Jeff looked at Lisa, and they both nodded. "Yes, please," Jeff said.

Dillard took out his phone, stepped away to use it. He was well built for an older man, reminding Lisa of her father, a take-charge guy who kept in shape.

"I know this is a bad time," Judson said to her. "But give some thought to joining us at the homeowners' association. It's a fifty-dollar-a-year membership fee but comes with all kinds of discounts on restaurants, services. You get a newsletter to keep you informed on meetings and events, and there's information about our neighborhood-watch team. Right now we're running a fund to plant more shade trees in the neighborhood."

"I don't know…" Lisa said.

"Just think about it. It's also a good way to get to know more people here, feel connected."

Tripp joined in. "And you can join the watch through the association. We'd love to have you, too, Jeff. Usually people take a short night shift with a small team whenever they can."

"Thanks, but I'm kinda tied up with my new job."

"Where's that?" Tripp asked.

"Downtown with Asgaard-T-Chace," he said. "Advertising."

"Ahh," Tripp said. "What about you, Lisa?"

"I work at home. Telecommute with my old company in Cleveland."

"Cleveland." Tripp smiled. "Great town. LeBron reigned supreme there and here for a while before going to LA. What's your line of work, Lisa?"

"I'm a data analyst. We do research mostly for nonprofit groups, those advocating for improved health care or underprivileged people. We also do research for academic studies and government."

"Sounds like good stuff," Tripp said.

Dillard returned holding his phone to his chest.

"Jeff, Lisa, you can have Steel Sands Protection here in about two hours. They cost a bit more, but they're the best. They'll repair and change all the locks and give you an excellent system, fully operational today. Let me know if you want to green-light this."

Jeff turned to Lisa, who nodded.

"Absolutely," Jeff said. "We'll take it. I'll call Zolpatz and cancel everything with them."

"Thank you so much, Mr. Dillard," Lisa said.

"Roland," he said and winked at the Taylors.

Jeff exchanged a glance with Lisa, and she gave him the beginnings of a smile signaling hope.

8

That afternoon, a van with the Steel Sands Protection logo on its panels rolled into the Taylors' driveway.

The crew chief, Hector, according to the name patch on his branded shirt, introduced his team: Vicki, short hair and a nose ring, and Kyle, long hair with a ponytail. Lisa and Jeff had accepted Roland Dillard's friendly offer to help oversee installation.

As Dillard and Hector's crew began an assessment of the house, inside and outside, the cleaning company called. Jeff told them to come the next day after the security system was installed. Now, with the assessment completed, Hector advised the Taylors.

"We recommend our Steel Sands Armor Shield Package." He swiped through his tablet, showing them highlights with photos. "Wireless, with sensors, motion detectors, cameras. You can monitor in-house or remotely on any device. It's all linked to our emergency call center. There's a monthly monitoring fee, but the discount from your insurer will help offset it. We could be done today in three to four hours. With a full package installed, the door repaired and locks replaced, this is your total."

Jeff raised his eyebrows slightly at the figure, feeling another heavy expense they didn't need right now, but after glancing at Lisa, he said, "Yes, go ahead."

As they set out to work, Lisa contended with her feelings. This action, the fact they were doing something, had instilled in her a sense of fighting back, a turning point, a step toward recovering her peace of mind. But at the same time, having so many strangers coming and going on every floor, in and out of every room, was unsettling.

Dillard had read her reaction. "Don't worry," he gave her a warm smile when they were alone. "Everyone with the company undergoes extensive background checks. I know Hector, and I used Steel Sands for my own house, if that helps."

Lisa smiled. She liked Dillard. He struck her as a protective, capable man. "It does. Thanks."

Together they found Jeff, then Dillard led them through the house, room by room, explaining the system. They were installing sensors on every exterior door, every window, and the garage, which would alert the alarm system to unwanted entry. Motion detectors with infrared technology were also being installed to distinguish body heat and the movement of a prowler or intruder. The surveillance system involved having dome and bullet cameras strategically placed in every room and covering all exterior points outside the house, leaving no blind spots. The camera feed could be viewed on their TV or any portable device. All of it was networked through the master control panel to sound an alarm.

"Would've been nice to have this when we moved in," Jeff said.

"Can't turn back the clock," Dillard said. "I understand from Cruz and Reddick that you don't have a gun. I could help you if you're considering getting one now for protection?"

"No. Thank you, no," Lisa said. "We don't like guns."

"Even now?"

"Yes. Jeff's father was killed in an accident while hunting with his friend when Jeff was a child."

"I see."

"My mother never recovered from it," Jeff said. "It destroyed us. I don't want to have anything to do with guns."

Dillard nodded his understanding.

"So you're a retired detective," Lisa said. "Do you have a gun?"

"I do. I have a concealed-weapons permit."

"Were you with police here in Miami? I detect a bit of an accent…"

Dillard smiled. "NYPD. Five years as a beat cop, twenty as detective. Dealt with everything. Homicides, robberies, drugs, organized crime. Handled cases in all five boroughs. Retired ten years ago. Moved down here, where I do consulting and contract work, travel to security conferences. It's a nice life."

"What do you consult on?" Jeff asked.

"Everything. Lately it's been cybercrime, investigative techniques, how to cultivate CIs."

"CIs?"

"Criminal or confidential informants—intel, sources, that sort of thing."

"Guess you're still in the mix," Jeff said.

"I am."

"Are you married, Roland?" Lisa asked.

"Happily. To the same woman for thirty-five years."

"That's nice. Do you have kids?"

"No, no children. You?"

"Not yet, but soon, we hope," Lisa said.

The crew had worked for nearly two hours when Jeff's boss called to see how the Taylors were doing and to let Jeff know that he'd managed to push back the South American presentation by a few days. After the call, Jeff retreated to his office to do some work on it.

A little over an hour later, the installation was complete.

Hector very patiently guided Jeff and Lisa through creating and entering pass codes in their control panel. He showed them how to arm and disarm the system and monitor all their cameras and control their system on mobile devices. He watched as Vicki and Kyle spiked a security sign into their front lawn and placed stickers on their windows.

"Those security signs alone can be a deterrent," Dillard said.

"This package also includes alerts to your smoke and water detectors to alert you to a potential burst pipe or flooding," Hector said, explaining how, when an alarm is triggered, the call center would check with the homeowner in seconds and dispatch a security team or call 9-1-1, depending on the emergency.

He promised to send them an invoice, then turned to Dillard. "Give my best to Nell, Roland."

After the crew was gone, Dillard pulled out his phone.

"You've got a veritable fortress now. Give me your numbers, and I'll send you mine, so you guys can contact me anytime. If anything happens, you know I live behind you."

They gave their numbers to Dillard with their thanks.

"Now you can get back to normal." He smiled at both of them. "Give some thought to joining the watch patrol and reaching out to the folks here. They're good people."

"We will," Lisa said.

Dillard's phone vibrated, and he checked a message.

"There you go," he said. "I got nothing on my cameras, but it looks like one of our neighbors captured some security footage of the suspect."

Dillard showed it to them, a granular, dim image of a figure.

"It's not too clear, but it's got to be a break, right?" Jeff said.

"It's a start," Dillard said. "The fact this happened in my backyard is something I don't take lightly. I've got contacts in law enforcement and on the street—I'll be working on this, believe me." He looked at Jeff, then at Lisa. "We'll get this guy, folks. You'll see."

9

Palm Mirage Creek slept in the still night.

Pretty houses. Well-kept yards.

Then a flash.

A dark figure outlined against a stucco garage wall blazes across the frame.

Then nothing.

Detective Camila Cruz tapped on her keyboard, freezing the surveillance footage image on her computer screen. She leaned closer to study the suspect. The grainy image offered no details.

Shadow Man.

She made a note.

It was the day after the Taylor burglary. Cruz and Reddick were at their desks at Miami-Dade's Midwest District Station in Doral, a modern-looking building of glass and concrete squares. Through the window, she glimpsed the palms out front nodding in the breeze as she worked. They'd set their ongoing investigations aside, concentrating on the new Taylor case, working well into the night, talking to neighbors, street officers, returning this morning before their shifts to share information at roll call with patrol units.

They didn't have much.

White male, six foot, one-seventy, armed with serrated knife, small tear near eyelet of left dark blue sneaker. Shadow Man.

Taking a hit of coffee, Cruz surveyed her tidy desk, her awards and the framed family photo with her husband, Paulo, and her eleven-year-old son, Antonio, taken at the Grand Canyon. The calendar clipped to her low dividing wall had previous days crossed off with Xs. The days ahead held penned notations flagging her courses, appointments and Antonio's Little League practices and games. His birthday was marked with a happy face and candles.

Turning back to her monitor, she ran the footage again. "Not much here, Joe."

"I know." Reddick was finishing off a bagel with cream cheese. His desk was cluttered with fast-food wrappers and tepid take-out coffee. A picture of Reddick when he was a linebacker for the University of Miami Hurricanes was pinned to his desk wall. He'd had a shot at the NFL; in fact, the Saints had invited him to try out, but he'd decided to be a cop, like his old man, his uncle and his brother. "I had to think about the long run. Injury and career brevity versus a pension and the odds of getting shot," Reddick had told Cruz when they'd been partnered a year ago.

"And now you're living the dream," Cruz had said.

Reddick had allowed the hint of a smile.

They fit well together.

Cruz felt vibrations on their conjoined desks as Reddick typed with force on his keyboard while scrutinizing the security-camera images again.

"Yeah," he said, chewing on the last of his bagel. "There's little there. I'm thinking our guy knows the neighborhood and planned a hideout and escape route. He got by us. He got lucky."

"We've run down every tag we could obtain of every vehicle parked in the vicinity during the time frame. Zilch so far."

"Maybe he was on foot, had a bicycle, who knows," Reddick said.

"I'm surprised he got by Roland's place. His yard adjoins the Taylors', and he's a watch captain."

"The direction of his cameras was off. Besides, he's got plenty on his plate without having to watch his yard for assailants."

"I heard. That's so sad about his wife." Cruz flipped through her notes and forms in a file folder, went back to her computer and ran down the status of the investigation.

They'd found no latents or traces. The lab was still analyzing Lisa's nightgown. Nothing concrete had emerged from the neighborhood canvass. No witness accounts, no unreported incidents that could be related. They'd also shared their information with other investigative units. They'd requested to be alerted to anyone recently arrested

that they could question about knowledge of burglaries or sexual assaults in the area. They were
going through the Taylors' phones, computers
and routines for the past days and weeks to see
if they'd encounter anything that stood out. They
were working through the list of contractors: a
landscaper, a window washer, a pool company. No
flags so far. They were also preparing to request a
warrant for all phone communication in the area
within the time frame of the attack.

"Why were they targeted? Did they have any
enemies?" Reddick asked.

"New arrivals, no security—they were vulnerable. Crime of opportunity," Cruz said.

"Nothing taken." Reddick nodded. "They likely
interrupted him."

"What troubles me is the sex assault," Cruz said.
"What if he was counting on Lisa being alone, and
he wasn't there to steal anything?"

"Or he planned to bind and kill them?" Reddick typed commands on his keyboard. "I'll take
another run through other reports and field interviews for suspicious people, vehicles, disturbances
and neighbor complaints to see if this is similar to
any others in proximity."

"We've had burglaries in Coral Terrace and
Coral Gables," Cruz said, typing. "I'm going to
sift through local systems for recent cases. Then
I'll submit our case to the national databases."

After combing through the local, regional and
state crime repositories, Cruz began submitting

all the information she could on the Taylor case to national networks, starting with the National Crime Information Center. Operated by the FBI out of Clarksburg, West Virginia, NCIC was the federal government's central database for tracking crime-related information. Cruz used the appropriate codes that applied to the Taylor case for Burglary–Forced Entry–Residence, Sex Assault and others, adding remarks on the case where she could.

Once she was done, she moved on to the Violent Criminal Apprehension Program. She scrolled through the form. ViCAP was the nationwide database that gathered and analyzed details of missing-person cases and unsolved violent crimes, especially murder, and linked them to others with similar patterns. The FBI in Quantico ran the system.

ViCAP's aim was to detect signature traits that would pinpoint the crimes committed by the same offender. The submission process was meticulous and time-consuming, and Cruz knew her case didn't apply to every section of the form. It didn't involve murder, sexual homicide or anything ritualistic, yet instinct told her they should get the Taylor case in all systems, including ViCAP. Other investigators monitored it for updates.

Cruz moved quickly through the administrative section, then described details of the incident, noting the offender's exact words during the attack, including those directed at the victim.

When she finished she turned.

Reddick was behind her, reading over her shoulder.

"You're submitting this to ViCAP?" he asked her. "That's largely for serial offenders."

"Maybe that's exactly what our guy is, Joe."

10

On the morning of the third day after the assault, Lisa kissed Jeff goodbye as he headed for his office downtown.

"You're sure you're going to be okay?" he said. "Be honest."

"No." She released a nervous laugh. "But I've got to do this."

He searched her eyes, failing to mask his own unease. "All right, well, we've got our impenetrable, state-of-the-art security system. Cruz and Reddick arranged for extra police patrols in our area. You've got Roland's number, and I can be home in twenty minutes. Twenty-five tops. It's going to be fine."

"I'll be okay." She adjusted his new tie, one she'd picked for him. "You're going to knock 'em dead with your presentation."

"Thanks. I want you to text me every hour or so."

"Okay," she said and patted his chest. "Get going."

They kissed again, and he left. Lisa locked the

door behind him, leaned on it, then reached for her phone.

My lifeline.

The detectives had taken her damaged phone as evidence. Yesterday, she'd gone with Jeff to their service provider's outlet where they'd transferred all of Lisa's contacts to a new, better phone. It was among the things they'd done to get their lives back on track.

The previous afternoon, they'd met their neighbors to the right, the Mortimer sisters, Virginia and Anne. Both were in their seventies but didn't look it. They were retired teachers who lived together and had just returned from a long vacation in New England. Jeff and Lisa had introduced themselves as they'd finished unloading their SUV in the driveway, informing them of events and that police would want to review their security-camera footage. "Of course, we'll help," Anne Mortimer had said, after the sisters had responded with a chorus of *Dear Lord*, *How horrible*, *Poor thing* and *Thank heaven you're okay*, ending with *What's the world coming to?*

And last night Jeff and Lisa had gone shopping for a new sofa at Merrick Park. Strolling through the upscale shops and being among people had helped Lisa feel safe. But at the same time, she found herself studying the faces of strangers, wondering if her attacker was among them, watching them. Jeff was uneasy, too. Their underlying sense of vulnerability became evident as they both continually glanced at their phones, checking on the house. It was a move Lisa had mastered, and she used it now, monitoring the cameras as she watched Jeff wheel out of their driveway and disappear down the street.

For the first time since the attack, she was alone in the house.

Take a breath. You're a big girl. Get busy doing whatever you need to do.

What she needed to do was assure herself that she was *alone*. She went from room to room, checking closets, behind doors, tubs, showers, under beds, anywhere a person could hide. Sure, it was silly, but she had to do it. And each time she checked a room, she went to the window, scanning the street for anything strange: a parked car or a suspicious-looking person. She saw a woman walking her dog, an older couple strolling along. A courier truck passed by, then a marked patrol car, which gave her a measure of relief.

But as quickly as the police car came, it vanished.

She then saw a solitary runner—a woman in a ball cap, T-shirt, shorts—and felt a pang of envy. Lisa loved running. She'd kept her routine in the first days after they'd moved in, getting to know their pretty neighborhood through the jogging paths she'd chosen. She wanted to resume her running routine, wanted to explore the new trails in the links Michelle Judson had sent her.

But she was afraid to go running alone.

Because he's still out there.

Her fear evolved into anger at her attacker for what he'd done to her life.

I've got to get past this.

Work.

She made fresh coffee and went to her desk to resume analyzing high survey-nonresponse rates and sampling errors concerning studies from regions with slightly higher-than-average traces of pesticides in drinking water. It had been days since she'd worked on this. She took her time rereading and reacquainting herself with the material, trying to recall where she'd left off on her draft report when her phone vibrated.

A text from Jeff.

How're you doing?

Had it been an hour? She checked the time: closer to ninety minutes.

Fine, actually. How're things there?

Good so far. Stay strong. Love you.

She sent him a heart and smiling face.

She loved him so much. It felt so right to be with someone who understood her. Their relationship was not like most others—they were welded by childhood tragedies.

Lisa never talked about everything that had happened the day Stacey was killed, but when she'd first met Jeff she had sensed something different about him, different from the other men she'd known. On their third date, she told him about Stacey, sobbing as she relived the horror of the car accident.

Stacey's dad was driving them home from Tiffany's ninth-birthday party. Lisa and Stacey were in the back seat of Stacey's dad's car, laughing, teasing each other, when her father cursed, the brakes screeched, the car crashed and Stacey shot from the vehicle.

There was an investigation—another car had run a red light—but that date night, Lisa revealed something to Jeff she'd never told anyone before about why she carried the guilt of Stacey's death with her every day. Jeff was so understanding as he comforted her.

"I know what you're going through." Then, fighting his own tears as Lisa rubbed his shoulder, he revealed how his father had been killed.

Jeff was eleven when he had gone hunting with his dad and his dad's friend Charlie. At one point Jeff had been running toward his dad, when he fell and a shot echoed.

"They say I blacked out for a moment because I hit my head when I fell. But when I came to, my dad was on the ground," Jeff said. "Charlie had accidentally shot him. I don't remember much. Sometimes bits of what happened come back to me in flashes, and sometimes…" Jeff paused. "Charlie always said that he shot my dad, but… I remember kneeling over my dad and crying as he spoke his last words to me, and… I just don't know."

Jeff stopped, searching for some composure before he resumed.

"After my dad died, we lost everything. There was no insurance—my mom lost her job, then the house. We ended up living in shelters, in a van, on the street." Jeff brushed at his tears.

Jeff told her about how he still sometimes blanked out, had anger issues and sleepwalked sometimes. "I'm a real piece of work. Does that scare you?"

"No," she said. "It only makes me feel closer to you."

They were psychologically scarred people, but that night when they'd shared what they guarded in the most private corners of their fractured, guilt-laced hearts, they'd bonded.

Lisa blinked several times at the memory.

She resumed working, but her thoughts drifted to the people she had supervised in Cleveland. She missed her team: Cheyenne, the eco warrior who rode her bike, always harping about SUV owners, coming in with her backpack stuffed as if on alert for deployment; Dorian, the guy always dressed impeccably even on casual Fridays; Leena, the goddess who knew everything about beauty products; and Danuta, the soft-spoken vegan.

In Lisa's recent exchange of business emails, she hadn't told them about the intruder. She didn't feel comfortable opening that door. Now, here she was alone, grieving her lost human connections, unable to concentrate on her work. She tried consoling herself with the fact her report was nearly done and wasn't due for another two weeks when her phone vibrated.

Her sister, Joy, had sent a text.

Hey, I'm free for a video chat if you are.

In the past days, Joy was the only person Lisa had told about the attack, pouring her heart into a torrent of texts, hoping they'd find time for a video call.

Less than a minute later Joy's face filled Lisa's monitor.

"Oh, Lisa, it just sucks. I'm so sorry. How're you holding up?"

"Doing my best. At first I wanted to move back to Cleveland."

"How did that sit with Jeffrey?"

"He's against it. He's right. It's not an option. I get it. But I'm afraid."

Something blurred behind Joy, who turned. Then Lisa's niece's face filled the screen, her little hand waving.

"Hi, Aunt Lisa!" Six-year-old Charlotte pulled down her lower lip, showing the gap of a missing tooth. "The tooth fairy took my tooth, see?"

"I see, sweetie!"

"Bye."

"Bye, honey." Charlotte vanished.

"I know you're afraid," Joy said, "but you can't let your fear run your life."

"I told you what he said. What if he's out there?"

"I know, but you're strong. We come from fearless stock. Look at Mom and Dad, retired and building houses in some of the roughest parts of El Salvador."

Something bumped Joy, then five-year-old Carter got in front of her.

"Aunt Lisa! Aunt Lisa! Look!" A bandaged index finger blocked his face. "I got a cut, and there was blood!"

"Wow! Did it hurt?"

Carter shook his head. "Bye!"

"Bye, buddy."

Carter vanished, and Joy leaned closer.

"Sorry," she said.

"No, no, don't be. I love seeing them. I wish I were there. This whole thing has left me angry, feeling violated and paranoid, like a prisoner."

"That's perfectly understandable, but you can't let it control you. You're a fighter. You have to take control."

"I know."

"Want me to fly down? I've got vacation time banked and I can get Brad's mom to watch the kids."

"No. That's nice, thanks. But I don't want this disrupting your life, too."

"Believe me, I could use the break, and we have a lot of points."

"Let's put a pin in that for now."

"All right."

A doorbell sounded at Joy's end.

"That's probably the furnace guy, to give us an

estimate for a new one. He was supposed to come later. I'm sorry, I better go."

"Sure, I understand."

"My offer stands, sis."

"You're so kind. Hug everybody for me. Bye."

The call ended.

Lisa sat alone in the silence of her empty house, gauging how Joy's vibrant, kid-filled life in Cleveland accentuated the desperation of hers.

Wallowing isn't going to solve anything. Joy and Detective Cruz are right. I can't let this consume me. I won't let it take over my life.

Her coffee cup was empty.

On her way to the kitchen to get more, Lisa passed the great room and stopped.

Scene of the crime.

It was the one room, the one place she didn't check. She'd avoided it since the attack.

She thought for a moment, went to the security system's control panel and disarmed the sliding door and then returned to it.

This is where it happened.

On the other side of the glass, the pool water sparkled in the sunlight.

Lisa opened the door, stepped into the warmth, but felt a chill slither up her spine as she looked at the poolside spot where he'd dragged her, continuing to grab her breasts and between her legs before vanishing.

She froze when she heard a small, mechanical whirr.

Lisa turned, looked up. One of their new dome

security cameras with its automatic motion sensor had locked onto her, doing its job as the intruder's threat suddenly echoed in her head.

I know everything about you. I'll be watching you. I'm going to come back and—

11

The office of the Asgaard-T-Chace Group was on the fifty-first floor of the new Coral Cloud Tower, which jutted sixty stories up from downtown Brickell.

It was among the tallest of the city's skyscrapers, and Jeff was awed by the spectacular view it gave him of Miami's world-class architecture: condos, hotels, soaring construction cranes, scaffolding-clad towers and other high-rises. He could see the water to the horizon, the cruise ships at the port, the stadiums, and expressways weaving through the metropolis at his feet.

He'd come a long way from Cleveland and that drafty fifth-floor office in the crumbling brick building on East Ninth Street. He shuddered at how the place rattled whenever winter winds knifed through the city.

Looking out over the water, he was carried back in time to when he was a boy, living in a van with his mother on a Chicago street. It held a foul smell of sleeping bags, fast-food containers, heaps of clothes, empty liquor bottles and drug crap. A curtain divided the front cab from the back where they slept on a mattress. Jeff would wear headphones to shut out the moaning whenever his mother was behind the curtain with a man. Listening to music, Jeff would ache for his dad and for the time when his parents worked in the appliance factory, when they had money and a house, when they were happy. Until that morning...

That morning had been different. They were up before the sun, shivering in the cold gray pre-dawn light, Jeff's heart nearly bursting with excitement because he was now old enough to hunt with his own gun.

His dad had shown him everything, taught him to respect his gun, drilled into him how safety was paramount. It had been a glorious, surreal day until the sound of the shot shattered the calm and changed Jeff's life forever...

The happiness he and his mother had known died with his dad in that Wisconsin marsh. Soon after they'd buried him, the factory had closed. His mother, without a job, had complications with the insurance and trouble with paying bills. They lost the house, and she couldn't cope. She drank, took drugs; they ended up on the street, and she did what she had to in the back of the van for them to survive.

He tried to find work, going to stores and restaurants begging to scrub floors or clean bathrooms. He went to car dealerships and offered to wash cars in the lot, anything for cash, anything to climb out of the hell that, in his heart, he felt responsible for. And with every car he washed, every toilet bowl he scoured, he vowed to do whatever he needed to do to make a better life for himself and never come back to the one he was living.

Never.

Now, he thought of Lisa, how she missed Cleveland and wanted to return, and the toll the attack was taking. He thought of her home alone. After texting her and seeing her responses, he resumed reviewing some of the data for his presentation. He needed to be confident his figures were accurate.

"Knock, knock." Leland Slaughter, his director and the number-two man in the Miami office, entered, shaking Jeff's hand and patting his shoulder.

"Happy to see you, Jeff. You're okay? And Lisa?"

"We're taking it one step at a time."

"That's a helluva thing to have happened, a helluva thing. The police are on it?"

"They have some video footage from a neighbor, which may give them a lead, and we've installed a good home-security system."

"Good, good. I hope they catch the animal that did this. If there's anything we can do, just let me know. Come straight to me."

"Thank you, sir. Again, I'm sorry for delaying the presentation."

"No, no, couldn't be helped. I called in some favors, took care of it." Slaughter indicated the slides looping on Jeff's monitor. "You've come up with a brilliant concept, Jeff. They'll be here in an hour. All set?"

"Just fine-tuning."

"I'll send Martinez in. He needs to be on the same page for translation. Oh, and a last-minute addition. Your presentation will be webcast live to their affiliates in Bogota, Lima, Caracas, Santiago and Guatemala City."

No pressure. Jeff swallowed after Slaughter left. He'd resumed working for ten minutes when Fred Bonner, a longtime senior manager, stuck his head into his office.

"Got a sec?"

"Sure."

"I heard what happened to you and your wife. Everything all right?"

"We're a little shaken, but we're getting back to normal."

Bonner folded his arms, lowered his head of slicked-back, silver-streaked hair, then looked hard at Jeff. "Delaying your presentation threw a wrench into things."

"I know, and I feel terrible about that."

"Bet you didn't know that the delegation was pissed off, threatened to fly back to South America, taking with them our shot at a multimillion-dollar account. Leland had to call in some big favors, do some swift, creative diplomacy."

"No! What happened?"

"He called some of our airline and hotel clients and arranged to send the delegation to the casinos on Paradise Island in the Bahamas to keep them happy while he waited for you."

"I had no idea."

"He went out on a limb for you." Bonner nodded to Jeff's work on his monitor. "This is the concept you developed in Cleveland that Leland fell in love with, the one that got you here?"

"It is."

"And it's all yours?"

"What do you mean?"

"It's your idea."

"Yes, well, the concept came out of a brainstorming session in Cleveland, but I ran with it, took it further and developed it. So yes, it's my idea."

Bonner shook his head slowly. "I don't quite grasp it, but Leland seemed impressed enough to bring you down here." He sucked air through his teeth, gazed out at the view. "These days, we just don't do this sort of thing, move people around anymore. When I started with the group here, we had over one hundred and fifty people in this office. Now we're down to—what, forty-five, fifty? And we're fighting to stay alive, to understand what's happening to advertising and marketing." Bonner turned to him. "Guess what I'm trying to say is Leland's put his ass on the line for you, Jeff. Don't let him down."

"I appreciate what's at stake here."

A soft knock at the door sounded.

"Sorry to interrupt, but Leland sent me," Nick Martinez said, "to check the updates for translation."

"Go ahead, Nick. I'm done here." Bonner moved to leave. "Good luck, Jeff."

Martinez came over to Jeff's monitor. After Bonner's departure, he said softly, "Don't worry about Fred."

"You heard?"

"Enough," Martinez said. "Fred Bonner's a dinosaur, thinks he's in *Mad Men*. He started in the business long before the digital age—before cell phones, if you can believe it."

"I got a sense of that from his hair," Jeff joked.

"He looks like a Wall Street villain," Martinez said. "Look, Leland's smart, he's adapting to the evolution of the industry. He sees how the New York, LA, London and Paris offices are adapting to change, that we need perspectives like yours. When Leland saw your work, he feared we would lose you to some other ad or tech company in California. That's why he went after you. I heard him say there's a lot of unharnessed talent in that Cleveland office."

"A lot of problems, too," Jeff murmured to himself.

"Sorry?"

"I've seen the changes, too. It's moving fast," Jeff spoke up, smiling.

"Yes. So, speaking of changes…"

Jeff and Martinez polished the presentation until it was time.

There were three women and three men in the delegation, largely from Buenos Aires. Most spoke English but with another forty or so on the video link from the other Latin American offices,

Slaughter wanted Martinez to provide translation, which the delegation accepted.

The group was from Globo Aedifico, a Latin American–based construction conglomerate seeking to establish a positive brand in order to compete around the globe. They'd already seen presentations by top agencies in New York and Los Angeles.

After introductions and checks that all links to the cities online were clear, Jeff commenced his slide and video presentation.

"In order to best tell the story of Globo Aedifico, we propose you tell a story—a truthful, honest story—but not what Globo Aedifico is. No. You don't create a brand that people will respect by promoting yourself. Never."

Jeff paused for effect. Some of the delegation looked puzzled. Jeff was certain Fred Bonner winced.

"You tell the story of how Globo Aedifico makes the lives of people in need better. Not who you are but what you do."

Jeff's presentation started by showing that most of the world's poorest people don't have access to hygienic toilets and often suffer from poor health, outbreaks and higher mortality rates as a result. He noted that several companies under Globo Aedifico were currently using their clean-water technology to address the issue in remote areas, but no one knew about the work they were doing in this regard.

He then outlined a campaign that would bring

the effort to the attention of international media, buy strategic ad space, and employ social-media influencers to spread the word, while also reaching out to the United Nations, the World Health Organization and expert NGOs, to make public-service videos with them.

The campaign would be framed as a humanitarian effort and would set Globo Aedifico apart from other corporations, branding it with the highest order of social awareness.

When his presentation ended, Jeff, Slaughter, Bonner and Martinez took questions and made notes before the delegation left, genuinely impressed.

"You hit it out of the park." Slaughter slapped Jeff on the back. "One of the best presentations I've seen in a long time. Their reactions were heartfelt, emotional. I got a good feeling."

"I agree." Bonner slapped Jeff's back, too. "Excellent job."

After accepting praise, Jeff stole away to the bathroom, splashed water on his face and texted Lisa.

How's it going on the home front, honey?

Still good. How'd it go?

Great, and I owe it to you. It was the tie.

Ha. Glad it went well.

Want to go out for dinner tonight?

Love to.

On his way to his office, Jeff saw Vanessa at reception holding the phone receiver and giving him a little wave. "Excuse me, Jeff. I have a call for you."

"Who?"

"Vida Warren."

Jeff caught his breath. "I'll take it in my office."

By the time he closed his door, his pulse had kicked up. He swallowed and picked up the handset.

"What is it, Vida?"

"All settled in there in Miami with Lisa?"

"Vida—"

"I know what you did in Cleveland, Jeff."

"Vida, please. You have to stop this."

"I know what you did, and I swear to God you're not going to get away with it. *Do you hear me?*"

The line went dead in his hand.

12

FBI special agent Terri Morrow let out a slow, even breath.

The First SkyNational Trust Bank in Fort Lauderdale, the one she was watching right now, was going to be robbed.

Morrow's heart beat a little faster as she reviewed what she knew.

In Macon, Georgia, the ex-girlfriend of a member of a criminal crew faced losing custody of her child for a drug charge. In exchange for immunity or a suspended sentence, she'd revealed that her ex's gang was set to pull off the heist. "And it's not the first one," she added. "I know because I've done research for them."

Macon police then alerted the FBI.

With less than twenty-four hours to act before the heist, the FBI had moved quickly to lead a multiforce operation on the bank to catch the suspects in the act and to secure an ironclad case against them. Their subjects were ex-convicts who had belonged to white-supremacist prison gangs and were believed to be behind at least four other commando-style armed bank robberies in Texas, Alabama, Georgia and Mississippi.

The FBI's information gave them the specific targeted branch, located in a strip mall not far from where the I-95 and I-595 intersect. Time of the robbery would be within fifteen minutes of opening, with the crew posing as tradesmen and construction workers. They had good descriptions of the suspects.

Last night the FBI had alerted bank management who contacted staff informing them not to report for work in the morning because the branch would be closed due to a computer failure. The FBI working with other police agencies moved in early to place armed law enforcement, hastily trained in bank procedure, to work as bank staff so the bank remained open for business.

Other agents, posing as customers or bank staff, would protect any customers who arrived early by taking them out a rear entrance. FBI SWAT team members were also nearby in concealed positions surrounding all entrances.

Fort Lauderdale police and Broward County sheriff's deputies had taken up concealed points forming an inner and outer perimeter around the strip mall using unmarked vehicles.

Morrow was with the Miami field office's violent-crimes squad, positioned with a radio and earpiece and reading her phone on a bench at the edge of the parking lot. Not far from her mind was the 1986 shoot-out at a bank heist in Pinecrest that left two FBI agents dead and five others wounded. She was wearing body armor under a baggy sweat-shirt.

Eight minutes after the bank opened, Morrow and others watched a Ford SUV and a GMC pickup truck arrive and park. Two men got out of each vehicle. Two of the four were wearing overalls, while the others looked like construction workers and carried sports bags or large backpacks over their shoulders as they walked across the parking lot to the branch.

When the men entered, police casually moved unmarked cars to block the parked pickup and SUV to hinder their escape.

At that moment, Morrow noticed something in an adjacent parking lot. Through a landscaped island holding a stand of palms and a dense, waist-high hedge, she saw a paneled van, driver's window down and a bare arm resting on the frame. She casually walked closer, spotting the tailpipe jitter of an idling engine. She requested an urgent check of the Florida tag.

Moving closer, Morrow now clearly saw the driver's tattoo, a shield bearing the number *1666*, a known supremacist, prison-gang symbol.

Her radio crackled.

The van's plate had come back: stolen out of Tampa.

Her radio then transmitted a static-filled update that all four suspects had been arrested without in-cident. Morrow's pulse quickened, her eyes sharp-ened on the van's driver. This was the getaway vehicle. Morrow called for backup, pulled out her chained badge, then drew her weapon, aiming at the driver's head.

"FBI! Put your hands outside the window now!"

The driver, Caucasian, in his early forties, with a scarred face bearing teardrop tattoos, eyed Morrow without moving. A siren yelped. Two unmarked Fort Lauderdale units appeared within inches of the van, doors opened, shotguns aimed at the driver.

He cursed, then got out as ordered, got down on the ground on his stomach. Morrow pulled his arms behind him, snapped handcuffs on him while he growled at her.

"I would've enjoyed killing you, you—"

"Shut up!" Morrow said, then read him his Miranda rights.

Standing up and catching her breath, Morrow felt her phone vibrate.

A text from Addison, her ten-year-old daughter.

Mom, Dakota just invited me to her birthday party sleepover can I go? Please, please, please!

Morrow exhaled and closed her eyes.

She needed a coffee.

Some twenty miles north of Miami on twenty acres of reclaimed wetland, the FBI's South Florida headquarters ascended seven and six stories in an H-shaped complex of undulating glass and aluminum.

The futuristic Grogan and Dove Federal Building was named after the two agents killed in the 1986 shoot-out, a fact Terri Morrow never forgot, even as she changed from her sweaty clothes and got into fresh pants, shirt and a new jacket, then washed her face in the bathroom sink.

Now, as she completed her report on her part of the operation and finished her coffee, she contemplated getting more before catching up on her other cases. One of the ASACs voices boomed from where he stood across the floor.

"Listen up, everybody," said Scott Wood, one of the FBI's Assistant Special Agents in Charge of Miami. "Outstanding work on this morning's takedown at First SkyNational Trust—five arrests, a major case cleared. The director called with congratulations. Superb performance."

Isn't that sweet. Morrow shrugged it off as she got fresh coffee and settled in to check her emails and the system for updates. She had a court case to work on. Her squad was preparing for an upcoming surveillance job concerning subjects linked to an armored-car heist. She checked her subsequent texts from Addison and thought that the surveillance timing might work out with Addison being at Dakota's sleepover party.

Morrow resumed working. All was quiet for her at the moment, until she caught sight of the small yellow note she'd posted to her monitor as a reminder.

Right.

Morrow was the FBI's South Florida agent on

a national task force investigating a series of unsolved homicides committed by one killer.

So far, the task force confirmed that over a span of six years, at least five women had been murdered and one had been attacked and had survived. Half of the cases were in Midwestern states. The others were in Pennsylvania, New York and Kentucky. The bureau had assigned agents in every state to the task force to scrutinize details that might arise in their jurisdictions. Morrow monitored the case regularly, checking with analysts and reviewing updates on all databases.

She entered her password to access the encrypted file, bracing herself as she started to review the first case. Her monitor filled with color photographs of the corpse of a naked white woman under a pile of branches. Her hands were bound behind her back with a cord stretching to wrap around her neck. Connie Ware, age twenty-five. A dog walker had found her August 4, 2012, in a wooded area of suburban Pittsburgh. Autopsy showed she had been sexually assaulted and stabbed nearly fifty times with a serrated blade. Her attacker had used a condom. She was last seen leaving her waitressing job at Super Ray & Dave's Family Eatery. Her wallet, including cash, bank and credit cards, was found at the crime scene. Her driver's license and phone were missing.

One month after Ware's body was found, someone used a burner phone to call Ware's home. Her mother had answered. She heard nothing but hard breathing. She insisted someone was on the line, refusing her demands to answer her questions. Investigators determined the call had been made from an untraceable phone and were unable to pinpoint the location. No other calls were ever made. An ex-boyfriend, who was solidly alibied and passed two polygraphs, had been ruled out.

Morrow moved to the second case, which began with a woman's naked torso on its back in a shallow grave in a vacant wooded lot of a Detroit suburb. On June 23, 2013, a local community group cleaning up the neighborhood discovered the body of Tammi-Sue Bellow, age twenty-four. She was bound in the same way and with the same type of cord and knot used in the Ware case. Bellow had been sexually assaulted and her throat had been slashed with a serrated knife. She had worked part-time as a drugstore clerk while studying to become a nurse at college. Her bag was found intact at the scene, but her driver's license and phone were missing.

The case was submitted to the FBI's ViCAP system for comparison with others. Investigators discovered that a foot impression found in the mud at the Detroit crime scene matched one found at the Pittsburgh scene, linking the first two cases.

In the next case, a wooded trail appeared on Morrow's screen. The display advanced to an empty field and the naked corpse of a white female, covered with a discarded rug.

On September 14, 2014, in Buffalo, NY, a group of birdwatchers found the body of Debra Lee Plager, a twenty-seven-year-old librarian. She'd been sexually assaulted, bound and strangled with the same type of cord and knot as in the previous cases. Plager's wallet was found at the scene. Only her driver's license and phone were missing. Plager's ex-husband, known to have abused her, was questioned but ruled out as a suspect.

The fourth case file began with photos of an abandoned apartment complex and a rusted trash bin that contained a woman's corpse. On May 19, 2015, in Chicago, two teenage boys, flying a drone that crashed into the bin, discovered the body of Nina Kaye Wilken, age thirty, a law student who'd been working in a bar. She had been sexually assaulted, strangled and bound with the same type of cord used in the other cases. Family members helped confirm her remains through dental records. Her purse was found with her, but again her phone and driver's license were missing.

The fifth case showed images of a two-story home. Then Morrow's monitor showed a bedroom with a naked woman on a blood-soaked bed, her limbs tied to each corner. On October 22, 2016, a neighbor discovered the body of Jasmine Maria Santos, age thirty-one, in her Indianapolis home. Santos was a bank teller and the divorced mother of a son, seven, and daughter, five. She had been bound in the same manner, sexually assaulted and stabbed more than three dozen times with a serrated knife, according to the autopsy report. Her phone and driver's license were missing.

Morrow clenched her eyes for a moment to process the horror of what she was reading before moving on.

The next case changed everything.

In the early hours of April 8, 2017, Rhondell Felicia Hinson, age thirty, was alone and asleep in her town house in Louisville, Kentucky, when she was attacked by a man with a knife and wearing dark clothing. Hinson, a security officer who'd served with the Army National Guard, fought for her life, struggling with the intruder. She clawed at his masked face, neck and hands, tearing one of his latex gloves, then smashing a lamp against his head before jumping from her window. She fled to a neighbor's house and suffered only lacerations to her arm and a sprained ankle.

But evidence recovered from the scene aided the investigation. It included a partial print. Investigators also recovered a section of cord, identical to the type used in previous attacks, and a partial shoe impression that, while a different shoe, was the same size as the impression recovered in earlier cases.

The quality of the partial fingerprint proved challenging for examiners. To date they had not succeeded in finding anything similar on record.

But interviews with Rhondell Felicia Hinson, the only known survivor, advanced the investigation, confirming a key fact common to all the cases. Prior to the attack, Hinson, a single woman, had frequented online-dating sites. When she'd arranged to meet a man, Ritchie Lee Bellanerd, at a restaurant, he failed to show up, leading Hinson and investigators to later suspect the attacker had targeted and stalked her.

Online-dating-site use was also a factor in three of the earlier homicides. And in the two other murders, the women who were living alone had conversed online about moving into a new residence. Again, this led investigators to suspect the killer hunted for victims online.

The FBI obtained court orders to examine all records of the dating sites and social-media sites used by the victims and visited by the suspect. The investigation yielded no concrete results. In the Hinson case, Ritchie Ray Bellanerd didn't exist. In the other cases, investigators suspected the killer had used stolen or fictitious IDs and burner phones to communicate with, stalk and attack the women.

Morrow surveyed recent comments posted by other task-force investigators. Some were concerned that they only knew of the six confirmed cases. There may have been more. Others observed that the killer appeared to be dormant after the Kentucky case, and they speculated that, having been thwarted, he'd been thrown off his game. An FBI agent in Chicago wondered if it was time to go to the media with the case.

The Behavioral Analysis Unit, in its study of the offender, noted that he kept the driver's licenses and other items of his victims as trophies and as a means for him to relive and fantasize about his acts and to possess his victims again.

That prompted an agent in Buffalo to nickname their unknown subject The Collector.

Morrow felt her gut tighten with anger at how this monster preyed upon lonely, vulnerable, beautiful women, and how he was outsmarting law enforcement, getting away with his crimes.

We've got to catch this guy.

She'd been working with Jake Zhu, an FBI analyst, to monitor the crime databases of the three metropolitan counties, Miami-Dade, Broward, and Palm Beach, and Monroe in the south, along with several others for any similar key details found in crimes committed in her area. She knew it was hit-and-miss because not every jurisdiction or police department was thorough or had the resources to keep their systems detailed and current.

She made one last check for any alerts or updates.

Nothing.

She exhaled and logged out of the investigation.

At least we have no connection to The Collector in Florida.

13

Jeff took Lisa to a French restaurant not far from the Venetian Pool in Coral Gables. Nick Martinez, from his office, had recommended it. It was cozy with elegant wood paneling, ornate mirrors and candlelight flickering on their table. The aromatic air held the promise of delicious food.

"This place is *so* expensive," Lisa whispered behind her menu after they were seated.

"We've earned this. We've had a wild ride these past few days."

They selected a red house wine and the six-course option that began with an appetizer of grilled octopus, pine nuts, potatoes and romesco sauce. It was delicious, but at the outset of their evening Jeff seemed distracted.

"Jeffrey." Lisa tapped his hand playfully as he swiped his phone's screen. "You've checked it several times since we arrived."

"Sorry." He slipped his phone into his jacket pocket.

"Is it the house? Is it work?"

"Everything, I guess. There's a lot riding on the South American account, and I was checking the security system, you know. Tell me how things went for you today."

The next course came, and Jeff started on his small portion of tangerine-roasted Alaskan king crab. Lisa tasted her warm potato salad with smoked salmon, then related her day.

"I worked on the pesticide data for a while, then I had a video chat with Joy."

"How're things with her?"

"Good. Carter and Charlotte are so adorable. I wish I were there. She offered to come down for a few days but I said no."

They both knew there was more, that Lisa was scratching the surface.

"What else did she say?"

Lisa took a moment as she ate. "She told me not to let my fear run my life, that I should take control."

"Sounds like good advice."

"I knew you'd say that."

The next course was warm creamy egg and sea urchin on a salt bed.

"Lisa, you have to take things one step at a time. But Joy's right. Get out there. Meet the neighbors, join the groups, get connected. Live your life."

"But I—I…"

"What?"

"I miss my life in Cleveland, Jeff—my family, my friends, my job. I'm sorry, but that's the truth."

Jeff's face went taut as he topped his wineglass, gulped some.

"What about you?" she asked.

"What about me?"

"Don't you miss Cleveland, too?"

"Not really. I needed to get out of there."

"That's an understatement. Our move was so fast we must've set a record. I know things weren't great in your office, but why did we have to move so fast?"

"You know why. There were problems there. I was busting my behind, doing the best I could. I was covering for people, carrying people, and I was going nowhere. I needed to make something happen, if I was ever going to get someplace." Jeff swallowed more wine. "You know most of this."

"Not all the details."

"I worked hard, came up with new concepts, and I was secretly talking to top people in the marketing divisions at Google and Apple about positions in California."

"California? I didn't know that."

"Only early-stage discussions. Anyway, that's when Leland Slaughter saw my work. He loved it. He made the fantastic offer to come here. It meant more money, and God knows we need it with our debts. I couldn't refuse. He needed me right away for the South American proposal. I told you, there's a twenty-million-dollar account on the line. The stakes in this are huge, not only for me or the Miami office but for Asgaard-T-Chace."

"You never told me about California. Why did

you keep that from me?" Sadness washed over her face.

"It was just some preliminary stuff, nothing concrete. Honey?"

Lisa looked at him, the candlelight reflecting in her glistening eyes.

"What is it?" he asked.

"I have a bad feeling about being here. I can't explain it."

"It's understandable, after what's happened."

"We're supposed to start a family."

"We will."

"You keep saying that."

"Just give me a little time."

The next course came, a small portion of foie gras for Lisa and seared sweetbreads, asparagus, quail egg and ham for Jeff. They ate in silence with Lisa taking small bites until Jeff's fork chinked as he set it down.

"What happened was horrible," Jeff said, "and it enrages me when I think of what that asshole did to you, to us. But we have to step back."

"What do you mean?"

"We need to appreciate our lives, what we have," he said. "The projects we're each working on highlight just how fortunate we are, compared to so many others. Look at what your folks are doing in Central America, then look at where we are and how we live."

Jeff paused, reached for his wine, gazed into it, thinking, then studied her, his eyes burning.

"Lisa, you gotta remember where I came from. How I had to fight for everything. We both know how life can take everything away from you." He snapped his fingers. "Like that!"

"But it almost did." Her voice nearly broke and trailed off to a whisper. "The other night in our home, Jeff, it almost did."

He got up, moved around the table and hugged her.

"We're going to get through this. Consider how, ever since you were nine, you've carried guilt over your friend's death. Consider everything I went through after my father's death. We've both survived the worst life has thrown at us, and I swear we'll survive this, too."

She nodded, embarrassed, urging him to get back to his chair.

She needed to collect herself. She went to the washroom. Navigating around the tables in the dim light, she felt the attention of other diners had subtly turned to her, and she was hit with a sudden wave of unease.

Is he here, watching me?

Alone in a locked stall, she sat down and took a few slow breaths.

What's happening to me? Joy's right. Jeff's right. I've got to get a grip.

She took out her phone and checked the security system, examining the exterior and interior of the house until she was satisfied, regained her composure and returned to their table.

* * *

After dinner they went for a drive along the water.

They found an inviting spot where they got out and walked on the beach holding hands, enjoying the soothing caress of the breeze.

They got home late. Jeff checked the system and then, at Lisa's insistence, inspected every room. As they got ready to turn in for the night, Jeff went to the bedroom window and looked down at the street. After a minute, Lisa joined him.

Two men in reflective vests were talking to an officer in a marked Miami-Dade car near the front of their house.

"What's going on?" Lisa asked.

"Looks like the crime-watch people. I'm sure one of them is Roland Dillard. I'm going out there. Stay here. I'll be right back."

She watched Jeff approach the men. She cracked the window. Scratchy bursts of police radio chatter made it difficult for her to comprehend the parts of the conversation that drifted up from the street. Jeff nodded as the men and officer pointed here and there. Then everyone shook his hand, and he waved to them and returned to the house.

One of the men looked up at the window, directly at Lisa. She recognized him as Dillard. He gave her a friendly wave. She waved back.

"What's up?" she asked after Jeff returned and undressed for bed.

"It was Dillard on the watch patrol with some other guy, Jed Purcell. They were just talking with the cop who told me they may have new leads on our suspect."

"Good. I feel better with Dillard's posse out there."

"He asked me again to join the watch patrol."

"Are you going to?"

"Yes, I told him I would."

"Really? With everything you've got going?"

"I thought about how he helped us with the system, how our neighbors are out there, you know, everyone doing their part. He's going to talk to me about how it all works in a couple days."

"Officer Jeff Taylor on the beat." She got into bed, wrapped her arms around him. "It's kind of a turn-on."

He hugged her. "I'm sorry about tonight," he said. "I need to be more understanding of what you're going through."

"I'll get control of things."

"We'll start a family. I promise."

She kissed him. He kissed her back.

"You know, we could practice right now," she said, reaching for him.

Lisa woke. It was nearly 2:00 a.m.

She turned, having expected to hear Jeff snoring, which he always did after sex. His side of the bed was empty.

She looked to the bathroom. Empty, too.

Jeff was gone.

She got up to look for him, pulling on her new robe, switching on the lights and padding down the stairs. Jeff was in the living room, sitting on the sofa. She approached him, but he didn't acknowledge her or react. His eyes were glassy and open, staring at nothing, with his arms at his side like a zombie.

She'd seen this before—he was having a sleepwalking episode.

It happened a few times a year. She knew that the best thing to do was leave him alone and go back to bed. She was a little uneasy doing that now, but she was tired and decided to head back upstairs. She'd just managed to fall back asleep when she was awakened again.

Jeff had returned to bed, but now his side of the room was awash in the light of his phone.

He was wide-awake, tense as he scrolled.

The sleepwalking, the phone. What's going on?

Lisa turned back to her side pretending to be asleep while staring at the wall, too tired to ask him and risk starting something.

She tried to get back to sleep, but the questions kept coming.

Why had he kept California a secret? Is he keeping something else from me?

14

The next morning, Lisa woke determined to start reclaiming her life.

After breakfast and seeing Jeff off, she launched into a morning workout of leg lifts, squats and push-ups. Then, holding her light weights, she punched at the air and her frustration.

Joy and Jeff were right. She had to get control. And Jeff was doing his best to be supportive. He was. But she couldn't dismiss feeling a bit neglected these days because he was married to his ambition.

Lisa got that.

Switching into a shoulder stand to bicycle her legs, she remembered how they'd met nine years ago at a party for one of his clients, one that her company had also done research for. He had those Bambi eyes, full of feeling, yet there was a quiet mystery about him.

"I'm a street kid from Chicago," he'd said after they'd started dating and opening up to each other. He'd told her how his parents were blue-collar factory workers before his father was killed, how he and his mother ended up on the street, living in their van and shelters.

Jeff was smarter than most kids and, despite his hardships, did well in school while working at jobs to help with bills. As he got older, he continued helping his mother until she died of heart failure. He earned scholarships, worked part-time, took out loans and put himself through college, determined never to work in a factory or be on the street again. He excelled in advertising. And after interning at Asgaard-T-Chace Group in Chicago, he landed a job in the company's Cleveland office.

Lisa couldn't help herself. At times she thought of him as a quiet, mistreated pup no one wanted. She had so many reasons for loving him the way she did. He was the only person who knew and truly understood the secret guilt she carried for Stacey's death because he carried the same feeling over his father's death.

She also loved him because he was so capable of surviving. She felt safe with him. Look at all the heartbreak that life had thrown at him, and he not only survived but triumphed. And he had a good heart. She saw it when she went with him to the Chicago cemetery to visit the graves of his parents, watching him tenderly caress the headstone as he placed flowers and fought his tears. Yes, he had a good heart. She knew it and trusted him completely with hers. Jeff was not perfect. He had a temper, issues—the sleepwalking among them— but she loved him with everything she had.

Still, in all the time she'd known him, there was something beneath the surface that she didn't fully understand.

She knew he'd vowed to never be poor again and would do anything to prevent that from happening. Yet he seemed to hold a grudge against the world, while a dangerous inferno raged in his heart.

And now I can't shake this feeling he's keeping something from me.

But why would he do that, when things were going so well for him?

Breathing hard after her workout, Lisa asked herself if she was resentful of Jeff now that she was the one facing challenges. She'd worked hard, too. She had a master's degree from Yale where she'd studied statistics and data science. But the move from Cleveland had cost her her manager's status, something she'd striven for and earned. She had given that up, along with her family and friends in Ohio, to follow Jeff's dream, with the promise of starting a family.

And now she was grappling with the assault and the intruder's threat to return.

"Stop it. Stop complaining, count your blessings and get on with your life!" Lisa told the woman in her bathroom mirror, convincing herself that she knew her husband and that he wouldn't keep secrets from her.

They'd both faced profound tragedy and carried the pain of it with them. Jeff was right: they were survivors, and they understood each other. That's why she'd married him.

Lisa reached for her phone and as she ran a check of the security system, she got a text from Jeff.

Everything good?

Yes. Fine. How're things there?

Got a big meeting coming up, gotta go. Love you.

Love you, too.

Before Lisa got into the shower, she placed her phone on the counter within reach.

You've got to think positive, be strong and brave, and quit thinking of yourself.

But it was not easy.

The ghost of her own childhood tragedy was ever present, and it began haunting her now. Her mind called up images of her riding in the back seat of the car with Stacey. She couldn't bear to relive the details again.

Even now, everywhere I go, I see Stacey. I see her at the mall, in parks, on the street, in the faces of little girls who look like her and of women who are the same age that Stacey would be had she lived. I see those women with their husbands and children, and I wonder about the life Stacey would have had if I hadn't—if I hadn't... It just hurts so much. I feel that I don't deserve a happy life, that karma's going to get me, going to exact a painful toll for what I did to Stacey.

Lisa shifted her focus and considered her parents who, after working so hard on their business for decades, after putting her and Joy through college, set out devoting their lives to helping people less fortunate in the world. Drawing on her mother and father for inspiration helped Lisa focus and get to work.

She finished writing her report on the survey data relating to traces of pesticides in drinking water. She polished it, then submitted it and moved on to her next assignment. It involved working with a state government and a number of health groups to design a survey to help with the study of people who have emerging diseases. Lisa's Cleveland office had sent her a file with twenty-six attachments of material of various sizes. She dived in, reading each file and making notes. It was midafternoon by the time she'd finished.

Her neck and shoulder muscles were knotted.

She'd worked through lunch and went to the kitchen to eat some fruit, happy that her work had taken her mind off of her troubles. Eating an apple, she walked to the sliding door, disarmed the security system, unlocked it and stepped into the warmth of the sun shimmering on the pool.

So inviting.

Admitting that since the attack she had not resumed her running routine because she was still afraid, she decided that until she climbed back on that horse, she'd get her exercise by swimming ten, fifteen, twenty lengths, whatever she could handle. She changed into her swimsuit, then got a big towel and placed it next to her phone at the poolside and stepped into the water.

It was liquid heaven against her skin, magically melting the tension. After ten lengths, she began to tire, but the no-pain-no-gain mantra kept her going. While turning her head automatically for air with every other stroke, Lisa had just begun her twelfth length when she was pierced with a spear of fear.

What was that?

She plunged underwater, frantic for her feet to find the bottom, crouching below the surface, swirling her arms and hands, steadying herself, turning toward the edge of the pool. Looking up through the water, she saw a distant, blurry face.

Someone was in her backyard.

15

Lisa's heart pounded in her chest.

She didn't know how much longer she could stay underwater.

I've got to get to my phone!

It was at the opposite end of the pool, near the house and opposite to where the figure was.

Lungs nearly bursting, she swam underwater toward the far end. Surfacing then scrambling from the water, she seized her phone. Leaving wet tracks, she ran toward the sliding door, preparing to dial when—

"Hello, Lisa!"

The voice stopped her in her tracks—it was her neighbor Roland Dillard.

"Oh my God." She released a deep breath. "Roland, it's you!" Abandoning her call, her panic subsiding, she returned to her poolside chair and reached for her towel, pulling it over her shoulders. "Gosh, you startled me."

"I'm so sorry. I didn't mean to scare you."

Dillard was standing in his yard, his head and

shoulders visible above the shrub-encased fence that divided their property.

"I was working on my garden, heard splashing and thought I'd check. You know, keeping watch. Forgive me, please. I didn't mean to startle you."

"It's okay," she said, wrapping her towel around her, tucking it under her arms. "Thanks. Oh, I wanted to tell you again how much we appreciated your help with our security system."

"Don't mention it. Look, if you have a minute, why don't you come over. I'd love for you to meet Nell, my wife, have a proper hello."

Lisa nodded. "I'd like that. How about in an hour? Let me dry off and change."

"Sounds fine. Just go around the block. We're one-sixty-eight Sunhaven."

Lisa had a quick shower, dried her hair, put on a summer top and shorts, grabbed her car keys, armed the security system and drove to the big strip mall where she visited a couple of boutiques before making a purchase.

Soon after that, she pressed the doorbell at the front of the Dillards' beautiful, sprawling bungalow. As the door opened, Lisa's smile retreated slightly. An older woman stood before her wearing a floral muumuu and matching head scarf. The skin on her face was tight to her skull, making her oversize glasses look even bigger. Lisa thought she looked ill.

"Hi, I'm Lisa Taylor, your backyard neighbor."

A gnarled hand was raised to open the door

wider as Lisa met the woman's fierce, dark eyes and the hint of a smile.

"I'm Nell Dillard. Please come in. Rollie, she's here!"

Cellophane rustled as Lisa stepped into the house carrying a gift basket.

"What have we here?" Nell said.

"This is for you and Roland. Jeff's at work, but it's our way of thanking you for Roland's help with our home-security system, for being good neighbors. It's just wine and chocolates."

"Thank you. Very thoughtful. It wasn't necessary." Dillard emerged, smiling. "But I'll take it." He headed to the kitchen.

Nell led Lisa to the living room. "It's terrible what happened, that sleazeball breaking in, assaulting you, all right behind us. Just disgusting. Miami-Dade's good. Rollie's got his sources. They're working on it. Sooner or later they'll get that loser."

"Hope it's sooner."

"You'll see," Nell said upon arriving in the living room. "I made some fresh lemonade. Bring it out, Rollie," she called to her husband.

Lisa loved Nell's New York accent. "You have a gorgeous home," she said, looking around.

"I'll give you the grand tour later, if you like." Nell eased herself into a chair. "First, I'll get to the point about me." Nell pulled off her head scarf, revealing nothing but small islands of downy hairs on her scalp. "I've got cancer. It's terminal. I have good days when I'm strong and bad days when I'm not. Not sure how much time I have left—days, weeks, months, maybe a year, but that's it."

Lisa put her hand on Nell's knee. "I'm so sorry."

"Don't be. Death has been my life."

Not understanding, Lisa glanced at Dillard, back at Nell and said, "What do you mean?"

"I worked in the New York City medical examiner's office as a forensic mortuary technician, assisting the MEs with autopsies. It's how I met Rollie. We stood together over many bodies. I also worked death scenes across the city. You wouldn't believe the things I've seen."

Nell leaned closer to Lisa, dropping her voice. "I know the unimaginable things humans are capable of doing to other humans."

Lisa nodded at Nell's intensity as she continued.

"The job gave me a different point of view. Not much in this world gets to me. So no, dear, don't be sorry for me. Rollie and I have had a good run. We're at peace. Aren't we, Rollie?"

"We are." He set down a tray of some cookies alongside glasses filled with ice and lemonade.

"My, my," Nell's focus sharpened on Lisa, her high cheekbones, her thick hair and her pearl stud earrings. "You are a pretty one, aren't you?"

Lisa smiled, blushed. "Thank you."

"Rollie, get my pillow, will you?"

Dillard fetched a large pillow from behind Nell's sofa chair, slipped it behind her, gently fluffing and positioning it just so. Lisa was touched at how tender he was with his dying wife. He stood in healthy contrast to her. He had sharp, squinting eyes and the knotted face of man who had experienced a hard life, a capable protector who reminded Lisa of her father.

"Thanks," Nell sighed. "So Rollie tells me you and Jeff don't have any kids?"

"Not yet, but we're working on it. Roland told me that you don't have any children."

Nell shook her head. "That's right, I lost three. I couldn't carry to term. No relatives either. It's just going to be Rollie when I'm gone, but he'll manage to find someone else to marry."

"No need to talk such nonsense." Dillard bit into a cookie and shifted the topic. "I'm glad Jeff's going to join our neighborhood watch."

"Me, too," Lisa said. "He wants to pitch in, do his part. As you said, it's only a few hours now and then, even though he's pretty busy at his job."

Lisa helped herself to a cookie, then tried Nell's lemonade as they talked about what she and Jeff did—*statistician and advertising*—life in Cleveland—*won't miss the snow*—and whether the Browns would ever make it to the Super Bowl. They talked about life in Palm Mirage Creek. How Dillard's consulting work meant a lot of travel. Sometimes Nell went with him. But lately they'd slowed things down a bit; they arranged a nurse for Nell whenever she was not feeling strong and Dillard had to leave on business. And how Dillard was confident Miami-Dade would arrest Lisa's attacker; how he was pressing every source he had to help track down the suspect.

"I'm sure he's done this before, and he'll try

to do it again," Dillard said. "But we're going to catch him."

Lisa found comfort in Dillard's assurance. Melting ice shifted in her now-empty glass, most of the cookies were gone and she glanced at her phone.

"Look at the time," she said. "I'd better be going. Don't want to overstay my welcome."

"You're not leaving," Nell said and pulled herself to her feet, "until I give you that little tour."

"I'd like that."

Starting with the living room, Nell swept an arm to the white mantel fireplace with its soft gray and white tiles. They moved to the modern kitchen with wooden cabinets, granite counter and island. The home had polished marble floors, a mix of vaulted ceilings and exposed beams. As they continued, Nell, who clearly loved her home, explained what was original, restored or replaced.

The great room opened to a small pool and an Eden-like yard of palms and thriving flower gardens. The dining room had a carved mahogany table and six Queen Anne chairs. Throughout the house, Lisa saw stunning white porcelains, which Nell said she'd collected from Thailand and China. There were a number of white accent chairs with a red-coral needlepoint design evoking a tropical look. One small room was finished in a tranquil shade and had a beautiful old rocking chair next to a large window. "My great-grandfather made that chair for my great-grandmother," Nell said.

The master bedroom was huge with a king-size bed. Lisa noticed a forest of pill bottles covered one of the night tables and assumed it was Nell's. The walk-in closet went on forever. The en suite bathroom was spacious. The second and third bedrooms had a sort of art-deco feel and were done in shades of *verde agua* and turquoise.

"It's more room than we need, but we like to spread out. We like our space. Last stop."

They went across the house to the far end where they came to the fourth bedroom. The guest room. It had a queen-size bed, coral accented walls, a matching love seat at the foot of the bed and twin bamboo night tables.

"Pretty," Lisa said. She glanced at the closed closet door and stopped.

Something about the door was unusual. At first it looked like a regular door. The coral shade matched the room, yet it seemed...*fortified*. It was a solid door with a steel handle. A foot above the handle was a dead-bolt, then another near the top of the door and another at the bottom of the door. Nell saw Lisa's curious expression.

"It's a safe room," Nell said. "They're fairly common."

"A safe room?" Lisa stepped to the door, touching it with her fingers.

"The original owner had it put in when he repaired the place after Andrew," Nell said. "That door is fourteen-gauge steel, with triple locks. Nothing can penetrate it. The room itself is enormous, built with its own concrete footings and steel, its own A/C, ventilation and water. It can withstand any hurricane or home invasion. We don't have to pack up and sit in evacuation traffic with every storm. Still, I prefer to evacuate, but if we can't get out, we have this room. Rollie keeps it locked and stocked, takes care of everything."

"Wow. That's thinking ahead," Lisa said, turning, surprised to see that Dillard had joined them for this part of the tour and was watching from the guest-room doorway.

"Because you never know what's coming," he said.

16

"So I shouldn't put through any calls from Vida Warren?" Vanessa at reception repeated for Jeff, who was standing at her desk after arriving at the office.

"That's right. Say I'm unavailable or you've passed her message to me. You know, something like that."

"I'll take care of it." Vanessa typed a note on her keyboard.

"Thanks."

When he got to his office, he set his bag down near his desk. Before he could deal with everything on his mind, his email chimed with a priority alert from Leland Slaughter's assistant.

The director has called a meeting in the board-room in ten minutes. RE: Globo Aedifico. If you've received this message, your attendance is required.

Forcing himself to remain calm, Jeff checked his other messages, texted Lisa at home, downed the last of the coffee in his commuter cup, then went to the meeting.

Fred Bonner was already there, checking his phone, as was Nick Martinez and a handful of colleagues from other departments who Jeff didn't know that well yet. Leland entered, taking his place at the head of the table. He was not wearing a jacket, his sleeves were rolled up, his tie loosened.

"Last night, Antonella Benitez, one of the executives of Globo Aedifico, called to inform me her team loved our proposal. They want it."

Cheers rippled around the table.

Slaughter raised a palm. "There's more. Her team will urge Globo's executive approval committee to accept our proposal. A formality, she said. And they want to add another five million to the account. Approval may take longer, but she assured me nothing will prevent Globo Aedifico from giving us the twenty-five-million-dollar account."

"Jeez," someone said.

Someone else whistled.

"They were blown away by our presentation," Slaughter said. "Foster and I were on the phone to New York early this morning conveying the news. We beat out some really heavy hitters, and New York was pleased, very pleased. Excellent job, everyone, and to you, Jeff, given all that you had going on at the time."

Jeff nodded his appreciation. Martinez slapped his back.

"This week we'll start planning meetings to

initiate some of the preliminary work," Slaughter said. "So again, congratulations on a helluva job, team. Now we get down to it. Jeff, can you drop by my office in a minute?"

"Yes, sir."

As the meeting concluded, Jeff accepted handshakes, backslaps and attaboys. In the hall, Bonner pulled him aside.

"I have to confess I was skeptical," he said. "That concept you developed—well, what can I say? It's something." Bonner gave him a once-over and winked. "It's something, all right."

Unsure if Bonner was challenging him or complimenting him, Jeff accepted Bonner's hand, shook it and thanked him.

Slaughter was on the phone, standing at his desk, and waved Jeff in as he ended the call.

"I want to emphasize that I'm very pleased with your work." Slaughter rolled down his sleeves, fastened his collar button, stretched his neck, then tightened his tie. "In the short time you've been here, you've proven to be a vital asset to this office."

"Thank you, sir. I appreciate all you've done for me."

"Your concepts are marvelous, brilliant. We'll expect more work of that caliber from you. It's why I brought you here."

"Yes, sir."

"Now, this is premature because the Globo Aedifico contracts haven't been signed yet. But there will be a bonus for you, a very healthy bonus.

Foster and I convinced New York of this, so keep it confidential, please."

"Of course, sir. Thank you."

"Just keep up the good work, and give my best to your wife."

Alone in his office, Jeff drank a cold glass of water and tried to sort out the thoughts whirling in his head. Last night with Lisa, her wrestling with the assault and wanting to start a family, him joining the patrol, and here he was performing like an all-star, succeeding beyond his expectations. If this played out right, if nothing got in the way, his dreams were in his grasp.

A knock sounded at his door. "Hey, superstar," Martinez said.

"Hey, Nick."

"You're killing it, man."

"It's unbelievable. Thanks for your help."

"Don't thank me. It was all you. Hey, sorry, but there's this woman on my line who somehow got me. She says she really needs to talk to you. Won't say why, but I got her name. Vida Warren."

Jeff's face whitened. "Really? On your line?"

"Yeah. Her name sounds familiar. I think she's from the Cleveland office. I might've sat in on conference calls with her a while back. She insists she talk to you. Want me to transfer it to you?"

Jeff hesitated, then said, "Sure, transfer her to me. Sorry."

"Hey, no worries. Oh, one quick thing. I wanted to tell you my sister's a criminal defense attorney, a lot of rich clients. Anyway, she's got Marlins season tickets, so if you ever want to see a game, maybe celebrate the deal, let me know."

"That's fantastic. Very generous. Thanks."

"Sure, pal. I'll send that call to you." Martinez left.

Jeff closed his office door. A few seconds later his line rang, and he grabbed it. "Vida?"

"I know what you did, Jeff."

"Stop calling me."

"I won't stop until everyone knows."

Jeff stood, glanced around to ensure no one heard as he lowered his voice. Gritting his teeth, he said, "You better stop. I'm warning you."

"Or what? What're you going to do?"

"Don't push me."

Jeff ended the call.

He turned to the magnificent view, but all he saw was the beginnings of a crisis.

17

"The club looks good. What're you getting?" Joe Reddick said.

"Cobb salad." Camila Cruz ruminated as she swiped on her iPad. "What the hell did Taft mean?"

The Miami-Dade detectives were returning from Hialeah where the police department had alerted them to the recent arrest of a suspected car thief, one Grover Garfield Taft. He'd claimed to have information about recent burglaries in Coral Terrace and Palm Mirage Creek and wanted to exchange it for a reduced charge. "You got a lot of movement in the trade in the Terrace, the Creek and the Gables, a lot of strange shit, man. It's why I moved my show to Hialeah."

But the twitching thirty-year-old refused, or was unable, to elaborate or provide names, details, anything of value, and after thirty minutes Cruz and Reddick left empty-handed. They'd been putting in long hours and were grabbing a late lunch at the Denny's east of the Palmetto Expressway by the airport.

Cruz, frustrated at Taft's cryptic, all-but-useless information, went back to square one with a vengeance as she worked on her iPad.

Earlier that morning, Frances Thorne, a crime analyst, had provided them with a fantastic geo-statistical timeline breakdown of burglaries that were similar to the Taylor case. Thorne drew upon data from Miami-Dade and those supplied by other jurisdictions. Her analysis covered Palm Mirage Creek, Coral Terrace, Coral Gables, South Miami, Pinecrest west to Olympia Heights and south to Palmetto Bay and Cutler Bay.

"You think we'll pull something from all of those pretty maps, graphs, pies and summaries?" Reddick bit into the first quarter of his club.

"It's another tool we need to use, Joe, because so far we got nothing solid."

Cruz stabbed her salad, shaking her head as she inventoried the status of the case. The video of *Shadow Man*—the name Cruz had given their suspect—had yielded nothing so far. The lab's analysis of Lisa Taylor's nightgown resulted in detailing some fibers but no DNA, nothing promising. Study of the Taylors' phones, computers and list of contractors had not led to any leads, nor did the warrant on phone communication in the area for the time of the crime. No hits or flags from any of the regional or national databases so far.

"But the analysis we got from Frances this morning is custom-made specifically for us." Cruz turned her iPad, giving Reddick a better look. "It's very good. Thorne's analysis went back three years, two years, one year, six months, then one month, breaking it down with dates, addresses and details, but only cases that have key aspects similar to the Taylor case."

Cruz swiped through the information showing residences with no security system, then those where point of entry was a sliding door, those where it was a back door or window, those where little or nothing of value was stolen. She showed Reddick how they could superimpose any of the maps and data over any of the others. She noted that, of all the cases, the Taylor case was the only one where the residents confronted the intruder.

"Go back three years." Cruz was chewing thoughtfully. "House in Cutler Bay, no security, side door, bedroom dresser rummaged, nothing stolen. Resident was away. Go back two years. Olympia Heights, no security, back window, nothing stolen, but while residents slept, house was messed up, even a girl's bedroom while she was away." She swiped. "A year ago, Palmetto Bay, residents absent, no security, side door, house ransacked."

"But we don't know if it's the same guy. No evidence linking these cases," Reddick said.

"That's right. We cannot say with one hundred percent certainty that this is all one guy. All we have is behavior that is similar. Now—" Cruz swiped again "—six months ago in Coral Gables, a house with no security, entry through sliding pool door, house was ransacked while residents were away. Now things change dramatically."

"What do you mean?"

Cruz slid her finger across the screen.

"Just under a month ago, South Miami, no security, side door, residence ransacked, but a female resident, away at the time, reports her underwear was taken."

"What the hell?" Reddick said.

"Two weeks ago, in Pinecrest, no security, side door, female resident away at the time with her husband reports all that's missing are her bras and panties."

"What do you make of that?"

"If it's the same guy, he's got a fetish for women's underwear, and we both know that's how many serial offenders evolve—Bundy, Golden State, BTK, that guy up in Canada, and a lot of others. In our situation here, the pattern fits. And if it's the same guy, something's happened. Something's changed in the last month or so, because he's escalating things."

"Then we have the Taylor case."

"The pattern fits there. Look at what he did to Lisa Taylor, what he said."

"Yeah, it fits, all right. He seems to like places with no security system. Maybe he stalks people online, scouts the community. Maybe we should alert patrols, neighborhood-watch block captains, set up bait houses."

"Yeah, because I think the Taylors interrupted him. I think he's becoming more dangerous, and he's going to strike again very soon."

18

That afternoon, Jeff arrived home, stopped cold in the foyer, worry etched in his face as he read new messages on his phone.

When he looked up, Lisa was standing in front of him.

"Everything okay?" she asked.

As if caught red-handed with a secret, he slid his phone into his pocket, shook his head, his face blossoming into a broad smile.

"Everything's terrific. We got the South American contract."

"Are you serious?"

"You bet. And get this: they upped the deal to twenty-five million."

"Wow! That's just—wow!" She threw her arms around him. "You worked so hard on this."

"There was a lot of pressure and strong competition."

"I was going to make spaghetti for dinner, but we should celebrate."

Jeff kissed her. "Your spaghetti with mushrooms is one of my all-time favorites. It'll be perfect. We can celebrate when it's official. There's talk that Slaughter and Foster Shore might throw some kind of shindig in a few days. Besides, we can always celebrate in other ways." Jeff caressed Lisa's back.

"More baby-making practice?"

"Practice makes perfect," he said and kissed her.

During dinner Jeff kept his phone on the table.

Given the celebratory air was something they both needed, Lisa refrained from requesting he shut it off and put it away.

"Oh, I almost forgot to tell you," Jeff said. "I've got a bonus coming from the South American deal, so we can pay down some of our debts and definitely get that sofa set we looked at in Coral Gables."

"Gosh, it's so expensive."

"It's going to be a big bonus." Jeff took a forkful of spaghetti. "This is excellent. So tell me about your day."

"Well, I worked right through. Finished the pesticide job, then started another assignment, then went for a swim."

"Nice, wish I was with you for that."

"Someone was."

Jeff stopped chewing. "What?"

Lisa told him how Dillard had given her a start, how she'd visited with him and Nell.

"It's good that you're getting out there, connecting with our neighbors," he said. "It's sad about

Nell being terminal, but it sounds like she appreciated the company, too."

"With all they're facing, they're such an extraordinary couple," Lisa said. "Nell worked in the medical examiner's office in New York. Roland's an ex-detective. I mean, she's dying but still a firebrand, and he's so vibrant, and the tender way he cares for her..." Lisa blinked her glistening eyes. "I know this sounds dumb, but they remind me of how swans are devoted to each other and mate for life, you know, stay together until death." She paused. "Did you hear what I said?"

He looked up from his phone. "Sorry, Dillard just sent me a message about my patrol shift. He needs to come over this weekend, something about a form."

Lisa stared at him. Behind his eyes was a half-hidden intensity betraying that something was going on with him.

"What is it, Jeff? What're you not telling me?"

"Nothing. It was just Dillard. Go on, I was listening."

"It's not important."

The mood had sobered, and they finished their dinner with little conversation.

"I'll clean up," Jeff said.

"No, I got it."

Jeff hesitated, knowing it would be wise to back off. "All right. I've got some work to look over."

He went to his office, shut the door and studied his phone.

Since he'd hung up on Vida Warren earlier that

day, she'd sent him more than two dozen emails
and texts.

Each one the same.

I know what you are, and I know what you did in
Cleveland. Soon everyone else will know. Time is
running out on you, Jeff.

19

"Come on, Addie!"

Addison Morrow turned the ball away from the pressure point so her team could maintain possession. Her dribbling skills were stronger than before, and so was her love for playing in the under-twelve group of the girls' soccer league, Terri Morrow thought, watching from the bleachers.

Two years since the divorce and Addie had been resilient adapting to what had become their new reality. Morrow had custody, but the terms meant Addie pinballed every third weekend and every second holiday from her home to her father's place in Hallandale, where he lived with his girlfriend and her two boys. But Addie had rolled with it.

"I've got one big family, Mom, like a lot kids in school," she had said.

Watching her, Morrow accepted the old truth: they grow up too fast. Now she stood, placed two fingers in her mouth and whistled a cheer. As Addie moved the ball down the field, Morrow's phone vibrated in her pocket delivering a secure message from her supervisor.

Terri: task force conf call in 1 hour. Need you to take it in the office.

Morrow calculated the distance and time. She'd pretty much have to leave now to make it.

Stephanie Gleason was standing next to Morrow. Gleason was her neighbor and Gleason's daughter was on the field, on Addison's team. She turned to Morrow and asked, "What's up, Terri?"

"Work."

"On a weekend?"

"Yup. I've got to go. Steph, can you take Addie? I'll catch up with you guys later. I shouldn't be more than a couple of hours."

"You got it."

"Thanks."

Stepping down to the sideline, Morrow waved, caught Addison's attention on the field, held up her phone, pointed to Stephanie. Addison, understanding her signal, nodded. This happened when your mom was an FBI agent.

Driving across the sprawling metropolis, Morrow was frustrated that she had to leave her daughter's game to take this call at the FBI office. But that was where the encrypted system was, and this was the job.

She glanced at the image of her and Addie on her phone's home screen and thought *Yes, they grow up too fast, and all you want to do is pro-*

tect them because—her mind flashed on images of all The Collector's victims—*because there are monsters in this world.*

Morrow made it in with fifteen minutes to spare. As she expected, no one was in the office.

She made coffee. At her desk, she logged in to her computer, put on her headphones, went to the secure app for video conference calls and punched in her password and today's code.

Staring at the FBI seal and the motto Fidelity, Bravery, Integrity on her screen, she sipped coffee, wondering why no advance information was given on who was leading this and why the urgency.

A static click sounded, and the seal was replaced with an image of several men and women at a conference table.

"Okay, everyone, we'll get to it. I'm Eva Sawyer, ASAC in Cleveland, and we have with us our colleagues with Cleveland PD and the Cuyahoga County Sheriff's Department. We'll dispense with introductions—people can identify themselves as they speak, and an attendance list will be circulated afterward. The FBI is leading and coordinating, but I'll pass this to Cuyahoga for an outline."

"Thank you. Detective Reese Tiller," the next person said. "We'll have accompanying slides and videos as we go, and you will all receive reports. Approximately six months ago, Maylene Marie Siler, age twenty-six of Cleveland, was reported missing by her family and friends after she'd finished her shift as a clothing-store clerk at one of the city's malls."

Photos of Siler, smiling and pretty, were displayed.

"Shortly after she went missing, investigators found no activity on her phone or her credit or bank cards. Approximately two months prior to her disappearance, Siler had broken up with a boyfriend—who has been cleared—and begun using online-dating services. In the days leading up to her disappearance, we determined she was in communication with a man named Luther Chase Lycek and had planned to meet him after her shift. Working with the online service, we've since confirmed the Lycek identity is fictitious and the phone he used was a burner, untraceable.

"Two weeks ago, a man walking his dog in the wooded edges of Tiffin Field discovered a partially clothed body, in a makeshift grave covered with underbrush. Subsequent investigation and autopsy confirmed the identity of the deceased as that of Maylene Marie Siler of Cleveland."

Images of the decomposing body were displayed, including those showing investigators in full bio suits processing the scene.

"Cause of death: stabbing with a serrated knife. Key facts: cord and knots used to bind the victim are consistent with those in the previous cases. The victim's cell phone is missing, and efforts to locate it have so far been unsuccessful. The victim's wallet with cash and credit and bank cards were found at the scene. Her driver's license is missing."

Slides showing the cord, the wallet, financial cards and other crime-scene material were displayed, and Morrow found herself nodding.

The Collector had definitely surfaced again.

"But we found something in one of her shoes," Tiller said.

Crime-scene photos showed a piece of paper, creased from folds. The next was a full screenshot of the words scrawled on it in black felt-tip pen. *I want to stop. Why can't I stop?*

Morrow cupped her face with her hand.

"There were no security cameras anywhere near that area," Tiller said, "leaving us to speculate that the suspect knew or had researched the area. We'll discuss other theories before we wrap up."

More aerial images from a drone of the crime scene were shown.

Eva Sawyer came back on. "Thank you, Reese. Now, we have our people processing the note, our BAU people working overtime on this. We have our forensic people going flat out on all the trace that surfaced in the previous homicides. It is clear, by the display here in Cleveland and the note, he's communicating to us. It is also clear that he will continue. He's intelligent. We know he's a traveler. We need each member of this task force to take a good, hard look—and I mean really hard look—at all the key facts and apply them to your respective jurisdictions across the country. We need to find a connection. There is one. It's out there. It's our job to find it and to stop him, because he's going to do it again."

The call then evolved into a Q and A session and discussion of theories and possible strategies. After it ended, Morrow got up from her desk, walked to the window, staring at nothing as she gathered her thoughts.

Bit by bit, we're getting more evidence, but we're not getting any closer, and he's collecting more victims.

Before leaving the office, Morrow went back to her desk to check the system for any updates or new internal emails for her. She found a few announcements, then one from Jake Zhu that had been sent late Friday.

Hi, Terri:
Still checking with the SF counties for any similar key facts; nothing hot surfaced. Then I got word from a colleague of mine with Miami-Dade on a case she recently investigated. There might be something interesting there. We should talk. How about Monday morning?

"How about now." Morrow clicked onto the FBI master contact list and scrolled to the bottom for Jake Zhu's private contact information.

20

Dillard cued up a page, then slid his tablet to Jeff.

"First thing, you have to complete this volunteer application for me," he said. "Miami-Dade requires it for all civilians who participate in the watch program."

"Now?"

"We should get it done before I take you out. Standard stuff, Jeff. Won't take long. I'll wait."

It was Saturday morning, and they were at the Taylors' kitchen table. Jeff scrolled through the form's questions about his address for the past five years, his employer, his medical-insurance provider, if he'd ever been arrested and convicted, if he abused drugs or alcohol, had any mental disabilities, was a registered firearms owner and so on. Jeff pulled out his wallet to reference his cards and began typing on the tablet while Dillard sipped coffee Lisa had made.

She was at the sink washing fresh vegetables she and Jeff had bought at the market that morning. She stopped, dried her hands and, while tightening her ponytail, asked, "So how's Nell doing?"

"The same. We take things one day at a time."

"I guess that's the best thing you can do."

"We go out when she's up to it. We'll go shopping, take a walk, go to dinner or see a movie, that sort of thing. Depending how she feels."

"Is she in any pain?"

"At times. Her drugs help, but some days nothing helps. You know, she was thinking of having you guys over for dinner sometime."

"I'd like that."

Then they talked a little about the investigation, with Dillard saying he'd heard the detectives were working hard on a few leads. By the time Dillard's cup was empty, Jeff had completed the application, and the two men left.

"Palm Mirage Creek, as you probably know, is unincorporated. Doesn't have its own police department and is covered by Miami-Dade."

Dillard wheeled his SUV from Jeff's driveway to take him through the neighborhood as an emergency scanner mounted under the dash spurted out transmissions.

Jeff felt like he was riding in a patrol car.

"Now—" Dillard lowered the scanner's volume "—I'm required to give this spiel about how watch members are only the extra eyes and ears of police, that we're to report any suspicious activities to 9-1-1 and never take action. But I'm telling you, we draw the line if a life's at risk."

He looked at Jeff for agreement. Jeff nodded.

"We patrol twenty-four seven, we use radios, we wear reflective vests so you know it's us out there as we watch for suspected criminal activity. And some of us are armed." Dillard opened the console between the seats to show his holstered handgun. "You with me so far, Jeff?"

"I am."

"There are regular community meetings with Miami-Dade that cover this, but since I'm a block captain, you're as good as deputized." Dillard winked.

In this introductory tour, they rolled along streets arched with tall shade trees, with Dillard noting the banyans, oaks, palms and occasional orange trees. Contemporary houses and those built in the Mediterranean Revival style of architecture sat on landscaped yards.

"Your night shift is coming up, so I'm going to let you in on something, given how it relates to what happened to you and Lisa."

"What's that?"

"My sources tell me that the investigators have a few theories based on their analysis of similar crimes here and in surrounding cities and counties."

"What're they?"

"The no-brainer is the burglars target homes without security systems and may go online to search for people who may be away."

"All right."

"Since your incident, they've been working with us and residents to set up bait houses."

"Bait houses?"

"A couple of homes without security systems are currently vacant, their residents away. We've advertised that fact on social media, citing vacations, sabbaticals in Europe, extended medical leaves, and hinting—lying, actually—that the homes have valuables—coin collections, jewels, that sort of thing. We have the agreement of the homeowners."

"To draw the burglars there."

"That's the point. But Miami-Dade has embedded GPS tracking chips in some items, set up cameras and silent alarms in the homes, cameras in the neighboring homes. The neighbors will watch, and so will we."

"Not bad. Think it'll work?"

"Time will tell." Dillard's face hardened as he searched the neighborhood, then looked at Jeff. "I will not accept what happened in my backyard on my watch."

"Believe me, I get that. I don't like it either."

"We're going to catch this guy. When I think about what he did and what he said to Lisa…" Dillard shook his head.

"Wait, you know what he said to her?"

"I'm an ex-cop. People trust me. They tell me stuff." He looked at Jeff. "Doesn't it piss you off that the asshole who assaulted your wife is out there?"

Jeff searched the neighborhood as a vein in his neck throbbed.

"More than you know."

21

A pair of crutches was leaning against Jake Zhu's workstation when Terri Morrow approached his desk at the FBI office Monday morning.

Bandages covered Zhu's forehead and elbow.

"What happened to you?" Morrow asked.

"Fell off my bike on the weekend." He turned from his keyboard, revealing red scrapes on his cheek. "Banged my head and elbow, sprained my ankle. They kept me overnight in the hospital for observation and wouldn't let me near any devices. Got to your messages on the task force this morning. All six of them."

"Sorry, Jake. I didn't know. We've got a new case out of Cleveland."

"No problem. I read the report this morning when I got in."

"You're okay to do this now? Can I get you anything?"

"A little sore, but I'm fine. Pull up a chair, Terri."

Soft-spoken, Zhu had been recruited by the FBI

from Caltech after his team was a runner-up in a hacker competition. Now, two years out of Quantico with top secret security clearance, Morrow thought he looked no older than fifteen, making her feel old.

"Okay, so…" Zhu began by pulling up a number of maps on his monitor. "You'd asked me to take key facts of the task-force cases and look for similarities in South Florida."

"Right."

"Been doing that all along, and we haven't got much to get excited about. As I'd mentioned, when you get to local levels, the quality of databases varies."

"I understand."

"I've been reaching out to other jurisdictions. Late Friday, I got an interesting response from Frances Thorne, a crime analyst with Miami-Dade. Recently, she'd completed an analysis for an ongoing investigation into a series of burglaries that may or may not be linked to each other."

"Burglaries?"

Zhu pointed a capped pen at one of the maps on his monitor. "In Thorne's analysis of Miami-Dade and neighboring jurisdictions, we have aspects of collection. In these cases, it's not IDs but rather undergarments. Still, it's collection. But there's more."

Zhu clicked, enlarging the map with locations and boxes containing dates and case summaries.

"Here and here, South Miami and Pinecrest, all within the last month."

"Yeah, but to link them to our guy is a bit of a stretch, Jake."

"Wait. A new case surfaced last week in Palm Mirage Creek. In this one, an intruder appears to have been interrupted. Nothing was taken, but the suspect, wearing gloves and face covered, held a female victim at knifepoint and sexually assaulted her by grabbing her briefly in front of her husband. Before escaping, the suspect threatened to return and assault the woman. The weapon was reported to have been a serrated knife."

"That's a serious crime, but I just don't know how it relates..." Morrow leaned closer to Zhu's monitor to read the case summary, then her breath caught. "The victim just moved to Palm Mirage Creek from Shaker Heights. That's Cleveland."

"I know. Could be a coincidence," Zhu said.

Morrow thought for a moment. "It probably is."

"But look at the other aspects—the collection, the sexual assault, covered face, wearing gloves and the use of a serrated blade. He could've stalked the property online. Remember, our task-force guy's a traveler, been active in a lot of states over the years."

Morrow continued thinking.

"Look," Zhu said, "it's not like TV, movies and books. Things don't always connect neatly, perfectly."

"This is something," Morrow said. "I don't know what, but it's something. Good work. Keep monitoring, and keep me posted."

Zhu nodded.

Morrow pressed her lips together, studying the maps and summaries and wondering about the potential threads to the Cleveland case.

22

Is Jeff keeping something from me?

Lisa inched her Chevrolet Cruze into a parking space at the Palm Creek Mall, wondering what was going on with her husband. She couldn't shake the feeling that the way he'd been behaving lately went beyond the disruption of the move or job pressure, even their home invasion.

He's been so distracted, and when I push him on it—he's secretive. Maybe we're both still grappling with the assault, or it's just me.

I don't know.

Her mind drifted to Stacey. What would her life be like now, if she had lived? Would she be married with a family? Would she have a career?

Would she still be my friend?

Is the attack payback for what I did in the back seat of the car that day? Why do I have this feeling things are going to get worse?

Stepping from the car, Lisa double-checked to ensure each door, including the hatch, was locked. She'd studied some self-defense tips online. Taking care to be vigilant had become second nature. She scanned the parking lot in every direction. Heading to the mall entrance, she kept a tight grip on her bag with one hand. The other was closed in a fist around her longest key, the sharp edge sticking out near her pinkie.

Ready to stab flesh and hit bone.

It was Monday afternoon. She'd risen super early that morning, dived into her work, saw Jeff off. *Did he even know I was there? His nose was glued to his phone during most of breakfast.* After he'd left, Lisa resumed toiling full bore, getting another huge chunk of the emerging-diseases job done so she could get to the mall.

It felt good getting out, being among people. Today was another step toward regaining confidence and control. Still, she wondered again about Jeff and considered his recent demeanor, like how when they'd first moved to Palm Mirage Creek, he'd get up in the night to work.

He'd even go out for a walk or a solitary drive, be gone for a few hours.

"I'm just wound up about everything," he'd told her.

At times, when Lisa took a sleeping pill, she wouldn't know if he'd gone out or had a sleepwalking episode. Then she thought about how Jeff had behaved over the years. Yes, he'd had a hard life and would sink into moods where he'd become quiet, pensive, withdrawn.

Or guarding some secret.

In his professional life, he always seemed to be

under pressure, always traveling to conferences or making presentations to clients. Because he was often up at all hours and going out in the middle of the night, there was a time when Lisa had jokingly called him The Vampire. But after sensing that he didn't like it, she'd stopped. And in the last year or so, before they'd left Cleveland, Jeff was having a hard time with some people at his office. He'd never elaborated, only hinting at it. Just the other night, he'd said, "I was covering for people, carrying people."

And now Lisa believed that Jeff was troubled by something, and that as his wife, she knew him, knew instinctively that something was going on.

She pushed it all aside as she meandered through the furniture showroom, glancing around warily at other customers, especially men.

He's still out there.

After browsing for a time, she decided she liked several sets, a sectional with ivory fabric, then a leather three-seater with recliners and small chrome-plated features that gave it an art-deco look. The last was a cream-colored sofa, love seat and chair collection with a soft floral pattern.

She couldn't decide. She needed Jeff's opinion, she thought, as she moved through the store, finding herself in the nursery section. Watching pregnant women with their husbands, relatives or friends, Lisa felt a strong maternal ache. She wanted to be pregnant. This was the time. Jeff was making more money, he had a bonus coming and she was working at home. She had to nudge him to keep his promise.

She wanted to stop taking the pill.

Lisa traced her fingers over the cribs, changing tables and dressers. She moved to one end of the showroom and stood before a full-length mirror. She turned sideways and imagined herself pregnant, smiling at her reflection until another face appeared in the mirror. Watching her.

A man's face.

He was standing outside the showroom, at the window—

Lisa turned. Roland Dillard was staring at her.

He gave her a little wave. She left the store and went to him.

"Small world, isn't it?" he said. "What're the odds?"

"Hi, Roland." Lisa looked around.

"I hope I didn't startle you again?"

"No, not at all."

"Just waiting on Nell." He indicated the sign across the hall for the restrooms. "And I saw you."

"Oh, right." She smiled.

Dillard nodded to the nursery furniture. "This an indication of big news?"

Lisa blushed, shaking her head. "No, just browsing before I leave."

"That security system working okay for you?"

"Works fine. I'm glad we have it. Well, I should be going."

"Remind Jeff his patrol shift is coming up."

"I will. Give my best to Nell."

Dillard gave her a little salute, and she could feel his eyes on her as she walked away. Before leaving, Lisa stopped at the food court to get a smoothie for the drive home.

Outside, cutting across the lot, she watched for strangers while wrapping her key in her fist. Glancing at her whitened knuckles, she thought about her encounter with Roland Dillard.

He's like a cat. A tiger. And he's everywhere.

She walked around her car before unlocking it, checking the hatch and back seat. Then, she got in and locked the doors before starting it. As she sipped her smoothie, she noticed Dillard across the parking lot.

He was walking to his SUV.

Alone.

That's odd. He said he was waiting for Nell.

Lisa shook her head, fastened her belt and drove off, debating whether she should ask him if everything was all right. Before she reached a decision, she saw him drive off alone through the lot.

Now, that's strange.

23

The house sat back from the street shaded by tall palms hissing in the breeze out front. The left side of the yard was cloaked in darkness by shrubbery that brushed the rooftop.

A burglar's dream.

But the grainy, greenish glow of Dillard's night-vision binoculars gave them visibility in the darkness. "Your turn to watch." His voice was soft as he passed them to Jeff.

They were three hours into Jeff's first late-night patrol, and as he took the binoculars from Dillard he thought of Lisa, home alone for the first evening since the attack. He could still hear the unease in her voice, feel her kiss on his cheek.

"I'll be all right. I'm glad you're doing this," she'd told him.

"It's only for a few hours," he'd said.

In the time Jeff and Dillard had been patrolling, they'd driven and walked throughout their zone of Palm Mirage Creek, listening to the scanner and maintaining radio check-ins with the other neighborhood patrols, before taking their shift *surveilling*—Dillard's word for it—the bait house.

It was a ranch-style bungalow, and subtle indications that the owner, who had antique jewelry, was convalescing in hospital, while her flight-attendant daughter stayed at the house off and on, had been posted online. All of it fiction. In reality the house was a rental, and the owners had agreed to help police.

Jeff and Dillard watched from the gazebo in the backyard of the house across the street, where they had cover and a direct line of sight on the house.

"Look at it," Dillard whispered. "Sitting there like a fresh slab of cheese for the vermin."

"Think it's going to work?" Jeff said from behind the binoculars.

"It's a proven method." A tiny crackle of static leaked from Dillard's earpiece, then he whispered "Copy that" into his radio to the volunteers patrolling a few blocks away. Then to Jeff he said, "So. You don't like guns because your dad was killed in a hunting accident?"

"Yes."

"What happened, exactly?"

Jeff hesitated. "I'd rather not talk about it."

"It was a long time ago?"

"I was eleven at the time."

"I see. Were other people there, too, or just you and your dad?"

"Me, my dad, and his friend Charlie. Charlie accidentally shot my dad. Look, I don't like talking about it."

Dillard absorbed the response, and Jeff thought the discussion had ended.

"What happened, really?"

Jeff cursed under his breath, pressed the binoculars tighter to his head.

During the night they'd talked about sports, movies, politics, the cities they'd traveled to, but now, sitting here in the dark, Dillard had shifted the conversation, making it probing and personal.

Too personal.

"Give me a break, okay?" Jeff said.

"Just my detective's curiosity. How's the new job going?"

"It's going great."

"A lot of pressure, I imagine?"

"Nothing I can't handle."

"Lisa told us your move from Cleveland happened pretty fast."

"The company wanted me moved quickly."

"I've been to Cleveland a couple of times. I liked it. Has lots to offer. Did you leave anything behind that you miss?"

The question gave Jeff pause. He looked at Dillard, his lined face in the dark, then resumed watching the bait house.

"No, not really. Lisa's ties to the city were stronger than mine."

"How's everything going at home?"

"What?"

"Since the attack."

Jeff wasn't sure why he'd ask that. "Fine, we're doing fine."

"The security system working okay?"

"It is, and thanks again for helping us."

"Good. Your home should be a fortress. Lisa told us that you two want to start a family here."

"That's the plan."

"Have you started?"

"What?"

"Your wife's a very beautiful woman."

Jeff's head snapped to Dillard. "What the hell are you say—"

At that moment, Dillard's earpiece gushed with a loud, excited transmission. "Okay, copy," Dillard whispered into his radio. "Ned Tripp just spotted a man in black passing through the backyard behind the bait house."

Pulling the binoculars to his head, Jeff saw movement in the shrubbery. "I see something— someone's there!"

"Let's go!"

"Go where?"

"I'll go along the right side of the house by the carport, to close in on the backyard. You go directly toward the guy. It'll force him back where I am. With Ned on the other side of the house, we'll box him in."

"We're supposed to call police—"

"No time—he could get away. Let's go!"

Taking the binoculars, Dillard moved swiftly across the street, disappearing around the far side of the house. Alone and unarmed, Jeff searched the ambient light. Grabbing a croquet mallet from the gazebo, he headed for the house.

Fixing his gaze on the darkness, he crouched, rushed to the front of the bait house, wishing Dillard hadn't taken the binoculars.

Keeping his back to the house, making his way to the corner, he heard the soft clink of metal against metal, like a tool bag had been set down.

Pulse racing, Jeff edged his head around.

Under the narrow beam of a small headlamp, the masked intruder, dressed in black and wearing gloves, was working on a window. Angered by the creep's brazenness, knowing Dillard and Tripp were there in the darkness, Jeff gripped the mallet tighter and shouted, "Hey! Watch patrol!"

The intruder looked up as Jeff stepped toward him, blocking his escape. Jeff raised the mallet, but it lightened as the hammer broke off with a thud, leaving a wrinkled ribbon of duct tape and the twig-like remnant of the handle.

The intruder lunged at Jeff, who glimpsed the flash of a blade in time to grab the guy's wrist and throat. They fell to the ground, fighting, clawing, kicking, wrestling for the knife, the headlamp making everything convulse and strobe.

Where the hell were Dillard and Tripp?

Jeff's heart hammered, his fingers slipped on the knife as he tried to loosen the guy's grip, but the attacker was strong, agile, slowly turning the serrated blade to Jeff, poising it at his face. Jeff's head was locked in a vise grip, the blade drew closer and he braced for it to plunge into him when the entire side of the house blossomed in blinding white.

"Freeze, asshole!"

Dillard aimed his tactical police flashlight at them. The muzzle of a gun pressed into the attacker's head, and a lightning kick knocked the knife free. Dillard picked it up with his flashlight hand and pocketed it. As Jeff stood up, Dillard delivered another kick to the attacker's side, causing him to grunt.

"On your stomach, asshole!" Dillard dropped plastic cuffs on his back, keeping his gun trained on him. "Pull his wrists behind his back, and put those on him, Jeff."

Breathing hard, bleeding and sweating, Jeff zipped the cuffs on him as another flashlight lit the scene.

"Jeez, you got the guy." Tripp arrived, panting.

"Jeff got him," Dillard said.

Tripp raked his light over Jeff. "You all right?"

"Yeah." His pulse galloping, Jeff dragged his hand across his face. "Thanks, Roland. It was close."

"Get him on his feet," Dillard said.

Tripp and Jeff hefted the guy up. Dillard yanked off the man's balaclava. He was a white guy in his late thirties, with the scarred face and expression of a human nightmare. Dillard patted him for weapons and ID but found nothing.

"Is this the guy who invaded your home and attacked your wife, Jeff?"

"Could be. The knife looks the same. I don't know. Say something, dipshit, so I can hear your voice."

He sneered at Jeff and remained silent.

"Light up his shoes," Jeff said.

He wore dark blue sneakers. The left shoe bore a small tear near a left eyelet.

"This is the guy," Jeff said.

"We need to call 9-1-1," Tripp said.

"Hold on, Ned." Dillard stepped closer, keeping his gun on the suspect. "So this is the guy. You're sure?"

"Zero doubt." Jeff was still breathing hard.

"Know what I think, Jeff? I think it's time for payback."

"What do you mean?"

"He broke into your house and assaulted your wife, and he just tried to kill you. Are you going to stand for that?"

"What, you want me to beat him up?"

"You'd be right to do it."

"No. We'll let the cops handle him."

"He's right, Roland." Tripp was uneasy. "We need to call police now."

"Shut up, Ned. Jeff, you know you want to do it."

"It wouldn't be right. He's handcuffed—"

"Do it for Lisa."

Dillard reached into his pocket for the knife.

"I'll cut the cuffs off him, to make it fair. I'll keep my weapon on him. And I will shoot you, asshole. Nobody's going anywhere. Go on. Take a piece of him."

Breathing hard, Jeff stared at the guy.

"Jeff," Dillard said. A soft snap sounded, the guy's shoulders rolled as Dillard sliced away the plastic cuffs. The guy didn't move. "He wanted to rape Lisa. He promised to come back to your house and fuck her. Are you okay with that?"

The veins in Jeff's neck and jaw began throbbing as he glared at the guy. Jeff tasted blood webbing from a cut on his cheek, and something quaked deep, deep in a black, secret chamber of his heart. Something thundered. The feral force he'd fought all his life to keep chained was raging again—images blazed before him of the guy with the knife on Lisa, his hand all over her, molesting her, while Jeff stood useless to stop him. The cage exploded.

Jeff saw white and blanked out.

He didn't know what happened in the next few moments, but when he became aware again, he was on the ground smashing his fists into the guy's face, his gut, his back, his groin. The guy groaned, never fought back as Jeff beat him in a frenzy bordering on insanity.

"Stop! Lord, stop!" Tripp said.

But Jeff was crazed, couldn't stop himself and continued hammering the guy until Dillard and Tripp pulled him off.

"All right, I think we're done," Dillard gasped. He turned to Jeff. "Are you okay?"

Jeff blinked, coming back to himself. "What—what happened?"

"That was frightening," Dillard said.

"I never saw anyone act like that before," Tripp said.

The suspect, his face bloodied, stared at Jeff in silence.

Once they'd restrained him again and called it in, they walked him to the sidewalk. Sirens sounded and two Miami-Dade marked units arrived, lights flashing, radios alive with static chatter. Some neighbors ventured from their homes, others peered from windows. The officers who approached them knew Dillard.

"What've we got here, Roland?" one of the uniformed cops said, before saying *ten-four* into his shoulder mic. Then he added, "This is one of our houses."

"This man was witnessed burglarizing this home. When our patrol member here—" Dillard nodded to Jeff "—came upon him, the subject attacked our member with a knife with the intent to kill him, and there was a struggle."

The uniformed officers, four in total, had arrived and looked at the suspect. Blood cascaded from the guy's face, drenching his shirt. His lip was split, his mouth and nose were bleeding, his eyes were swollen. Then the cops looked at Dillard, Tripp and Jeff.

"Is this what happened, sir?" one of the officers asked Jeff.

"Yes."

"And you, sir?" The officer raised his chin to Tripp. "This is what happened?"

Tripp took a moment, shot Dillard a glance. "Yes, that's what happened."

"You know you should've called us, Roland. You're not vigilantes out here," one of the older officers said.

"Yeah, well, it happened fast, and we didn't want to lose him."

"And you've got the weapon, Roland?"

Dillard pulled it from his pocket.

"Would've been better if you hadn't handled it. You know that," an officer said.

"He was in the process of using it on my neighbor. I had to take it away."

"Did you fire your weapon, Roland?"

"No."

"Will you surrender your gun to us, as a matter of routine?"

Dillard handed it, grip first, to the officer. Another officer preserved the knife in a bag, then got yellow tape from the trunk to cordon the scene.

"Okay, we're going to need ID and statements from each of you independently," one officer said. Another took the suspect's arm, leading him to the back of the patrol car. "We'll take you to the hospital so they can take a look at you. Then we'll get your statement."

Before the car holding the suspect pulled away, he glared from the caged rear at Jeff. The wild rage that passed between them was not lost on Tripp, as he struggled to blink away his worry over what he'd witnessed.

Nor was it lost on Dillard.

After Jeff watched the patrol car round the corner, he lifted his bloodied face to the sky, took in a deep breath and let it out slowly.

24

Lisa's sleep was fitful.

With Jeff gone in the night, she kept her phone in her hand.

But every time a dog barked or the air conditioner kicked on, she'd wake and check the security system. She was on edge.

She tried to relax by thinking of the baby furniture she'd seen the other day and how badly she wanted to start a family. She wondered again if she should stop taking the pill.

Without telling Jeff? Wouldn't that be wrong? Would it? He promised to start a family as soon as we moved. It was part of the deal. Now he says he needs time.

But now's the time.

Lisa tensed.

She heard a new noise. It was 3:41 a.m. She took up her phone, checked the security cameras and saw a figure at the front door.

It was Jeff.

She sighed with relief and went to him.

"What're you doing up so late?" he asked, standing in the foyer, placing his keys on the entrance side table.

"I couldn't sleep." She took in his face, laced with scratches, his hair mussed, shirt torn and blotched with dirt and grass stains. "What happened to you? Are you okay?"

He smiled at her.

"We got him. We got the guy who broke into our home and assaulted you."

"*Really?* You got him?"

"He's in custody."

"But how—what happened? Wait, go sit down. I'll get some things to clean you up."

They went to the living room. Jeff eased onto the sofa. Lisa got a washcloth, a towel, their first-aid kit and a glass of water for him. As she tended to him, he related how the night had unfolded.

Listening and nodding, she delicately removed some of the now-damp bandages police had applied to Jeff's head and knuckles, cleaned his wounds with antiseptic wipes, put on fresh bandages. Pieces of skin had been scraped from his knuckles, and she washed and blotted them dry. She could feel him shaking, adrenaline still driving through him.

"I swear to God he would've killed me, Lisa." A vein stood out throbbing on his forehead. "I blanked out. I can't remember everything except that all I could think of is what that animal did to you, what he wanted to do to you, what he took from us. Something detonated inside me, and I wanted him dead. It was like an out-of-body thing. The intensity of it just took control."

Lisa stared at him, searching his eyes as if the man she knew was gone. He cupped his battered hands to his scraped face, still shaking, chest heaving.

"This anger, this rage, just grew in me," Jeff said. "A dark need to hurt someone because I was hurt. I knew it was wrong, but that's how life has wired me. For the most part, I always controlled it, but not tonight. Tonight it got loose again, and I swear to God, Lisa, if Dillard and Tripp weren't there, I would've beat that asshole into little slimy pieces and fed them to the dogs."

Lisa swallowed hard at Jeff's revelation.

My God, she thought, *this is not the Jeff I know. I'm seeing a part of him I've never seen before.*

When they were finished, he went to their bathroom to take a hot shower, leaving her to consider what he'd told her. She knew nothing of this dark, violent side that he'd kept locked away.

It frightened her.

But it also excited her.

For tonight he'd risen to her ultimate defense, defeating the dragon who'd threatened her life.

Lisa stripped off her T-shirt and got into the shower with him.

25

The next day Lisa kept pace with Jackson Browne's "Running on Empty" flowing through her headphones as she ran.

She loved that old song.

Breathing in the scent of the flowering trees lining the wide streets with their beautiful homes, she ran with purpose and a sense of freedom.

The creep who'd attacked her was in jail.

And it sounded to her that Jeff had beat him up pretty badly, too. On a moral level she didn't *really* approve of what Jeff had done or the way it was handled, with Roland holding his gun, giving Jeff an advantage. It seemed savage, kind of Neanderthal.

Just plain wrong.

But when she resurrected the memory of the intruder's hands on her and what he'd said, part of her was secretly glad he'd got his ass kicked.

The creep had it coming.

She turned into a large park with vibrant gardens and massive banyan trees that created cool, dark tunnels of green canopy, shading her way. Each time she met other people jogging in the opposite direction or passing her, she'd smile and wave, offering a fellow runner's sign of friendship.

Lisa was buoyant: she felt her confidence restored, felt free to live her life again. And best of all, this morning, Jeff had agreed that she should stop taking the pill, that it was time to start a family. She had an appointment to see her doctor.

The intro guitar riff of "Radar Love" by Golden Earring, another classic from her playlist that she loved, began throbbing in her ears, and she increased her stride, picked up speed and smiled to herself. The sex she and Jeff had had the previous night had been the release both of them had needed.

Meandering into a darker part of the park, Lisa glimpsed the fluorescent orange shirt, white cap and dark glasses of a woman jogging behind her.

I saw her going in the opposite direction. Now she's behind me.

Lisa shrugged it off, figuring every runner has their own route, and kept going, thinking about the future and having a child.

She thought of Jeff and his revelation, and how he'd kept his dark, dangerous persona hidden from her. It just went to show you that when you think you know a person, something happens to prove that you don't.

He wouldn't keep secrets from me, would he?

Her right shoe became loose. Broken laces flapped. As she stopped to tie the frayed ends together, the woman in the glowing shirt came up and passed her. Lisa offered a friendly wave. The woman ignored it and disappeared around a bend, leaving Lisa alone to cope with her broken lace.

It took longer than expected to repair it. Frustrated, she pulled off her headphones to concentrate. In the quiet calm, she found herself completely alone. She welcomed the birdsong from the dense forest, then the rustle of branches and a crisp snap stopped her cold.

Is someone in the brush?

Lisa quickly tied her lace together and resumed running.

26

The offender's name was Clete Younger Loften.

He kept his handcuffed hands on top of the veneer table in the stark interview room of Miami-Dade's Midwest District Station. His knuckle tattoos spelled *HELL FIRE*.

Loften's eyes took a walk all over Cruz when she entered the room with Reddick. Cruz ignored his leer as the detectives rolled up chairs and placed a clipboard, yellow legal pad, iPad and phones on the table.

Staring at the suspect, Reddick released a low whistle.

Cruz glanced at Loften's pocked face. With the bandages, his swollen blackened eyes and crusting lacerations, Loften looked as if he had been torn apart then mashed back together, like a hastily made scarecrow.

"Mr. Loften, I'm Detective Camila Cruz, my partner is Detective Joe Reddick. We understand you've already been read your Miranda rights?"

Loften locked his eyes on hers for a long moment before nodding.

"Answer yes or no, Clete," Reddick said. "You know this is being recorded."

Loften shot Reddick a look. "Yes."

Cruz turned the clipboard to Loften. "And this is your signature acknowledging you understand your rights?"

Loften glanced at the document, then stared directly at Cruz. "Yes."

"We'd like to talk about a few things, the charges against you and additional charges you're facing. Understanding your rights, do you wish to talk to us?"

The veins in Loften's neck pulsed.

It may have been the beating he'd taken, or his failure to overpower Jeff Taylor and escape or the cold, hard fact he'd been caught. Or it may have been all of these elements coming together that had Loften seething beneath the surface with such ferocity his skin should've been bubbling.

"Clete," Reddick said, "the witness statements we have indicate you used a knife to attack a community neighborhood-watch member who caught you in the act of breaking into a house. The member fought back and disarmed you. Do you wish to dispute the statements?"

Loften gave the detectives a look that conveyed that everyone knew what really happened, but for Loften to dispute it was futile. He grimaced and shook his head. "No."

"Mr. Loften," Cruz said. "We have information that needs to be addressed. We need a clear response that you either wish to talk to us, to help us get to the bottom of things, or not."

Loften stared at her without speaking.

"It's your right to remain silent, and to end this interview at any time and request an attorney," Cruz said. "But that leaves us no choice but to pass along your decision not to cooperate to the State Attorney's Office. You understand the ramifications of that, Mr. Loften?"

Loften didn't respond.

"Clete, think about this," Reddick said. "You're facing a long list of first-degree felonies, armed burglary, burglary with assault, to name a few. We're working on more. Don't help us and you're facing up to thirty years in prison, but if you cooperate, help us clear cases, that could be reduced to seven or ten. So you see, this is your onetime chance to help yourself. You want to do seven years, or do you prefer thirty? Think about that because, when we walk out of here, your one and only chance goes with us."

Loften blinked, then his swollen lip began to move. "Ask your questions."

"All right," Cruz said. "Let's confirm a few things. We understand you work in construction. Are you currently employed?"

"I'm between contracts."

"What is your specific line of work?"

"I'm a framer for new houses. I do the doors and windows."

"Would you consider yourself an expert at doors and windows?"

Loften shrugged. "Sure."

"You currently reside in the Oceanwave Gardens, a motel residence in Allapattah?"

"Yes."

"How long have you resided there?"

"Three or four months, maybe."

"Where did you live before that?"

"Atlanta."

"So you don't stay in one place long?"

"I go where there's good-paying construction work."

"You own a twenty-sixteen Dodge Ram fifteen hundred, white with gray on the bottom?"

"Yes."

"All right. I'm going to show you a few things." Cruz swiped through files on her iPad and came to photos of a serrated knife. "This was recovered in your possession at the location of the most recent offense. How did you acquire it?"

"I don't know anything about that knife."

Cruz moved to photos of Loften's shoes, dark blue sneakers, then to close-ups of the left one, the lower-left eyelet with a tear running near it.

"These are your shoes. Were you wearing them the night of the eleventh, morning of the twelfth?"

Loften didn't respond.

"Can you account for your whereabouts on those dates?"

Loften didn't answer.

"We can put you in those shoes with that knife

attacking a woman in a residence in Palm Mirage Creek on the morning of the twelfth."

Loften was silent.

"We found your bag with burglar's tools," Cruz said. "These were also found in your bag."

She swiped at her iPad and photos of a package of condoms appeared on the screen.

"You weren't there to steal valuables, were you?"

Loften swallowed.

"Mr. Loften, we have you for two separate events in Palm Mirage Creek." Cruz swiped to the maps, timeline and summaries the crime analyst had created for them.

"Within recent weeks in Pinecrest, someone broke into a residence through the sliding door on the side. Residents were out at the time but report the only items missing were bras and panties.

"Just prior to that, a residence was burglarized in South Miami. The resident, away at the time, reported her underwear was stolen. We're going back and looking at similar cases in Coral Gables, Coral Terrace, Olympia Heights, Palmetto Bay and Cutler Bay.

"I'll ask again. You're not breaking into homes to steal valuables at all, are you, Mr. Loften?"

He didn't answer.

"We understand if you have, let's say, compulsions that you can't control, an overwhelming need that must be satisfied. We can assist you in getting the help you need."

Cruz looked at Loften long and hard, then

nudged her iPad a little closer to him so he had a better view of all the mapped crimes, webbed like a digital splatter on the screen.

"Why don't you help us clear all these cases, make a formal admission detailing all of your activities in South Florida. We'll inform the State Attorney, and I'm confident it'll help you in the long run."

Studying the map, Loften's breathing quickened.

Reddick stood and leaned into Loften's space.

"Clete, we're running your prints and DNA through every data bank we can. We're in the process of securing warrants to search your room at Oceanwave Gardens, your truck, your phone, laptop. What do you think we're going to find?"

Loften swallowed. His neck muscles spasmed, and despite the air-conditioning, he was sweating.

"I want to exercise my right to remain silent, and I want a lawyer."

27

In the days after Jeff had battled with Clete Loften, the twenty-five-million-dollar contract with the South American conglomerate had been signed, and work had begun.

By now, the scratches on Jeff's face had started to fade, and everyone in his office had heard his telling of his ordeal or learned of it from conversations while getting coffee in the office kitchen.

Winning the huge Argentine deal and fighting and arresting a criminal had earned Jeff the admiration of most people in Asgaard-T-Chace's Miami branch. While he enjoyed his elevated status, he downplayed it because there was much work ahead, and they couldn't afford to become distracted.

"I can't emphasize this enough. Our goal is to humanize Globo Aedifico with a campaign that creates an uplifting moral experience for the audience. One that not only works globally but translates locally," he said at one of the planning meetings.

And there were many meetings. Jeff's day would begin early with meetings and usually end with a late one. Teams met to lay out a launch schedule and coordinate it with a media schedule. There were calls and discussions to ensure all the specialty groups were working in sync and on the same page. Meetings were held to discuss the research data that had been mined, then others to screen preliminary video-production ideas, still others to develop concepts for logos and visuals.

But from time to time, Jeff's concentration would drift as it did today during the meeting on the status of engaging the international news media. Jeff was looking at the damaged skin on his knuckles, thinking about how close he'd come to losing it and killing Loften.

I wanted him dead.

A thunderclap of realization forced Jeff to flinch as his rage and the guilt that had consumed him for so many years boiled inside, compelling him to admit what he was and would always be.

The truth that had tormented him much of his life had broken free.

Again.

"So what do you think, Jeff?"

Someone had said his name. He heard more words but was lost. "Pardon me?"

"I was saying we've also spoken to the international desks at the BBC, CNN and the *Wall Street Journal* and Bloomberg. They all expressed interest in sending news teams to see Globo Aedifico's new sanitation systems and clean-water projects in development in the remote regions and—" Carlotta Diaz interrupted herself to stare at him. "Jeff, are you all right? You look pale."

"I'm sorry, Carlotta. I'm not feeling well." Jeff got up. "Excuse me."

He left the meeting and went to the washroom, leaned over the sink and ran the water until it was cold, cold like it was that morning he was hunting with his father and Charlie. Remembering now kneeling over his dad...

...bleeding on the ground...his dad's face ashen...eyes burning with surprise and sadness in the cold of the marshy riverbank...where his father lay dying...the brilliant red of the blood...

Coloring his world, scarring him, changing him forever.

It left him without a dad, forever.

Suddenly, he was pierced with the memory of the time he'd found a measure of happiness when he'd joined the Boy Scouts. But within weeks, the Scouts had planned a father–son event. His mother, mildly drunk at the time, had suggested that one of her new drug-addict boyfriends stand in with Jeff for the event. God, how Jeff roiled with pain he couldn't contain.

"He's not my father, he's your customer," he'd spat at her.

Her palm on his face stung.

He quit Scouts and, after lying about his age, got a job cleaning shoes in a bowling alley.

His father's death was a tragedy he could never escape. It had broken his mother, annihilated her will, forcing her to do the vile things she did for money so they could survive. And he'd seen her taking drugs, drinking herself into a stupor. He'd seen her with men, seen what she did on her knees and on her back, and he burned with shame, anger and guilt.

Guilt because it was his fault she had become what she had.

Shame and anger at his mother because she had not been strong, had not striven to overcome their tragedy, had not fought back at every turn, like he'd done. He had stood fearlessly against the schoolyard bullies who'd mocked him, and he'd defeated every person who he'd deemed an enemy. He was determined to rise above the catastrophe, had refused to let it destroy him by destroying anything that threatened him or got in his way.

All his life he had fought to never return to the black hole of his childhood that he'd crawled out of. Yes, he'd loved his mother, but he couldn't rid himself of the simmering rage he felt at the woman she had turned into.

Because—God help me—it was my fault. I can never undo what I did.

Jeff leaned into the sink and splashed water on his face until the heat of his anger had subsided.

By the time he'd found his composure, the meeting had ended, and Jeff returned to his office.

Where Vida Warren was waiting for him.

28

"Hello, Jeff."

Vida Warren was at ease seated in one of the chairs in front of his desk. Fred Bonner happened to be walking by and glimpsed her, did a double take, grinned and winked at Jeff as he closed the door.

Jeff then leaned against his desk, folded his arms across his chest and looked down at Vida.

She smiled. "It's been a while, hasn't it, Jeff?"

"How did you get in here?"

She reached into her bag, withdrew a laminated Asgaard-T-Chace employee-ID card with her photo and name and held it up.

"Nobody knows details of other branch offices. I made a duplicate. Nobody checks if cards are expired. Besides, I can usually talk my way past anybody." She dropped the card into her bag and took in the glorious view of Miami's skyscrapers, the water and the metropolitan area sprawling to the horizon. "You've got it good, don't you?"

"Why did you come all this way, Vida?"

"You left me no choice. You kept refusing my calls."

"We have nothing to talk about. I want you to leave."

"We have business to discuss."

She still had that silky, seductive voice that he'd always thought was affected. She was attractive and had a reputation for being flirtatious. She looked good in her well-cut dark suit. Her face didn't betray the ravages of her disgrace.

Mourning the death of her marriage after her husband left her for another woman, Vida was driving home one night after drinking at a bar and wrapped her Subaru around a tree, breaking several bones and leading to her addiction to pain-killers, then illicit drugs. She began borrowing money from coworkers. At times they found her sleeping at her desk or passed out in the bathroom.

Her work began slipping. Some female cowork-ers were sympathetic at first—"that dick of an ex did this to her"—and tried to protect her, until she begged for money, calling at all hours and finally stealing it from them.

Then came the time they found her in the alley behind the building on East Ninth Street, which led to her in-laws taking custody of Lucas, her little boy. She'd sought help, but it was futile.

She was quietly fired.

That had been about nine months ago.

"Just hear me out, Jeff. Would you be decent enough to do that?"

He stared back in silence, her cue to continue.

"I haven't used in over four, almost five, months now. I'm getting things together, and I need to show that I'm on the right track so I'll get Lucas back. To do that, I need you to help me get my job back but here, in this office, because my in-laws who have my son live in Florida, in Boca."

Jeff gave his head slow, little shakes.

"It's admirable that you're getting clean, that you're pulling your life together, but I can't recommend you be hired back."

"You don't understand. I have no options. This is my only hope."

"*You* don't understand. I helped you in Cleveland. I covered for you. I gave you money. All of your favors with me have been used up." Jeff stopped, softened his tone. "I'm new here, Vida. This office is different from Cleveland. I have no say in hires. You've been through a rough time, but you have to get on with your life, start fresh. Somewhere else."

Her face became stony.

"All this—" she stabbed her chin at his office and view "—your job, your move here, all this should be mine, and you know it."

"What?"

"You know what you did. What we did."

"What're you talking about, *what we did*? Nothing happened."

"Something definitely happened, Jeff, and there's nothing you can do to change that."

He dragged both hands over his face. "You were sick, Vida. Your work suffered. I had to pick up your projects, and that's what happened, nothing else. There's no *we*. We're done here. I listened. It's time to leave."

"Not yet." She looked at him for a moment. "I know about your new twenty-five-million-dollar campaign."

"From who?"

"I have my ways of finding out things. More important, the concepts you used are the ones I created in Cleveland. You stole my work."

"Stop right there. Those are my concepts. I finished your sloppy, half-developed work for you when you were sick. You had created nothing when I took over your stuff. *You had nothing.*"

"Bullshit. You stole my work and used it to get this promotion and the campaign. I want you to go to Leland Slaughter and Foster Shore and tell them the truth—that I created the brilliant concepts that you presented. And then I want you to demand they hire me for a position here."

"Leave."

"I need this to happen, and it will happen."

Staring at her, Jeff felt she was unbalanced. "You need help, Vida."

She reached into her bag for her phone, swiped the screen, held up pictures.

"You've got a nice house in Palm Mirage Creek," she said, "and a nice wife—Lisa, as I recall. You know, Jeff, when you slip into the gutter like I did, you meet all kinds of people with all kinds of connections willing to help you for a little quid pro quo, you know, a little something for something. Oh, here she is." She held a picture of Lisa running near their house. "Pretty."

The muscles under Jeff's jawline began to spasm.

"And it's too bad about your little burglary."

Jeff stared, surprised that she knew.

"Your neighbors post things online." She smiled. "Besides, you forget, I know all about you. What you're really like. And you know what else I have in here?" Vida patted her phone, then typed a quick message before slipping it back into her bag. "The truth. I don't think you'd want me to share it with Lisa, or anybody really. But I will if I have to."

Jeff's expression was devoid of emotion. Glaring at Vida, something inside was on the verge of erupting. Then his smartphone pinged.

"There," Vida stood, moving close enough for him to smell her perfume. "You've got my contact info, and I've got yours. I'll give you one week to make things right, Jeff. If you don't, then I'll tell everyone *everything*."

29

The toothpick in the corner of Lex Prewitt's mouth moved up and down as he studied the documents on the counter.

It was a search warrant concerning Clete Younger Loften, the current tenant in unit 45 at the Ocean-wave Gardens, a motel residence in Allapattah, of which Prewitt was manager.

Prewitt scratched his stubbled chin, then his belly, which stretched the stained Marlins' T-shirt he wore.

"Come on, Lex," Detective Reddick said as he and Detective Cruz looked around at the tiny lobby with its duct-taped chairs, figuring they'd likely been damaged in a brawl among hookers, pimps or other people who frequented the establishment. "This can't be the first warrant executed here."

"First one this month," Prewitt grunted, then reached under the counter.

Reflexively, Reddick and Cruz stiffened, ready to reach for their weapons, until Prewitt produced a key with a cracked tag. It bore a strip of masking tape with *#45* in blue ballpoint pen.

"This way."

Prewitt led them across the courtyard, dotted with patches of dirt where there used to be flower gardens. Pieces of trash were scattered about the property. The motel's stucco walls were blistered and chipped; beer cans bobbed in the deep end of the pool's greenish water.

"This is where dreams come to die," Reddick said to Cruz.

"Be nice, Joe." Cruz was monitoring her phone for updates.

They came to unit 45, where the door, like those for most of the other units, was fractured from previously being kicked in.

"Place hasn't been cleaned," Prewitt said. "The tenant is on the weekly plan, so it won't get service for two more days."

"Kill the cleaning service. We're going to have other people joining us shortly. We own this room until we release it," Reddick said as he and Cruz slipped on shoe covers and snapped on latex gloves. "Got that, Lex?"

"Got it." Prewitt slid the key into the lock.

The air in the darkened room was a mix of body odor and bug spray. Cruz hit the light switch. It was a standard motel room of substandard quality. The floor had peeling laminate. The unmade bed revealed a mattress with yellowing sheets. The walls were stained with something. The air conditioner rattled as if it were about to quit. A plastic bucket had been positioned under it to catch dripping water. The tub in the bathroom was chipped, stained and ringed with mold.

"Looks like heaven, don't it?" Reddick said.

Detailed street maps of Miami and surrounding cities, with handwritten notations, were pinned to one wall.

"We'll need these for sure," Cruz said.

Clothes were strewn about. The furniture was cracked. An array of empty take-out food containers and a stained paper bag of rotting fruit covered a table. The desk near it held a selection of cell phones and a laptop.

"Let's get to it," Cruz said.

They began by taking photos and making a video recording, then searching everything and everywhere—the trash, the clothes—collecting what they needed for further processing like the maps, phones and laptop. They found worn work boots, gloves, an assortment of tools and supplies, utility knives, a roll of cord, screwdrivers, a bevel, a measuring tape, a bubble level. One of the cell phones, a prepaid, throwaway version, was not locked. They swiped through photos, mostly of the beach, then of a middle-aged woman walking with a young boy, taken at a Boca Raton strip mall.

"Could be a stolen phone?" Reddick showed Cruz.

Working in Loften's room, Reddick and Cruz took care logging and describing everything they seized on the inventory sheet.

Across the city, Loften's Ram pickup had already been impounded and was being processed by crime-scene techs. They'd already collected his knife and tools to be analyzed for prints and trace. Soon, a team would arrive at Loften's motel room to start work.

Cruz had moved to the bathroom, logging Loften's toiletries to be processed. When she finished, she lowered herself to the area under the sink near the toilet, her attention going to the wall plate that covered access to the room's plumbing.

Cruz pried the plate away, used her penlight to search the space in the wall. Her focus sharpened when the beam reflected something in clear plastic. Before removing it, she took photos with her phone. Then she reached into the wall and pulled out a large resealable, clear plastic bag, filled with colored items.

"Well, would you look at this, Joe?"

Cruz held up the bag. It was jammed with women's panties, bras and condoms.

"How about that," Reddick said.

"I'm telling you, Joe. I got a bad feeling about our guy," Cruz said.

"Me, too. We've got to get this place processed by Crime Scene and update everything you submitted to ViCAP and all the other databases."

"Now you're a believer," Cruz said. "I told you that what we have here might be more than a burglar."

"I've not only seen the light, Camila, but I'm thinking it's showing us the tip of the iceberg."

"Yeah," Cruz said, nodding, taking stock, fearing that what she was standing in was akin to a wild animal's lair.

30

"Did you hear me?"

In the kitchen, Jeff sat at the table. Lisa was making banana smoothies and turned from the counter to see him on his phone.

"Jeff?"

"I'm listening." He looked at her. "So you went to the doctor."

"Yes, I'm now officially off the pill." She smiled, turned back to pour milk into the blender. "The doctor said some women can conceive as soon as they're off it, but for others it can take a couple months. I can't believe we're finally doing this."

She turned for his reaction.

"That's good," he said to his phone.

Lisa pivoted back to the counter, slammed the lid on the blender, jabbed the switch inciting a near-deafening whining and grinding of blades. She looked out the window to the yard, willing away her frustration.

Moments later, sitting together at the table with

their smoothies, her disappointment abated when Jeff put his phone down and turned it over.

"Sorry, got a lot of things going on," he said, drinking from his cup. "This is really good."

"Have you heard anything more from Cruz on the guy?"

He shook his head with a glint in his eyes. "Only that he's facing felony charges and a lot of prison time and they're looking at him for other crimes. The prick."

"But he's still in jail?"

"Yes."

"Good." She sipped her smoothie. "It was good to get out of the house and go running again, to get my life back."

Jeff's phone vibrated with a message, and his fingers nudged the surface of it. He glanced at Lisa and didn't answer it.

"When we finish these, I want you to come with me," she said. "There's something I want to show you."

They went upstairs to the bedroom directly across the hall from theirs. Since the move, it had become a storage area for unopened boxes, but before the smoothies, while Jeff was in his office, Lisa had repositioned some of the boxes as if they were furniture. Taped to each of them was a sheet of paper identifying the boxes as *crib*, *changing table*, *rocking chair*, and *dresser*.

"Like we talked about when we first saw this house, we can make this the nursery."

"Boy, you're going full steam ahead on this."

"It's way too early, I know, but I saw some great-looking furniture at the mall the other day, and I got dreaming, or a little carried away. But this is the layout I had in mind. What do you think?"

Jeff was staring at his phone, running one hand through his hair.

"Come on," Lisa said. "This has got to stop."

Jeff didn't react. It was as if he hadn't heard her. *"Jeff!"*

"What?"

"What's going on with you?"

"Nothing." He switched off his phone and shoved it into his pocket. "I'm sorry. Nothing."

"Nothing? Ever since we moved—no, ever since we learned we had to move—something's been off."

His Adam's apple rose and fell. "I'm sorry I've been distracted. It's work."

"It's more than work, more than the move, even more than the break-in. Don't lie to me."

He took in a deep breath. "It's this campaign— it's overwhelming. I've never handled one this big before, and it's got me worried."

Lisa searched his eyes for deception. She shook her head. "No. Something else is going on. And not only won't you tell me about it, you *lie* to me instead."

She stormed past him, tears in her eyes.

"Lisa."

He followed her down the stairs.

"Get away from me."

"Lisa, come on."

She went to the foyer, jerked on her sneakers, tied them with a vengeance and picked up her phone and keys.

"Where're you going?"

"I need to think."

"About what?"

She glared at him, shaking her head. "It's almost like another side of you is emerging, and I don't like it. It's scaring me, Jeff, because I don't know where the hell that leaves us!"

The mirror over the entrance table rattled when the door slammed behind her, leaving Jeff to stare at his reflection.

His phone vibrated in his pocket.

Vida had sent him another message.

Ticktock, Jeff.

31

Biting her bottom lip, the heels of her sneakers hammering the sidewalk, Lisa felt unsteady and confused.

What was wrong with Jeff? She was talking to him about the most important thing in their lives, and he ignored her? Then he refused to tell her why.

As she walked, she struggled not to scream in frustration.

What's he keeping from me?

She closed her hands into fists and stifled a sob as she rounded the corner of her block and approached the Dillards' home.

Oh no, I should've gone the other way. She didn't want them to see her this way—not like this, not now.

Too late.

Roland was in the front yard, working in the garden, and noticed her just as she cupped her hands to her face and swept away her tears.

"Lisa? What's wrong?"

Dillard left his flowers and moved toward the sidewalk. She accomplished a weak smile with a measure of composure.

"I'm okay."

"You seem upset."

"I was just thinking about something sad, that's all."

"Maybe I can help?"

"No, thanks, Roland." Lisa blinked a few times, checked the yard. "How's Nell?"

"Oh, pretty much the same." He tugged off his gloves. "She's resting now."

"The other day when you were with her at the Palm Creek Mall, I saw only you in the parking lot, and you drove away alone. I was worried that something had happened to her because you had indicated she was in the restroom."

Dillard's face held a question as if searching to understand, then he found the answer.

"Oh, yes. Nell was tired and went to the front entrance. It was a shorter walk. I got the car and drove around to get her."

"I see. I was worried I didn't see her, and I guess I thought that because of her condition you'd have a permit to park closer."

"No, she didn't want to get one, always prefers to make the walk whenever she can." Dillard took stock of Lisa. "Are you sure you're okay? You seemed troubled."

"I was thinking that I'm so lucky that you and Jeff got the guy who attacked me and he's in jail. Do you think he'll get bail?"

"Loften?" Dillard shook his head. "Not likely."

"How do you know?"

"From what I heard, he's a drifter with no ties to Florida. That makes him a flight risk. He's facing more charges. He'll be jailed right through to his trial or his sentencing if he pleads. Don't worry, that guy's going to be locked up for a long time."

"Good."

Dillard looked at her, trying to make eye contact.

"That's not all that's troubling you, is it, Lisa?"

"Oh," she exhaled, looked off and released a little laugh. "I just had a little disagreement and needed to clear my head."

"Well, it's none of my business, but did you disagree with Jeff?"

She met his probing blue eyes and nodded.

"Well, he's probably dealing with the aftereffects of Loften."

"What do you mean?"

"Jeff did quite a number on him." Dillard gave her a little sideways grin. "Not only did he put him in jail, he would've put him in his grave if I hadn't stopped him."

"He told me."

"In my time on the job, I've seen a lot of things, but Jeff was a little unnerving. He sure has an animal inside, doesn't he?"

"Evidently."

"I don't blame him for going nuts on Loften for what he did." Dillard looked hard at her. "You know what I mean?"

Not sure that she understood, an awkward moment passed with Lisa grappling to find the best way to respond.

"I should let you get back to your flowers," she said. "Give my best to Nell."

"I will. And, Lisa?" Dillard pulled on his gloves. "You keep a close watch on Jeff."

"Why?"

"His violent streak and that eye-for-an-eye thing can be dangerous. Never know where it could lead."

"Okay, I'll do that. Thanks, Roland."

Lisa resumed walking around the block trying to fathom what Dillard meant about Jeff's violent streak and *where it could lead.*

32

Staring at Vida's last message, Jeff's breathing quickened.

Okay, okay. Lisa's gone to cool off. Use this time to think.

Kneading the tension knotting in his lower neck, he tried to remain calm. But how could he? Vida knew where they lived, had been by the house, knew about the break-in *and had taken pictures of Lisa.*

That pissed him off so much.

Vida had accused him of stealing her work, wanted him to get her a job, then suggested they had done something together, something that could hurt him. *I know all about you. What you're really like.*

Jeff stared at himself in the mirror.

Admit it. There is truth in Vida's lies.

All the saliva in his mouth evaporated.

If this gets out, it could destroy everything I've worked for.

Anger rolled over him, and he cursed into the mirror.

He had to keep it together. There had to be a way to get through this. He had to find it.

Time was working against him.

First things first.

He went to his office, sat at his desk and unlocked his drawer with the false bottom. He pressed the hidden spring-release latch, slid open the top of the secret compartment. His fingers probed his memory cards and flash drives. Each bore tiny labels with dates. Throughout his life, he had saved everything he'd ever created. Everything he did in college, his internship, all of his work in Cleveland and his most guarded, private things.

His fingers brushed against one drive he'd labeled *Pain*.

No one knew the horrible truths he'd stored in there.

Jeff stared at it. Considered what it contained, could feel its pull but resisted.

Not now. Focus on the Vida issue.

Again, he counted the drives and memory cards. Everything was here.

He shuffled through the dates of files saved from his Asgaard work in Cleveland, found the stick he needed. He inserted it into his computer, scrutinizing with intensity all the files. Clicking through folder upon folder, file upon file, until he came to one labeled *Food VW*.

It was a scan of a handwritten, four-page draft of an Asgaard file concerning a project for a surplus-food redistribution campaign. The marketing approach involved storytelling married with media, on a local and national scale.

Reading through it, the truth squirmed in the back of his mind.

This was Vida's draft; this was her idea.

Jeff remembered how he'd found the discarded draft in the recycle bin in Vida's office when she'd been falling apart. He was certain no one had seen it or knew of it. It was pretty good stuff. Fair game, he'd thought at the time. So he took the paper out of the bin, and late one night, he scanned it into his computer and shredded the hard copy. And after Vida was fired, he began adapting the strategy.

Who would know? *I built on it, applying other dynamics, essentially creating a solid new concept.*

But the new concept was a factor in getting him his Miami job.

Jeff rubbed his lips with his fingers.

Look, he reasoned, *ideas pop up from all kinds of people in all kinds of ways. It's common practice for someone to improve on them. It happens all the time.* And this concept was exactly what he needed to get out of Cleveland and climb higher, to get control of their mounting debts. *No one will ever know*, he'd thought then.

No one will believe her, he thought now.

He froze.

Lisa was home.

Jeff closed down the files, put everything back into its hiding place and braced himself.

* * *

He met her in the kitchen.

She was drinking ice water from the fridge, her back to him.

"Lisa, I'm sorry—"

She held up her palm, then whirled to him, her face taut with anger.

"You tell me everything that's going on with you right now, or I swear I'll go back to Cleveland and stay with Joy until you get your shit together."

He stared at her.

"Jeff, I moved here for you. I gave up so much for you. *I was attacked in my home!*" She took a breath and kept going. "We're planning to have children. My God, I'm your wife! I deserve to know the truth."

The anguish in Lisa's eyes was more than Jeff could bear. She was right. Pushing back his emotions, he gestured for them to sit at the table.

"Do you remember a woman I worked with, Vida Warren?"

"Yes," Lisa said, trying to decipher what was coming. "You said she was a little off, she had problems and they had to let her go."

"Right. Drugs and drinking after her husband left her. Well, at first, people tried to help her, you know, cover for her at work. I felt bad for her. Then Vida got worse. She'd pass out at her desk, in the bathroom, in an alley. She stole money."

"I remember you telling me some of this. Okay, so?"

"Shortly after we moved, she started calling me."

"Why?"

"She wants me to help her get her job back so she can regain custody of her son."

"Are you going to help her?"

"No, she's unbalanced. For instance, she'd spew shock talk to get a reaction from people in our office. Once, she said she had friends in prison, only to say later that she was joking. Another time, she said her brother was in prison, then she said that she didn't have a brother at all. No, you would not want her working with you, believe me."

"So you told her you won't help her?"

"Yes, but she's relentless. The other day she showed up in my office."

"Here, in Florida?"

"Yes, she says her in-laws have her son and live in Boca Raton."

"What did she want?"

"She made accusations, claims that I took her work, her concepts, and that's how I got my promotion here and the South American campaign."

"Did you steal her work, Jeff?"

"No. She had concepts, but I overhauled them, improved them. It happens in the business. I didn't steal her work."

"All right, but is that why we moved so fast, before someone found out you used her concepts?"

"God, no!"

"Swear to me you're telling the truth."

"I swear it's the truth, but—"

"But what?"

"Vida and I had worked together a couple of

times, but that was when she was starting to fall apart. She could barely function. I did all the heavy lifting on the concepts. There's no way anyone could say I stole her work."

Lisa took a moment to assess what he'd said.

"She's been by our house," he said.

"What? *She knows where we live?*"

"Must've had a friend from the Cleveland office willing to look us up."

"Why would she come by our house? What else is going on?"

"She's threatening to tell everyone in the Miami office that I stole her work to achieve what I have, unless I get her a job there."

"This is ridiculous. Tell Reddick she's harassing you."

"No, we don't want police involved."

"Then, tell your bosses what's going on before Vida does."

"I don't want to do that. She's given me some time, a week."

"And you trust her to wait? What will that accomplish—what exactly are you waiting for?"

"She needs my help. A week gives me time to work something out with her."

"How? What do you plan to do?"

"I've got some ideas I need to sort out."

"What exactly?"

"Will you just let me work on this?"

"Jeff, you're making me nervous. You need to tell people about Vida now. I don't understand why you won't."

"Because I can't let this thing snowball and implicate me in any way. The break-in almost derailed things at work, almost cost us the campaign. I can't have this crap with Vida surfacing, not now."

"The break-in." Struck by a sudden fear, Lisa said, "What if Loften's connected to Vida—helping her? What if she does know guys in prison? We need to tell the detectives."

Jeff shook his head. "Vida spews a lot of bullshit. Besides, Loften's locked up."

"But, Jeff, what harm would it do to tell them?"

"I told you, it's too risky at this point. I'd have to say how all of this is connected to my job. Cruz and Reddick would need to question people in Cleveland, in Miami. If it leaked out, it could have an impact on the South American campaign. There could be headlines, a scandal that would injure the company's reputation. Globo Aedifico could cancel their contract. We could lose other contracts. Asgaard-T-Chace would surely fire me. Then where would we be, Lisa? No job, hundreds of thousands of dollars in debt? We'd be on the fucking street! And don't say that won't happen— I know it will, it's happened before!"

A moment passed.

Lisa turned from him, her eyes stinging.

"I'm sorry," Jeff said, standing, cursing under his breath. He thrust his hands into his hair. The veins in his temple throbbed as he went to pour himself a glass of water. "I'll talk to Vida." He gripped the glass hard, drinking to douse the inferno raging inside. "I'll handle it. I've worked too hard, come too far, to let this bitch ruin my life!" The glass cracked in his hand but stayed intact, and he set it down.

"Okay, okay." Lisa was unnerved by Jeff's rising anger. "Take it easy."

His phone vibrated, and he picked it up.

He had a new message from Leland Slaughter.

Meet me in Foster's office first thing tomorrow. We need to talk about an important confidential matter.

33

FBI agent Terri Morrow stopped typing at her desk to cover a yawn.

She'd been out all night on the streets of West Flagler with the violent-crimes squad surveilling suspects believed to be conspiring to commit an armored-car heist. They'd gained strong leads on new players. The next step would be warrant applications for wiretaps.

Unfortunately, the timing of the surveillance operation hadn't coincided with Dakota's sleepover birthday party after all, which meant Addison had had to spend the night in Hallandale with her father.

Morrow was nearly done but needed more coffee before she could finish her report. Stiff, she got up, surprised that the office, so peacefully empty in the predawn, was now filled with the nine-to-fivers.

She was returning to her desk and pondering taking Addie to the beach on the weekend when Jake Zhu waved her over to his cubicle.

"Good morning, Jake. Still using the crutches, I see." Morrow sipped from her mug. "What's up?"

"You know the Miami-Dade burglaries you'd asked me to monitor?"

"Yeah, for the task force."

"I just got a heads-up from my colleague there. They've made a recent arrest." Zhu swiped through his phone. "Clete Younger Loften."

"Really?"

Zhu held up Loften's mug shot. "Looks like they executed warrants in Allapattah in the motel where he lived."

"All right, send me everything you can on this. I'll need to alert my supervisor." Morrow looked around unsuccessfully for Weggnor. "I've got to finish something. This is good. Thanks, Jake."

At her desk, Morrow downed half of her coffee. With renewed energy, she wrapped up her report. Then she began reading the material on Loften that Zhu had sent to her. One of the first things she did was submit Loften's name to the data bank for the task force pursuing The Collector. Then she submitted it to other national systems.

It would take a little time to process.

Morrow then read through all the key points of what she had so far: that Loften had been arrested, found with a serrated knife, and identified as the subject behind the Palm Mirage Creek attack; that it was believed he stalked and studied his targets online; that he appeared to be a drifter who'd traveled to a number of states.

After digesting what she knew of Loften,

Morrow sent off an urgent note to her supervisor, Sebastian Weggnor, requesting she talk to the Miami-Dade investigators with an eye to interviewing Loften in relation to her work on the task force.

Several moments later, Weggnor answered.

Interesting. I'll call my counterpart at Miami-Dade now and get right back to you.

Weggnor's reaction to her information and request was somewhat deflating. He was known to be a straitlaced, by-the-book type who rarely left his desk. In the time she waited, Morrow reread everything with a growing feeling that Loften's arrest was a potential lead in the case. Then she went to Zhu to see if he had been able to dig up anything more from his sources.

"Working on it, Terri."

"Thanks."

Before she returned to her desk, Weggnor stood at his door and called her into his office.

The air smelled of Old Spice. As he returned to his chair, Morrow's eye went to the brochures on condos in Key West and cruises in the Caribbean. Weggnor's mind was on retirement. When she moved to take a seat, he stopped her.

"This won't take long." He leaned back, making his chair springs creak.

"You spoke to Miami-Dade?"

"I did. Now, from your note, and in addition to my understanding of the case, the possibility of a connection between Loften and the task-force cases is tenuous at best."

"*Tenuous?* But, sir, I don't think—"

Weggnor held up a finger.

"Let me be clear. I'm not ruling out any action on our part. Miami-Dade has Loften in custody, and they're working on charging him with other crimes. They have a very active investigation, and he's not going anywhere. Now, I understand they've got a backlog in processing some of their evidence. Our best course of action is to let Miami-Dade do their thing before we move. We've got to respect their jurisdiction and the fact that it is their case and Loften is their guy."

"But, sir, did you tell them about the task force?"

"I made them aware of our interest." Weggnor turned to his keyboard. "We've got time. We'll just wait and let them get on with their work."

Morrow strode back to her desk in disbelief. Weggnor was the consummate bureaucrat—a hindrance, not a leader. Why didn't he just get out of the way? She was considering a few choice words for her supervisor when her phone rang.

"It's me," Zhu said. "Just sent you more stuff. Take a look."

She opened the files to see the inventory list on the search warrant Detectives Cruz and Reddick had executed on unit 45 of the Oceanwave Gardens, Loften's residence. She studied it until her heart skipped. There on the list was *cord*, along with *women's underwear*. Nothing directly linked to The Collector's murder victims, but maybe there was something else.

She continued studying the list until her computer pinged with notifications on her submission of Loften's name into national crime data banks.

He had driving infractions in Kentucky and Indianapolis.

Morrow entered her password to access the encrypted data bank for the task force to check the dates against the cases. It didn't take her long to learn that Loften was in each state around the time of the most recent Collector incidents.

One was the murder of Jasmine Maria Santos, October 22, 2016, in Indianapolis, bound with cord, sexually assaulted and stabbed more than fifty times with a serrated knife. Her phone and driver's license were missing. The other was the case of Rhondell Felicia Hinson. On April 8, 2017, she survived her attack in her Louisville, Kentucky, home. A shoe impression found at the scene was the same size as the one recovered in earlier cases.

Morrow covered her mouth with her hand as she absorbed the information, then glanced to Weggnor's office. No way did she want to deal again with Mr. Tenuous who'd retired on the job. One thing working for her was the fact Loften was in custody.

How am I going to play this? I need to get around Weggnor.

She picked up her phone and called her friend in admin.

"Hi, Muriel, this is Terri. I'm planning some courses and vacation and need to know Sebastian's schedule for supervisor sign-offs. Do you know the next time he's off and who's my go-to person?"

"Hold on, sweetie, I'll check." A keyboard clicked. "In two days, Sebastian will take a week. Your go-to is Scott Wood."

"That's great. Thanks."

"Anytime."

Morrow tented her hands before her face.

A couple of days would be all right. She'd wait and present her information to Scott, a hard-core agent.

In the meantime, she'd just have to pray Loften didn't get bail.

34

Jeff had got to the office early and was seated at his desk.

But he wasn't there, not mentally.

He barely remembered driving to the Coral Cloud Tower downtown, had hardly touched his coffee and couldn't focus on today's upcoming development sessions for the South American project.

All of that had been eclipsed by his pending meeting.

What's the "important confidential matter" with Foster and Leland? Is it Vida? Did she go to them?

If she did, was he ready? What was his plan? Tell them the truth? That he'd refined Vida's concept. Have them talk to Cleveland about the disaster she had been and continues to be.

It wasn't that simple, was it?

Jeff took a breath, placed his hands flat on his desk.

He tried to relax to be ready for the meeting,

but he was consumed by Vida's intention to ruin him. Yesterday, in revealing to Lisa as much as he did, he'd dismissed her fear that Vida was linked to Loften. The truth was he had the exact same concern. Vida had mentioned criminal friends. Her words came back to him.

When you slip into the gutter like I did, you meet all kinds of people with all kinds of connections willing to help you for a little quid pro quo, you know, a little something for something.

Other tentacles of Vida's threats wriggled across his mind.

You know what you did. What we did.

He had no idea what she was talking about. Yes, she was a bit of a seductress, a tease. But it had never gone anywhere with him. Was she implying they'd had an affair? That was insane because nothing had ever happened between them.

Ever.

Not at work. And he'd only seen her at a few social gatherings he'd gone to, most of them with Lisa.

So what else could Vida have?

He leaned his elbows on the desk, drove his knuckles into his temples.

What was he going to do? He knew some people with other agencies, maybe he could arrange something...

He flinched when his phone rang.

"Jeff Taylor."

"Hi, Jeff, this is Gwen in Mr. Shore's office. Foster and Leland will see you here now."

"Thank you. On my way."

Jeff took out a small mirror from his top drawer, checked his hair, tightened his tie and left his desk.

On his way down the hall, he passed the conference room where he'd made his successful presentation; he assured himself that he could handle whatever awaited him. But his gut tensed when he spotted Fred Bonner, who appeared to have just exited Foster Shore's office.

"Hey there, big guy," Bonner flashed a grin, glanced around and lowered his voice. "Tell me, who was that woman I saw in your office the other day?"

"Oh, just a former business associate."

"She's a real looker. Be nice to have someone like that here, huh?" His chuckle echoed as he left Jeff alone outside the door to Foster Shore's office.

What a pig.

He pushed through his unease, knocked on Shore's door then entered. Gwen smiled at him from her desk in the outer office.

"Go right in. They're expecting you."

Jeff's shoes sank in the plush carpeting. The huge corner office smelled of fresh flowers and featured matching mahogany credenza, bookcase and oversize desk, leather sofa and chairs, and a majestic view of the city and the water.

"Have a seat," Shore said.

Jeff took the sofa chair next to where Leland was sitting.

"We wanted to congratulate you again and tell

you we're pleased with your work and how things are progressing with Globo Aedifico."

Jeff looked at Leland, then back to Shore. "Thank you," he said.

"Don't look so surprised," Shore said. "Getting that contract was a huge win for us, and the big guns in New York and London have taken notice. Your name is on the lips of some powerful people."

"That's great."

"Now, Jeff, we know you just arrived, your star is rising fast and we appreciate what you're doing for us here."

"I appreciate everything that you and the company have done for me and my wife."

"Good," Shore said. "Now, as to the reason we asked you to come in—all this is strictly confidential—Lee mentioned the bonus you've got coming?"

"He did."

"Everything's been approved and finalized, so you'll see sixty-five in your bank account by month's end."

"Sixty-five hundred? Thank you so much."

Shore exchanged a look with Slaughter.

"Jeff," Slaughter said, "Globo's a twenty-five-million-dollar account. Your bonus is sixty-five thousand."

Jeff's jaw dropped. "You're serious?"

"Quite serious," Shore said.

"I don't know what to say."

"You've earned it, Jeff," Shore said. "You might

want to talk to an accountant about sheltering it against the tax hit."

Shore and Slaughter stood, ending the meeting with handshakes and shoulder pats.

"Just keep up the stellar work," Shore said. "And if there's anything you need, anything you want to discuss, you can come directly to Lee and to me. Okay?"

Jeff hesitated, thinking of Vida Warren.

"Is there something on your mind?" Shore said.

"Uh, no." Jeff smiled. "It's all just a little, well, overwhelming."

"Completely understandable."

"Enjoy it. Take Lisa on a trip," Slaughter said. "But only after you've got the campaign nailed down."

Jeff left to the sound of their laughter.

He was elated and relieved as he settled back at his desk, ready to focus on the work ahead for the day. Rolling up his sleeves, he thought of texting Lisa about the bonus when his line rang.

"Got a call for you, Mr. Taylor," Jane, the temp receptionist, said.

He picked up, but before Jeff could say anything, her voice came through.

"Time's up," Vida said.

It took a moment for Jeff to shift his attention. "It hasn't been a week."

"I can't wait. I need to get things on track, to make things right."

"Vida, give me just a bit more time."

"For what? You're stalling."

"I'm working on an idea I need to discuss with you. You're going to like it."

Silence hissed. "What is it?" She sounded different: colder, desperate.

"Not over the phone," he said. "Let's meet, today."

He heard a muffling sound at her end as if she'd covered her mouthpiece to talk to someone.

"All right. There's a café, Romero Sunrise, on the waterfront at Bayside Marketplace. Meet me there, five thirty. But this is it. If you don't deliver, if you don't own up to your responsibilities, then everyone will know everything. And that'll only be the start."

Vida ended the call, and Jeff's cell phone pinged.

The message from Vida opened to a photo of Lisa jogging alone through Palm Mirage Creek.

35

Four miles north of the Coral Cloud Tower where Jeff Taylor ended his call with Vida, Clete Younger Loften waited for his cell door to open in the Miami-Dade County Pre-Trial Detention Center.

The Y-shaped complex across from the criminal courthouse was in Overtown, one of Miami's poorest neighborhoods and a world away from the gleaming skyscrapers of Brickell.

There was an electric buzz-click, followed by a heavy thunder roll, and the gunmetal steel doors opened simultaneously along the block. Loften, dressed in orange prison scrubs and tennis shoes, stepped out with accused murderers, rapists, robbers, carjackers and other inmates.

Under the watch of security cameras and correctional officers, they filed by the cream-colored cinder-block walls, along the polished floors to the dining area. Loften held no expression. He knew how to survive, how to keep from being blinded by his anger.

It enraged him that he was here, that he'd been

stopped by some suburban snowflake named Jeff Taylor.

I shoulda killed that motherfucker and tapped his wife when I had the chance.

The more Loften chewed on it, the more intense his anger grew.

I've got needs. Painfully powerful needs.

After breakfast, Loften reported for work in Sanitation. Call it providence or call it good luck, but after the booking process and Loften's first court appearance, which resulted in nothing but a new court date because he didn't have an attorney yet, he was assigned, probably incorrectly, to the trustee program. There, because he knew the rules, he exercised his right to volunteer for a job that gave him mobility in the institution. He chose Sanitation.

Every day, all the garbage in the jail was removed by trustees from inmate units, collected and stored in containers, then moved to storage areas, dumpsters and compactors for transfer. As Loften worked, he watched and listened until he became expert in the patterns, rhythms and timing of the process.

He rolled with the frequent personal searches and surprise shakedowns of housing units for contraband. Each day passed the same way, until a CO took him aside.

"Attorney visit, Loften. Let's go."

He was escorted to a secure area and one of the private booths, separated by a glass partition with a phone on each side.

Waiting for him on the opposite side was a woman who looked to be in her teens. Long dark hair and bangs framed her face, and oversize glasses took over half her face.

He sat and watched as she reached into her briefcase for papers but dropped them, causing them to spill on the floor. Flustered, she collected them, retrieved a legal pad and pen, then picked up her phone.

Loften picked up his.

"Mr. Loften, I'm Tarrah Pond from the Office of the Public Defender. I'll be representing you."

Loften's scarred, frightening face was stone cold. He said nothing, and Pond diverted her attention to her notes.

"Let me bring you up to speed on where things are at," Pond said. "I've gone through the criminal report affidavit. The prosecution's pushing for continued pretrial detention. They argue that the nature of the charges against you, the fact you're unemployed with no family or ties to the community, and the fact they continue to investigate you for additional crimes make you a flight risk."

Loften stared at her, his nostrils flaring a little. He said nothing.

"They've executed search warrants on your residence and your truck and argue that evidence linking you to other crimes has been found. However, we believe they've failed to provide a basis solid enough to support a strong case."

Loften said nothing, but his mind was racing.

With the search warrants, the heat was going to find out what he'd been up to.

"We believe, at this stage, their case against you is not that strong, and I promise we'll continue to press for bail."

Pond brushed back her hair, offering a timid smile to indicate she had provided what her young-attorney heart believed was a glimmer of hope.

"Do you have any questions, Mr. Loften?"

He tightened his grip on his phone and leaned forward.

Instead of speaking, he hung up, signaled the CO and left.

Returning to work, he let his thoughts caress what he'd been on the brink of saying to Tarrah Pond.

Tell me about the panties you're wearing. Next time you come, can you arrange a contact visit? I want you to slip them to me so I can smell them.

Loften's neck muscles throbbed as he shifted from fantasy to reality.

Gritting his teeth and grunting as he hefted a full bin of stinking trash into a dumpster, he thought of Jeff and Lisa Taylor.

I've got unfinished business.

36

"Something's come up with the campaign—got to work late. Let's go out or order in later. Okay?" Jeff said on the phone.

"How long do you think you'll be?" Lisa asked.

"Two hours, max."

After the call, Lisa was unable to shake her unease about Jeff's tone, which sounded almost deceptive, as she tried to comprehend the trouble plaguing their lives. Just when she was coming to terms with the attack and how Loften's arrest had helped put it behind her. Just when she and Jeff had made it official that they would try to get pregnant and live the life they'd dreamed of living, this new, ugly threat had surfaced.

Was this it? The karmic payback she'd feared all her life?

She remembered Stacey's funeral. How Stacey's broken mother had stooped down and crushed Lisa in her arms. "Thank God you were with her at the end, thank God my angel had you. Thank you, Lisa."

No, no, don't thank me. How she wanted to

scream back the truth—the horrible truth—that it was her fault Stacey had flown from the back seat through the windshield. And how badly she wished she could pay for the pain she had caused.

Lisa closed her eyes and took a breath.

Then she closed the files she'd been working on and searched old social-media posts for Asgaard-T-Chace in Cleveland. She dug into some of the personal photos and updates that Jeff's colleagues had put up over the years, looking for Vida Warren. She combed through images of people gathered at office events, at bars, at parties.

And there she was.

Lisa found photos of Vida at a Christmas party that were only a few years old. Staring at them, the memory of meeting her came back. Vida was attractive, but she was also kind of out there. Lisa saw it again as she met Vida's gaze on her screen: that wild glint in her eyes went right through you.

This woman is trouble.

Lisa's worry about Vida and Jeff gnawed at her.

The way Jeff had kept things from her, the way he'd grown so angry, so intense, beating up their home invader, ranting about Vida until he nearly broke a glass in his hand. Throughout all of their lives together, she'd known Jeff to be calm, reticent, almost withdrawn. But these days, something was raging in him. Lisa had never known this side of him, as if he'd become Jekyll and Hyde.

And what if Vida is connected to this Loften creep?

She stood, went to the window, cupped her hands to her face, thinking of how Jeff had come home all bloodied the night they caught Loften, then of his insistence not to tell the police about Vida. *I'll handle it.*

Roland Dillard's caution about Jeff came back to her, too. *His violent streak and that eye-for-an-eye thing can be dangerous. Never know where it could lead.*

But she'd known Jeff for nearly ten years now; they'd been married for seven years. He was a decent, honest guy who'd survived a horribly hard childhood. Like her, he'd been unable to escape the specter of the death of someone close to him.

Lisa didn't know what to do or where to turn.

Staring out her second-floor office window, she glanced at the security sensors and the strategically mounted surveillance camera, so thankful to have one covering every room of the house. Staring out, she was pleasantly surprised to see Roland working in his backyard garden.

Her surprise deepened when she saw Nell digging vigorously alongside him, like a strong, healthy woman. *She must be having a good day*, Lisa thought.

Dillard stopped, drank from a water bottle, checked his phone, then, by chance, turned and looked up at her watching him from her window. As if busted, she flushed with guilt. He smiled and gave her a little wave. She waved and smiled back, noticing that Nell had turned, looked up at her, too.

But Nell did not smile or wave.

At that moment, Lisa's computer and phone pinged. She left the window to see a message from her sister.

Free for a quick chat?

Lisa typed several commands on her keyboard and soon Joy's face appeared on her monitor.

"Hey, how was your trip to Niagara Falls?" Lisa asked.

"Exhausting but wonderful. The kids loved going on the *Maid of the Mist*. We all got wet. Then in Toronto, we went up the CN Tower—everyone loved that. We had a blast. It's so beautiful. You have to go. What about you? All I got from you were texts. Fill me in."

Lisa recapped and elaborated on most of the things she'd told Joy: how she'd stopped taking the pill—"I'm so happy," Joy said, "not because I'm going to be the best aunt ever, but because I got all these baby clothes to give you!"—then how Jeff got the big contract, then how her attacker had been arrested.

"So he's definitely in jail?"

"Yes."

"And you're serious, Jeff beat the guy up?"

"Yes. My neighbor, the guy I told you about, was there kinda helping arrest the creep, and he saw it all."

"Wow. Compared to Cleveland Jeff, Miami Jeff is a badass. Who is this guy you're married to?" Joy laughed.

"I know. Seriously, though, it's like he's got this dark, violent side to him. I mean, it's disturbing. And there's more."

"More?"

"I need your advice on something troubling me."

"Sure. Shoot."

"Ever since we moved, Jeff's been acting weird, like he was keeping something from me. I finally got it out of him."

"What is it?"

"There's this woman from his Cleveland office." Lisa related everything she knew about Vida Warren as her sister listened. "So here's the thing—she didn't show up in Jeff's office until after Loften was arrested. That's why I think that there's a possibility Vida could be connected to him."

"Oh my God. What does Jeff think?"

"He doesn't think they're connected. But here's the other thing—Jeff's still acting like he's hiding something, and he says that Vida knows where we live and she's been by our house. Once I saw this woman with a ball cap and dark glasses while I was running in a park. She seemed to be watching me."

"You've got to tell the police."

"Jeff says we can't. He says he has to *handle it*."

"That's stupid. Just tell the detectives, 'Hey, by the way, check out this wacko who's threatening me and my husband.'"

"I can't."

"Why not?"

"Jeff says that if we did that and police started questioning people at his office, it would create a scandal that could ultimately cost the company the big contract and cost him his job. But... I feel he's not telling me everything about Vida. Like today, he just called to say he has to work late, but I feel something else is going on. Now I'm so afraid because anything could happen. I don't know what to do."

Joy thought for a moment. "You want my advice?"

"Yes."

"Go to your neighbor, the ex-cop. Tell him confidentially. He'll know what to do and how to keep it quiet."

Lisa took a moment to consider the suggestion. "That's not bad. Let me think about that."

"And, Lisa, don't let Vida make you a prisoner. Fight back. The jerk's in jail. Keep running. You can protect yourself, right?"

"Now I keep spray and a panic alarm with me when I run."

"Good. If she confronts you, get in her face. Don't let that woman control your life. You've always been a fighter."

"Thanks."

In the background on Joy's end, Lisa could hear her kids calling their mom.

"I have to go, but keep me posted."

"I will. Love you, sis."

Lisa felt better after talking with her sister.

She stood and returned to the window and looked down into the Dillards' backyard.

Roland and Nell were no longer there.

Lisa returned to her computer, resurrected the photos of Vida Warren and focused on her eyes. Staring into them, Lisa felt a stirring, and for the first time in her life, she wondered if she should get a gun.

37

While Lisa Taylor was video chatting with her sister in Cleveland, Agent Morrow was in Doral, reviewing her task-force files and information on Loften in a second-floor interview room at Miami-Dade's Midwest District Station.

Morrow didn't know where this would lead, but her instinct had told her to follow it through. She was on the right track and shouldn't give way to hurdles.

She shook her head at how she'd come to this stage. Cases reaching across jurisdictions involved excessive bureaucracy. Desk jockeys like Weggnor reflected the FBI's sensitivity to respecting local authority and adhered to formalities, which ensured nothing got done. Thank heavens for people like ASAC Scott Wood, a guy who still had street cred and contacts. He cleared the way for Morrow to consult the investigators leading the Loften case.

The rest is up to me, she thought, as Detectives Camila Cruz and Joe Reddick entered with files, notebooks and coffee.

After introductory handshakes, they seated themselves opposite Morrow.

"Our supervisor knows yours," Reddick said, "and after she got a call from him, she directed us to talk to you. You're looking into Loften in relation to an FBI task force?"

"That's correct," Morrow said. "Our task force concerns an ongoing investigation into a series of unsolved homicides across the US committed by one individual. Loften's a person of interest. I'll background you, but this is highly confidential."

Morrow began swiping at her tablet and, for the next twenty minutes, provided a detailed history of The Collector case, showing them geo-timelines, case summaries and key-fact evidence.

Then she highlighted factors in Loften's arrest, his use of a serrated knife, his possession of condoms and women's underwear; how it was believed he stalked and studied his targets online; how Loften appeared to be a drifter who'd traveled to a number of states; how they could place him in Indiana and Kentucky within the time of two attacks; and many other points, like the type of cord found in Loften's motel.

"That's a lot of cherries coming up for him," Reddick said.

"A disturbing number," Morrow said.

"But our guy collects underwear; your guy collects driver's licenses. That's a distinction," Reddick said.

"Yes, but the trophy-collection element fits with the pattern," Morrow said. "And here's another one of our challenges that prevents us from ruling him out. Going back to the case in Louisville, Kentucky, we got a partial thumbprint, but the quality was poor. When you grabbed Loften and printed him, we ran his prints against the partial, but it doesn't give us enough for our examiners to suggest consistency with Loften. So we're thinking about his serrated knife. What have your people pulled from it?"

The detectives traded glances. "Still being processed," Cruz said.

"All right," Morrow said. "But you collected Loften's DNA when you arrested him, right?"

"We did, but we haven't submitted it to CODIS or the other data banks yet because it's still being processed, too," Cruz said.

Thinking, Morrow tapped her pen on her file. "What have your forensic people found on his laptop and phones? Anything showing how he stalked targets and others?"

"Not much so far because nearly all of his devices are locked," Reddick said. "It's frustrating for us, too. We got three homicides from an arson in South Miami-Dade and four homicides from the warehouse shooting near Cutler all being processed ahead of us. It's going to take time.

"And it wouldn't be a good idea for the FBI to pull our Loften material out of the queue to process it yourselves because, if nothing comes of it, it could muck up chain-of-evidence when things get to court for the case we do have."

"No," Morrow said, "I agree."

"We could try to push things, but it would be futile," Cruz said. "The other cases are multiple homicides with grieving families waiting."

"I understand, believe me," Morrow said.

"Besides," Reddick said, "Loften's in the Dade county jail, or what we now call the Pre-Trial Detention Center. He's not going anywhere."

"That brings me to another question," Morrow said. "I'd like to interview him while he's locked up. Would that be detrimental to your case?"

"Shouldn't be a problem," Cruz said. "I'll get you his attorney's contact info. We could go with you. It should be arranged in a day or so."

"Good. Thanks."

"I'd like to go back over a few things about Loften and The Collector," Cruz said. "With the most recent killing in Cleveland, can you put Loften there?"

"We're working on that with our Cleveland office."

"As we mentioned, and it's noted in our report, when we questioned Jeff and Lisa Taylor as to whether they knew Loften or had had any contact or history with him, they both insisted that he was a stranger to them."

"I read that."

"But they recently moved to Florida from Cleveland, and Cleveland looms large in The Collector case."

"It certainly does," Morrow said. "It's almost like we're missing a puzzle piece."

"Right," Cruz said. "We need to determine if the

Taylors have any knowledge or link to the victim in Cleveland, Maylene Marie Siler."

"I agree," Morrow said. "We've got a lot of dots here, but little by little, I feel we're getting closer to connecting them."

38

By 5:20 p.m. Jeff was threading his way among the boat groups, tour people and shoppers at Bayside Marketplace, Miami's busy waterfront plaza.

The aroma from the restaurants mingled with live Latin music, creating a carnival atmosphere, while a storm churned in Jeff's gut as he contended with the menace Vida posed to his life.

He was consumed with guilt for not telling Lisa everything, like how Vida had taken pictures of her jogging. At the same time, he felt his control slipping, control over all he'd worked for, over all he'd achieved, over everything he cherished and all the risks he'd taken.

I've got to put a stop to this now, before I lose everything.

His mind raced as he worked his way to the Romero Sunrise. He scanned the café's cluster of outdoor tables topped with yellow umbrellas that looked out to Biscayne Bay and the marina, until he spotted a woman sitting alone, wearing dark glasses and a floppy straw hat. On the table before her was an empty glass, and beside it stood another, half-filled with what appeared to be a mojito.

"Vida," he said.

"Hello, Jeffrey. You're on time."

He looked around. "We're going to end this right now," he said.

"Got that job lined up for me?"

"I can't help you with that. Why are you doing this?"

"I need a good job to get my boy back, and I need you to make it happen."

Vida touched her phone, gently, but Jeff could see her hands were shaking. He also noticed a bruise under her left eye, peeking out from under her glasses.

"It just hasn't sunk in yet, has it?" he said. "I can't get you a job with Asgaard. They fired you. They're not going to hire you back."

"They will when you confess to stealing my work."

His conscience raced, his moral compass spinning out of control.

But Vida's notes had been in the trash. And they were just the beginnings of an idea he'd run with, turned into what it was… But the truth—the truth he couldn't face—was that her idea had been brilliant.

Vida was tugging on the bottom card of his house of cards, a house he'd worked so hard to build.

"I didn't steal your work!" Jeff shouted.

People at tables near them turned to the drama unfolding.

"I *know* you did." She threw back a good long drink of her mojito, and he realized she was under the influence—the drink or something else.

She rubbed the back of her hand across her mouth, like a trucker finishing a beer. "You said you had something for me?"

He looked at her for a long time, then reached into his jacket pocket and passed her an envelope. She looked inside—it was filled with cash.

"That's one thousand. And I'll give you another four thousand contingent upon the guarantee you never again contact me, my wife, my office or anyone, concerning me."

"I'll take it because I need it." She put the cash in her bag. "But I don't agree to any of your terms until you do your part, Jeff. Because I'm not some kind of whore you buy off. Do you understand?"

Whore?

Jeff saw himself reflected in her dark glasses as she slowly tilted her head to stare at him. Suddenly, he realized he'd made a mistake.

"Do you have any connection to Clete Loften, the prick who broke into our home?"

Vida leaned back in her chair, and as she weighed the question, a smile crept across her face. "Maybe I do, and maybe I don't."

With the speed of a cobra, Jeff seized Vida's wrist, jolting her so that her hat and glasses fell from her head and onto the table.

"You're hurting me!"

People turned, but he ignored them, gritting his teeth, growling.

"I should've killed him when I had the chance. Now, you listen to me. You're not getting another cent from me! Stay the fuck away from me. You're sick—get help!"

As Vida tried to replace her glasses, he saw the discoloration around her left eye. Tears rolled down her face.

"Is everything okay here?" A waiter had materialized, his attention on Jeff's grip until he released her wrist.

Vida smiled, replacing her glasses and hat, and nodded weakly to the waiter.

"We're fine," Jeff said. "Just having a discussion."

"Can I get you anything?" the waiter offered.

"We're good. Thanks," Jeff said.

After the server left, Vida leaned in to Jeff.

"How can you treat me like this?" she asked. "After what you did, after what *we* did—"

"We didn't do anything! I don't know what you're talking about."

She picked up her phone, scrolled through it until she came to a series of photos and turned the screen to him. The images showed a naked Vida with a dressed Jeff on a sofa, them kissing, Jeff's hand on her breast, Jeff with his pants unzipped, her head in his groin.

"That was fun, wasn't it?" Vida smiled.

All the blood drained from his face. "What is this?"

"Remember Artie's party a few years back in Cleveland? You and me, when the wife was away?"

"I drank a lot at that party—I passed out. You staged these."

"Did I? Will it look that way to Lisa when she sees them, or to Foster Shore and Leland Slaughter or the rest of the world when I post them online?"

"My God, why would you do this?"

"Because I liked you. Because it was fun, and you never know when something like this will come in handy."

"You're unbelievable!"

Vida closed her phone, secured it in her bag, stood to leave.

"I'm giving you forty-eight hours to make things right. If I don't hear from you by 5:00 p.m. the day after tomorrow, your world ends."

She turned and walked away, moving fast around the tables. Jeff moved faster, grabbed her arm roughly and turned her around.

"Don't do this, Vida."

"Let me go!" She slapped his face hard and struggled free.

"Vida!"

"You leave me no choice, Jeff!"

"Okay, I'll—I'll talk to some people. I'll help you."

"You've got until five in two days. Ticktock."

Vida disappeared into the market crowd, leaving Jeff stunned, standing alone in the café. People were staring at him, shaking their heads. The café music throbbed with an ominous beat, scoring the nightmare future uncoiling in front of him.

39

Jeff texted Lisa when he started walking to his car: Heading home now.

Lisa responded quickly.

I'll order pizza. It'll be here when you get home.

Jeff arrived to the smell of baked spicy meat and onions. When he got to the kitchen, Lisa turned away from the kiss he tried to press on her cheek. She slapped a slice of pizza on a plate, nearly slamming it on the table.

"What is it?" Jeff asked, chewing on his first bite.

"Did you fix the problem that kept you late at work?"

He nodded as he chewed.

"Funny. After you called me, I called your office back to ask you about getting something else instead of pizza for dinner. They said you'd left your office for the day and that you had no late meetings."

Jeff's chewing slowed.

"Why were you late, Jeff?"

He reached for a napkin and wiped his mouth. "Vida called me. I went to meet her."

"Why didn't you tell me?"

"I didn't want to worry you."

"I'm beyond worry." Tears brimmed in her eyes. She was at the sink and turned her back to him. "How can I trust you with anything?"

He went to embrace her from behind, but she pushed him away.

"Where did you meet her? What did she want?"

"At a café in Bayside Market. I tried to make her agree to stop harassing me."

"And?"

Jeff didn't respond.

"And?" Lisa repeated.

"It didn't go well."

"What do you mean?"

"It's complicated."

"Uncomplicate it, and tell me what's going on."

"I gave her a thousand dollars to leave us alone."

"Oh my God! Where's your brain? You gave money to a disturbed woman like her, *a woman who could be connected to the man who broke into our home and assaulted me*? What're you thinking?"

"I was desperate. She just keeps pushing and pushing and won't give me time to clear it up."

"Did the money work?"

"No."

"You have to tell your bosses. We have to tell the detectives."

"No—"

"*No?* Are you kidding me?" Lisa's eyes drilled into him. "What's really going on here? Did you steal her work?"

"No."

"Because if you didn't, if you're innocent as you say, and this is a case of a troubled woman Asgaard has already fired, then you've got nothing to be concerned about. Your star's rising. They love you— they moved you here, promoted you and gave you a huge bonus for your work that they love. They'd believe you. They'd take your word over that of an unbalanced ex-employee, wouldn't they? So why are you so reluctant to blow the whistle on her?"

"She has these pictures..."

"Pictures? What pictures?"

"They're not real. Do you remember a couple of years ago when you went to visit Morgan in Philadelphia?"

"Yeah."

"Artie Corinda, a graphic designer at the office, threw a huge party. Everyone went. Vida was there. I'd been working long hours, and even though I was exhausted, I went, too. I got plastered. I passed out and slept it off at Artie's place."

"And that's all that happened?"

Jeff swallowed. "Vida must've come into the room where I was passed out, then took off her clothes and got these photos of me with her."

Lisa's face burned as she fought to stay calm. "You've seen these photos?"

"She showed them to me today. I never knew

they existed or what she'd done. I swear, *nothing* happened between us. My eyes are closed in all of the pictures. They're staged. She's a sick woman. If I don't get her a job, she's going to send the pictures to you, to Foster Shore, Leland Slaughter and post them online along with the claim that I stole her work. It'll destroy everything."

Seconds passed with Lisa staring hard at him as if he were a stranger, her face fracturing with anguish. "Did you fuck her?"

"No, Lisa—God, no! I swear."

She scrutinized him for deception through her hot tears. "I don't know what to believe," she said. "If you've got nothing to hide, if you've done nothing wrong, then tell your bosses, and tell Cruz and Reddick."

"I can't. If Vida's lies got out, they could destroy everything." He took her shoulders. "Can we sit down, Lisa, please?"

She shrugged him off.

He blinked several times, searching for the right words. "You have every right to be angry with me, to think I'm a fool. But I swear with all my heart, I never slept with Vida. I know you're scared. I am, too. This is a nightmare. As for Vida knowing where we live, I'll talk to Cruz. I'll say we're still a bit jumpy, which is true, and ask for extra patrols. As for Loften, he's locked up. Besides, I think the detectives would have come to us if he had any connection to Vida, right?"

Lisa said nothing.

"Lisa, look at everything we suffered through

when we were kids. Things that scarred us. Things we've never told anyone. You know how I lived, how I really lived, after my dad was shot, and how it shaped me, and how I carry everything from that day—you've felt similarly shaped by a childhood tragedy, right?"

She closed her eyes and nodded because it was true.

"Our bond is so strong. I'm not perfect, but I would never do anything to hurt you, okay?" he said. "Now, I know you don't believe this, but we're living a fragile financial existence. When you take everything into account, we have several hundred thousand dollars in debt. I'm making more, but you're making less. Even with the bonus, we're only a few months away from having nothing and, my God—" Jeff's voice cracked "—that terrifies me more than you'll ever know. Vida Warren could set in motion events that will ruin everything, that will catapult us into that kind of life, if I don't stop her first. I can't let her go around depicting me as a thief and adulterer. I just can't. If I tell people what I did, it'll still look like I took her work, and the damage will be significant. It'll mark me when I try to find other work." Jeff wiped at his eyes. "She's given me two days. All she wants is a job. I have a plan that should work."

"And if it doesn't?"

"I'll tell Leland and Shore everything."

That night, Lisa went to bed early and alone. Sleep was a fugitive as she lay awake, anguished at how things were spinning out of control. And most frightening was the realization that she could no longer trust the things she had believed in.

Everything that mattered to her was crumbling.

Who was her husband? Did she really know him?

Alone in his office, Jeff worked at his computer, drafting emails to colleagues he knew from college, from conferences, from his network of professionals in the industry.

Many were with agencies or corporations with advertising and marketing departments in-house, which had offices in South Florida. Cathy Millard, whom he knew from Chicago, was with SkyHi-Media, Reed Kassan with NineStar Amazing International in Los Angeles, and Shelley Rozart with Smith-Wren-Fujama Global in New York, along with several others. All were huge operations with offices in the Miami area.

Earlier, he would never have considered taking this step, but Vida had pushed him into a corner. He hated her for it.

He made urgent appeals that sounded like exclusive tips, touting Vida Warren as a brilliant ad exec he used to work with who was seeking a position in Miami, and highlighting how she'd be an asset to any agency. In all, he'd sent out about a dozen requests, knowing he could face fallout if someone did hire Vida and she proved to be useless…or worse.

That's not my concern. Not now.

Jeff sat back in his chair, his thoughts galloping in a thousand different directions. What more could she possibly know or fabricate about him? Dragging his hands over his face, he tried to quash every fear.

One way or another, he was going to end his problem with her.

40

Every morning of incarceration was the same for Clete Younger Loften.

The electronic buzz-click, the heavy roll of the steel doors opening, joining the other inmates watched by cameras and correctional officers as they filed by the cinder-block walls to the dining area for breakfast.

"Loften." The CO who the inmates called Brutus pulled him from the line. "You got a message. Call your attorney. Let's go."

Brutus escorted him to the dayroom of his housing area and the phone where he made his call to Tarrah Pond at the Public Defender's office.

"Mr. Loften," Pond said, "the FBI and Miami-Dade detectives have requested to interview you with respect to several ongoing investigations."

Loften was silent on the line.

"I advise that you grant the request. I'll be present. You do not have to answer questions that may incriminate you, but this would be a good step in demonstrating cooperation to the court."

Loften said nothing.

"Mr. Loften, it would help our case for pretrial release. Do you agree to meet with them?"

Loften's thoughts shifted to his memory of Tarrah Pond, all bangs and frames. The sound of her voice gently stroked his imagination. He envisioned the color of her bra and panties, their delicate lace design and what they smelled like.

"Mr. Loften? Do you agree?"

"All right."

"Good. They'll send me a summary of questions. I'll be there tomorrow afternoon, in advance of them to prepare you."

Loften hung up, turned to Brutus, then joined the others for breakfast.

He picked at his scrambled eggs while his anger and frustration ate at him. His attorney figured that helping the FBI would demonstrate cooperation. Loften sneered to himself. Young Tarrah Pond knew nothing. The way he saw his situation, if the FBI was knocking on his door, he might as well help them put a noose around his neck.

After breakfast, Loften reported for work in Sanitation.

The crew of trustees started the morning routine, which Loften knew by rote. Every morning, with little scrutiny, the trustees went floor by floor, block by block, collecting all garbage, trash and rubbish from all inmate units and residential areas. The trash was stored in wheeled bins that they rolled through the institution to the rear dock of each block.

The docks were secured within the jail complex and had an industrial-size stationary compactor with an open chute. The trustees emptied the bins into the chute. When full, the metal ram was turned on to compress the trash, crushing it under thousands of pounds of pressure.

The compactor had a tailgate that extended through the jail wall, topped with barbed wire, to the outside where a sanitation-company truck would collect the compacted trash and haul it away without entering the institution.

That the FBI was now on his case was all Loften could think about as he worked. Well, he also thought of Tarrah Pond's underwear, which was why he agreed to the interview.

As he rolled his first morning load of garbage to the dock and positioned his bin to dump into the chute, he seethed at the fact he faced thirty years behind bars.

He had unyielding, aching needs and unfinished business with the Taylors. Loften's problem so engrossed him that he failed to pay attention to his job, which registered when the bin slipped from his grasp into the compactor, crashing into it with a *thud*.

Staring at it lying five feet below, atop the small heap of rotting garbage with flies and wasps strafing it, he cursed. He looked around. He was alone but for the security cameras.

The bin had to be retrieved.

Grumbling, Loften lowered himself into the trash, forcing himself to breathe through his mouth to deal with the gag-inducing stench. The plastic bin was large but relatively light, and if he got his shoulder under it, he could heft it back up to the dock. The problem was traction: he was slipping on God knew what and the wasps were buzzing around him.

As he worked to get a better hold and grip, something furry with a tail scurried from the heap toward the far end. Loften leaped back to avoid a pair of big rats.

That's when he noticed it.

The morning trash had been heaped at the front. The rear of the compactor, the end that extended through the wall to the outside, was still empty. A thin, fibrous curtain hung down from the far side, where a bar of light spilled into the compactor.

Stepping carefully around the stinking garbage, Loften moved to the curtain and pushed it back to discover a gap about eighteen inches wide and chest-high running horizontally across the locked steel doors. He peered through the gap and had a clear line of sight to an alley and saw traffic passing by a block away.

He couldn't believe it.

A plan began taking shape, when suddenly he heard a noise near the chute. Fearing the compactor was about to be switched on, he scrambled back toward the dock before it was too late.

41

Home alone, Lisa struggled with work at her desk all morning but accomplished little.

Her concentration had been overtaken by her anxiety. Troubling thoughts about Jeff, Vida and Loften flew at her in clusters. Unable to focus, she'd stare blankly at her monitor, the window or nothing at all.

Jeff had been up all night. She never heard him come to bed, and he left so early for work in the morning she never saw him. What was he going to do about Vida? Lisa couldn't stop worrying.

For lunch she managed a small salad, half a cup of yogurt, then tried to continue working, but it was hopeless. Her concern about Vida dominated every thought.

Jeff had said she'd given him a few days to get her a job. Then what? Problem solved? Lisa doubted it. That woman was unbalanced, and this thing between her and Jeff, whatever it was, went deep.

There had to be a way out of this.

Lisa couldn't stand it any longer. She couldn't just sit in the house fretting. Her sister's words came to her, how she should not let Vida make her a prisoner.

Running will help me think. It will help me decide what to do.

She changed, checked to be sure she had her spray and panic alarm—secretly wishing she had a gun—then armed and locked the house, and left.

The Talking Heads' "Once in a Lifetime" thudded through her headphones as she ran. The fresh air, the fragrant smell of flowers and the wide streets made her feel good as she listened to the song.

Lisa could not let Vida and everything her demands entailed ruin everything. She had to trust Jeff. As hard as it was, she had to trust him. Yet she was terrified that Vida, given her background, might very well know someone like Loften and could've possibly sent him to their house.

She knows where we live, Jeff had said.

Jeff.

He was a bigger problem.

Lisa struggled to believe that he'd told her the truth about his relationship with Vida and his story about her pictures.

He held back the truth from me before. Is he lying about Vida now? Did they have an affair— is that what this is really about? Why he's so desperate to keep things quiet? No, no, no. I've got to stop thinking the worst about him. In my heart, I do know him. He wouldn't cheat on me. Deep down to his core, he's not a dishonest guy. He's just under so much pressure right now. That's what I have to believe.

Entering the big park with its huge trees, thick shady tunnels of green, she switched off her music and pulled out her plugs to enjoy the birdsong of the woods. It was early afternoon; few people were around today. She passed a mother with her little girl, a child who looked so much like—

Suddenly she was in the back seat of Stacey's car again, Stacey's dad driving and drinking from a can, playing the radio loud. Stacey playing a game with her… Stacey's turn…now her turn… her father cursing…brakes screeching…metal and glass exploding… It was just a game…

Lisa knew it was her fault.

She didn't deserve to be happy considering what she'd done, and everything that was happening with Jeff and Vida was the price she had to pay for the pain she'd caused.

And things could get worse.

Lisa then thought of Jeff's violent streak and his determination to handle Vida himself without telling his bosses or the detectives. Nothing made any sense—

She stopped in her tracks, hesitating.

She'd heard a sound ahead, in a darker section of bush.

Like a child's cry. Maybe a lost little boy or girl?

Breathing steadily, Lisa left the running path

and, pushing away branches, moved closer to where she'd heard the sound.

"Hello?" she called.

Step by step, she progressed into the cool, darkened corner of the forest until it swallowed her.

A distance ahead, a branch quivered.

"Hello?"

Lisa made her way to the area from which she was certain the sound had emanated but found nothing. She swallowed, turned in all directions until she heard another branch snap. Not far off through the leafy growth, she saw a flash of orange.

A jacket, shirt or cap?

The tiny hairs on the back of her neck stood up, and her scalp tingled.

There was no child. Something, or someone, was watching her.

Slowly stepping back, she reached for her spray, positioned it in one hand. She then reached for her panic alarm with her other hand as she turned and rushed away through the brush, branches slapping and pulling at her, as if trying to prevent her from returning to the path.

Her heart hammering, she ran as fast as she could without looking over her shoulder, running until she got home.

Once inside, she locked the door behind her, slammed her back against it and worked to catch her breath.

Was that real? Was there someone there? Am I losing my mind?

She stayed at the door until her breathing subsided.

Using her phone, she ran a check of her home-security system, scanning all the cameras until she was confident the house was empty. Then she went upstairs, removed her clothes and got into the shower. As the steaming water rushed over her, she began to shake uncontrollably.

She began sobbing, huge gasping sobs.

Hugging herself, she slid to the floor of the shower like a broken woman, knowing there was one person she could turn to for help.

42

Stepping from the shower, Lisa picked up her phone and found Roland Dillard's number and sent him a text.

Hi Roland, this is Lisa Taylor, your neighbor. Sorry to impose, but I'd like to see you about a confidential matter. Are you free?

While waiting for his response, she toweled off, dried her hair and got dressed. She was pulling on a shirt when her phone pinged with Dillard's response.

I'm free. Come on over.

Fifteen minutes later, she was at his doorstep and rang the bell. Dillard opened the door, wearing khaki shorts and a navy polo shirt.

"Forgive me for disturbing you."

"Not at all." He gestured to the living room.

Lisa glanced around before she sat on the sofa. "Where's Nell?"

"She's resting in bed. Can I get you something to drink? Coffee?"

"No, thank you."

"So what did you need to see me about?"

She bit her bottom lip and inhaled.

"This has to be confidential."

"Absolutely."

Fully aware she was betraying Jeff's trust, and because she was desperate and afraid, Lisa began recounting her husband's history with Vida Warren. Speaking through tears, Lisa told Dillard everything she knew, leaving nothing out. He nodded and asked an occasional question as she clasped and unclasped her fingers in her lap. When she finished, she stared into his craggy face, met his eyes—calm, confident and full of understanding.

"It concerns me that this woman is causing you so much anguish," he said. "You need her to stop, but it appears nothing will stop her."

"Yes." Lisa touched a tissue to her eyes. "This is going to sound crazy, but I was just out running in the park, and I felt like someone was watching me. It may have been kids playing or a bird or something. But... I don't know."

"You're upset, jittery. It's understandable."

He sat back and held a poker face for several moments.

"Do you think Vida could be linked to Loften?" Lisa asked.

"It's unlikely, but you shouldn't rule anything out."

"Should I tell Cruz and Reddick?"

"Tell you what. I could talk to them for you, suggest they question her quietly, and at the same time I could float the Warren–Loften link to them. That could be enough to get Vida to back off."

"That would be such a relief."

"But I don't think that should be the first step," Dillard said.

"Why not?"

"I think we need to let Jeff take his shot, let him handle it."

"But what if he fails? And he has this violent streak, he blacks out. You saw it yourself."

"I know. There's a bit of a risk there, but look, Jeff knows more about this than we do. We'll give him a little time. We don't want to make it worse if he can resolve it. Maybe he can find her a job."

A long moment passed before Lisa reluctantly nodded. She had to trust Dillard's judgment—she'd come to him for his advice, and he was giving it to her.

"Have you spoken to anyone else about this?"

"Only my sister in Cleveland."

"It pains me to see you so distressed. Especially in light of all that has happened to you. The move, leaving your hometown, the attack, the dream of a family and now this deranged person. If Jeff can't sort things out with her, I'll step in."

Lisa stood to leave, her mind racing at the whirlwind her life had become. Looking at Dillard, her heart warmed at the hope he'd held out for her, and she managed to voice a weak *thank you* before she was overcome with emotion and sobbed.

Dillard stood, took her into his arms, pulled her to him. She felt his strength as he comforted her, just like her dad would, making her feel as if nothing in this world could ever hurt her.

"It's going to be all right," he told her.

She sought her composure, smiling and nodding her appreciation.

"Why don't you and Jeff join me and Nell for dinner tonight—take your mind off things for a few hours?"

"But we can't tell Jeff what I told you."

"No, no. It'll help me get a read on him and where things stand."

Lisa nodded. "Okay, I'll ask him."

She thanked Dillard, then stepped away to leave, neither of them aware that Nell had heard them from the hall leading to the kitchen, where she stood wearing a Miami Dolphins T-shirt.

It was orange.

43

Time was ticking down for Jeff.

When he got to his desk on the fifty-first floor of the Coral Cloud Tower that morning, more than half of the dozen people he'd requested help from had gotten back to him.

It didn't look good. No one had anything.

Minutes were slipping by.

Meetings concerning the Globo Aedifico campaign took up much of his day as he battled to pay attention between yawning and checking his phone for other responses.

"You okay, there, Jeff?" Nick Martinez asked as a concept meeting ended.

Jeff rubbed the back of his neck. "Didn't get much sleep last night."

Martinez nodded, then changed the subject.

"My sister won't be using her Marlins tickets this weekend. Yankees are in town. If you're interested in going, let me know."

"Thanks, Nick. Sounds great. I'll let you know."

Jeff nearly made it to his office when Foster Shore caught up with him.

"Need to see you for a second."

Jeff's stomach knotted and his face whitened.

Shore entered Jeff's office with him and closed the door behind him.

"Wanted to give you a heads-up," Shore said. "Martin Nedwell in our London office has got several major projects coming and wants you to join his team in making presentations in Dublin, Edinburgh, London and Manchester later next month. You'll need to be there for a couple of weeks. There's additional compensation London will pay you, as well. You can take your wife."

Jeff took a moment to think.

"Are you all right, Jeff? You look a little pale."

"I'm fine. This sounds like a great opportunity, but I'm not familiar with their operations, and we have the Globo Aedifico campaign."

"Don't worry, we'll have more information for you on London, and by then the South American work should be well underway. We can video conference with you while you're overseas to keep things moving. Can you handle this?"

"Yes, sir. Thank you."

"Good." Shore slapped Jeff on the back and left just as Jeff's line rang.

Anticipating a call from Vida, his stomach tensed. "Jeff Taylor."

"Hey, Jeff, Shelley Rozart with Smith-Wren."

He could hear an echo of PA announcements in the background.

"Hi, Shelley."

"I'm in preboarding at Kennedy, so I'll get to it. Got your message, and it just so happens we have an opening coming up in our Miami office. So have your friend send her résumé, then call Delores Shutter to arrange an interview. All the contact info is in the email I'm sending you now."

"Thanks so much, Shelley."

"Not a problem. I'll see you at the next conference."

Jeff's phone pinged with Shelley's email, then it pinged again with an email from Reed Kassan at NineStar in California.

Yo, Jeff. Talked to our Florida people and pitched your friend to them. Our office in Lauderdale would like to see her CV to set something up. Here's the contact info. When you coming to LA?

Jeff thanked Reed, then immediately sent Vida the information about two job possibilities in South Florida, relieved that his colleagues had come through. As the day rolled on, he checked the status of other requests. That's when he saw an email notification from his bank, alerting him to the recent deposit of sixty-five thousand dollars into his account.

He stopped for a moment to digest the significance of the bonus. Beyond the money, it was an acknowledgment of how hard he had worked to reach this point in his career, his life.

No way will I lose everything to Vida Warren.

But the fact remained: anything was possible with that woman.

I'm walking on a tightrope.

As he continued working through the day, Jeff grew uneasy because he hadn't heard back from Vida. Taking in the panoramic view from his office, he saw nothing but risk on the horizon.

Vida was unstable, uncontrollable. What if she was connected to people like Loften? And if she delivered on her threats, he'd be fired; they'd force him to return the bonus.

An ocean of fear swept over him, and suddenly he was back in Chicago, when his father was still alive and they had a house and he had his own room and was happy and safe, before a shotgun blast ended it all.

His mother's face aged; she wore her grief permanently as she lost her job, then the house and her dignity as they fell, fell, fell from the joy he'd known to that van. Their stinking cage of hopelessness.

One day at school, two girls had been following Jeff. "You smell like pee," one of them said before they ran off. Their giggles rang in his ears.

His phone vibrated with a text from Lisa.

We're invited for dinner tonight at the Dillards'. We should go. Be good to take our minds off things for a few hours. OK?

Jeff sighed then texted back.

Agreed. Sounds good.

By the time he left the office at the end of the day, he'd received responses from all of the people he'd contacted. All but Shelley's and Reed's answers were negative.

Far more troubling, he still hadn't heard anything from Vida Warren.

"How'd it go today?" Lisa asked him when he got home.

Jeff got a cold beer from the fridge, sat at the table, took a long pull, then ran a hand through his hair and shrugged. "I'm beat. It was busy, and I was up all night."

"Where do things stand with Vida?"

"I got her two interviews for possible jobs, one in Miami and one in Fort Lauderdale."

Lisa had leaned on the kitchen counter, her arms folded. "That's something."

"It's something." He took another drink. "How about you? You see or hear anything?"

"Do you mean did she send me the pictures?" Lisa's stare drilled into him.

"Yeah, did she send you the pictures?"

Her face reddened, and her jaw was firm. "Not yet."

Jeff nodded wearily. "In other news, my bonus was deposited. Maybe we could chip away at our debts, set up a college fund and set some aside for retirement?"

"Whatever. You earned it."

"Hey, what's that supposed to mean? I did earn it."

"Fine."

"Also, Foster wants me to go to England, Ireland and Scotland for a couple weeks next month to help our London office. You can come, too."

"Sounds like things are going gangbusters for you."

Jeff shook his head. "Tell me about your day," he said.

"It was rather crappy—had a lot on my mind—so I went for a run. When I went through that park, I thought someone was following or watching me."

Jeff sat a little straighter, careful to mask his alarm. "Did you see who it was?"

"No."

"What happened?"

"Nothing. I'm not even certain that I saw or heard anything, or whether I'm just a little on edge because of all this garbage going on with you, Vida and Loften. Did you ask the detectives about extra patrols?"

"Yes, I did. They've put in the request."

"I know you think that we'll end up destitute if the worst happened and you lost your job, but that's not rational, Jeff. I'm working. We could scale down."

"Scale down?"

"You know what I mean. It doesn't mean going to a shelter. We could ask my parents for help. We could be smart about spending."

"No one would hire me, Lisa. Word would get around, my career would be over and I'd never be able to earn the same. We owe so much as it is."

"We could declare bankruptcy, start over—"

"Just stop. I don't ever want to hear talk like that again."

They both took a moment.

"All right," she said, "but sooner or later it has to end."

"I'm working on ending it."

They looked at each other in silence, each reading the fear in the other's face, each uncertain of what they could trust or believe in anymore. After several moments, the tension eased with an unspoken truce.

"You better get ready," Lisa said. "We need to be at the Dillards' in about forty-five minutes. I got some wine we can bring."

Lisa accepted Jeff's peace-offering peck on the cheek before he went upstairs to shower.

He checked his phone on the way. Still nothing from Vida.

Before he undressed, he closed the bathroom door and called her cell phone. It rang through to her voice mail.

This was not good.

The moment he set his phone down, Lisa knocked

on the door, and he opened it. She was holding her phone.

"Detective Reddick is on the line. He wants to talk to both of us now."

44

Jeff and Lisa went to their bedroom.

She switched her phone to speaker, set it on the dresser where they stood in front of it.

"Okay, Detective," Lisa said, "we're both here."

"Good," Reddick said. "First, I want to assure you that everything's okay. This is a routine check, all right?"

Lisa glanced at Jeff.

"Sure," Jeff said. "Is this about the extra patrols?"

"No, we've taken care of that. This is something else. We're going to send you some photos."

"Okay," Jeff said.

"Hold on," Reddick said something to Cruz, then Lisa's phone pinged. "There," Reddick said. "Now, earlier, you both told us that you didn't know Clete Loften, have any dealings with him or anyone who might know him, correct?"

Lisa turned to Jeff, jerking her head to the phone, her expression insisting that this was the time to tell the investigators about Vida. He shook his head.

"That's correct," Jeff said. "We don't know Loften or anyone who might know him."

"Okay. Now, we want you to look at the photos. Did you get them?"

Lisa picked up her phone, tapped, scrolled and swiped through photos of a smiling woman in her midtwenties. She was pretty.

"Are you looking at them?" Reddick said. "Does this woman look familiar to you?"

"No," Lisa said, then turned to Jeff who was still staring at the images, taking a moment longer than needed to decide.

"How about you, Jeff?" Reddick said.

"No. I don't know her. Who is she, and why are you asking us?"

"Her name is Maylene Marie Siler. She was twenty-six years old."

"Was?" Lisa said.

"She was from Cleveland, worked as a clerk in a mall before she was reported missing about six months ago. Recently, her body was found in a wooded area near the edge of the city. She was murdered."

Lisa's hand flew to her mouth, her eyes widened.

"I have to ask you," Reddick said. "You're absolutely certain that you did not know her?"

Staring hard at the photos and thinking, Jeff shook his head, then looked at Lisa who was shaking hers. "No, we don't know her," he said. "Why would we? Just because we're from Cleveland? It's a big city."

"Can you tell us why you're asking us this?" Lisa was uneasy.

"As I said, it's fairly standard," Reddick said. "We have nothing to confirm that this is related to Loften and his crimes against you. When we get cases like Loften's, we enter details into databases, and it's common that we get queries to check against cases from other jurisdictions. My apologies if we've alarmed you."

Jeff was nodding and beginning to remove his tie. "Okay," he said. "Is that it?"

"That's it. Thanks for your help, guys."

After the call, Lisa looked at Jeff, her face creased with worry. "Routine?" she said. "Something's happening."

He took her into his arms. "Honey, I know it's upsetting."

"I'm scared, Jeff. What if that woman's murderer is connected to Loften?"

"He didn't say it was connected."

"Not in so many words but—but—Loften threatened to come back and—and—"

"Lisa," he said and held her tighter. "Lisa. He's locked up, and he's going to stay locked up. It's clear that they're just checking him against other cases and, like Reddick said, it's routine. We've got enough to deal with right now. We don't need to imagine more trouble, all right?"

Lisa pulled away, touching the corners of her eyes, finding a degree of composure. "You better hurry up," she said.

45

It was late in the afternoon when Detectives Cruz and Reddick met with FBI agent Terri Morrow at the Miami-Dade County Pre-Trial Detention Center to interview Loften.

After they passed through the security process, a correctional officer led them to an administrative section of the institution and introduced them to a sober-faced young woman. She had large glasses and was wearing a blazer and skirt. She was talking with two grim-looking men. The white-haired man was Captain Jasper Smith. The man with salt-and-pepper hair was Lieutenant Deon Johnson.

"Agent Morrow, Detectives," Smith said. "As we were telling Ms. Pond here from the Public Defender's office, we're sorry to inform you that it appears that inmate Loften has been killed."

"What?" Reddick said.

"What do you mean by *it appears* Loften's been killed?" Morrow asked.

"Inmate Loften was working in Sanitation," Johnson said. "That's a volunteer detail of inmates who collect all trash from the facility. It appears that when Loften emptied a container into the compactor, he slipped, fell in and was subsequently crushed."

Reddick winced.

"When did this happen?" Cruz asked.

Johnson consulted his phone. "This morning."

"Has his death been confirmed?" Morrow asked.

"We're in the process of recovering his body from the compactor. We're working with the company, and we're investigating the incident," Johnson said.

"How are you investigating?" Morrow asked.

"We're working with Miami-Dade police and the medical examiner, in keeping with protocol, reviewing security cameras and questioning all facilities and management personnel."

"Can I observe the review of the security cameras?" Morrow asked. "Because there was a case in Texas—"

"Agent Morrow," Captain Smith's demeanor cooled, and he removed his glasses. "Inmate Loften's death was a tragic accident. He slipped on a substance on the dock, which resulted in his fall," Smith said as he assessed Morrow, then the detectives. "I'm sure I don't need to remind you that the FBI has no jurisdiction in this immediate ongoing matter. Now, I assure you that our investigation will be thorough, and when it's concluded, we'll let you know."

"That would be appreciated," Morrow said.

Reddick gave Morrow a little smile as they left the jail.

"You got balls, Morrow," he said.

Officers and medical-examiner staff worked in protective suits, with gloves, boots, goggles and masks, as sanitation-company experts went through the meticulous process of dismantling the compactor at the dock where Loften was seen falling into the chute.

The daily load from the unit had not yet been removed, but it was nearly full. The slow, careful work by the sanitation people allowed investigators access to the stinking, crushed garbage so they could use poles to probe it for Loften's corpse.

It was a drawn-out, stomach-churning process that would take several more hours.

Inside the institution at one of the jail's main security-camera hubs, Miami-Dade detective Frank Tester led the review of surveillance footage of the dock. He worked with correctional officers at the vast console of panels and monitors in the control room. They needed to ensure that Loften's death was an accident: that he was not pushed, and that his fall wasn't the result of an altercation.

"One more time," Tester said.

They reviewed the footage showing Loften's first trip to the dock, losing the bin in the chute, hopping in to retrieve it, then hopping out. On his second visit, footage showed him dumping his bin and slipping and falling into the chute without exiting. There were over a hundred cameras to monitor the entire institution, but no one actually had witnessed Loften's fall at the time it took place.

A few minutes later, footage showed another inmate dumping his bin, then a second and third each dumped their bins. After the fourth inmate dumped his, he switched on the compactor.

"Gruesome," Tester said as his phone rang with a call from his partner, Detective Hank Acosta, who'd gone to the security people at the criminal courthouse across from the jail to review their cameras.

"What's up, Hank?" Tester said.

"Loften's not dead! Look at the video clip I sent you that we pulled from courthouse cameras facing the street."

Tester clicked on the video, willing it to load faster. When it was ready, he saw the compactor's tailgate from the street, then movement at the small gap that ran horizontally across it.

A hand appeared, then a tennis shoe, then a head, as a man in an orange jumpsuit hefted himself through the gap, dropped to the street and fled. Tester cursed.

Loften had escaped.

46

Dillard handed Jeff a cold bottle of Heineken.

They stood at the barbecue in the rear patio. The aroma of steak, chicken and foil-wrapped fish sizzling and smoking on the grill was appetizing.

"How're things at work, Jeff?" Dillard drank some beer.

"We're pretty busy with a new contract."

"Yeah, you look stressed." Dillard flipped the meat. "Anything on your mind you want to talk about?"

Got a million things on my mind, Roland, Jeff thought. *Like Vida, my job, my marriage, and how in the moments before we caught Loften, you got all weird asking me about my father's death and saying how Lisa was pretty.*

"Not really, thanks."

"All right, but I'm a good listener." Dillard continued positioning the meat. "I gotta say that was quite a beating you gave Loften the other night. I think you would've killed him."

"I would have. I lost my mind."

"You sure did."

"And he didn't really fight back, with you holding your gun on him."

"We'll just keep that between us. Remember, he came at you with a knife. He deserved what you gave him for what he did to Lisa."

Jeff said nothing. Dillard continued working the meat while glancing at Jeff. Seeing he was checking his phone, Dillard said, "Something urgent?"

"Sorry." Jeff tucked his phone in his pocket, then took a swig of beer and changed the subject. "You and Nell have a real nice house."

Dillard prodded the meat thoughtfully with tongs as the grill hissed.

"I'll show you around after we eat."

Jeff stared pensively at his beer, then said, "Can I ask you something, Roland?"

"Ask away."

"Before we came over, one of the detectives, Reddick, called to ask us if we knew anything about a woman who was murdered in Cleveland. A mall clerk named Maylene Marie Siler. They sent us pictures of her."

Dillard concentrated on the sizzling meat, listening.

"You heard anything on the grapevine as to what that's all about?" Jeff asked.

"No, I haven't."

"Why would they ask us about something like that? Because we're from Cleveland?"

"That could be. Or it could be a coincidence. What'd Reddick tell you?"

"That it was routine, a query from another jurisdiction."

"That sounds right. They're likely working with other agencies, running down Loften's history. They give you any details on this Cleveland case, anything about evidence or suspects?"

"No, nothing."

"Interesting. Something would've triggered the Cleveland query on Loften." Dillard took a slow sip of his beer. "I'll ask around, see what I can find out for you."

Lisa was in the kitchen with Nell drinking wine and helping with potatoes, vegetables and a salad.

Nell topped off their glasses with the bottle Lisa and Jeff had brought.

"I'm so sorry. Please don't feel obligated to drink this," Lisa said. "I should have thought before bringing wine."

"Why?"

"Well, your condition, your treatment."

Nell, wearing a head scarf, print shirt and slacks, waved off her concern and took a large drink. "Doctors told me that I'm so far gone, life's too short to deprive myself of a little happiness."

Lisa took quick stock of Nell as she expertly sliced and chopped vegetables with a large, serrated knife. Even though she was sick, and with her oversize glasses emphasizing her emaciated appearance, her motions and dexterity were fast and strong. It all conjured up an image of Nell assisting at an autopsy in the morgue, one which Lisa dismissed.

"All right, then." Lisa raised her glass to toast. "To life!"

Their goblets chinked when Nell raised hers. "To life!"

After another swallow, Nell looked at Lisa. "So, you knocked up yet?"

Lisa blushed. "Not yet."

"It'll happen and soon. Trust me, I've got a feeling," Nell said, her knife flashing as she cleanly divided a tomato.

By the time they sat down to dinner, it was near sunset.

Nell had dimmed the lights in the dining room, and they ate by candlelight. Small talk, beer and wine flowed.

At Nell's insistence, Jeff explained the South American project, then talked about possible travel overseas. Lisa talked about her work, then how she admired the Dillards' home and their gardens.

"I saw you outside the other day with Roland," Lisa said to Nell. "I think it's great that you're so active, you know, good that you get out to places like the Palm Creek Mall."

"The Palm Creek Mall? What do you mean?" Nell asked.

"Well, we didn't see each other, but you were there with Roland a few days ago."

Nell shook her head. "I haven't been to the Palm Creek Mall in months."

"But I—" Lisa threw a questioning look to Dillard.

"Nell's medicine sometimes causes her to forget," Dillard said.

A loud thump caused Lisa to flinch as Nell slapped her palm on the table. "I don't forget things, Rollie. *I never forget!*"

"It's all right, Nell," Dillard said. "It's not important."

A tense moment passed before Lisa, ever the diplomat, said, "I'm sorry. I think maybe I was mistaken." She tapped a fingernail to her wineglass and exchanged another glance with Dillard.

In that moment, Jeff caught something passing between Lisa and Dillard. The looks they'd exchanged betrayed an unspoken secret or some other familiarity that he found disturbing. Reaching for his beer, Jeff glanced at Nell, who was watching all of them. She had a haunting presence, the candlelight reflecting in her glasses, creating the impression her eyes were ablaze.

"I think we've all had a lot to drink." Dillard took the last bite of his dessert, apple pie.

"You know, Rollie—" Nell stared at him "—you can get married again when I'm dead and gone."

"Nell, this is not the time to talk about these things."

"It's the best time. I'm still here. There are plenty of wealthy widows in West Palm. You have my blessing."

"And I think you've had a lot of wine." Dillard picked up his plate and stood. "Jeff, how about that tour?"

* * *

Recognizing that Dillard was trying to defuse matters, Jeff and Lisa complimented their hosts on dinner and collected their plates. Jeff went with Dillard, while Lisa helped Nell clean up.

"I'm sorry if I upset you, Nell." Lisa began scraping and rinsing plates at the kitchen sink.

"You didn't upset me." Nell first patted Lisa's shoulder, then gripped it with such force it almost hurt. "You know what monsters men can be. And Rollie's no exception. I bet even Jeff has a dark side, right?"

"I'm not sure I know what you mean."

"All marriages have their secrets and complications. Would you like more wine?"

Lisa looked at her, then shrugged it off as an older woman's ramblings and searched for her glass.

"So, let's talk about Cleveland, your hometown," Nell said.

Dillard guided Jeff through the house, the living room, the great room, then the master bedroom where Nell's pills sat bunched together on her night table. They went to the other bedrooms, then the last which served as the guest room, with its queen-size bed and bamboo night tables.

Jeff did a double take at the door with the steel handle.

"What's that? Looks fortified, like a vault," he said.

"The door's heavy steel, triple locked," Dillard

said. "Nothing can get in. The room has its own footings and reinforced fourteen-gauge steel frame. It's got its own ventilation, water and A/C, built to withstand hurricanes. We don't have to face evacuation traffic. We keep it locked and stocked."

Jeff knocked on the solid steel door and nodded.

"So it's like a panic room or a safe room?" Jeff said when they'd returned to the living room.

"You should consider installing one." Dillard got more beer. "These days, our storms are getting more intense."

Lisa and Nell joined them in the living room, bringing more wine. Before sitting on the sofa, Lisa, hit by a wave of dizziness, swayed.

"Are you okay?" Jeff moved to help her sit.

Lisa rolled her head. "I just need a minute."

Nell sat next to her and touched her knee. "Can I get you anything?"

"No. Thanks, I'll be fine."

"Lisa and I were talking about Cleveland's virtues," Nell said. "I was telling her how, up until very recently, I liked to travel with Roland and help him at the conferences. I liked Cleveland." She sipped her wine and patted Lisa's knee again. "And you're both from there. Isn't it funny how, in some strange way, we're all connected?"

Nell grinned behind her glasses, drawing the skin on her face even tighter. For some reason, Jeff suddenly saw two blurred versions of her and began rubbing his forehead and blinking to sharpen his focus.

That's when his phone rang.

He answered without thinking.

"Jeff, this is Joe Reddick, Miami-Dade."

"Yes?"

"I'm calling to inform you and your wife that earlier today Clete Loften escaped from Dade county jail."

"What?"

Alarmed by Jeff's tone, Lisa asked, "What is it?"

Jeff held up his hand as Reddick continued.

"There's a major manhunt, and we're confident he'll be captured. We're putting even more patrols in your neighborhood. We don't think there's reason for you to be concerned. We believe he'll head out of state, likely Georgia."

"How did he get away?"

"Through a trash compactor."

"I can't believe this."

"I'm confident he'll be caught."

"I sure as hell hope so. Keep us posted, please."

Jeff ended the call and looked at the others. "Loften escaped from jail today."

47

Dillard switched on the living room TV and surfed channels until he found one reporting live.

A Miami station had a breaking-news banner topping the screen. Under it was footage of a helicopter, police K-9 units and officers at roadblocks stopping cars, while the news anchor's voice told the story.

"A massive search is underway across Miami for a prisoner who escaped the Miami-Dade County Pre-Trial Detention Center. Clete Younger Loften was in custody awaiting trial for a list of first-degree felonies that included armed burglary, assault and sexual assault."

Loften's photo filled a quarter of the screen.

"Officials first believed Loften had fallen into a compactor and was crushed to death while on cleaning duty. But later, a review of security cameras showed he had in fact escaped through a gap in the mechanism. Police are advising residents in the areas surrounding the jail to lock their homes and cars…"

"Oh my God." Lisa's hands were shaking as she covered her mouth.

"Reddick said they think he's heading for Georgia." Jeff rubbed his head. "I can't believe he escaped."

"I just got a text," Dillard said. He continued, reading from his phone, "'As a precaution, Miami-Dade will increase patrols of Palm Mirage Creek. We'll also make sure the neighborhood-watch team is extra vigilant.'"

"Good." Lisa let out a slow breath.

"Don't worry, they'll capture him," Dillard said.

"You don't look so well, Lisa," Nell said. "You sure I can't get you anything?"

"No, I'm just a little woozy from too much wine."

"Me, too. We should be going." Jeff stood but steadied himself on the sofa arm.

"I'll drive you," Dillard said.

"Why? We walked over. We're around the block," Jeff said.

"We'll drive you," Nell said. "You both seem a little dizzy. We don't want you falling and cracking your heads. No arguments. I'll go with you."

Jeff and Lisa climbed into the back of Dillard's SUV, with Roland at the wheel and Nell beside him. After everyone's door was closed, all the locks snapped shut. Lisa thought she saw Nell give Roland a worried look, but she couldn't be sure.

Then the neighborhood rolled by their windows in the night.

Feeling light-headed, Lisa was grateful to be

driven home. Despite their polite protests that it wasn't necessary, Nell and Roland walked with Lisa and Jeff to their front door where Jeff punched in their entry code. Roland and Nell entered with them, stopping in the foyer.

"We just want to be sure you rearm your system properly," Dillard said.

Key tones sounded as Jeff, blinking several times, rearmed their home-security system. Once completed, the Dillards said their goodbyes, with Nell hugging Lisa.

"Get some rest, dear. You'll feel better in the morning."

Lisa nodded.

"They'll likely capture Loften tonight," Dillard said.

"Thanks for the lovely dinner," Lisa said.

"Yeah, thanks," Jeff added.

Gripping the banister, they climbed up the stairs.

In the bedroom, they lost their balance a few times as they removed their clothes, crawled naked into bed, then switched off the lights.

"I overdid it on the wine," Lisa said, sighing.

"I lost count of the Heinekens I had," Jeff said. "I'm so beat."

"Oh no," Lisa said.

"What?" Jeff groaned.

"I'm pretty sure I'm ovulating. We should try, but I don't think I can."

"Lisa, I'm drunk, and I don't know if I... I'm so..."

Lisa's head was spinning. The bed became her pool mattress floating on sparkling water, taking her into sleep. Floating, floating as liquid thoughts and images swirled.

Someone in the woods watching her... Loften's face on the TV news, then his hands all over her... "I'll be watching you. I'm going to come back and fuck you"... Jeff's face laced with scratches, his hair mussed, his shirt torn after beating Loften... Vida Warren's face. Jeff's lies...

Floating and floating, time moving and moving.

...nine years old coming home from Tiffany's birthday party with her friend Stacey...in the back seat of the car... Stacey's dad driving and drinking from a can, playing the radio loud... Stacey playing with her...pushing the button... "Don't push the button, Stacey!"... But Stacey won't stop pushing the button...

Time was a river, and Lisa was floating along, watching scenes flowing by on the mist-shrouded banks.

Nell with the knife... "You know what monsters men can be...all marriages have their secrets and complications"... "Do you know this woman murdered in Cleveland?"... Nell in the morgue cutting into a corpse swiftly, surgically... Joy waving with her kids...happy, waving...no, Joy's face is a mask of worry...waving, frantically waving...a warning?

A shadow in the bedroom...a figure cloaked in the hazy darkness of the corner..."what mon-

sters men can be"... "Loften has escaped"... Now the figure moves in cloud mist toward her bed...a massive search for Loften... "I'm going to come back"... She's asleep, dreaming... He's next to her, touching her... Jeff...oh, Jeff...rubbing her shoulders and back so softly.

We should try for a baby.

His hand moves down along her body. It's so nice. Massaging her breasts tenderly, her stomach. So nice, moving lower, lower until he's caressing her with long, lovely pleasurable motions that become a sensual tingling between her legs, the stroking becoming firmer, more arousing, again and again until she moans, signaling that she's ready, please, oh please, now. She feels him, feels his warm hardness as he enters her, pushing in slowly, powerfully, as he lies upon her, crushing her breasts against his chest, then raising himself while rhythmically driving into her, pumping wonderfully into her, deep into her as if he might go through her, again and again and again and again...

It's so good, so good.

When it ends, she smiles.

Oh, Jeff, such a beautiful, heavenly dream.

48

The next morning Lisa stirred from sleep.

A moment passed before she sluggishly surfaced to consciousness, blinked awake and turned in the bed.

Jeff was gone.

Her head felt a little light and achy. She kneaded her temples, and it all came back to her: dinner at the Dillards, drinking too much, feeling dizzy.

Loften's escape.

She sat up.

The room spun a little, but she was okay. Thirsty, but all right, except that her body felt funny. Then she remembered her bizarre sex dream.

Weird.

Wait. Is it possible that maybe Jeff made love to me while I was out? No, he wouldn't. It was a dream. Wasn't it?

Shrugging it all off, she went to the bathroom, took three aspirin and showered.

Jeff sat at the kitchen table dressed for work, welded to his phone while drinking coffee.

Lisa had put on shorts and a polo shirt and pulled her hair into a ponytail.

"Did they catch Loften?" she asked from the counter where she poured coffee from the glass carafe into her cup. "Want some more?"

"I'm good, thanks. No arrest yet."

Lisa dribbled milk into her cup. "Have you heard from Vida on the job possibilities you arranged?"

Jeff's jaw muscles pulsed. He kept his attention on his phone. "Not yet."

"This whole thing scares me." She stirred. "We have to do something."

"Like what?"

"With Vida threatening you and Loften on the loose, you should tell people. Tell Leland Slaughter, and tell the detectives before something bad happens. You promised me you would."

"I did and I will, but there's still time."

"For what, Jeff? Time for what? What the hell're you waiting for? I feel like something is going to explode."

"Lisa, I can't wave my hand and tell everyone, 'Hey, there's an unstable woman spewing lies about me, who I think is connected to a fugitive criminal.' Don't you see how that would play? How that would unfold?"

"But, Jeff, I'm afraid of those people. Loften was in our home!" Her voice broke. "You know what he did, what he said!"

"I know. I know. I'm uneasy about all of this, too. But we've got security, extra patrols and assurances he's headed out of state." Jeff softened his voice. "Listen, we have absolutely zero evidence that Loften is connected to Vida in any way. And I'm working on getting her a job. It's coming together."

They paused, reading the uncertainty in each other's eyes.

He reached out and took her hand. "Look, this whole thing will pass if we just wait it out."

Her thoughts spinning, Lisa shook her head. She couldn't argue with him anymore. She peered into her coffee for a long time, deciding on how to ask him something she needed to know.

"That was some night last night," she said.

"Sure was," he smiled.

"Did we have sex last night?"

He looked at her, not comprehending the question.

"You don't know if we did or not?" he asked.

"No, I drank too much, and I was exhausted," she said.

"If we did, I was too wasted to remember," he said.

"Do you remember me telling you I was pretty sure I was ovulating?"

"Yes."

"Maybe you went on autopilot and tried to make a baby, because I had this wild dream that you made love to me."

"Oh, really?" Jeff smiled. "How was I?"

She smacked his hand.

"No, seriously, Lisa. I wouldn't do that. It's

creepy and just plain wrong. It probably was a dream brought on by all the wine."

She gazed into her cup, contending with how she felt funny, a little different down there when she woke.

"Maybe you're right," she said, not believing what she was saying.

"I should get going," he said.

Lisa went with him to the door, and they kissed.

She glanced to the street, hoping to be reassured by the sight of a patrol car. Jeff followed her gaze.

"Do me a favor," he said. "Just to be safe, I don't think you should go running today."

"I wasn't planning on it."

After Jeff left, Lisa shut the door and leaned against it, again ruminating over feeling funny when she woke. Now, on top of all her other fears, she was afraid that she couldn't trust her own memory.

49

The moment Jeff stepped into one of the elevators at Coral Cloud Tower, he sent his first message to Shelley Rozart, asking if she'd heard from Vida.

Time was winding down on Vida's deadline.

If she gives Lisa and the whole world those pictures, if she tells Leland and Foster her lies about me...

I can't let that happen. I just can't.

By the time Jeff got off the elevator, he'd sent a second message, to Reed Kassan. He went straight to his office and shut the door.

At his desk, he immediately studied every Miami news site he could think of to see if Loften had been captured. All the stories he found had reported the escape but nothing about him being caught. Using Loften's full name and keywords like *inmate*, *escape* and *capture*, Jeff set up a news alert to send him notifications.

He took a breath and scrolled through his emails, scanning his meetings and work for the day. But his troubles yanked his thoughts away, first to Lisa.

He didn't remember them having sex. What was that about?

And what about the Dillards?

Lisa seemed to like them, seemed to get along well with Roland. Maybe *too well* from what he'd seen with those little looks they'd given each other. Jeff could barely endure the evening. Thank God for alcohol.

Jeff hadn't liked Dillard telling him that he looked stressed and that they should talk about it, like they were all buddy-buddy. Dillard was an oddball, with his questions, his storm room and his sheriff-of-the-block thing. Then there was Nell, half-crazed and staring at everybody like some mystic witch. She just creeped him out.

A chime sounded with an email notification on Jeff's computer, a message flagged confidential. It was from Foster Shore.

The subject line read *You Need to See This*.

It had attachments.

Jeff's gut lurched, thinking Vida had pulled the trigger, had delivered on her threat to destroy him.

He braced himself and opened it. Reading as fast as he could, his heart rate subsided as he recognized it as preliminary material for next month's trip.

You've got to calm down, he told himself, undoing his collar button and loosening his tie. He was opening his door to get some air just as Nick Martinez happened to be approaching.

"Good timing, Jeff," he said. "I got to know if you're up for the Yankees before I commit to the tickets. Got a lot of other people who want to go, but you're first in line."

"Thanks, Nick, but I'm going to have to pass on this one."

"Not a problem. Hey, you okay?"

"Sure, why?"

"You look a little tense."

"The guy who attacked us escaped from jail."

"That's the guy? I saw it on the news. Wow."

"He's the one."

"I'm sure they'll catch him." Martinez patted his shoulder. "Hang in there. Do you have a gun?"

"No."

"Look, if you're thinking about getting one, my sister, the attorney, might be able to help you with the permit, expedite things, you know. Just let me know."

"Okay. I know nothing about guns. Still, it should be fairly easy for me to get one, right?" Jeff said. "I mean, if I wanted one?"

"That's right. Just let me know."

"I will, Nick. Appreciate that."

"Oh, before I forget. Whitney told me to remind you she has more demo figures for local and international marketing to share with you before the Globo Aedifico meeting later this morning."

"Okay, thanks, Nick."

As Jeff returned to his desk, Fred Bonner materialized at his door. "Hey there, superstar."

"Fred."

"Hey, you know that woman I was asking you about, the hot one?"

Jeff tensed. "Yeah?"

Bonner closed the door, then lowered his voice. "I finally figured out who she is."

"What do you mean?"

"I thought she looked familiar so I did a little digging."

"Why?"

"Why? Are you blind? She's a knockout. Anyway, she's Vida Warren from your Cleveland office, right?"

Jeff swallowed. "Yes, so?"

"I met her once on a business trip. Oh man. Listen, Jeffster, I'd like you to do me a solid. The next time you see her or she plans to come in, let me know, and we can make it a business lunch." Bonner slapped his back. "My treat, okay?"

"But you're married, Fred."

"Sure, sure. Don't get me wrong, it's not what you think. But we're always looking for new talent, especially when the talent looks like Vida, huh?" Bonner winked.

The man's a pig, Jeff thought after Bonner left a wake of overpowering cologne.

Jeff tried to work, but it was futile.

He tried texting Vida but got no response.

Then he called her, and as it rang repeatedly, the images of Vida's photos and the news footage of Loften's escape gnawed at him, while Lisa's words echoed in his head.

I feel like something is going to explode.

50

"A state trooper stopped a stolen Mustang northbound on I-75 south of Ocala," Reddick read from his phone. "Suspect thought to be Loften. ID confirmed as Arlo Reemus Rains out of Jacksonville. Not Loften."

Cruz was at her monitor. "Here we go," she said. "Tampa police arrested a man stealing food from a Mobil gas station and resembling M-D fugitive inmate. Subsequent arrest confirmed he was not our subject."

It was the afternoon after Loften's escape. Cruz, Reddick and Morrow were working together in Doral at Miami-Dade's Midwest District Station.

"Last night, Daytona Beach PD arrested a man suspected in a burglary of a residence." Morrow scrolled through her phone. "A white male fitting Loften's description—no, wait, there's a supplemental update. Suspect confirmed to be Cody Edward Jarmette."

They were scrutinizing scores of tips, sightings and reports coming in the wake of Loften's jailbreak, confident one would lead to his capture. But so far, everything they had was a false lead or dead end. Despite a major dragnet and high-profile coverage, nothing had emerged to put them on Loften's trail, and every hour that passed worked in his favor.

"I can't believe that Corrections let him walk out like that." Cruz leaned back in her chair, cursing under her breath.

"He's smart, and he's long gone," Reddick said. "But sooner or later, he'll mess up."

Miami-Dade was working with investigators from several jurisdictions across South Florida as the search for Loften had expanded into a statewide manhunt. But the detectives and Morrow had little background from the Miami-Dade County Pre-Trial Detention Center, nothing on any of his communication while incarcerated. His attorney, Tarrah Pond, had no record of any family.

Reddick had gone back several times to their records on Loften, noting that their inquiries with contractors Loften had worked for provided nothing. "We struck out there," he said, adding that they'd found no activity or useful information at any of the banks Loften had used to cash paychecks. "This guy's light. He was practically living off the grid."

Before meeting with Morrow at their station, Cruz and Reddick had spent a good part of the morning in Allapattah working with investigators from Miami PD's central district canvassing the Oceanwave Gardens.

"You've got mostly transients there," Reddick told Morrow. "Some with warrants, a couple of registered sex offenders. We'll continue canvassing because a few people were not present. Just sent you the list of residents still to be interviewed about Loften."

Morrow gave the list a quick scan: Bodine Hewett Carr, Naomi E. Ellerd, Jevon B. Cummings, Donna-Anne Fran Wellsley, Gertha Janice Fox, Vida Warren, Virgil Martin Grubb and Harry Carlos Herto. None of the names jumped out at her.

Morrow then reviewed the inventory list on the search warrant Cruz and Reddick had executed on Loften's unit. Again she scanned through the items, including the women's underwear, the phones and the laptop. They were still being processed. Then there were work gloves, boots, utility knives, a roll of cord and various tools.

"What about the serrated knife you recovered when Loften was caught by the neighborhood-watch people? Is that still being processed?"

"Yes, still waiting in the queue with our other material," Cruz said. "The lab's still backlogged with multiple homicides."

Morrow tapped her forefinger against her chin as she returned to an aspect of the investigation that niggled at her.

"What is it?" Reddick asked.

Morrow recapped her thoughts on how The Collector's most recent known victim was from Cleveland. Loften was a person of interest in the case.

The couple he attacked in Palm Mirage Creek had recently moved from Cleveland.

"Are we missing a possible connection?" Morrow said.

"But the Taylors assured us that they know nothing of Loften," Reddick said.

"Did we ask them if they knew of Maylene Marie Siler?" Morrow asked.

"Yes," Cruz said. "Their response was negative."

Morrow resumed tapping her chin.

"What about those pictures you found on a phone in Loften's unit, a woman and child?"

Cruz's keyboard clicked, and she cued up pictures taken at the beach, then images of a middle-aged woman walking with a young boy outside a strip mall that, judging by the names on the business signs, was in Boca Raton.

"And you suspect Loften took these photos?" Morrow asked.

"Yes," Cruz said.

"Have you determined who the woman and child are and their relation to Loften?"

"No, we have no information, but we haven't dug deep yet."

Morrow leaned toward the monitor. "Do you mind if I take a closer look?"

"Be my guest." Cruz gave up her chair.

Morrow continued standing, leaning forward and using the mouse to click through the pictures. "I think there might be something there," she said. "Is there a bigger monitor we can use?"

Cruz and Reddick exchanged a glance.

Minutes later, they were in a meeting room, using a large video screen to examine the photos of the woman and child as Cruz clicked through them on the laptop she'd connected to the meeting room's screen.

"Stop." Morrow walked up to the frozen image of the woman helping the boy into an SUV. Morrow blinked, then pointed to a grainy section. "Right there. See it?"

Cruz and Reddick focused, nodding slowly.

"Right there, that's our key to identifying the woman. It may take us right to Loften and maybe bust this open."

51

Earlier that day, shortly before six, fugitive Clete Younger Loften stood in line for breakfast at the Blessed Light Mission Center, several blocks north of the MacArthur Causeway.

Groggy, yawning and keeping to themselves, close to a hundred people waited for the doors to open. No one gave Loften a second look.

Immediately after he had escaped, he had tossed his prison scrubs, stripped down to his boxer shorts and turned his orange prison T-shirt inside out so the jail abbreviation didn't show. He'd pulled down the brim of a soiled ball cap he'd found. With his face unshaven and looking like he could use a shower, he blended in with others at the mission.

Now in the breakfast line, Loften eyed the heavyset haystack of a kid in front of him. The kid was talking softly to himself and, according to the conversation, was counting the money he'd earned from panhandling the previous days.

After he counted the coins, he counted his fistful of bills and folded them tightly together. When he stuffed them back into his pocket, some of the bills fell together to the ground. The kid didn't see them.

Loften covered them with his stained tennis shoe.

He let a minute pass before he casually crouched down to tie his shoe and collected what turned out to be three ones and a crisp twenty from a generous donor.

Inside, the walls of the shelter were covered with thank-you notes in crayon and finger paint from children, next to passages from Scripture.

The thing about shelters was that nobody asked many questions. Loften liked that. And the thing he knew about being on the run was that no one paid attention to you if you kept to yourself.

You just have to look people in the eye and act naturally.

Carrying his tray of hot food, Loften found a seat at the end of a table in a far corner where he kept his back to the wall and his eyes sharp. As he ate scrambled eggs and toast, he considered the line of prayer from St. Francis posted on the nearest wall.

It is in dying that we are born into eternal life.

Loften liked that one, and he had one of his own.

People who fuck with me will pay a price.

He took stock of the scores he needed to settle with Vida and Jeff and Lisa Taylor.

God, that Taylor woman.

Loften closed his eyes to savor his memory of her, how she felt, how she smelled.

One more time. If I could just have one more time with her.

Something throbbed inside Loften as he ached to go back again and give that woman more—something she would *never* forget.

"The Lord loves you."

Snapped from his thoughts, Loften looked at the white-haired woman wearing a cross around her neck who was standing in front of him and holding a carafe.

"More coffee, dear?"

"Sure."

"You're new to our mission."

"Yes."

"Welcome. I'm Sister Emily. We have beds and showers, if you're in need, and a thrift shop for clothes, toiletries and other things. Just help yourself. And we have a jobs board. Landscapers are always looking for help."

"Great."

"We want you to know that you're safe here, dear."

Loften nodded.

Good, because I have a lot of work to do before I leave Florida.

52

Roxanne Peallor.

Reaching her was Jeff's single occupying thought when he got home.

With his temples pounding, he walked into the house and called upstairs to Lisa, "It's me! I've got some work to do!"

"What happened with Vida?" she called back down to him.

He didn't answer—just went directly to his office and shut the door.

At his desk, he sent another message to Roxanne Peallor. Then he ran a hand across his throbbing brow. Vida's deadline had passed, and he'd heard nothing from her. Neither had Shelley or Reed.

This was not good.

Jeff couldn't reach Vida. He had no idea where she lived. She'd indicated she had in-laws in Boca Raton, but he didn't know their names or address. He couldn't track her location through her phone. Nothing he tried had worked. Before he'd left Asgaard for the day, his need to find her had grown into desperation.

Someone has to know where she is.

That's when he'd thought of Roxanne Peallor, who still worked at the Cleveland office.

If Vida had one friend back there, it was Roxanne.

So from the moment he left the Coral Cloud Tower, he'd besieged Roxanne with messages, sending them from the elevator, then just before he entered the parking garage, and checking his phone at every red light.

Nothing.

He wouldn't give up.

Roxanne, who worked in human resources, was the one person who, even after all the crap Vida had pulled, like passing out at work, lying and stealing money, had remained steadfast in her sympathy for her. If Vida had kept in touch with anyone in Cleveland, it would've been Roxanne.

His phone rang, jolting him before he answered.

"Hello, Jeff? It's Roxanne. I got your message to call."

He sighed with relief.

"Thanks for getting back to me. Hope you're doing well."

"I'm fine. You said you're trying to reach Vida Warren. Why?"

He took a breath.

"You probably know she's here in Florida?" Jeff said.

His question was followed with silence, and he

pressed the phone harder to his ear, wrestling with the fact that he didn't know how close Vida may have been to Roxanne or what she may have confided to her.

"You know, Jeff…" Roxanne's voice was shaky as if she were struggling with something she'd been holding inside for a long time. "It was so unfair the way everyone, and I mean *everyone*, treated her here. She was going through a rough time. She wasn't a criminal. She was sick. I lost my brother to his addiction, you know?"

"I know, and I'm so sorry. You're right. Vida faced a lot of hardship." He cleared his throat. "Listen, she may have told you I saw her here in Miami. She looked good. She's trying to get her life back on track. I'm trying to help her get a job, and I need to find her."

Roxanne said nothing.

"Do you know where she's staying?" he asked. "Do you have an address for her? Because two companies want to see her for interviews."

Roxanne remained silent, leaving Jeff to hope she was considering helping him while, at the same time, he feared Roxanne might know all about Vida's threats against him and may, in fact, have been helping her.

For all I know, Roxanne could've given Vida my address here. But I can't accuse her of anything. I need her.

"Roxanne, please. I'm trying to find her," he said.

"Everyone here was against her. She was treated like garbage. Jeff, are you aware of the fact that I was in charge of handling all her files and folders on her computer after she was terminated?"

Jeff froze.

"No. I thought the IT guys just deleted everything, purged it all."

"First we have to go through everything. Some files we delete, some we keep. I read through a lot of her work. While I don't know the inner workings of campaigns, from what I could tell, she had some good ideas."

"I guess so, yeah."

"I get the feeling that people never appreciated how good she was."

A bead of icy sweat trickled down Jeff's back. "I agree."

Did Vida put her concept, the one that I found discarded, into the system, in one of her folders? Is it in the Asgaard system somewhere?

"And all she's doing now," Roxanne said, "is trying to get her son back and trying to get her life back together."

"What files of hers did you keep?"

"I can't tell you that because it's confidential in the case of a termination. Why would you want to know that?"

"Sorry. I mean, it could be useful to have examples of her work. For the job opportunities. I'm trying to help her, so help me do that, please. I need to know where she is."

"I haven't heard from her in a while."

"Did she ever tell you where she was staying?"

"She wasn't happy there. She was planning to

move out. It was some motel. She said it was filled with all kinds of misfits, but it was all she could afford."

"Where?"

Roxanne took a moment.

"It's called the Oceanwave Gardens in a place called—I don't know if I'm saying it right—Allah Pattern or something."

"Allapattah?"

"Sounds right."

He found a pen and wrote it all down.

"Jeff, she's been through hell. Her sickness brought her in touch with some pretty bad... Let me just say not the best people in the world. All she wants is to get her boy back, get her life back."

"I know, I understand and I'm trying to help her."

"I pray that you do that."

"I appreciate this. Thanks for helping me, Roxanne."

Jeff ended the call, blowing out a breath. He went online, typing quickly, just as his door swung open and Lisa entered the office.

"Was that Vida on the phone?"

"One of her friends in Cleveland. I found out where Vida's living in Miami. I'm going to talk to her tonight."

Lisa could see the anger seething in Jeff as he left his desk.

"Is this a good idea?" She followed him to their

bedroom, where he changed into jeans and an old T-shirt.

He didn't answer, hurrying down the stairs with Lisa behind him.

"Jeff, I'm afraid. Don't do this."

"I'll be fine. One way or another, I will end all this tonight."

He kissed her cheek before he left.

Lisa watched him drive off, his taillights disappearing into the dusk.

Then she immediately armed their security system.

53

Lisa's pulse hammered, fear gnashing at her.

Everything was whirling out of control.

Loften had escaped, Vida had vanished and the ghost of a woman murdered in Cleveland loomed over them. Now Jeff had lost his mind, rushing into the night with a vengeance.

What was he going to do when he found Vida?

Paranoia crept toward Lisa like a wolf emerging from the darkness.

I've got to put a stop to this.

She felt her phone in her hand. Pursing her lips, forcing herself to steady her fingers, she scrolled through her contacts to the number for Detective Cruz. She hesitated.

Tears stood in her eyes as she pressed the number.

The line rang three times before it was answered.

"Cruz."

Lisa didn't speak.

"This is Detective Cruz… Is this Lisa Taylor?"

She must have caller ID, Lisa thought, her anxiety rising as she tightened her grip on her phone. "Yes."

"Hi, Lisa. How can I help you?"

Apprehension flooded her mind with Jeff's warning beating against her like a foreboding drum.

What if Jeff is able to fix things with Vida? What if alerting police now triggers the process which ultimately does destroy everything, as Jeff says?

"Is everything all right, Lisa?"

"I was wondering if you're getting closer to catching Loften."

"We've got a lot of people working on it."

"Any idea where he might be?"

"He could be anywhere, but we believe he's trying to get out of Florida."

"I see. Well, okay."

"Is that it, Lisa? Was there anything else?"

She hesitated. "No."

"Are you sure?"

A moment passed between them. "No, I'm just a little anxious. Sorry to bother you."

"No need to apologize. We'll call you with any updates. Okay?"

"Okay, thanks."

She dropped her phone in her lap and thrust her face into her hands, feeling helpless and fighting tears.

Joy. I could talk to Joy.

She seized her phone and began texting her sister in Cleveland when she remembered that Joy had told her that she was going to a movie tonight with friends from her book club.

Lisa abandoned the text.

She went to the kitchen for a glass of wine to calm her nerves. At the window she glanced outside. The evening light shimmered on the pool as she looked across the backyard to the Dillards' house. The lights were on. Someone was moving around inside.

I could talk to Roland.

Lisa texted him.

When she didn't get a response for a few minutes, Lisa called him and it rang through to his voice mail.

But they're home. I saw someone moving around inside.

With Jeff out there looking for Vida, Lisa felt a measure of urgency, enough to fuel her need to see Dillard. She collected her phone, rearmed her home-security system, locked up and left.

A few minutes later, she walked up to the Dillards' door and rang the bell. She waited. No one responded.

She rang the bell again and waited.

Nothing.

What's going on?

Lisa drew her face to the nearest window. The lights were on. She couldn't see anyone. She turned away, but before she left, she was struck by the thought that something could be wrong.

Navigating the tall shrubs in the flower bed at the front of the house, she came to another window, the one that opened to Nell's tranquil room. Carefully, Lisa inched her way to the edge of the window, peered inside and caught her breath.

Nell was in her chair, rocking back and forth, rhythmically as if she were in some kind of trance. Her face was lifted to the ceiling, her eyes closed. Her arms were wrapped around a huge black Bible as she rocked away.

On the table next to her was a handgun.

This is no time to disturb her, Lisa thought, swallowing and backing away, nearly screaming when a palm frond slapped against her face. Brushing it away, she started for home in the darkness, trying to make sense of what she'd seen, while wondering why the Dillards' security lights and alarm hadn't gone off.

Lisa hurried to her house, all of her fears pursuing her.

Loften was still out there in the night, and he'd vowed to return. Jeff was gone. She couldn't find Dillard.

She was alone.

Cruz's words about Loften echoed in her head. *He could be anywhere...*

Then Loften's threat. *I'm going to come back and...*

She spotted a figure down the street, uncertain if it was a man or woman. The person was approaching. Getting closer.

Her pulse pounded.

Relieved to arrive at her driveway, Lisa raised her phone and began submitting the entry code to unlock the front door. When she reached it, the door failed to open. She flinched when, behind her, the sound of growling and a jingling chain pierced the night.

Lisa turned as a German shepherd and its owner strained the leash between them.

"Sorry," the dog's owner said. She scolded her animal. "That's not nice, Rusty!"

Lisa then manually entered the code, and it worked.

Once she got inside, she checked the security system and set the alarm again. Then she took a breath and texted Jeff.

Did you find Vida?

A full minute passed then another without his response.

When're you coming home?

A minute passed, then two, three, five without Jeff responding. She knew that even if he were driving, he'd respond at a red light.

Answer me please! she wrote in her third text.

But he didn't respond.

54

The faltering neon sign read *O...wave...den* in the early-evening dark when Jeff pulled up to the office of the Oceanwave Gardens Motel.

Two men bent with age wearing torn floral shirts and ripped pants drank from a shared bottle in a paper bag, beside the office door. A splashing sound drew Jeff's attention to a third old man relieving himself against the wall near the ice machine in the breezeway by the door with the word *Laundry* scrawled on it in black marker.

Jeff's car chirped when he used his key fob to lock it.

The office doors and windows were open, and a radio tuned to a conspiracy-theory show spilled from it. The reception area, with its tape-patched furniture, smelled of something unpleasant and leathery. Jeff could see the unshaven night manager, his stained T-shirt stretched over his belly, seated behind the counter watching porn on a laptop while sipping from a ceramic coffee cup. Next to the man was half a bottle of Coke and half a bottle of whiskey. His chair creaked when he swiveled.

"Need a room?"

"I need your help."

The toothpick in the corner of his mouth shifted. "You a cop?"

"No. I'm looking for my cousin—her family's concerned. We understand she's a guest here. I need to check on her. Her name's Vida Warren."

"We got rules about privacy. We don't give out that kind of information."

Jeff saw that the man's eyes were glassy and he was struggling to appear sober.

"I know, but she's been going through a very dark time. She's suicidal. I need to check on her before it's too late."

The clerk's head bobbled as he burped.

"Suicidal? Those can be messy."

"Can you just take me to her room? You can go with me. It would mean so much to her family."

The clerk scratched the whiskers on his chin, then sipped from his mug. "How much would it mean to her family?"

Jeff was glad he'd stopped at an ATM on the way. He reached into the pocket of his jeans, counted five twenties and put them on the counter. The clerk's eyes went to the cash.

"If you doubled that, I might be able to find the key to her unit."

Jeff put down another hundred. As his eyebrows climbed, the clerk stood. He clamped down on his toothpick, swept up the cash, went to a keyboard, sniffed and blinked several times at a computer monitor.

"Vida Watson?" the clerk said.

"Warren."

"Warren. Got her in number twenty-nine." He belched, reached under the counter for a key with a tag that had a strip of masking tape with *#29* inked in blue. "Let's go," he said.

After chasing away the drinking party outside the office, the clerk led Jeff across the courtyard, along the islands of dirt and trash and past the bottles and cans floating in the pool. The motel's walls were pocked and stained. The doors were scarred and needed painting. Jeff could almost hear the motel groaning from neglect. For a moment, his heart went out to the old Vida he'd known in Cleveland, the Vida who was bright, funny and talented, before tragedy had put her here in this hellhole. They stopped at a door identified by the weatherworn *29*.

"This is it." The clerk knocked, then used a moment to think before he said, "Ms. Warren? You have a guest."

No response.

"It's Jeff, Vida. Please open the door. We need to talk."

Nothing.

It took the clerk a few attempts to steady his hand and insert the key.

They entered. The clerk switched on the lights. The room was unoccupied. Jeff went to the bathroom. It was empty, too.

"All right, there you go," the clerk said. "No one home, no suicide, no nothing. We checked. Let's go."

"Can I have a minute?"

"For what—" A cell phone rang, and the clerk reached into his pocket and answered. "Jocko, I told you, I'll have it for you—stop—no, you listen..."

While the clerk dealt with his caller, Jeff took further stock of the room. The bed was made, the air held a mingling of cigarettes, air freshener and perfume. Her suitcase was put away. The luggage rack was not in use, which suggested a long stay. On the closet rod he saw various shirts and slacks, as well as the blazer and skirt she'd worn when she'd come to Asgaard.

A framed picture of a freckle-faced little boy stood on the night table beside the bed. Notes were written on the pad next to it, a motel pad with stylized palm trees bookending the name Oceanwave Gardens. Jeff read Vida's handwriting: *Jeff, 5:30, Café Romero Sunrise, Bayside Marketplace.* He turned, blocking the night table with his body so the clerk couldn't see while on his call. Then, attempting to erase a thread connecting him to Vida, Jeff pocketed the pad. Next, he browsed through magazines stacked on the desk and stopped when he came to a closed laptop under them.

While driving to the motel, his strategy had been to urge Vida to follow through on the job interviews and sell him her phone, laptop and any other devices. Everything he needed to shut this whole thing down was likely on those devices. He knew she'd probably stored things online—maybe he could find them with her laptop. He was desperate. His pulse started to gallop. It was now or never.

Jeff took the laptop.

The clerk pointed at him and ended his call. "No, no, put that back!"

"I'm taking this in case she left a note for her family. This actually belongs to them."

"No, put it back."

"She may have gone off somewhere to end her life."

"And she might come back any moment." The clerk pulled the computer from under Jeff's arm where he'd tucked it. "No, you're not taking anything. If she did off herself, the laptop will be right here. I've let you in to check on her. She's not here. Now, I really don't know who you are, but I'm asking you to get out now before I call the cops. They've been here almost nonstop for the last few days."

"Why? What's happening?"

"I don't know why. Now, let's go. Out, before I call them."

Jeff walked back to his car empty-handed, got behind the wheel and started the engine. Defeated, he prepared to head home, when he changed his mind.

I can't give up. Not when I'm this close.

He drove down the street, pulled a U-turn, then found a parking spot across from the motel that gave him a direct line of sight on unit 29. Digging through his glove compartment, he got his charger and connected it to his phone.

He responded to Lisa's texts.

I'm waiting for Vida. Not sure when I'll be home.

The night ticked away, one hour bled into the next, with Jeff shifting in his seat to get comfortable while keeping vigil for Vida's return. But with all of his problems, stress and exhaustion weighing on him, his eyes grew heavy, and sometime after midnight his body surrendered to sleep. His muscles, his mind, had shut down to luxuriate in rest until dawn, when the sounds of voices and slamming car doors pulled him awake.

It took him a few moments to regain full consciousness, to recognize where he was and why. He sat up, rubbing his eyes, freezing in midyawn at what he saw.

Across the street, in the motel lot, people wearing Miami-Dade PD raid jackets were carrying clipboards, going door-to-door, waking guests and talking to them. Jeff caught his breath when he recognized one of them as Detective Cruz.

What the hell? Did Lisa call her about Vida?

Jeff shook his head, rubbed his eyes again, then started his car and drove home to get ready for work. He'd gone six blocks, constantly checking his rearview mirror, when a horn blast alerted him to the fact he was about to run a red light. He braked with a second to spare.

Heart thudding, he gripped the wheel and took a long, slow breath.

Why is Cruz at that motel?

55

The condo was tucked in a pleasant, tree-lined corner of Boca Raton known as Bonita Verde.

It was a pretty two-story attached home, with a Spanish-style clay roof, peach stucco and stone construction, fronted by a single-car garage with a neat brick driveway.

After helping with the early-morning recanvass at Oceanwave Gardens, Reddick and Cruz parked in front of the residence.

Morrow pulled up behind them.

She had excavated the address after examining the photos found in the burner phone among Clete Loften's items in his motel room. She'd noticed that in the photos showing a middle-aged woman and boy getting into an SUV, the plate was reflected, albeit backward, in the window of an insurance office. She noted the plate number. Cruz and Reddick ran it through the state database, and it came back for a 2019 Ford Edge, platinum white, registered to Lamont and Ellen Hagen of Boca Raton.

Neither Lamont nor Ellen had outstanding warrants or criminal records.

"You didn't call ahead?" Reddick said as the investigators headed up the driveway.

"Nope," Morrow said. "Don't want people to have a chance to leave."

"No Ford Edge in the driveway," Cruz said.

"Maybe it's in the garage?" Reddick said.

When they reached the door, Morrow rang the bell. No response. After waiting, they tried again. The home was silent.

"No one home." Reddick turned when a different doorbell rang. Cruz had gone to the attached condo next door, and a man in his seventies opened the door. Reddick and Morrow joined Cruz.

"Sorry to trouble you, sir," Morrow said, taking the lead. "We're looking for your neighbors, Lamont and Ellen Hagen. Would you know where they are?"

The older man's eyes skipped to each of them, his jaw clenched. "Who are you?"

Badges were produced, IDs conveyed. The man scratched his head. "Well, they left on a vacation to Canada and Alaska several days ago."

"Did they leave you a contact number?" Morrow asked.

"Hang on. Dottie!" the man called, and a woman, also in her seventies, appeared, assessing everyone as her husband explained.

"Ellen gave me a number. I'll get it," she said.

"Might be hard to reach them," the man said. "They flew to Montana or Alberta, not sure. Then they were supposed to rent an RV and drive to Alaska, so the phone might not work if they're in the mountains."

"Here it is." The woman gave Morrow a slip of paper.

"Thank you." Morrow pressed the number into her phone, then, without stepping away, held it to her ear.

"Does a little boy live with them?" Cruz asked.

"Yes. Lucas, their grandson. He's five," the woman said.

"Do you know if they traveled with him?" Cruz asked.

"Yes, they took him on their trip."

Morrow was listening and watching as her call rang several times.

"Do you know why Lucas has been living with them?" Cruz asked.

"Not really. They're fairly private," the woman said.

"Well, Lamont once told me they had some sort of tragedy with their son and his ex-wife," the man said, "and that's why they have custody of the boy."

Morrow ended the call, shaking her head.

"I couldn't reach them," Morrow said. "What sort of tragedy?"

"I don't know," the man said. "Lamont didn't get into details."

"Would you know if the Hagens are familiar with Clete Loften or Maylene Marie Siler?" Morrow said. "Do those names ring any bells?"

The man stuck out his bottom lip and shook his

head as the woman shook hers. "What's this all about?" he asked.

"Just checking a few things," Morrow said. "Have the Hagens always lived in Florida?"

"No, no, they retired here a few years ago," the man said. "They're from Boston. Lamont was in insurance, and she was a teacher."

"Boston?" Morrow repeated, thinking, turning to Cruz and Reddick in case they had questions.

"Can we get your full names and contact information?" Cruz said.

After they took down their information and passed cards to them, Morrow said, "If you hear from the Hagens, tell them we'd like to talk to them."

"We will," the man said.

The investigators were halfway down the driveway to their cars when the man followed them.

"Agent Morrow! My wife just told me to let you know that the boy, Lucas, isn't from Boston."

"Where's he from?"

"She thinks that Ellen once said he and his mother were from Cleveland."

"Cleveland?"

Morrow, Reddick and Cruz exchanged glances. "Thank you," Morrow said.

56

"Jeff?"

A hand gently gripped his shoulder.

"Jeff."

He raised his head from his arms, disoriented until realizing he'd been asleep at his desk. Nick Martinez stood over him, a file folder under one arm.

"Man, are you okay? I haven't seen you all morning."

Jeff sat up, massaging his face, blinking into focus. It was midafternoon. Every part of his body ached from being out until early that morning in his futile effort to find Vida.

"What's this?" Martinez pointed. "Looks like you hurt your hand."

Jeff looked at the fresh bandage on his right palm.

"This? Oh, I didn't get much sleep last night and was a bit drowsy while cutting up an apple this morning."

"You gotta be careful," Martinez said. "We've got a graphics meeting in ten minutes."

"Right. Thanks. Sorry, Nick. Is the meeting in the big conference room or the small one?"

"Small."

"I'll see you there. Just need a few minutes. Got to splash some water on my face."

Martinez held his gaze for a long time. "Is everything all right with you, Jeff?"

"It's just that they still haven't caught the guy who attacked us. It's freaking my wife out. Plus, this campaign is ramping up, and I've got a lot of other stuff on the go."

Martinez weighed his explanation. "All right. Well, try to take it easy. I'll see you at the meeting."

Alone in the bathroom, Jeff ran the water to get it as cold as possible, while thinking about last night and Lisa.

She'd confronted him when he'd got home just after sunrise. He was sitting at the kitchen table studying his phone, and she'd come down from having a shower.

"Please, forgive me. I'm sorry I was out so late."

"I was sick with worry, and I was afraid with Loften out there."

"I'm so sorry. I just lost it. I shouldn't have left you alone like that. I'm losing sight of my priorities, losing my mind. God, I don't know what's happening to me. I can't think straight. I was consumed with finding Vida and ending this mess."

"And did you? Wait—" Lisa seized Jeff's right hand, stared at the fresh bandage across his palm. "This is new. What happened?"

"I was slicing an apple, and the knife slipped in my hand."

Lisa stared at him.

"I was starving when I got home. I made a sandwich, too." Jeff nodded to the unwashed plate in the sink.

"So did you find her?"

"Yes and no."

"What's that mean?"

"I found where she's been living, but she wasn't there, so I waited."

"All night?"

"I fell asleep."

Lisa stared at him. "I can't believe you. With Loften on the loose, Vida threatening to ruin your life and detectives asking us about a woman murdered in Cleveland, you refuse to tell them and—"

Blinking back tears, Lisa had looked closely at Jeff's hand. The wound on his palm was bleeding through the bandage.

"Jeff, what did you do last night?"

What did I do last night?

Now, as the water hissed in the bathroom, Jeff stared at his bandaged palm.

Did I sleepwalk? Did I blank out?

He splashed cold water on his face, and as it dripped along his temples, cheeks, jawline and chin, he stared at his reflection. While the scratches from his fight with Loften had faded, Jeff's rage hadn't.

Why is my hand bleeding?

57

Landscaper Alfred Wilson had more contracts than he could handle and needed help.

"You lost everything in a fire?" Wilson asked the man at Blessed Light Mission Center who wanted the job he had just posted on the board.

"Yes, sir." The man's eyes held a measure of sadness. "Lost my dog, my wallet, everything in a fire. I'm still working on getting my new license issued to me. It was the apartment fire in Wynwood, was in the news."

"I don't have time to watch the news. You say you worked in construction near the airport?"

"Yes, sir, and before that I did landscaping work in Georgia."

Wilson rubbed his chin, assessing the man—his stubbled beard, bandages on his fingers, the hint of desperation in his face. Like most people at the mission, he looked like he'd had a hard life and needed a break. Wilson needed help so he decided, as he always did when he hired from the street, to roll the dice.

"What's your name again?"

"Henry, sir. Henry Call," Loften lied.

"All right, Henry. We'll try things for a week, see how it goes. I'll pay you twelve bucks an hour in cash to start. You can start with me today."

Wilson extended his hand. Loften shook it, then got in Wilson's pickup.

"You got any ID at all, Henry?"

Loften showed him a Miami-Dade Public Library card he'd found on the street with Call's signature. "That's all I got."

"All right, first thing we'll do is get you some new ID if you're going to work with me. There's a place I use at a strip mall. Let's go."

Loften had taken every precaution he could while staying at the mission because he believed the staff would've been alerted to his escape. He let his beard grow to cover his pocked face. He bandaged his *HELL FIRE* tattoos or kept his hands in his pockets. He'd found a pair of framed reading glasses and wore them.

Miami police made routine passes through the mission, staying a short time, talking to the managers or casually observing things. Nothing ever came of those visits. Loften knew that people never really looked at you here, especially if you looked them in the eye—and he'd altered his appearance.

He knew he had to be smart at every turn.

Wilson picked him up early every morning on the street outside the mission. He had other crews, but new hires worked with him for a week or so.

The work was hard and hot, hefting fifty-pound bags and installing mulch, stone and sod, or taking care of lawns, trees, shrubbery and perennials.

"It's going well, Henry," Wilson said to him a few days in. "Next week, I'll assign you to work with my crew chief, Delbert, for jobs south of downtown."

One morning, while Loften waited on the street for Wilson, a Miami patrol car stopped next to him, and two uniformed officers approached him.

"What are you waiting here for, sir?" one of them asked as radio transmissions spilled from the car.

"My boss is picking me up. I'm a landscaper."

"You have any ID?"

Loften gave the officer the temporary ID Wilson had helped him get, and the cop studied it, then looked at him. Loften looked at him directly.

"Okay, all this ID says is that you're an employee with a landscaper. Got anything with an address, Henry?"

The radio hissed and crackled.

"No, not yet. I lost everything in an apartment fire in Wynwood. That's why I'm living here in the mission for now."

At that moment, Sister Emily was arriving at the mission and approached the officers, recognizing one of them.

"Good morning, Officer Denley."

"Sister Emily."

"Is there a problem?"

"Is this man a resident at the mission?"

"He is. Why do you ask?"

At that moment, Wilson eased his pickup behind the patrol car and walked up to them, as well.

"May I ask what's going on?" Wilson said.

"And you are?" Officer Denley asked.

"Alfred Wilson. I'm a landscaper." Automatically, Wilson produced ID, while one of the officers glanced at the company logo on his truck. "And Henry here is one of my employees. I'm here to pick him up for work. Is something wrong?"

Denley exchanged a look with the other officer.

"Mr. Call here doesn't have any other ID."

"I know," Wilson said. "He lost everything in a fire, even his dog. He's trying to get back on his feet. Give the man a break. What did he do? Why're you questioning him?"

Denley looked at Loften.

"What kind of dog did you lose?"

"A Lab. Her name was Daisy. She was three."

Denley nodded. "I had a Lab. Sorry to hear that." He handed Loften his ID. "We had a report of a car prowling near here, and you fit the general description."

The radio crackled with a new call for the officers.

"We have to go," Denley said. "Have a good day."

The matter ended with everyone going their way, but watching unseen from a far corner of the mission was another resident, one who was struggling to understand why the officers left without taking away that guy in the glasses and beard—because he knew he was a bad man.

58

Detective Camila Cruz arrived at her desk at 7:00 a.m.

She put her coffee down, reached for the calendar clipped to her dividing wall, then took her marker and put an X through another day. It had been two weeks since Clete Younger Loften had escaped from Dade county jail.

Two weeks.

She sipped coffee and pushed back her frustration as she reviewed messages and database updates. The tips on Loften and the reported sightings were drying up. They'd pursued every possible lead in vain.

She opened file after file.

All the physical evidence they'd collected in the Loften–Taylor case—the serrated knife, all the material from Loften's vehicle and his unit at the Oceanwave Gardens in Allapattah—was still in a holding pattern for processing for his DNA, prints, trace and other matter because of the enormous backlog and because this was not a murder case.

So far, none of the residents at the motel that they'd interviewed had any connection to Loften. There were still four residents they needed to locate and interview: Gertha Janice Fox, Vida Warren, Virgil Martin Grubb and Harry Carlos Herto. They made every attempt to locate them, leaving messages, going to previous addresses. All to no avail. All were believed to be unemployed transients who had likely moved on.

"You're in early, partner." Reddick settled into his desk.

"Got to leave early to take Antonio to the dentist."

"Right." Reddick peeled the lid from his takeout cup. "What's got you shaking your head?"

"Loften. The way he escaped. Two weeks now, and he's still at large. He's one of the smarter ones."

"He's lucky." Reddick downed some coffee. "Don't worry, something will pop. Or he'll make a mistake, and we'll grab him. He has to be lucky at every turn. We just have to be lucky once. Meantime, we've got a lot of other work."

True, Cruz thought, exhaling. She and Reddick had to prepare to testify at the upcoming trial of two men charged in the armed robbery of a grocery store and needed to review the case in detail for an upcoming meeting with the Miami-Dade State Attorney's Office. She and Joe also had to follow up on the armed robbery of a jewelry kiosk at a flea market. They'd also caught the case of the armed carjacking of a bank teller.

Cruz knuckled down and got to work. Still, with

everything on her plate, she kept coming back to Loften. Later in the day, she found a free moment to replay the video of the first interview she and Reddick did with him.

She studied Loften's pocked, bandaged face, his swollen eyes and the patchwork of lacerations from the beating Jeff Taylor had given him. All the while she watched, she thought again of all the items they'd linked to him: the serrated knife, condoms, his collection of women's underwear. How Loften's icy demeanor exuded some sort of immeasurable darkness, something beyond anything she'd experienced with other suspects.

Could he be The Collector? The killer Terri Morrow and the FBI have been hunting across the country?

Cruz shook her head in anger.

And did we capture him without knowing it before he slipped through our fingers?

It was midafternoon when Reddick's phone rang. He took the call, his face serious as he listened for a few minutes before he smiled and said, "Hold on, Melvin, I gotta put you through to my partner." Reddick punched a button on his phone. "Another wild one from the tip line, Camila. No call display on where it's coming from, but you gotta hear it."

She grimaced and picked up her line. "Detective Cruz."

"It's like I was sayin', my name is Melvin, no last names, please. I am a guest at the mission, and Jesus told me to call you."

"Jesus told you to call?"

"That's right. I asked Him why, and Jesus said that the man police are looking for is at my mission. But they're not looking very hard."

"Sir, what man and what mission?"

"Also, one of my friends said that this man police want stole my money that fell from my pocket, so that's breaking the commandment *Thou shalt not steal*, right?"

"If that's what happened, yes. Melvin, what mission are we talking?"

"Now, Jesus and His Father work in mysterious ways, do they not?"

"Yes, they do. Can you tell me the address?"

"I surely can, but first, I want to report that last month I was taken aboard an alien craft. I swear to the Lord I was, and they studied me before they released me. It was unpleasant but necessary. They told me they were from Mars and could read my thoughts. That is the reason I have taken the precaution of lining my hat with foil. It deflects their mind-reading capability..."

Cruz looked at Reddick, shaking his head and laughing soundlessly. After several minutes of bizarre accounts from Melvin, she ended the call without obtaining a shred of useful information. "Melvin the Martian," Reddick said. "He's called twice before."

59

Waves of nausea roiled through Lisa.

Bile rose at the back of her throat as she knelt at the toilet and vomited into the bowl. This was the third morning in a row she'd thrown up.

Rinsing her mouth at the sink, her heart was leaping as she stared at the two home pregnancy tests she'd bought at Walgreens the night before. She'd gotten two different brands. She'd followed the directions, peeing on the absorbent test sticks, positioning them as directed.

I can't believe this is really happening.

She waited the required few minutes before the timer she'd set on her phone sounded. The first test showed two pink lines in the result window. The second test showed a blue plus sign.

Oh my God.

She was pregnant.

Lisa steadied herself, taking a moment to process the result and trying to think. She knew from her sister that home tests were not always 100 percent accurate. But she'd missed her period and knew that it was possible to get morning sickness not long after conception.

She went to her home office, logged on to her computer and began searching for a doctor from the links Michelle Judson, from the community association, had shared with her after the attack.

What if I'm not pregnant? What if my illness is an aftereffect of that time I felt queasy after dinner with Roland and Nell? I need confirmation.

Dr. Niki Tanaka had recently joined Palm Mirage Creek Total Medical and was accepting new patients. Lisa called. The clinic's rates were expensive. Fortunately, she was covered through Jeff's insurance at Asgaard. Someone had canceled, and there was an opening on Thursday, the receptionist told Lisa, and she arranged for an appointment.

She decided not to tell Jeff.

I want confirmation first.

Total Medical was in a new jade-tinted six-story professional building near Palm Mirage Creek's border with Coral Gables.

Lisa entered through the frosted-glass doors on the third floor and reported at the curved marble-topped reception counter. She was given forms to complete while she waited on one of the comfortable sofa chairs next to a potted plant.

After she'd filled out the forms and returned them, Lisa reflected on her life and how she'd dreamed of starting a family with Jeff.

Funny how things had unfolded—she never thought they'd be having a child in Florida, or that she'd be living in such a beautiful home. Never thought she'd be attacked by a monster who'd vowed to come back and attack her again. Never thought Jeff would keep secrets about a beautiful, deranged woman from his past, lie to her or have such a violent, dark streak.

I've got to stay calm, think positively.

In the last couple of weeks, things were almost normal again. Jeff had heard nothing more from Vida. Was it possible she'd backed off? And while Loften was still at large, it was looking more and more like he'd left the state. Jeff seemed to have gotten a grip on his anger and anxiety. Things between them were civil, tolerable, as they strove to regain a sense of normalcy. Jeff focused on work, talking about their upcoming trip to Europe and possibly squeezing in a few days in Paris.

She'd never been to Paris.

"Lisa Taylor?"

A nurse guided her into an examining room where she took blood, requested a urine sample and recorded vital signs. Then, after asking Lisa a number of questions and noting her answers on a chart, the nurse explained that Dr. Tanaka would examine her. She directed Lisa to get undressed and put on the hospital gown. Lisa braced for the unpleasantness of the examination.

"It's perfectly natural to be nervous," the nurse said.

Not long after the nurse left, the doctor entered the room.

She was not much older than Lisa. Her hair was

tied back in a neat ponytail. She wore frameless glasses. Lisa thought she had a lovely smile and a calming bedside manner that helped put her at ease.

Dr. Tanaka began by talking to Lisa, addressing any concerns, then moved on to obtaining her health and medication history, taking notes of her responses. She asked about her periods, any fertility issues, her sexual history, then about any discomfort, pain or other gynecological problems, before conducting an abdominal exam, then a breast exam.

"The pelvic exam is last," Dr. Tanaka said. "I'll need you to lie back, put your feet in the stirrups and spread your legs."

The doctor helped Lisa into position, putting a pillow under her head and ensuring she was comfortable before she explained the procedure. She conducted an external exam before concluding with the speculum internally. When the procedure ended, Lisa was given privacy to get dressed.

Lisa was sitting on the exam table when Dr. Tanaka returned. The doctor held a tablet, looked at it and then at Lisa. "Congratulations," she said. "You're pregnant."

Tears welled in Lisa's eyes. "Really?"

"Yes, really," Dr. Tanaka said, smiling. "We still need to wait for your blood and urine results, but all signs and indications are good."

"Thank you!" Lisa hugged Dr. Tanaka, who hugged her back, then gestured to a box of tissues.

In the parking lot, Lisa sat behind the wheel of

her car thinking about how her life had suddenly changed for the better.

I'm going to be a mother.

This was a dream she'd had all of her life. She wanted to tell her sister, her parents and her friends back in Cleveland. But she had to wait. She needed to tell Jeff first—but not by text or phone.

She had an idea.

Smiling, she eased her car out of the parking lot, nearly bursting for the moment he got home.

Jeff got home around five thirty. "Lisa! I'm home!"

Tie loosened, he went to the fridge for a beer and froze.

A pair of baby shoes were tied to the handle.

Puzzled, he touched them tenderly, then turned around to see Lisa standing behind him, smiling.

"I went to the doctor today."

"You're not—" His face was brightening.

She responded with big nods. "Hi, Dad."

"Hi, Mom!" Jeff's smile grew as he took her in his arms, lifted her and spun around in the kitchen. "I can't believe it!"

"I needed to be sure."

He kissed her, then set her down. "Oh, how're you feeling? Do you need to sit down?"

"I'm fine, silly, just fine."

"You're going to be the best mom. I love you so much!"

"I love you, too, future Best Dad!"

"When?"

Lisa looked at the calendar fixed to the side of

the fridge and began flipping through it, stopping. "My due date is here, on the twentieth."

"I'm so happy."

"Me, too."

"See? I told you. I told you."

"What?"

"That this is where we'd start the next and best chapter of our lives. I got that bonus. My star's rising at work. We're going to Europe, Loften's long gone and Vida's out of our lives. I said we'd get through everything, and we have. The worst is all behind us now."

60

Lisa found it challenging to work the next morning.

It was difficult to analyze the data on her screen when her pregnancy was occupying her mind. There were so many things to look forward to—and to watch out for.

It was overwhelming.

But in a good way. She smiled to herself while eating lunch at the kitchen table. She was feeling so euphoric she had even invited the Dillards over for dinner. As weird as they were, she felt they owed them a dinner. Now she needed groceries and to get things ready. She decided to knock off for the day, changed and got into her car.

As she drove down her street, she passed a battered landscaper's pickup truck parked half a block from her house. Lisa signaled to turn a corner without noticing the pickup's engine starting.

The truck followed her.

Clete Younger Loften was behind the wheel of the pickup. Dark glasses, dirty ball cap and a thick stubble made him unrecognizable.

He had waited patiently while watching the Taylor home, using the time to bandage his right hand and forearm to his elbow. To anyone meeting him, he appeared to have broken or sprained something.

All part of the plan.

Alfred Wilson had recently assigned him to work with Delbert, a longtime employee. The thing was, Delbert had recently lost a lot of money gambling, was always hungover and couldn't get up for work. The new guy having promised to keep it just between them, Delbert agreed to give Loften the keys to the truck and a list of jobs to do alone, even though Loften—aka Call—was still waiting on his new license. It was all to save Delbert's ass.

Now, here Loften was following Lisa Taylor, all the way to the Palm Creek Mall, where he saw her park and enter. He stopped in a far section of the lot, waiting for cars to move until a space opened up behind Taylor's car. He backed his truck into it, the rear bumpers about a yard apart.

Then he got out and dropped his tailgate; the truck's bed was a jumble of lawn mowers, trimmers, shovels, gas cans and assorted tools. He pulled out a large tarp, spread it out on the ground, grabbed some tools, got down under the truck and began working—at nothing.

Anyone who saw Loften would think he was a guy repairing his battered pickup.

From his vantage point, he would see Lisa Taylor's legs when she returned to her car. *This is how it's going to happen.*

Loften's pulse picked up as he replayed his scenario.

He'd bang on his axle, drop tools loudly on the ground and ask Taylor to help, showing her his busted wrist.

When she leaned down to hand the tools to him, he'd smash a wrench against her skull, roll her up in the tarp and heft her into the bed of the truck.

Then she'll be mine.

His heart thumped when he thought of getting another shot, of what he was going to do to her this time when he got her to the secluded spot he'd selected.

This is for what your husband did to me.

Then he'd take care of Vida—the whore who'd caused him so much grief. He knew how to take care of whores.

Then I'll be gone, gone, gone.

Rising voices startled him.

Dozens of people were flooding the lot. An alarm sounded. Then he heard the distant approach of sirens.

What the hell?

He climbed out from under the truck. People were talking about a fire at one of the restaurants in the food court, sprinklers activated, people ordered to evacuate. Loften saw Lisa Taylor approaching her car.

He ached to take her right there. But there was no way he could go through with his plan now. Not with so many witnesses and fire trucks. He pulled up the tarp, put it and the tools into the truck bed, slammed the tailgate.

Driving away, he tore the bandage off his arm.

He pounded the wheel with his fists, cursing. *I was so close, so damn close!*

A police car raced by in the opposite direction.

Loften would regroup and try again. For now, he needed to track down that whore Vida.

61

Agents from the FBI's violent-crimes squad had set up a stakeout box on their target vehicle in Fort Lauderdale—a woman driving a silver metallic 2018 Jeep Patriot.

It was parked in the driveway of a duplex not far from Las Olas Boulevard.

The woman was associated with subjects conspiring to commit an armed robbery of an armored car. New intel indicated that the woman with the Jeep was the mastermind and the plan had changed to the robbery of the armored courier's depot, where hundreds of millions in cash was stored and processed for distribution.

Agent Terri Morrow and Agent Dez Gilfoyle were in the Charlie car parked on the street some distance from the Patriot, waiting for the woman to get in and start driving to meet her coconspirators. Other unseen FBI vehicles had taken up points in the vicinity. Morrow had insisted on dropping all the windows to catch the sound of an engine turning.

"We've been sweating here for nearly three hours, proving the old adage." Gilfoyle's eyes never left the mirrors.

"What's that, Dez?"

"Police work is five percent adrenaline, ninety-five percent boredom."

"I hear you."

Morrow had used the time to review other cases on her tablet. Clete Loften had been a fugitive for weeks now, and she couldn't stop thinking about him and The Collector case. Pictures of how he'd murdered those women had haunted her sleep, along with one question: Was Loften The Collector? Or were they chasing a false lead with him?

Morrow felt her phone vibrate with a text from her daughter.

Can I go to the movies tomorrow with Kaylee and her mom? Please?

Morrow smiled.

As long as you get your report finished tonight, it should be fine.

Thanks Mom! Love you!

Addison's message blossomed with floating hearts as Morrow's phone vibrated again. This time it was a call, and she didn't recognize the number.

"Morrow, FBI," she answered.

"This is Lamont Hagen." The man was almost shouting. "I'm in Whitehorse, Yukon. We got your messages to call. Why is the FBI contacting us?"

Morrow set her phone to record the call, cranked up the volume, then powered up all the windows.

"Thank you for calling, Mr. Hagen. We're making a routine follow-up on a case and seeking your help."

"Certainly, but I don't think we'd know anything the FBI would be interested in."

"Sir, do the names Clete Younger Loften or Maylene Marie Siler mean anything to you and your wife?"

"No, never heard of them." Hagen covered the phone to talk to someone. "My wife hasn't either."

"We understand you have a little boy with you."

"Our grandson, Lucas."

"And he's from Cleveland originally?"

"Yes." Hagen's tone changed as if a light went on. "Has this got something to do with Lucas's mother?"

"And who would that be?"

"Vida Warren."

Morrow blinked. That was one of the names connected to Loften.

"Can you tell me a little bit about Vida's background? Is she from Cleveland? Would she have any relationship with the names I mentioned?"

Hagen said something to another person at his end and let out a long, exasperated breath. "Vida's our daughter-in-law—well our ex- or estranged daughter-in-law, whatever you want to call her.

Yes, she lived and worked in Cleveland. That's where she met and married our son. They had Lucas. But Vida was a drug user and unfaithful. That's not how she'll tell the story, but we know. Our son tried to save his marriage. It was futile. So he tried to start a new life and found Cynthia, a wonderful woman. But they—" his voice broke and he struggled for a moment "—but they were both killed in a boating accident while on vacation in Greece." He paused. "Vida's life—well, she associated with the wrong people, used drugs and was fired from her job in Cleveland. We got custody of Lucas. She followed us to Florida and was going to attempt to get custody of him. As for whom she may or may not know, we can't tell you. We just don't believe she has the stability in her life to be a good mother to our grandchild."

"Would you know if Vida is the type of person to use online-dating services?"

"No, I would not know. But I'll tell you, nothing that woman does would surprise me."

Something was happening in Morrow's mind; something was hammering away.

"Mr. Hagen, would you happen to know how I can reach Vida? I'd like to talk to her, as well. Do you have a number for her, or an address in Florida? Do you know who she worked for in Cleveland?"

"Hold on, just a moment."

Hagen was talking to someone. Morrow assumed it was his wife. In Morrow's experience, she'd learned that in many marriages women tended to be the record keepers. She waited, feeling like someone who knew the combination was opening a vault for her.

"Here we go. Last we heard, she was staying at the Oceanwave Gardens in Allapattah. That's in Miami."

Morrow squeezed her phone, feeling a breeze, glancing at Gilfoyle fanning himself with a tourist map.

"And when she worked in Cleveland," Hagen said, "it was in advertising or marketing. The company was called the Asgaard-T-Chace Group."

"Thank you. This has been very helpful."

Morrow ended the call, swallowed as her thoughts swirled.

Cleveland, Cleveland, Cleveland.

The Collector's last known victim was found in Cleveland.

Loften attacked the home of people from Cleveland. He resided in the same motel as a woman—potentially a vulnerable, troubled woman—from Cleveland and took stalking-type photos of her child, her in-laws.

Pieces were coming together fast—connections were clicking.

Another detail floated across her mind: Asgaard-T-Chace.

Why do I know that name?

62

Dammit, Reddick thought to himself. *This isn't funny anymore.*

Melvin again.

The guy was calling on the anonymous tip line almost every day now. It was untraceable to protect those who used it.

"I told you, Detective Reddick, I save newspapers, you know," Melvin said. "I read horoscopes so I know what the stars are warning us. Anyway, I clipped the picture of the guy police are looking for. It's him. You should arrest him because he stole money from me at the mission, you know. He doesn't know I'm calling you. He's not a very nice person. He doesn't follow the commandments."

"Melvin, you have to give us more information. We're looking for a lot of people. Who is this guy, and where are you?"

Without answering Reddick's questions, Melvin continued. "Jesus told me to also report on my meeting with the Emperor of the Moon about future events for the world."

When Melvin was pressed for information, his thoughts pinballed into the galaxy. Reddick squeezed his handset in frustration. As ticked as he was, he got to thinking about what a grizzled old flatfoot had advised him about following all tips, *no matter how crazy they sounded*, because you never knew where they could lead. But Melvin was exhausting. Reddick wanted to toss the phone.

Then he noticed that Cruz was making big waves to him after ending a call she'd received.

"Melvin, sorry to stop you, but I have to go," Reddick said. "But I need you to write everything down, all the details about this guy and the mission you saw him at, so you have it the next time you call me back, okay?"

Offended by the abrupt end of the conversation, Melvin hesitated. "Okay," he said.

"Okay, thanks, buddy. I'm counting on you."

Reddick hung up and turned to Cruz.

"I just talked to Terri Morrow," Cruz said. "The FBI's got something on Loften's pictures and a new link to Cleveland. It sounds good, Joe."

63

Early that evening, Lisa Taylor was in her kitchen cutting romaine lettuce, preparing to host the Dillards for dinner.

Lisa had been buoyant ever since learning she was pregnant. The darkness that had enveloped her life had been overtaken by light. Her sister was ecstatic when she told her the news.

"I'm over the moon, thrilled for you!"

And there were tears when she'd reached her parents in El Salvador for a static-filled video chat.

"This is the most wonderful news, sweetheart," her mother had said. "We'll definitely be home when the baby comes, and I'll come to Miami to help you."

Lisa then told most of her friends, aware that many expectant women usually waited until after the first trimester before revealing their pregnancy, but she couldn't bear not sharing her news. It was cathartic, as if she needed to disperse something positive to counter all the gut-wrenching trouble she and Jeff had been enduring.

For his part, Jeff was truly happy, genuinely content and relaxed. He was focused on her and more engaged with their life. They discussed a college fund, planned getting the nursery ready and started kicking around names. For the first time, Lisa felt that she had driven all of her doubts and fears back into the shadows.

Or was at least keeping them at bay.

Grating some Parmesan, she glanced at the guidebooks she'd ordered online for London, Dublin, Edinburgh and Paris. Their trip was only a few more weeks away.

Things really are getting better.

Lisa's happiness had prompted her to invite the Dillards for dinner and to consider reaching out later in the week to their other neighbors, like the Mortimer sisters next door. She thought seriously of joining some of the Palm Mirage Creek community associations to feel more connected.

She was living in hope now.

She spread the remaining sauce over the top layer of lasagna, sprinkled it with mozzarella and put it in the oven, setting the timer for forty-five minutes. She expected the Dillards to arrive at any moment, when her phone rang.

"Hi, Lisa, this is Dr. Tanaka. How are you doing?"

"Just great."

"Good. We got the lab results from your blood and urine tests. I went through your chart. Lisa, are you taking any prescribed medication that you forgot to tell us about?"

"I was on the pill."

"No, we've got that. Anything else?"

"I sometimes take sleeping aids that I buy off the shelf."

"Anything else?"

"No. Why?"

"Your tests show a concentration of JXQ-two-eighty-one."

"JXQ… I'm sorry, what? I don't understand."

"It's epotrienoprox. It's a strong sedative."

"No, I don't take anything like that."

"Okay, well, if you are, I want you to stop. It's a powerful sedative, not good for you during pregnancy."

"I don't take anything, and honestly I feel just fine."

A moment passed while the doctor contemplated Lisa's answers. "All right," she said. "I know the lab can, on occasion, get false positives. We'll retest you next time you're in. I just wanted you to know what we found."

"Okay, thanks, Doctor." Lisa hung up, stared at nothing and thought.

Jeff came into the kitchen and stole a cherry tomato from the vegetable platter Lisa had prepared. "Everything all right?" he asked.

"Yes, I think so," she said as the doorbell rang.

The Dillards arrived.

Nell, in light wide-leg pants with a paisley-pattern top and matching bandanna, looked strong, almost healthier. But it could've been makeup. Roland, in khakis and a navy polo shirt, let a smile grow on his rugged face as he presented Jeff with a bottle of wine.

Dinner went smoothly. The salad and lasagna turned out beautifully, and the conversation remained light.

"That was absolutely delicious, Lisa," Nell said.

Roland had indulged in a full second helping and a large slice of key lime pie for dessert. Afterward, Jeff topped everyone's wineglass, with the exception of Lisa, who was having water.

"And how are you doing, Nell?" Lisa asked.

"Good days, bad days. On bad days, I just go to my chair, rock and pray the pain away."

With a gun at your side? Lisa thought, wondering if Nell was contemplating taking her own life, before pushing the thought away.

"Roland, do you think they're any closer to catching Loften?"

Dillard peered into his wineglass, as if the answer was there. "Sooner or later they'll find him." He swallowed some wine.

"You hear anything more from your sources about any link to Loften and the woman murdered in Cleveland?" Jeff asked.

Dillard stared at him for a few seconds, then shook his head. "And how are things going for you in the high-pressure world of advertising and marketing?" he asked. "Is that South American deal working out all right?"

"Yes, it is. Work is good." Jeff nodded. "Busy, but good."

"How about everything else, Jeff?" Dillard cooled slightly as he stared at him, then he shot Lisa a quick, subtle glance before drinking from his glass.

"Everything's fine." Jeff's gaze bounced to everyone. "As a matter of fact, Lisa and I are going to Europe in a few weeks."

"Oh, that's splendid," Nell said. "I saw some travel books in the kitchen."

"London, Paris, Dublin and Edinburgh. It'll be exciting," Lisa said.

Jeff raised the wine bottle. "More wine?"

As he poured, Nell glanced at Lisa. "You're only drinking water—why's that, dear? If you don't mind me prying."

Lisa blushed, smiled and looked to Jeff who nodded. "I'm pregnant."

Nell clapped her hands and laughed. "Fantastic!"

"Congratulations." Dillard raised his glass, inviting the others to join him in a toast. "Here's to the best for Lisa, Jeff and their gift from heaven!"

Nell got up and hugged Lisa. "You see, I told you it was going to happen."

The conversation shifted to baby talk—names, schools and a variety of other child-rearing subjects. Jeff loved the sparkle in Lisa's eyes when she talked, something that had been missing for too long. What made him uneasy was the way Dillard was watching her. Something seemed off.

"Roland," Jeff said, "how are things going for you? Are you consulting or traveling much?"

"A little bit of both. Mostly I'm preparing."

"Preparing?"

"The safe room," he said. "Hurricane season's approaching, and you never know what sort of nasty forces are coming for us."

The doorbell rang. Jeff went to the front door and opened it to Detectives Cruz and Reddick and another woman.

"Hi, Jeff," Reddick said. "Sorry to interrupt your evening." Reddick nodded to the woman. "This is Agent Terri Morrow with the FBI. We're hoping you can help us answer a few questions."

64

Jeff invited the investigators into his house. They were in the foyer when they saw the Dillards and Lisa in the living room. Cruz nodded to them.

"Hi, Rollie," Reddick said. Addressing the rest of the group, he continued, "This is Terri Morrow with the FBI. Terri, this is Lisa Taylor, Roland Dillard, who is retired NYPD, and his wife, Nell, also retired from, if memory serves, the New York City ME's office?"

Nell nodded.

"Rollie is one of Palm Mirage Creek's watch captains. He helped Jeff take down Loften," Reddick added.

"Good to meet everyone," Morrow said.

"Well, look, this won't take long," Reddick said. "Sorry to disturb your evening by showing up unannounced like this. But we were sort of in the neighborhood and had a few quick questions."

"Sure," Jeff said.

"Would you like some coffee?" Lisa asked. "I've got a fresh batch."

"Coffee would be great," Reddick said.

They went into the kitchen and sat at the table, setting down notebooks and tablets. Lisa and Jeff served the investigators coffee, while the Dillards joined them.

"I assume this is about Loften?" Jeff said.

"Yes. We're following strong leads that could yield results soon."

"I hope that means you're going to put him back in jail," Lisa said.

"That's the plan," Cruz said.

"We're also working on other cases that Loften could be connected to," Morrow said.

"Are you talking about that case in Cleveland?" Jeff asked.

"That one." Morrow nodded. "And a few other matters."

"Jeff, Lisa—and Rollie and Nell, you, too," Reddick said, clicking his pen, "do you know a woman by the name of Vida Warren?"

Feeling the eyes of the two detectives and the FBI agent on him, Jeff's face whitened ever so faintly, and he swallowed. Lisa's eyes threw a silent question to Dillard, who blinked calmly while watching Jeff and the investigators.

"No, we don't know her," Dillard said.

"Never heard of her," Nell said.

Reddick nodded and looked to Jeff.

"I know Vida Warren," Jeff said. "Why do you ask?"

"Could you tell us how you know her, your relationship with her?"

"I worked with her in our Cleveland office."

"And you, Lisa, do you know her?"

"Only socially through Jeff. I met her a few times at parties." The shaky tone of her voice betrayed her anxiety.

"Jeff, Lisa, have you had any recent contact with her?" Reddick asked.

"I haven't," Lisa said.

"Vida visited me at our Miami office," Jeff said.

"When was this?"

"Oh…" Jeff looked down at his hands; his cut was fading. Reflexively he kept them flat on his upper legs under the table. "I guess it would've been over two or three weeks ago. Not sure when exactly."

"Why did she visit you?"

"She wanted me to help her get a job in our Miami office. She had a lot of trouble in her life with drugs in Cleveland. Asgaard let her go. I believe her relatives here in Florida have custody of her son. She was getting her life on track, trying to regain custody, something like that."

"And did Vida ever mention to you if she had any sort of relationship with Clete Loften?"

"No."

"Was there anything else Vida told you when you talked with her in your office?"

Lisa looked at Jeff as if silently urging him to reveal everything about Vida, how she had threatened him. Without returning Lisa's gaze, Jeff blinked a tense acknowledgment and told the investigators, "No."

Reddick took a moment, nodded and looked at the other investigators.

"Do you know anyone else in Florida Vida may have associated with?" Morrow asked.

"No," Jeff said.

"What's this about?" Lisa asked. "Does Vida have a connection to Loften?"

"We're not clear on that," Reddick said. "We've learned that she was staying at the same motel as Loften, and that recently one of Vida's relatives, or someone claiming to be a relative, was there looking for her."

"Oh my God," Lisa said. "So Vida and that creep could've had some kind of relationship?"

"It's possible," Reddick said. "Jeff, you worked with Vida Warren. You've had recent contact with her. We're trying to locate her. Would you have a number for her, one that we may not have?"

When Jeff picked up his phone, Morrow noticed the cut on his hand. So did Cruz and Reddick.

"How'd you get that, Jeff?" Morrow touched her palm.

"Slicing an apple. Damn thing keeps opening on me and won't heal," Jeff said, scrolling through his phone. He recited a phone number. "That's the one she gave me," he said. "Why're you looking for her?"

"Thanks. We can't go into details," Morrow said. "But we're concerned about her safety and her possible connection to Loften. So if you hear from her, let us know as soon as possible?"

"I will," Jeff said.

After seeing the investigators out, Jeff rubbed the back of his neck and rejoined the others in the kitchen. He leaned against the counter, folded his arms across his chest and briefly withdrew into his thoughts, then said: "I don't understand how Vida fits into this, how it's all connected."

Dillard finished his wine, set his glass on the counter, contemplated it, then said, "They know far more than they're indicating. They always know more. I suspect they were feeling you out, Jeff."

Hearing his name pulled Jeff from his thoughts. "Feeling me out? For what?"

"Likely to see if what you told them is consistent with what they know."

"What're you implying, Roland?"

Dillard shook his head casually. "Nothing. Just telling you what my ex-detective gut tells me."

"Thanks, but I didn't ask—"

"Oh dear Lord!"

Everyone turned to Nell, who was shaking as she stood, revealing bright red damp splotches staining her light-colored pants. A toppled wine-glass was at the table's edge dripping where she'd sat.

"I'm sorry, my glass slipped," Nell said.

"Goodness, don't move, Nell." Lisa took the glass. "I'll get a dishcloth." She went to the sink.

"No, don't worry. I'll throw them in the wash," Nell said. "I think this is our cue to thank you for a wonderful evening."

"Yes," Dillard said. "It was a fantastic dinner."

Jeff and Lisa saw the Dillards to the door where

the men shook hands and the women hugged. Then the Taylors watched their guests walk into the darkness.

But the night was far from over.

65

Lisa grappled with the storm twisting in her head as she cleaned up.

Foil snapped from the roll as she wrapped leftovers. The garbage disposal growled as she cleared scraps. She loaded the dishwasher, hip-slammed the door, switched it on, then went upstairs to confront Jeff before bed.

He wasn't there.

Searching the house, she called for him, but he didn't respond.

She noticed his office door was closed. She knocked, then opened it to darkness. Thinking it empty, she turned to leave.

"I'm here," he said.

"What're you doing sitting there in the dark?"

"Thinking."

Lisa turned on a light, dimmed it. She stood before him, hands on her hips, taking stock of him sitting there. "We need to talk."

"So talk," he said.

"They're looking at a Vida–Loften connection."

"Evidently."

"So why didn't you tell them the truth?"

"The truth?"

"That she's trying to extort you. That she threatened your job, threatened you with false accusations and horrible pictures?"

"I didn't think it was relevant."

Lisa's jaw dropped. "What's wrong with you? *It is relevant!* Besides, isn't it against the law to withhold information from the FBI?"

Jeff sat up, anger bubbling beneath the surface. "Look, if she hired Loften or convinced him to scare us so that she could destroy me, then that's for the detectives to discover. We don't need to make this public and part of the story. Don't you see, Lisa? Right now, Vida's gone, Loften's gone. We're out of the picture."

She began shaking her head. "You're not making sense. If you did nothing wrong, if everything is as you say, then you should be helping the police, telling them everything. And did you forget what happened to me?" She pounded her chest as tears came.

"I didn't forget."

"Then, call the detectives, call that FBI agent. Tell them everything!"

"No."

Lisa stared hard at him.

"Did you sleep with Vida? Is that why you want this kept quiet?"

"How many times do I have to tell you? No."

"I want to believe you, but how can I with the

way you're acting?" Tears rolled down her face as she shook her head slowly. "Where did you go, and what did you do that night you went out looking for her?"

"Again, I found Vida's motel. I went to talk to her. She wasn't there."

"And it took you all night?"

"I was waiting for her to return. What is it with all these questions? What about you?"

"Me?"

"I see the weird way you and Dillard look at each other. I saw it from the first time he set foot in our house. It's like you two have some little secret going on."

"What? He's a good neighbor, he's helped us and his wife is dying. Don't try to turn this on me. You're keeping something from me, something terrible."

"You're dead wrong, Lisa."

"Why were you out all night?"

"To confront her, and I fell asleep."

"And you've got that cut on your hand."

"Cutting an apple! Dammit, Lisa!" Jeff took a long breath and let it out slowly. "I'm sorry," he said, his tone softening. "We're both going a bit crazy here. I'm sorry."

He stood, tried to comfort her, tried to take her in his arms, but she refused.

"Listen," he said, "I'm upset, and I'm not thinking clearly. But you've got to believe me. We've got to hang in there. We'll get through this, I promise."

She looked at him, searching his face as if assessing a stranger.

That night, Jeff slept in the guest room, while Lisa cried alone in their bed, aching for her real husband, the Jeff she knew, to return.

66

The next morning Reddick was at his desk paging through his notes on Loften and working on his still-warm take-out coffee.

Set against the most recent Collector killing, Loften's link to the woman and her kid from Cleveland and the woman's link to the Taylors were interesting elements of the investigation, but the detectives were not yet sure where each one fit.

Cruz was on the phone with Miami PD's central district, which last night had made another fruitless attempt to locate Vida Warren at Oceanwave Gardens. The fact her phone went unanswered and emitted no signal was a concern. Reddick wanted to go to the motel this morning, get into her room if possible.

Maybe he'd find something to point them to Loften?

His line rang. He answered and immediately regretted it.

Melvin again. "Hello, Detective Reddick."

"Hey, Melvin, I don't have much time. I have to go."

"I did what you asked me."

"What's that?"

"I talked to Jesus, and he guided me."

"Guided you to do what?" *Go to Mars?* Reddick felt sorry for the kid and checked the time.

"I wrote everything down like you said. I looked at all the newspaper stories about the man you're looking for. Then I looked real close at the man who stole my money. His name is Clete Loften."

"Sure. Everyone knows that from the stories, Melvin."

"He's got a tattoo on his fingers that he tries to cover with bandages, but I saw it, and it spells a bad place." Melvin dropped his voice. "*Hell*, then *fire*."

Reddick sat straight up.

"Melvin, you say you're at the mission—which mission?"

"I wrote it down like you said. The Blessed Light Mission Center."

Now Reddick was writing things down. "Is it the one just north of the Causeway?"

"Yup."

"Are you there now?"

"Yup."

"Is this man there, too?"

"Yup. We're getting ready to have breakfast. He's always there for breakfast."

"Okay, Melvin. I want you to write my cell number down, and I want you to go to the center's office and stay with a manager there. Tell them to call me and meet me at the office. I'm on my way."

"Will you be able to get back my money he stole?"

"We'll work on it. Don't tell anybody anything. Just do what I asked, okay?"

"Yup."

"Here's my number. Take it down, and read it back to me."

67

Go slow. Take it easy. Take your time.

Buster Etter, an apolitical, beer-loving, die-hard Dolphins fan, adhered to the wisdom he'd gained from twenty-five years as a heavy-equipment operator, specifically a motor grader.

The engine of his Cat hummed, and he checked his grip on the controls. Other guys on the site considered Etter odd, called him the Morning Maestro because he always started around dawn and listened to classical music in his air-conditioned cab. He shrugged it off because his priority was the work, and the music in the morning helped.

Imagining what the finished job would look like, he lowered the toe of his blade, then eased his machine forward for the first pass to build a new residential street. He eyed a stake down along the ditch line to keep it straight.

Etter loved his job, considered himself a craftsman and was giving it his all on his current contract: Phase Three of Stonewater Meadows. The new subdivision and golf course had been approved for a rezoned, undeveloped swath of land near Miami International Airport, or MIA as many people called it.

Etter had already worked on Phase One in the distance where the newly built homes were completed. Families had moved into some of them. He liked being part of creating new neighborhoods and often envisioned the lives that would evolve in them.

Now he had to focus because there were a lot of variables, and he never wanted to work the earth more than what the job called for. All the while, he had to be mindful of slopes, moisture in the soil and how it reacted to the blade.

The specifications of the job called for him to skim to a depth of twelve inches, and he'd anticipated what his blade would do before he dropped it. Figuring on six or seven passes, he'd watch for high spots, or areas that needed cutting, and areas that needed filling. He'd work passes in both directions to avoid deadheading and watch for side drift.

It was going well, and the sun had climbed by the time he made his fifth pass. He was being careful to see how the soil rolled. He liked to have it well compacted because it made trimming easier. If there was one thing he disliked, it was carrying large clumps of material for long stretches.

Like now.

Etter cursed. It had been too good to be true. He had some serious clumping going on.

Studying the pile growing before the blade, he suddenly stopped. *What is that?* He'd caught something. Cursing again, he shifted to Neutral, letting the big engine idle, engaged his brake and opened the door of his cab to inspect what he'd unearthed.

In his years on the job, Etter had dug up just about everything. You name it. Dogs, cats, deer, cows, old stoves, washers, fridges, cars, even a steel safe.

As he climbed down, wispy clouds of dust pushed by hot, humid wind swirled around his machine. Jetliners roared overhead. The rattle-grind, clanking, thudding and staccato thwopping of nail guns sounded in the distance, where work on new homes was going full throttle. The echo of it underscored that Etter was alone where he stood.

He turned to the clumped earth expecting to find a dog, a deer, maybe a cow, when he blinked as if his eyes were wrong.

What the hell did I churn up?

The first thing Etter saw was a partially buried shoe, a woman's low-heeled casual shoe, and for a moment he thought he'd just dug up clothes until he saw that a foot was wearing the shoe. Then, half-submerged in the dirt, he saw something brightly colored, like a shirt, then an arm. Earth shifted, and the thing turned, just rolled, the way someone asleep would roll in bed.

That's when he saw a woman's face and hair, veiled in dirt like she was breaking the surface of a shallow grave.

"Dear God!"

Etter reached for his cell phone but didn't have

a good hold, and it fell on the woman's foot. Part shock, part reflex, he apologized, then picked it up, forced his fingers to stop shaking and called 9-1-1.

68

The aroma of bacon, sausages and coffee filled the dining room of the Blessed Light Mission Center.

Loften sat alone, back to the wall, stabbing at his food as he scanned the hall, trusting nothing. Other than that close call on the street with those two cops—*Man, I was so lucky there*—he never faced trouble here, except for that big kid, the one who was always talking to Jesus or aliens. The kid was always staring at Loften and making him wonder if he knew that he had stolen his fallen cash that day.

Nah, the kid was too stupid.

At that moment, Melvin was in the outer office talking with a supervisor and detectives Reddick and Cruz.

They'd confirmed that Henry Call, the man suspected to be the fugitive Clete Loften, had been residing at the mission, then pinpointed his location in the dining room. The detectives had called for support from Miami PD, who'd dispatched plainclothes officers in unmarked units to seal all exits. The SWAT team was rolling to the center, but breakfast was coming to an end. The guests would soon disperse.

Action had to be taken now.

Cruz, Reddick and two other officers in plain clothes entered the dining room, moving casually among the guests toward the corner where Loften sat.

As he chewed, Loften thought of that money-dropping kid and how he saw him every morning at breakfast. Sometimes the kid stood right next to him, always looking him over and talking to himself. Funny, Loften didn't see him this morning.

Where is he? Gone with the aliens?

And where was that nun, Sister Emily, who always came around with the coffee?

Something was different today.

Loften stopped chewing.

He saw a couple of people walking his way through the dining room. His eyes narrowed. Their faces didn't bear the downcast, weather-beaten look of most of the sad cases here. And the way they held themselves as they walked…

Those guys didn't belong here—those guys were cops.

They had come for him.

After cancer took her husband, Willow Dureegar had faced huge medical bills, forcing her to sell her home. Alone with two children, she needed a job and was surviving at the mission. Finishing breakfast, Willow was telling her boys things would get better for them, when she felt her hair being torn from her head, as she was lifted by an arm crushing her neck.

The steel point of a knife was pressed hard to her throat.

"Mom!" Lonny, her nine-year-old son, screamed.

Willow pulled at the arm around her throat.

Reddick and Cruz drew their weapons, pointing them at Loften.

"Drop the knife, Clete! Everybody on the floor!" Reddick called. "It's over, Clete! Drop the knife. Let the woman go."

The other officers inched closer, guns drawn. Reddick holstered his weapon and approached Loften, showing him his palms. "You're not getting out of here," he said. "Drop it and let her go."

Sweat beaded on Loften's brow as he searched in vain for a way to escape. When he relaxed his arm to reposition it on the woman's throat, she bit him and stomped his foot. Loften yowled, and she broke away with Reddick flying at Loften, slamming him facedown to the floor. The knife went flying. Loften groaned and cursed as a metallic click rendered him handcuffed.

69

Yellow plastic police tape bowed in the wind as it stretched around the motor grader and the swath of desolate earth that had given up a body at Stonewater Meadows.

A knot of Miami-Dade emergency vehicles, lights flashing and wigwagging, was parked approximately seventy-five yards away.

Stepping from an unmarked sedan, lead detective Jack Bogan slid a stick of Juicy Fruit gum into his mouth. He offered a piece to his partner, Dev Zelinski who, as usual, declined, thinking it somewhat disrespectful to the deceased. Bogan believed it sharpened his powers of observation and kept the rejected stick for himself.

They tugged on blue latex gloves, collected their tablets and notebooks, and then, so as not to disturb evidence, they followed the route used by the officers at the airport district station who had first responded to the 9-1-1 call made by the grader operator.

"They did a nice job protecting the scene." Zelinski surveyed how the tape seemed to stretch forever. "The more they rope off the better."

"I seriously doubt we'll get much evidence out here." Bogan chewed. "Looks like a straight-out body dump in the middle of nowhere with a whole lot of nothing. No security cameras, no wits, no tire or shoe impressions likely, seeing how the entire area's been graded."

"Stay positive, Jack. We live in hope."

"And we die without it, Dev."

They joined other investigators and crime-scene techs huddled at the grader near the blade where a yellow tarpaulin covered the body. Most everyone knew each other, and after perfunctory greetings, Bogan and Zelinski steeled themselves.

"Show time," Bogan said, gnawing away.

Two other glove-wearing detectives removed the sheet, revealing the corpse of a white woman in her midthirties, partially embedded in dark soil, as if she were frozen in her bid to rise from it. Studying the body without touching it, Bogan's gum chewing slowed as he digested everything, while Zelinski made notes and sketches.

"She's a pretty one." Bogan drew closer to where the dirt yielded the first of her wounds. "She's been stabbed," he said. "Repeatedly." He continued looking with an expert's eye and compassion. "Who are you? Who did this to you?"

Zelinski made more notes and sketches. Then he started a video, even though the techs would make a meticulous visual record of every iota of the scene. Zelinski was thorough because, with a homicide investigation, you could never take enough notes and pictures.

All the investigators then set out to do the work that needed to be done.

They noted the position of the body and its condition. It was not badly decomposed, indicating death was recent. The woman was clothed, but to even suggest she had been sexually assaulted or not was, at this stage, a fool's guess, and something the autopsy would confirm. Cord bindings on the wrists led Bogan and Zelinski to speculate that the woman had been bound but the bindings were broken by the grader's blade.

In the hours that passed, they collected a statement from Buster Etter, then arranged for a grid search, using metal detectors. K-9 was brought in to determine if there was a scent to track to one of the properties nearby. The Federal Aviation Administration was contacted for the okay to use a drone so close to the airport to make an aerial video record of the scene.

When the time came to move the body, they carefully lifted it from its position, placing it on a clean blanket where Bogan began searching it. The soil under and around where the body had been would be sifted and searched for additional evidence afterward. For now, with Zelinski watching over his shoulder, Bogan began by sliding his gloved fingers inside a back pocket of the woman's slacks. He felt a thin, hard rectangle, then withdrew a phone. With a hint of a smile, he held it up for Zelinski to see.

The phone was photographed, bagged and documented for chain of custody to preserve its value as evidence. In the second back pocket, Bogan found a key affixed to a plastic tab with worn lettering reading *Oceanwave Gardens, Allapattah*. Again, procedure was followed to protect it as evidence.

In the front pocket, Bogan found a folded sheet of yellow paper. He unfolded it to read an invoice for a guest stay at the Oceanwave Gardens.

The guest's name read *Vida Warren*.

"Oceanwave Gardens," Bogan said, contemplating it for a moment.

Then he passed it to the tech to be preserved with the other items.

"The ME's team can take her now," Bogan said. "That's it."

Zelinski updated his notes. "These items are a gold mine for us," he said.

Bogan didn't answer.

He was staring at the horizon, looking at nothing, while in the back of his mind, *Oceanwave Gardens* pinged over and over. Like a pebble tossed into a calm pool, recognition rippled as he thought.

"Dev," Bogan said and, after peeling off his gloves, fished in his pocket for a fresh stick of Juicy Fruit. "I can't put my finger on it, but I'm sure this case is connected to another one."

70

Terri Morrow was pushing her grocery cart through a checkout line at Publix, when her phone vibrated with a message.

Three words from Joe Reddick: *Loften in custody.*

Morrow made a mental fist pump, welcoming the stars smiling from the magazine covers to rejoice with her.

We got him. We got him. We got him.

Morrow made calls. The first was to her neighbor, Stephanie Gleason, who agreed to pick up and watch Addison after school. She rushed home, put the groceries away, showered and got dressed.

As she trotted to her car to drive to the office, a concern about the case arose.

But where is Vida Warren?

As if on cue, Morrow's answer came when her phone rang. It was Scott Wood.

"Gotta call you in," he said. "Developments on one of your cases."

"Is this about Loften, sir? Miami-Dade alerted me to his arrest."

"That, and the fact we have a fresh homicide."

"Homicide?"

"The ME's working on confirming identification, but I just heard from a colleague at Miami-Dade, and it appears that a body unearthed this morning near MIA is that of Vida Warren, a woman you were seeking to interview in relation to Loften."

Morrow took a moment, absorbing the news, then said, "I see."

"Loften's a person of interest," Scott said. "He fits the pattern of your task-force unsub, and in light of these factors, Miami-Dade's creating a small joint-agency team on the new homicide. They're convening a case meeting in two hours in Doral. We need you there. I'm sending you an agenda and details now."

"Yes, sir."

As Morrow got behind the wheel, Camila Cruz texted her about Vida Warren, Loften and the meeting. Morrow responded before starting her car.

Thanks. ASAC told me. On my way.

She headed to Doral, driving with a surge of adrenaline, thinking a thousand thoughts, when really it all came down to one question.

Is Loften The Collector?

Investigators had filled the meeting room at Miami-Dade's Midwest District Station when Morrow arrived. A lot of new faces.

Tablets, laptops, notebooks, phones and coffee cups dotted the table. Someone was adjusting the teleconference octopus, while another person tested a laptop hookup to the large monitor covering one wall.

Morrow found a seat waiting for her beside Cruz and Reddick. They gave her a quick briefing before things got started. Then Morrow read a new text from Scott Wood and was pleased to learn that her FBI counterparts from The Collector task force in other cities would be on the line.

The meeting began with Lieutenant Len Tucker introducing detectives from Miami-Dade, the Miami PD, and several other jurisdictions at the table and on the line. He outlined the Warren–Loften cases before Jack Bogan and Cruz used slides of photos to present the status of the homicide investigation and its links to Loften.

"Right off," Cruz said, "we're working with the ME and human resources at Warren's former employer in Cleveland, using health-insurance claims to get her dentist to confirm identification. I'll note that we did show her photo from the scene to her in-laws, who are traveling in northern Canada. They made a visual confirmation."

"This will be boiled down to what we know, what we're doing and what we need to do," Bogan said, continuing the brief. "Because the homicide now encompasses Loften, processing of evidence from both cases has been accelerated, and we expect to be receiving ongoing new information from forensics, the lab and other sources. We're also seeking a number of warrants, including one to gain access to Warren's cell phone and laptop. Some of this stuff will take time. We don't have a murder weapon. Indications are that a knife was used. We have K-9 and drones, and we're gridding the scene with metal detectors."

On the line, Eva Sawyer, FBI ASAC in Cleveland, had sent attendees a digital file summarizing the entire Collector case: the attacks in Pittsburgh, Detroit, Buffalo, Chicago, Indianapolis, Louisville and, most recently, Cleveland.

"We're pulling together all the information we have so far," Bogan said. "But let's look at the facts of all cases and brainstorm."

Loften and Warren were both residents of Oceanwave Gardens in Allapattah. What was unclear was why Loften had taken photos of Warren's son in Boca Raton.

"We don't know if he was stalking her, planning to help her with a parental abduction or something else entirely," Cruz said.

Investigators had confirmed that Warren had been an employee in Cleveland with Asgaard-T-Chace until her termination and that she'd stolen money from coworkers to support an addiction to illicit drugs.

"We haven't determined if Warren knew Loften while she lived in Cleveland, nor can we place Loften in Cleveland at the time of the most recent homicide there linked to The Collector, that of Maylene Marie Siler. Work is underway with all Cleveland and other Ohio law enforcement to determine if Loften was in the area," Sawyer said. "We can confirm that the cord used for binding in the Warren homicide is consistent with the cord found in Loften's Oceanwave motel unit and the cord used in The Collector homicides."

Sawyer continued, stating that The Collector used a serrated knife in nearly all of his attacks, noting that Loften was in possession of a serrated knife during crimes in Palm Mirage Creek, specifically in his recent assault of Lisa Taylor. Loften also had condoms in his possession while committing crimes in Florida. The Collector used condoms when he sexually assaulted his victims. Loften was found to have stolen women's underwear. The Collector took driver's licenses from his victims. Not quite the same items, but the similar element of trophy collection was troubling.

"Loften's looking good for The Collector," one Miami detective said. "What about latents, DNA, trace? Where are we with all of that?"

"Not as far as we'd like to be," Sawyer said, launching into a summary concerning The Collector case and the survivor in Louisville, Kentucky, who'd clawed at her attacker, tearing one of his latex gloves.

"From Louisville, we got a section of cord, identical to the cord used in previous attacks," she said, adding that a partial shoe impression was also recovered and the size was consistent with impressions recovered in earlier cases. "As some of you know, we also got a partial thumbprint."

Sawyer noted that the quality of the partial fingerprint had thus far proved challenging for examiners. To date they had not succeeded in finding anything similar on record.

"As for Loften," Reddick said, "much of the material is still being processed. We've got evidence linking Loften to Warren but nothing conclusive."

"What about Loften's attack at the home of Warren's former coworker, Taylor, in Palm Mirage Creek? Where does that fit with all of this?" another detective asked.

"We're still working on that," Morrow said. "There's every indication there's some sort of Cleveland connection. Our understanding is Warren asked Jeff Taylor to help her find a job in Miami, even though the company had terminated her earlier. She was trying to regain custody of her son, get her life together."

"Do we know who this relative who came looking for her at the motel is?" a detective asked.

"We'll be putting a lot of these questions to Loften. We're preparing to interview him," Morrow said.

At that moment, Bogan's phone vibrated. He read the message, then leaned to one of the detectives operating the laptop and slide presentations and typed on his phone.

"We just heard from the medical examiner," he announced to the room. "We have a positive identification through dental records. The victim is Vida Warren."

Investigators nodded, some made notes.

"There's more," Bogan nodded to the detective

on the laptop, and a new image filled the screen: notepaper from a message pad bearing the stylized name *Oceanwave Gardens* in small green lettering between two palm trees on the top. It was creased from having been folded, but the handwritten words scratched in black felt-tip pen were clear. *I want to stop. Why can't I stop?*

"The ME found this tucked in Vida Warren's left shoe," Bogan said.

A few seconds passed, then Sawyer could be heard on the line, speaking briefly to someone, and the large screen split with a second image beside it of a different folded sheet of paper with the words scrawled on it using a black felt-tip pen. *I want to stop. Why can't I stop?*

"This was found on the body of Maylene Marie Siler in Cleveland. Until now, she was The Collector's most recent victim," Sawyer said.

Soft cursing mixed with awe floated around the table.

Morrow glanced at Cruz and Reddick, feeling her gut clench.

Loften is The Collector. And we've got him.

71

That same morning while Loften was being arrested, Lisa Taylor sat at her desk in her home office and stared at her monitor.

She was working on the survey about emerging diseases, but as time ticked away, she found it increasingly difficult to work. Jeff's refusal to tell police the full story about Vida frustrated her to the point of distraction.

Her phone rang with a call from Detective Cruz.

"Hi, Lisa. Thought you'd want to know that Clete Loften was arrested this morning at a Miami homeless shelter. He faces a list of new charges. He'll be in prison for a long, long time."

Lisa covered her mouth with her hand. "Really?"

"Really."

"Thank you! This is so—thank you, Camila!"

Feeling as if a mountain had been lifted from her shoulders, Lisa blinked with relief. Still holding her phone, she called Jeff.

"Jeff, did you hear the news? They got Loften!"

"Yes, Reddick just called me. He said Cruz was calling you."

"It's so great!"

"See? I told you. If we just hang in there, we'll get through this."

Maybe Jeff's right, Lisa thought after hanging up.

Floating on a cloud of happiness and wanting to share her good news, Lisa texted her sister. He's been captured!

Waiting for Joy's response, Lisa left her office and went to her bedroom window overlooking the Dillards' house. She didn't see any indication that they were home when her phone vibrated. Joy had texted back.

That's fantastic news! Go out and do something to celebrate.

Good idea. I know just what I'll do.

Lisa got dressed, then began driving to a mall she'd discovered online that was in South Miami. It had great reviews for nursery furniture and maternity clothes.

Stopped at a light, she was overwhelmed by the throbbing music of the car behind her. The windows were tinted. The deafening bass vibrated against her, evolving into the pounding of unanswered questions.

What about Vida? Where is she? Are police still

*looking for her now that they've arrested Loften?
Has she decided to stop threatening Jeff?*

Did he sleep with her?

Will I ever know the truth?

The questions hammered in time with the music until a horn behind her blared. The light had changed. Lisa's thoughts shifted, and she continued driving.

The mall had a variety of stores with a great selection. Lisa checked out changing tables, dressers, cribs and other baby gear like high chairs, strollers and car seats. She browsed in specialty shops looking at maternity and nursing bras and other maternity clothes: leggings, jeans, dresses and tops. She grew wistful.

Her dream of being a mother was coming true.

Yes, maybe Jeff's right, she thought as she left the last shop. *Maybe we will get through this.* She was thinking that they should go out for dinner that evening. They could resume discussing how to put his big bonus to use. A nursery and setting up a college fund would be nice.

Lisa made her way out of the mall, thinking she should be looking at some new clothes for their upcoming trip to Europe, when she passed an appliance store with the TVs tuned to a local news station. A breaking-news banner stretched across the top of the screens. A reporter was standing at yellow tape in an empty dirt wasteland with several police vehicles behind him. His tie was lifting in the wind as he spoke into his microphone. Lisa could not hear what he was reporting as he pointed to a spot in the distance. The camera tightened on a large piece of heavy equipment and investigators clustered around a yellow sheet.

The information banner at the bottom of the screen said *Body Unearthed near Miami Airport.*

Lisa slowed but didn't stop, thinking it looked like another murder in greater Miami. *Tragic,* she thought.

She didn't dwell on the breaking story while driving home because she was pondering how she'd place the baby furniture. As she neared her block, she saw the Dillards getting out of their SUV in the driveway of their beautiful bungalow.

Lisa tapped her horn, waved, parked on the street and walked to them.

Nell was carrying a small canvas shopping bag. Roland gripped a heavy piece of equipment by the handle. Lisa guessed it was a small generator. His eyes gave her a quick once-over.

"Hi. Sorry to interrupt you," Lisa said.

"You're not," Nell said. "We just picked up a few supplies."

"Storm season's coming fast," Dillard said. "Got to be ready."

"I wanted to share the news. Loften was arrested!" Lisa said.

"That's great. Where?" Dillard said. "Do you know details?"

"No, no details. Somewhere in Miami."

"That's terrific." Nell gave Lisa a hug. "You and Jeff must be relieved."

"I can't tell you how much."

"Good to have that animal behind bars again," Nell said. "Did you want to come inside? I can make some celebratory coffee?"

"No, thanks. I just wanted to share the news. I'll take a rain check."

"Next time, then."

Lisa returned to her car, smiling and waving to Nell and Roland as she drove off.

Everything's going to be all right.

72

Jeff arrived home from work later that day with his tie in his hand, his brow moist and his face laden with concern.

Shedding his briefcase in the foyer, he walked to the kitchen, glanced up from his phone, pecked Lisa's cheek, then returned to his device.

"I was thinking we could go out for dinner. Celebrate they caught Loften."

"Sure, yeah," Jeff said to his phone. "Wherever you'd like. Let me check something first, something I picked up on the radio in the car."

Jeff disappeared, then Lisa heard the TV and followed him to the living room, where he was searching channels.

"Was it something on Loften?" Lisa asked.

Jeff didn't respond. He was skipping through channels, stopping at one showing images of the scene where the body was found near the airport. The anchor at the news desk was speaking, and Jeff increased the volume.

"...return to a developing story. Investigators

have confirmed to our Brianna Billings that the body unearthed near Miami International Airport is that of a white female, and the case is now being investigated as a homicide. We go to Brianna, who is at the scene..."

"Tom, police sources have confirmed that the woman has been identified as thirty-three-year-old Vida Warren—"

"Oh my God!" Lisa lowered herself onto the sofa. "Oh my God!"

A head and shoulders photo of Vida was inset at the corner of the screen.

"...Warren's body was found by a grader operator at Stonewater Meadows, a new subdivision and golf course under construction near the airport. Sources say Warren was originally from Cleveland and had relocated to South Florida to be closer to her son, who was staying with family in Boca Raton."

"We understand a disturbing new angle has surfaced in this case, Brianna," the anchor's voice said.

"That's right. A stunning twist regarding Clete Younger Loften, the fugitive felon who escaped from Miami-Dade County Pre-Trial Detention Center while awaiting trial on burglary and assault charges..."

Loften's menacing arrest photo was inset next to Warren's image.

"...as we reported earlier, Loften was recently captured at a Miami mission, but sources have told us that Loften resided in the same motel as

Warren, the Oceanwave Gardens in Allapattah, and is considered a person of interest in her murder. We've also learned that the FBI is looking at Loften's possible connection to the unsolved murders of several other women across the country."

"What can you tell us about those cases?"

"Florida investigators and the FBI are reluctant to reveal details at this time, saying the release of additional information could damage their ongoing investigation, Tom."

"All right, thank you, Brianna. We'll be following this developing story closely. Now to Washington, where a Florida congressman..."

Jeff muted the TV.

Lisa stared in disbelief at the screen.

"Jeff, they're saying that Loften, the man who broke into our house and tried to kill me, the man you fought with, murdered Vida and possibly other women... I just can't believe it... Jeff?"

He was transfixed in front of the screen. The barely audible sound of the remote rubbing against his leg was all she heard. It was making that sound because Jeff's hand was shaking. All the color had drained from his face, and his eyes had widened— all he could see was the crime scene and Vida's grave.

73

It was a nonfolding knife, with a partially serrated blade of high-carbon steel measuring four and three-quarters inches.

A gnarled-texture black rubber grip made its total length nine inches.

Miguel Perez, a latent fingerprint examiner, wearing a white lab coat, blue latex gloves and plastic safety glasses, took measurements, photographs and notes.

He was working into the night in room 1126, the Crime Scene Investigations Identification Section in the Miami-Dade headquarters complex in Doral.

The knife was one of the first key pieces of evidence in the sexual assault/burglary cases he had gotten to. The Palm Mirage Creek material had been previously mired in a backlog at the section due to a mass shooting at a warehouse, an unrelated triple homicide from an arson, and three separate double homicides in Miami-Dade.

Now everything concerning Palm Mirage Creek had changed.

And in a big way, Perez had thought after he'd come out of the conference call with forensic personnel earlier that afternoon. Investigators now believed the Palm Mirage cases were linked to several unsolved homicides, which not only made it a priority but meant it had mushroomed, with multiple scenes in multiple jurisdictions.

This is a big one, Perez thought.

In Florida, there was the homicide near the airport, Loften's arrest at the mission, Loften's and Vida Warren's residences in Allapattah, not to mention several vehicles. Add to that the FBI had a mountain of material to compare from homicides and attacks in more than half a dozen states.

During the call, senior people had determined that for this huge case, material would be distributed for analysis and collaboration involving forensic experts with Miami-Dade, the Florida Department of Law Enforcement and the FBI's crime lab in Quantico.

Perez, one of the most meticulous examiners in his section, was tasked with collecting latent prints from the evidence in the burglary/homicide cases to be submitted to local, state and national databases for comparison.

To find a killer.

That was his job. Making the invisible known.

Working at his bench, Perez used the utmost care and attention. He applied cyanoacrylate, also known as superglue, to the knife. It was excellent for developing latent prints because it made the prints more durable. Allowing sufficient time for the glue to dry, he then reached for a plastic squeeze bottle. It contained a pinkish liquid, Rhodamine 6G. Perez used it as a tracing agent because it adhered to superglue.

After treating the knife and superglue with Rhodamine, Perez placed it in the fuming hood to dry. When the knife had dried, he removed it and took it to room 1125 for more processing by placing it on a small examination table and switching off the room's lights. He turned on a laser light, which bathed the knife in glowing green, rendering latent impressions visible.

Perez studied the blade and handle for friction-ridge detail.

He found prints.

"Oh no," he said aloud to himself.

It was just as he'd feared and something common at crime scenes. Yes, the tech's notes had indicated several people had handled the knife—Perez knew that—but the multiple prints were overlapping. He needed to separate the prints so they could not only be run through databases but could also be compared with the partial latent print the FBI had taken from an attack attributed to the unknown serial killer.

The one they called The Collector.

Perez took in a breath and let it out.

Separating the prints would not be easy.

74

The next morning, the steel door of the cinder-block interview room opened with the clinking of metal as two correctional officers deposited Loften into a plastic chair at a large table.

Loften wore an orange jumpsuit with a belly chain attached to leg-irons around his ankles and handcuffs around his wrists. Since his capture, he'd been isolated from the rest of the population at Miami-Dade County Pre-Trial Detention Center and held in a special maximum-security section.

Before leaving, the officers affixed a chain from his wrists to the steel handcuff loop on the table so Loften could rest his arms.

Detectives Cruz, Reddick and Bogan and FBI agent Morrow sat across from Loften, studying his pocked face. Several other investigators were watching from behind the one-way-mirrored glass of one wall.

"Welcome home, Clete. We missed you," Reddick said, then tilted his head, studying him with mock concern. "It's nice that every time we meet, you get yourself all prettied up for us."

Loften's expression tensed, aggravating the scratches webbing his face from his arrest at the mission.

"Let's get started," Cruz said and introduced the investigators. "There are a lot of us here because we have questions on a number of cases and jurisdictions."

Cruz propped up her tablet, unfolded the keyboard and typed.

"Mr. Loften," she said, "I want to remind you that you're still under the Miranda warning that was given to you upon your arrest and our conversation is being recorded. Please acknowledge that you understand and agree to this interview, which you can stop at any time."

Loften held each investigator in his gaze for a moment. "I do," he said.

"Good." Cruz turned her tablet showing a photo of Vida Warren to Loften.

"Describe your relationship with this woman."

Loften looked at the image but said nothing.

Cruz then displayed the photos Loften had taken of Vida's son, Lucas, walking with his grandmother, Ellen Hagen, at the strip mall in Boca Raton.

"Why did you take these pictures of Vida Warren's son and mother-in-law?"

Loften looked at the photos without responding.

"All right, Mr. Loften." Cruz tapped away, coming to evidence photos of bundles of neatly wrapped cord. "This cord was found in your motel room in Allapattah. It's blue, black and orange nylon five-fifty paracord. Guess where else we found nylon five-fifty paracord?" Cruz tapped to another photo showing severed black cord on dirtied wrists. "On the wrists of Vida Warren's corpse."

Loften looked at the photos without expression.

"Now," Morrow said as she sat forward and turned her laptop to Loften, showing him crime-scene photos and summarizing all The Collector cases, specifically the cords used on the victims in Pittsburgh, Detroit, Buffalo, Chicago, Indianapolis and Cleveland. "Nylon five-fifty paracord, the same type of cord found in your possession, sir, was used in the murders of all these women."

Loften said nothing.

"As well, we can place you at or near the locations of some of these cases during the time frame of the crimes." Morrow showed Loften photos of traffic tickets. "You were cited in Indianapolis and Kentucky."

"And guess what, Clete?" Reddick folded his arms across his chest. "One was missed, but not long ago, our friends with the Akron PD found you in their system. You were cited for speeding in your twenty-sixteen Dodge Ram fifteen hundred during the time frame Maylene Marie Siler, a clerk at one of Cleveland's malls, vanished after meeting up with a man on an online-dating site. Now, you visited online-dating sites, and Akron is like—what?—about half an hour, forty minutes from the Siler crime scene. Again, paracord was used with Siler."

Loften remained silent.

"Now," Bogan said, placing a stick of Juicy Fruit into his mouth, "this is where it gets real interesting, Clete." Chewing, he nodded to Cruz, who then cued up a new image that only showed the top of the sheet of stylized message paper from Ocean-wave Gardens found in Vida Warren's shoe—not the words of the note. "This was found with Vida Warren. She resided at Oceanwave a few doors down from you. I bet you know what we found on it."

No reaction from Loften.

"Because we like to be thorough," Bogan said, "and because we know you'd like to cooperate, we'd like you to provide us a sample of your hand-writing once we're done here."

"Mr. Loften," Morrow said, "we have so many more elements of concern. For example, you broke into the home and attacked the wife of Vida War-ren's former coworker in Palm Mirage Creek. We'd be interested in knowing why you chose to target Jeff and Lisa Taylor. You had condoms, cord and a serrated-blade knife when you were arrested at the bait house. Other elements are consistent with your compulsion to collect women's underwear and identifications in Florida, as was done in the cases in other states. Your mobility is aligning with the time frame and puts you at or near the locations of most other crimes. There's your use of online-dating sites."

The investigators let a long, tense moment pass.

Then Bogan's chair scraped as he stood, walked around the table and drew his face within inches of Loften's, invading his space.

"Clete, the noose around you is tightening." Bogan chomped on his gum. "As sure as the sun will rise tomorrow, you are on the road to Starke and your execution. But, if you help us clear the other cases, admit to your sickness, appeal for help and cooperate, well, maybe the system could somehow find a way to administer justice in a non–death penalty state like Illinois, Michigan or New York where, if you're lucky, you can die in your sleep."

Loften stared at the cinder-block walls that felt as if they were closing in. His Adam's apple rose and fell as he digested his predicament. His chains jingled as his cuffs knocked against the table.

"I want a lawyer. Then I'll tell you everything."

75

Jeff's sleep was thin and interrupted with night-mares.

He got up early, showered, dressed for work and kissed Lisa's cheek while she was still sleeping.

He didn't drive to his office.

He needed to think.

Traffic wasn't bad, and the sun had risen as he drove along the Causeway to Key Biscayne and entered one of the parks shortly after it had opened for the day. After parking, he walked to the beach, breathing in the sea air, listening to the gulls, watching them glide on the ocean breezes. As the waves caressed the sand, he stood there numb, fighting to keep it all together. He cut a lonely figure, a portrait of a solitary, well-dressed man looking out at the Atlantic and the horizon as if at a funeral or preparing to spread ashes.

Vida's dead.

Murdered.

Loften's arrested.

A sense of finality rolled over him, for ever

since Loften had attacked Lisa and Vida had surfaced to torment him, he'd been a coiled spring,
winding tighter and tighter. Now, for the first time
in a long time, the muscles in his gut loosened as
his body and soul found peace.

And with it came the realization that it was over
with Vida.

Like a sudden and swift amputation.

Still reeling, he couldn't believe it.

Then, for a moment, his heart wrenched for
Vida's little boy. Jeff knew what it was like to
lose a parent early in life, how your world went
dark and the earth stopped spinning. Your insides
just cleaved open, broke apart. Being fatherless
left you with an aching black hole. It shaped you,
weighing on everything you did for the rest of
your life.

In the midst of his whirlwind of emotions, a
faint alarm was clanging in a distant recess of his
mind.

*The pictures of Vida naked with me. I forgot
about her phone and her laptop. How could I forget?*

His phone vibrated, and he looked at it. A news
alert on Loften's arrest, a repeat of what he already knew.

Staring at his phone pulled him back to the night
when he went to Vida's motel. She wasn't there,
but he'd bribed the clerk to get into her room. He
was out of his mind with anger. He was going to
confront her, put a stop to all her bullshit.

But she wasn't there. So he'd waited.

But for how long?

Thoughts sparked in his head.

What happened? Did I fall asleep? Did I have an episode, black out and wake up? I don't remember. I was so angry that night.

Then he looked at the cut on the palm of his hand.

I got that slicing an apple in the kitchen.

Didn't I?

Fear shot up his spine and made the small hairs on his neck stand up.

He remembered driving home from Vida's motel and a vague memory of blood webbing down his arm. No, that was wrong. He was confused with slicing his palm in the kitchen later.

The knife was slippery with juice and had slipped.

That's what happened.

He dragged one hand over his face as the gulls screamed.

76

Later that morning at Coral Cloud Tower, Jeff stepped out of the elevator into the reception area of Asgaard-T-Chace, where several staff members were gathered in solemn discussion.

It broke off when Vanessa, the receptionist, spotted him, cuing the others to turn.

"Did you hear the news, Jeff?" Vanessa asked.

"What news?"

"A woman who worked for Asgaard in Cleveland was murdered here in Miami. Vida Warren. They found her body by the airport."

Jeff, his face sober, nodded. "I know."

"You came from our Cleveland office," one of the women said. "You must've known her?"

"She called here for you," Vanessa added. "Some people say that she actually, recently, came to this office."

"I knew Vida," he said. "Yes, she came here to visit me. She had moved here. She has a little boy and family in Boca Raton. I think she was trying to regain custody of her son."

"Oh no," said one woman, her eyes glistening. "Who would kill her? That's just so, so sad."

"Yes, uh, well, she had difficulties in her life and knew some sketchy people," Jeff said, blinking, and looked away. "Still, it's awful, just awful."

"Jeff?" Gwen from Shore's office emerged from the hall. "Excuse me for interrupting, but Foster would like to see you in his office as soon as possible."

When Jeff arrived, Shore was at his desk on his phone and waved to him to be seated. "That's right," Shore said into his phone. "We'll look after that here. All right. You can call me. Okay, thanks." Hanging up, Shore, his face grave, turned to Jeff.

"Just the most terrible thing." He looked at Jeff. "I can only assume you've heard about our former employee from Cleveland, Vida Warren?"

"Yes."

"Did you know her well from your time there?"

"I knew her."

"Terrible, just dreadful. I've been on the phone with our people in Cleveland. We understand she was dismissed some time ago for reasons related to her drug use. But to end up the way she did..." Shore's eyes went to the framed family photos on his desk. "I've got a daughter about her age. Dammit."

"It's very sad."

"To be murdered, dear Lord. Well, our HR people say she has family here. In-laws, I believe. They're flying back from a vacation in Canada, and there will be a service in Boca. I think we should send a delegation from our office. Leland and I should go, and I'd like you to join us, Jeff."

"Of course."

"Maybe we can set up a corporate contribution or some kind of online fund to help her little boy?"

"That would be thoughtful."

Shore's focus sharpened on Jeff. "Are you okay? Do you need some time or anything?"

"Thank you. I think I'll be fine."

"You and your wife have been through a lot since you moved here."

"Yes, but we're doing okay."

"I'm happy to hear that, and I'm pleased things are moving well on the South American project," he said. "Now, forgive me for talking business at a time like this, but the European trip is coming fast. Do you think you can still handle it, with all that's going on? I can call London, pull you off?"

"No, no, sir. I can handle it. In fact, it may be a good thing for us at this time, if you know what I mean."

"I do. All right, then. If there's anything you need, let me know."

"I will. And thank you, sir."

At his desk, Jeff undid his collar button and loosened his tie. He logged in to his computer to find new emails from Shelley and Reed respectively.

Our condolences, Jeff. I just got word about Vida Warren, whom we wanted to interview. Our hearts go out to her family, you and all the people at Asgaard.

Jeff, we're so sorry, so terribly sorry. Sending prayers.

At that moment, someone knocked at Jeff's open door.

It was Fred Bonner, who extended his hand and shook Jeff's, his cologne wafting into Jeff's breathing space.

"Jeff, I am at a loss. I am so, so sorry about Vida Warren."

"Thank you."

Bonner blinked, then turned to the empty chair facing Jeff's desk.

"It's weird. I mean she was here, sitting right here talking to you and, now, murdered. And dumped in some field at the airport. I just don't know what to say."

"It's horrible."

"What did you two talk about, anyway?"

Jeff searched Bonner's eyes, finding nothing but the bearing of a person unaware that they were being rude. "It was personal, Fred."

Bonner, a little disappointed, hesitated then said, "Sure." Then he patted Jeff's shoulder. "I'm really sorry. If you want to go out for a beer later or anything, let me know, huh?"

"Thanks."

After Bonner left, Jeff shut his office door behind him.

He had close to an hour before his first meeting, enough time to prepare. But instead of reviewing files, he went online for the latest news on Vida's murder. He found an update on the *Miami Herald* site, reporting that Loften was considered a person of interest. The report went on to say that Loften was also being questioned in the unsolved murders of several other women across the country, in what one source called *The Collector homicides* because the killer kept personal belongings of his victims.

Jeff stared at Loften's menacing, pocked face.

Remembering how he'd battled for his life with Loften, how he'd assaulted Lisa, rage began bubbling under Jeff's skin with sudden, startling fury, forcing him to grip the edge of his desk.

If they've got Loften in the crosshairs, is it finally over?

His phone pinged with an email message from Detective Cruz.

We'd like to follow up with you on Vida Warren at your earliest. Call me to arrange a time.

77

"Jay Thomas Ellsworth."

He had to be midfifties. With his wrinkled suit and short, graying hair curling in every direction, he exuded rumpled chaos. But behind his glasses were eyes as sharp as dagger points.

"My firm does pro bono work, and as I indicated to Detective Cruz on the phone, I've replaced Tarrah Pond of the Public Defender's office as Mr. Loften's attorney."

Three days had passed since Loften had requested a lawyer as investigators questioned him.

Now, Cruz, Reddick, Bogan and Morrow were again sitting across from Loften, who was in chains, staring at his pocked grimace in the same cinder-block room of the Miami-Dade County Pre-Trial Detention Center.

Several long moments ticked by with only the deadened sounds of prison life beyond the steel door and the crackle of pages as Ellsworth reviewed his extensive notes on his yellow legal pad.

"Clete left us hanging, Jay," Reddick said.

"When we last left off, he promised to tell us everything."

"Certainly. Thanks for your patience." Ellsworth uncapped a pen. "I've conferred with my client and worked with my firm's research team. We've provided the handwriting samples you requested. My client denies any role in anyone's death, and we're now prepared to help you get your investigation pointed in the correct direction."

"Oh, it's pointed in the correct direction." Bogan snapped his Juicy Fruit. "Isn't it, Clete?"

Loften remained silent, and Ellsworth cleared his throat.

"My client is prepared to cooperate, provided the State Attorney gives his cooperation consideration."

"Noted," Cruz said.

"Thank you." Ellsworth pulled a sheet of paper from his briefcase. "My client admits to the felonies in Palm Mirage Creek, the burglaries and assaults, and the escape from this very facility."

"That's a no-brainer, Jay," Reddick said. "Let's get to the good part."

"My client also admits to an association with Vida Warren, initiated by her through an online-dating site."

"Excuse me," Morrow said. "Would it be possible for us to hear your client explain that relationship in his own words while we question him?"

Ellsworth blinked behind his glasses, tapped his pen on his pad.

"It would demonstrate his cooperation," Morrow added.

Ellsworth digested Morrow's point, then nodded to Loften. His chains jingled slightly as he repositioned himself in his plastic chair.

"Yeah, well, we met online," Loften said. "Vida said she was coming to Florida to fix her life. She was lonely, hurting. She moved into the same motel as me, and we hooked up. She was trying to get clean, but I saw she was in pain and needed drugs. I got her drugs in exchange for sex."

"Wow, you're every girl's dream, aren't you, Clete?" Bogan said.

"Did you have unprotected sex with her?" Cruz was taking notes.

"You don't have to answer," Ellsworth said.

"The answer is no," Loften said.

"When's the last time you saw Vida?" Bogan asked.

"Before I was arrested in Palm Mirage Creek. I saw her at the motel."

Bogan leaned closer to him. "You're lying. You saw her after you escaped. You tracked her down and killed her because you got off on it, just like you did with the others."

Loften was silent.

"Mr. Loften." Morrow had her notebook open. "Why did you target the home of Jeff Taylor, Ms. Warren's former coworker, and attack his wife? This is something you admit to."

"You can refuse to answer that," Ellsworth said.

"I'll answer. I did it for Vida. I mean, we had a

relationship. She knew my line of work was breaking into houses, doing what I do. So she asked me to break in to the Taylors' home, to throw a scare into them."

"For what purpose?" Morrow asked.

Loften shook his head. "She wanted to get a job with her old company so she could get her kid back. She thought she could lean on this guy she knew from Cleveland. I guess she had a little thing with him in the past. Who knows? The woman was wired different. She said she'd pay me down the road. I said paying me with sex was good enough. I cased the Taylor place in Palm Creek. They didn't have a home-security system. And when I saw how hot the guy's wife was, well…"

"That was the reason?" Morrow said.

Loften said, "Yup."

"Why take pictures of Vida Warren's son in Boca Raton?" Morrow asked.

"For Vida. I said if things didn't work out jobwise and custodywise, I would help her with a parental abduction, and we could disappear in Canada somewhere."

"You're just the best boyfriend ever," Bogan sneered.

"Vida was crazy, but she was hot, and I had a thing for her, you know."

"Right, just look how choked up you are over her death," Reddick said.

Loften's chains jingled as he shrugged. "That's life."

"Can you explain something?" Morrow said.

"Why do you collect women's underwear and carry condoms when you break in to their homes?"

"Taking things for keepsakes is my weakness, my addiction, my hobby, whatever you want to call it. I go online. I shop and have sex with the pretty women I meet."

"You mean, you hunt for vulnerable women," Bogan said. "You stalk them, break in to their homes and rape them."

"And you kill them," Reddick said. "Just like you did in all those other cases. You murdered Connie Ware in Pittsburgh, Tammi-Sue Bellow in Detroit, Debra Lee Plager in Buffalo, Nina Kaye Wilken in Chicago, Jasmine Maria Santos in Indianapolis and Maylene Marie Siler in Cleveland. Where did you put their IDs?"

"This attempt to incriminate my client does not warrant an answer," Ellsworth said.

"I'll answer this bullshit," Loften said. "I never took them, because I didn't kill them."

"You're a sick monster," Reddick said. "Stop giving us this crap and admit what you are, Clete."

Loften's jawline pulsed.

"Mr. Loften. We've got substantial evidence. We can put you at or near many of these crimes," Morrow said. "The cord used in the murders is identical to the cord found in your motel room."

"That cord can be purchased anywhere," Ellsworth said. "My client's supply, which was seized, was never cut, never used."

"So?" Bogan said. "He could've purchased more

for killing Vida. And we've got the note. The note that was made on your motel's stationery."

A long moment passed in silence as the muscles in Loften's lower cheek spasmed.

"Clete, you're facing execution—now's the time to unburden your soul. Tell us how you killed Vida and all those other women," Bogan said, "because we've got an army of forensic people working on the evidence, and it's going to seal your fate at Starke and in hell, where you're going to burn for eternity."

78

"Bill, could you turn the TV down?" Rachel Burke called to her husband from the motel bathroom where she was fixing her hair.

Bill Burke muted CNN's report on the forecast for the Atlantic hurricane season. Experts were predicting more storms than the previous year.

Sitting at the room's small desk, Bill glanced at Rachel in the bathroom mirror—still gorgeous after all these years. He sipped some of the horrid coffee he'd made with the in-room machine.

Then he returned to his big laptop and visited news sites because, as a retired newspaper editor who'd worked at the *New York Post* and the *Daily News*, he liked to be informed. Much to his long-suffering wife's annoyance, even as they vacationed in Florida, Bill had to get his news fix, often verbally rewriting stories—"They buried the lede"—as he read them.

It was books, needlepoint and puzzle games for Rachel, who was sharper than Bill. She was always right about exits, distances and landmarks during their second-honeymoon drive from Corona Park in Queens to Florida. They'd meandered through South Florida, Miami and the Keys and were now on their way home. They'd stopped for a couple nights in Miami Beach and were staying at the Sleepy Palms Motel, where Rachel was getting ready before they went out to eat.

Bill used the time to check the news on the *Miami Herald*'s site, reading the latest about a homicide and an escaped convict.

"I think there's a Denny's on Collins Avenue," Rachel said as she left the bathroom and put on earrings. "We can walk to Walgreens after. I need a few—" Rachel stopped in her tracks. Her attention jerked to the headline and photo of Vida Warren on her husband's screen. "I don't believe it! Bill?"

"What? Denny's, then Walgreens. I heard you."

"That's her! Remember when we saw that couple fighting in Miami at the café in the market?"

Bill scrutinized the photo. "Yeah, sure looks like her."

"We were sitting beside them. They were having a fight. The guy grabbed her, knocked off her hat and sunglasses."

"And he grabbed her again when she left. They made a scene, all right."

"That's her, Bill! Oh no, she's been murdered?" Rachel joined him, leaning closer to the screen, both of them eating up the story.

"Says they're looking at this convict who escaped and was captured," Bill said.

"Call the police, Bill." Rachel went to her bag, sifting through a travel book jammed with receipts. She was a stickler for documenting all their spending.

"Tell them what we saw?"

"Yes, tell them what we saw. We have to report it. Here." Rachel held out a receipt. "See? It was the Café Romero Sunrise, Bayside Marketplace. We've got the time and date, here."

"Right," Bill said as he looked at it. "Okay. I'll call. They can check security cameras. Might help their case."

"My God." Rachel put her hand to her mouth as Bill got the number for the Miami-Dade police and reached for the phone.

Approximately ten miles west of the Burkes' motel in Miami Beach, Lex Prewitt, manager of the Oceanwave Gardens, was riding an alcohol-fueled buzz while dealing with what the Miami detective was asking.

"Listen," Prewitt said, "I lost count of how many cops have been in here these days asking me the same questions over and over. I mean, it's—" he raised his mug to drink "—it's insane, really."

"Isn't it early for that?" Detective Holbrent nodded to the booze-laced coffee.

"Working here, I need it. With all that's going on. Been like a damn police convention."

"This is important, Mr. Prewitt. So let's be clear, now you say you in fact remember a man aggressively asking about Vida Warren, and you took him into her residence, unit twenty-nine?"

"That is correct." Prewitt nodded with certainty. "Guy said he was a relative."

Holbrent held out his phone with Loften's photo.

"No," Prewitt said. "Not him. This guy was clean-cut, like he didn't belong here. Never saw him before."

"Did he give his name? Did you see his vehicle?"

Prewitt shook his head.

"Can you give more of a description?"

"White, about six feet, medium build, good-looking guy."

Holbrent took notes, then said, "Do you remember when this was?"

"I was watching my favorite adult-movie stars—nothing illegal about that. Then…then after—oh yeah, I remember, *True Grit*, the original, was on a regular channel, and I switched to that because I love that movie."

"We can check listings to narrow that down," Holbrent said. "Did he touch anything in Vida Warren's unit?"

"He touched a lot of stuff. Even tried to take her computer, but I stopped him. You guys have everything now, with your warrants and all."

"Yes, we do." Holbrent continued making notes. "This is very helpful, Mr. Prewitt."

"Isn't there a reward or something?"

"I'm not sure about that. You'll have to excuse me." Holbrent seemed a bit excited as he left the office and reached for his phone.

79

Dissatisfaction fingered its way into the air during the next case-status meeting at Miami-Dade's Midwest District Station.

Everything had pointed directly to Clete Younger Loften, but now an unspoken sense of unease grew among the investigators as they listened to the updates of forensic analysis.

Bogan and Cruz led the meeting, starting with the autopsy report. It found that Vida Warren died from multiple stab wounds, "at least fifty thrusts inflicted with a serrated blade four to five inches in length." There were scratches on the deceased's legs; however, no injuries to the genital organs were found. That did not rule out forceful penetration. However, no semen was found after swabbing, indicating that if there had been forceful penetration, a condom had been used.

No murder weapon had been located. Of course, the serrated knife recovered at Loften's first arrest in Palm Mirage Creek was not the murder weapon, but it was consistent with the type of blade used in Vida Warren's murder. But the Mirage Creek knife was still being processed. Multiple latent prints found on the blade were overlapped, and separating them for comparison and verification with other evidence in The Collector cases was a complicated procedure. More work was ongoing.

So far, no usable latent prints had been recovered from the motel-pad note found with the deceased. Samples of Loften's handwriting, along with the original motel-pad note, had been sent to the Questioned Documents Section at the Florida Department of Law Enforcement's lab in Pensacola. Loften's handwriting and clear copies of the note were also sent to the FBI's Questioned Documents Unit in Quantico, Virginia.

Analysis concluded that the handwriting in the new note matched that in notes found with previous victims of The Collector, but that Clete Loften did not write the notes.

A soft but audible groan went around the table.

As for hair, fiber and trace, Bogan and Cruz said that analysis had determined that some of Warren's hair was found in Loften's unit and some of his was found in hers. There was no evidence in either unit to indicate a struggle or attack.

"So far, it's loosely consistent with Loften's account and his claim of a consensual sexual relationship," Bogan said. "However, one outstanding avenue: late yesterday, we obtained the warrants for us to open up Warren's cell phone and laptop. Our digital-forensics unit started working on it this morning and expects to have something for us soon."

That might sound hopeful, Morrow thought, but her gut told her something was slipping away. As Bogan and Cruz continued the meeting with the status of tips—most were not valid—and recanvassing, Morrow forced herself to accept a cold, hard fact. So far, the evidence did not strengthen their case against Loften. If anything, it weakened it.

They had little on Loften that was substantial for a prosecutor.

And it hit her like a gut punch, a painful reminder never to get tunnel vision and become blind to other possibilities. At the same time, Morrow was angry at the outrage against Warren, dumped in a lonely stretch of dirt. She thought of those stomach-churning autopsy photos; then she thought of the tragedy visited upon Warren's little boy, who'd already lost his father, and her heart broke for the child.

Morrow tried to concentrate on her work. Flipping through her notes, she came to a section she'd underlined. Something Loften had said about how Warren had come from Cleveland, wanting a job in the Miami office of Asgaard so she could regain custody of her son. How she'd thought *she could lean on this guy she knew from Cleveland. I guess she had a little thing with him in the past.*

Well, that could be Jeff Taylor who'd recently moved from Cleveland.

They'd talked to Taylor—he'd admitted knowing Warren and having had contact with her in Miami.

Maylene Marie Siler's homicide was in Cleveland.

Again, Cleveland, Cleveland, Cleveland.

Have we been looking in the wrong direction with Loften?

"Really? Let's put it up," Bogan said, pulling Morrow from her thoughts.

"This just came in. Miami PD followed up a tip about a woman thought to be Vida Warren arguing with a man at a café at Bayside, at Romero Sunrise. The owners volunteered security footage—here it is."

The footage rolled on the room's large screen, showing two people at a table, when suddenly the man grabbed the woman, jerking her wrist so her sunglasses and hat fell off.

"That's her." Cruz's eyes darted from her laptop to the big screen. "That's Vida Warren."

Then it showed Warren finding something on her phone, holding the screen out to the man. She attempted to leave, when the man seized her arm yanking her around.

"And that's Jeff Taylor," Reddick said. "What the hell?"

"This is a nice catch by Miami," Cruz said. "We've got to look into it."

"Hold on." Bogan was reading from his phone. "Digital just pulled material from Warren's phone and laptop. They've got several messages she exchanged with a number assigned to Jeff Taylor."

"Well, he said he'd talked to her," Cruz said.

"Bet he didn't tell you this." Bogan held up a hand, indicating he had more as he typed and nodded to the investigator handling the laptop. "Take a look."

The laptop's keyboard and mouse clicked.

The security footage was replaced with a series of crisp color photos showing Vida Warren completely naked with Jeff, who was dressed, on a sofa. Other images showed them kissing, Jeff with his hand on her breast, then his pants unzipped with Vida's head in his groin.

Amazement rippled around the table.

"Wow," Reddick said. "Just like that—boom! Things turn on a dime. And I thought this sort of break only happened in the movies and on TV."

"Okay, this is critical," Bogan said, chewing his gum. "We're going to have to recalibrate this investigation and move very fast because Jeff Taylor from Cleveland just became a person of interest."

80

Lisa was running.

She needed to run to clear her mind.

With Florence + the Machine's "Dog Days Are Over" pumping through her headphones, she entered the park near her house with its lush gardens, giant banyan trees and tunnels of green canopy.

She should've been running with a renewed sense of freedom. She was going to have a baby. They were going to Europe. All their troubles were behind them. The worst was over.

So why can't I believe it?

In the days since Loften's arrest and Vida Warren's murder, Lisa had grown apprehensive. Whenever she tried talking to Jeff about baby stuff or their upcoming trip, he was distant. He was obsessed with every news report on Vida's murder. Jeff stayed up late at night, and one morning got up and disappeared to who knew where.

Then there were the concerns Roland Dillard had raised. How Jeff had a violent streak and was intent on handling his trouble with Vida himself.

How he'd never wanted to inform the detectives about her threats toward him.

This is all stupid—I know my husband. He's a good man. Loften's the guy police are focusing on, for good reason.

Still, she didn't like where her worry was pointing her and tried to shake it off. When she left the park and headed home, it had started raining. Rain was falling at the same time the sun was shining.

Typical Florida weather. They called it a sunshower.

It was beautiful, but Lisa remembered reading that according to some myths, a sun-shower meant the devil was beating his wife, angry because God had created a glorious day, and the raindrops were her tears.

What a terrible image, she thought. *Is Mother Nature trying to tell me something?*

Lisa actually enjoyed the rain because it took her mind away from her anxiety. It also signaled that the storm season was upon them. And as she neared her home, she remembered she had things to do.

In the house, Lisa pulled off her damp clothes, got into her sweats and an old Cleveland Browns T-shirt. In the bedroom, she grabbed all their clothes from the hamper and prepared to run a load of laundry.

As usual, she checked pockets. She found nothing in Jeff's clothes. Then, at the bottom of the hamper, she noticed a small message pad and withdrew it. It had a palm-tree logo from the Oceanwave Gardens and bore a handwritten message: *Jeff, 5:30, Café Romero Sunrise, Bayside Marketplace.*

Oceanwave? That's the motel where the news said Loften and Vida stayed. Why does it indicate a rendezvous with Jeff? What's this doing in the hamper?

Lisa stared at it, but it offered no answers to her questions.

The doorbell rang.

Lisa went to the door, opening it to Detective Cruz and Agent Morrow.

"Yes?" Lisa looked at the two investigators with a question on her face that darkened as she looked beyond them to several police vehicles in her driveway and on the street.

"I'm sorry, but we have a warrant to search your house and vehicles. Now." Cruz handed Lisa a folded official document.

When Lisa opened it, some of the words leaped from the pages. *In the Circuit Court of the Eleventh Judicial Circuit in and for Miami-Dade County, Florida...affidavit...search warrant.* There were other terms, like *probable cause, property* and *evidence sought.*

Lisa's back slammed against the wall, and the foyer began spinning.

81

Downtown at the Coral Cloud Tower, Jeff stepped into the bathroom to check his hair and tie before heading to Foster Shore's office.

The plan was to join Shore and Leland Slaughter there before they left together for Vida Warren's memorial service in Boca Raton.

Standing alone before the mirror in his dark suit, Jeff tensed.

It's wrong for me to go to this after everything that happened. How can I even look at her family, or Roxanne, who's flying in from Cleveland?

Shore had wanted him there, and executive orders had to be followed.

Jeff took a breath and let it out, then headed to the office, but Shore's assistant stopped him when he reached for the door.

"I'm sorry, but Foster said you should wait in your office, Jeff."

"In my office? But he asked me to come here."

"I know. Something's come up."

Gwen forced a small, unnatural smile, making

him wonder if it was due to the upcoming solemn event or something else.

"Oh," he said.

"And Foster also told me to tell you the trip to Europe's on hold."

"What? Why?"

"Sorry, he didn't say."

Jeff took a few moments. "Okay, thanks, Gwen."

Walking away, Jeff was puzzled at why Shore wouldn't have told him personally about Europe. He decided to stop at Leland Slaughter's office, to wait with him and maybe learn more about what was up with Europe.

Slaughter's door was closed, and when Jeff knocked, there was no response. He glanced down the hall. Fred Bonner had stepped into it but had immediately reversed upon seeing him, as if to avoid him.

That's a bit odd.

As Jeff neared his own office, he heard the faint, distant chime of the elevator indicating someone was getting off and approaching reception.

Jeff stepped into his office while checking the time on his phone to estimate the drive to Boca Raton when it rang.

Lisa was sobbing.

"Honey, what is it?"

"The police are here! Going through our house, my car, taking things—"

"Honey, slow down. Breathe. Tell me what's going on?"

"Cruz, Morrow and all these cops, they've got a search warrant!"

"A warrant? What for?"

"To search for things connected to Vida Warren's murder!"

All the saliva in Jeff's mouth evaporated, and his phone nearly slipped out of his hand when a knock sounded at his door.

Standing there were Slaughter, Shore, Detective Reddick and two other men. Jeff lowered his phone, Lisa's voice growing tiny and faraway as she called his name.

"Jeff," Reddick said, "this is Detective Bogan and Detective Zelinski. Please put your phone down, and step away from your desk with your hands out so we can see them."

"Why? What is this?"

The two men, Bogan and Zelinski, were tugging on latex gloves. Shore raised slightly folded pages.

"They've got warrants to search the office, seize your computer and phone, and search your car," Shore said, indicating more officers in the hall.

"But why?" Jeff's eyes flitted to each man, ending on Reddick.

"Jeff, before we proceed, I have to advise you that you have the right to remain silent."

"What?" All the blood drained from Jeff's face.

"Anything you say can and will be used against you in a court of law. You have the right to an attorney. If you cannot afford an attorney, one will be provided for you. Do you understand these rights?"

"Why're you telling me this?"

"Do you understand what I just said?"

"Yes."

Reddick produced a document. "This states that you've been advised of and understand your rights. I need you to sign at the bottom."

Jeff stared at it as one of the gloved men picked up Jeff's phone, looked at it, hung up and deposited it into a Miami-Dade police evidence bag, then made notes.

"I'm not signing anything," Jeff said, "until you tell me why you're doing this."

"It's best if you cooperate," Shore said.

"Am I being charged with something?"

"No. We're arresting you for questioning concerning the homicide of Vida Warren. At this time, we're executing search warrants on your home and your vehicles."

Jeff swallowed hard and bile rose at the back of his throat as shock rippled through him. Several seconds passed before he signed, and Reddick collected the sheet.

"Hold out your wrists," Reddick said, reaching for handcuffs. "This is procedure."

Jeff hesitated.

"Please, Jeff. I'm sure this will all be cleared up," Slaughter said.

Jeff's gaze met Slaughter's, then Shore's, and he was unconvinced that they believed in his innocence as he held out his wrists, feeling Reddick lock them in steel.

Reddick took Jeff's upper arm. "Let's go."

With Slaughter and Shore in tow, the three detectives escorted Jeff down the hall. People appeared in doorways to stare. Jeff searched for Nick Martinez but couldn't find him. Small groups had gathered in reception; some of the women covered their mouths with their hands. A few of the men were recording the scene.

"People," Shore said, "get back to your desks."

Everyone was slow to respond to the order.

In reception, the detectives didn't need to push the elevator button. It chimed, the doors opened, and Nick Martinez stepped out. Within seconds, he'd taken stock of Jeff in handcuffs, the detectives and Shore and Slaughter looking stone-faced.

"Nick," Jeff said, "your sister, the attorney—what's her name and firm?"

"Uh, Sabrina. Sabrina Martinez, at Fender, Palmera and Cardena."

Jeff and the detectives got into the elevator.

"Jeff, what's going on?"

The doors started to close.

"I'm going to need her help."

82

Jeff's heart beat a little faster taking in the room at Miami-Dade police headquarters.

He glanced at the fluorescent lighting recessed in the fiberboard ceiling panels, the camera suspended high in the corner, and the drab white walls, and thought how the air smelled like a musty battle of air freshener, desperation and lies.

He'd been fingerprinted and photographed but had refused to provide a sample of his handwriting. He had not yet made contact with an attorney. Maybe it was a mistake, but he'd agreed to listen to what the detectives wanted him to know because he didn't understand why he was here.

Yet, in a faraway corner of his heart, he knew exactly why he was here.

Tears stood in his eyes.

How had it come to this? He'd had it all, and he'd had it all under control. He and Lisa had left Cleveland to start a new chapter in their lives. Everything was going the way it should, going beautifully, until Vida got in the way. Yes, he'd thought he had it all under control, but the truth was he'd lost control, and now his world was crashing down just like it had that day when his dad was...

...bleeding on the ground...his dad's face ashen...eyes burning with surprise and sadness... his dad dying on the ground...his last words begging to know..."Why, son?...Why did you...?"

His father's death gasps dissolved into the air conditioner's hum.

And now here he was: a suspect in handcuffs.

"All set there, Jeff?"

Waiting across the table from him was Reddick. Beside him was the gum-chewer, Bogan. And beside him was Morrow, the FBI agent.

"You don't have to say anything," Bogan said, "but this is probably the best time to come clean, believe me, because we've got a shitstorm coming down on you."

The investigators let that sink in.

"We know you killed Vida," Reddick said. "We've got a lot of people doing a lot of work. The evidence against you is overwhelming, and it's building. Our team of detectives has talked to a lot of people. We'll give you a sampling of what we know." Reddick opened a folder with official summaries.

"We've gone through her phone, her laptop and yours. We know you worked together in Cleveland. We know you had a sexual relationship with her. We know that she came to your office and that she threatened to do more than reveal your affair."

Reddick set down a page, marked as evidence, a screen grab of a text Vida had sent.

I know what you are, and I know what you did in Cleveland. Soon everyone else will know. Time is running out on you, Jeff.

The investigators studied Jeff's reaction, then Reddick moved on.

"You pleaded with Vida, argued with her. You needed to silence her."

Reddick then played the footage of Jeff man-handling Vida at the café.

"Her body was found near the airport with a message written on stationery from the Ocean-wave Gardens, the motel where she was residing. We know you went to her motel. We found the exact stationery in your home.

"We know you have rage issues, Jeff," Reddick continued. "Roland Dillard and Ned Tripp told us how you nearly beat Loften to death the night he was caught. Heck, we saw the result of your rage on his face."

Reddick opened the file folder, then one by one placed on the table before Jeff photos from the crime scene and the autopsy of Vida Warren.

Jeff clenched his eyes for a moment, then opened them.

Vida's body was mutilated, perforated with stab wounds.

"This was a rage-filled, frenzied attack," Bogan said, producing a knife. "This knife is similar to the one used in the homicide. Now, here's the thing. You see, many homicides involve a struggle. Attackers can be injured, too: blood splashes, things get slippery." He gripped the knife. "The attacker hits bone, it stops the blade suddenly, and the hand gripping the handle slips onto the blade. I'll show you." Bogan demonstrated with his hand, sliding down the blade, then tracing with a pen the spot on his palm where his wound would be. "It's called self-wounding. Hold out your palm, Jeff."

Jeff hesitated, then held out his palm, showing the now-faded cut on his right palm in the same area as Bogan's pen mark.

"You said you cut yourself slicing an apple," Bogan said. "But you can see how our version of your self-wounding is consistent with the homicide."

"Jeff," Reddick said, "maybe you didn't mean for things to turn out the way they did, but—this is where it gets worse—we're investigating some other homicides that Agent Morrow here will tell you about."

Case by case, while showing Jeff photos from her tablet, Morrow recounted The Collector murders, beginning with the first in Pittsburgh and ending with the most recent prior to Miami, the case of Maylene Marie Siler in Cleveland.

"We checked with Asgaard-T-Chace, had them go through records," Morrow said. "And with the warrants, we also reached back over the years into your credit-card and bank-card records. Jeff, we can put you in most of the locations within the time frame of the other attacks."

Jeff stared at the photos of Vida Warren, the images of the other murders, then the investigators.

Morrow was not finished. "We've recently learned from Cleveland PD and the Cuyahoga County Sheriff's Department that the woman murdered in metropolitan Cleveland used illicit drugs for a time and once shared the same supplier as Vida Warren and the two women met at a party attended by people known to you."

She looked into Jeff's eyes.

"You see where we're going with this, Jeff," she said. "A little six degrees of separation. You resided in Cleveland at the time Siler disappeared. Then you moved—or should we say *fled*—Cleveland for South Florida. But Vida Warren, with all her problems, followed you, bringing your monstrous past with her."

Bogan shoved a stick of gum into his mouth, then tapped the most gruesome photo of Vida's savaged corpse.

"That left you with no choice, Jeff."

83

In the same complex where Jeff was being held, Perez continued his work in the Crime Scene Investigations Identification Section.

He was endeavoring to separate the overlapping prints on Loften's serrated knife, a difficult process.

Perez was under pressure because FBI investigators needed to compare every print Miami-Dade had collected with the partial print left by The Collector in the Kentucky attack.

As for Loften's knife, the police report from his arrest by citizens in Palm Mirage Creek stated that three people had handled the knife: Loften, Jeff Taylor and Roland Dillard, the block-watch captain. The FBI had recently compared the partial print from The Collector case to prints from Clete Loften's and Jeff Taylor's arrests, along with those from Dillard's prints, on record for his concealed-weapons permit.

In all instances, analysis was inconclusive, meaning none could be identified as a likely match or ruled out as being an unlikely match to The Collector print.

The reason was attributed to the quality of the partial print from Kentucky.

This ain't like the movies, Perez thought, studying the case notes as he worked, aware of the factors that made analysis so challenging, like the elasticity of human skin, which meant the size, pressure and depth of a latent print were variables that could reduce and distort accuracy, and hamper analysis.

Exhausting every avenue, investigators now turned to the prints on Loften's knife in an effort to determine if the quality of latents found there could sustain comparison with The Collector's partial print.

After putting in long hours, Perez came up with an algorithm to separate the photo images of the prints from the knife and divide them into overlapped, non-overlapped and background regions. Then he applied further analysis and used a specialized filter, which resulted in his collection of several isolated individual prints from the knife.

"At last! All right," Perez sighed with relief, reaching for his phone.

His next step was to work with Brittany Delarmo, a fingerprint analyst whose desk was down the hall. They would work on sharpening the images, then they would send the strongest ones to the FBI. Together they would run analysis to see if any of the prints from the knife were a likely match with The Collector.

84

While Jeff was in custody at the station, he was permitted to make and receive a limited number of calls.

By the time Lisa reached him on the phone, she was distraught.

"They arrested you? Then, it's true!"

"Lisa, listen, I have to—"

"After our call was cut off, police here took my phone, then Nell and Roland came over, and he gave me Nell's phone to use to call you at the jail—"

"Listen, I can explain. They brought me in—"

"Then I couldn't reach you. I called your office. They said they took you away *in handcuffs*! I couldn't believe it, I didn't believe it—"

"Lisa—"

"And they ransacked our home…" Her voice weakened and broke. "I don't know what's happening. Will they let you go? Can I see you?"

"They brought me here to Miami-Dade headquarters in Doral to ask me questions about Vida's case."

"But I don't understand. I thought Loften was—"

"It's complicated. Before you come to see me, there's something I need you to do. Okay?"

Lisa was crying, struggling.

"I need you to do this. It's important," Jeff said. "Are you listening?"

Lisa swallowed a large gasp. "I'm listening."

After Lisa surrendered her borrowed phone and her bag, removed her shoes for inspection and emptied her pockets of all items into the plastic tray as instructed, the female uniformed officer patted her down.

Lisa endured the momentary humiliation of the officer's gloved hands groping her.

Then, as another officer, a man with red hair and freckles, led Lisa through a secure section of the Miami-Dade headquarters complex, memories replayed in her mind: Jeff so thrilled at the promotion, their move to Palm Mirage Creek, their beautiful house and her pregnancy. Now, she was numbed by the surreal twist her life had taken.

I was attacked in my home, and now Jeff's been arrested for the murder of a woman he may or may not have had sex with. Is my husband— Did my husband—

Everything's so horribly wrong.

Reflexively, one hand went to her tummy as she forced herself to keep calm and stay strong. But fear gnawed at her, fear that now, with every step she took, she was losing a part of herself, that nothing would ever, *could* ever, be the same again.

They came to a visiting room with three small, portioned booths, each separated by a glass window that faced an identical opposite booth. Each side had a handset phone on the left wall of the respective partition.

The officer gestured for Lisa to select a booth.

She chose the middle one, and she took small comfort that she was alone in the room and was uneasy with its clinical brightness, void of empathy, void of warmth. Something cold and dark dwelled within these walls.

Keys jangled, a door on the other side of the glass opened, and Lisa caught her breath.

Jeff entered alone.

He was wearing a dress shirt with no tie, his collar open. His pants lacked a belt. He took the booth seat across from Lisa. As they both reached for their handsets, she saw that he was not handcuffed and that his five o'clock stubble had started, accentuating the lines carved into his face.

"Oh, Jeff." Tears filled her eyes—her life was out of control.

He pointed to the cameras and signs, noting all calls and actions were being recorded.

Lisa gave him a nervous nod. "I don't understand why you're here," she said.

"They want to question me about Vida in the wake of all that's happened," he said. "Did you do what I needed you to do?"

"Yes, I called Nick. I got hold of his sister, Sabrina. She said she'd be down to see you later today. She said she normally charges a ten-thousand-dollar retainer, but because you know her brother, she'll drop it to five."

"We'll use the bonus money. You know which account it's in, right?"

She didn't answer.

"Lisa, listen to me. It's going to be okay."

"How can you say that? This is exactly what you were afraid would happen. I begged you to go to the police from the start. Look around, look where you are. Police have searched our home, seized my car. I had to rent one. I'm terrified. I had TV reporters knocking on our door."

"Did you tell them anything?"

"No, nothing," she said. "This is a nightmare."

Through her tears, Lisa stared long and hard into his eyes.

"Tell me, Jeff. What did you do?"

"Stop."

Tears rolled down her face. "Because you know—"

"Stop asking me questions. Nothing is what you think it is. Nothing, I swear."

"—you know what I found in—"

"Lisa, please stop! Everything's being recorded!"

"I don't care! I'm your wife! I deserve to know the truth. Or else I walk out of here and get on the next plane to Cleveland!"

She searched his face, finding his desperation so intense that for an instant she no longer recognized her husband. A stranger was sitting on the other side of the glass.

"The truth," she said again.

"I believed Vida was going to destroy everything, and I believed—truly believed—we would end up with nothing, end up on the street. It terrified me. I panicked, tried to stop her. I looked for her but couldn't find her. I didn't hurt her, and I didn't have sexual relations with her. I took her concept, her idea, and built on it, and maybe I tried to pass it off as my own. But that's all I did." He looked at the ceiling; he was blinking back tears. "I know I'm asking a lot of you, Lisa, but we've built a life together. We're having a baby." Jeff rubbed at his haggard face. "In your heart you know me, like I know you. We've carried so much pain all of our lives. God knows I've got problems, and I don't have all the answers, but I'm telling you the truth, and I'm begging you to believe me."

Pushing back on her tears, she managed a tepid nod that wounded him.

"I have to go," he said. "I have to work on some notes for the attorney. They haven't charged me with anything. I don't know how long they can hold me. I hope Sabrina can get me out of here as soon as possible."

Lisa brushed at her wet cheeks.

Jeff put his palm up against the glass to say goodbye.

Lisa raised hers to do the same, hesitating when she saw the faint cut on his palm, feeling a shiver pierce her, before she placed her hand on the glass with his.

* * *

Outside, Lisa sat behind the wheel of her rental car in the Miami-Dade police visitors' parking lot with images, real and imagined, swirling in her head.

Their wedding day; the news footage of the place where Vida's body was found; those pictures of Jeff with Vida naked that she never saw; memories of herself with Jeff in the many happy moments they'd had over their life together; then images of her holding their baby.

Suddenly she shook with racking sobs.

Oh God, help me. I don't know that man in there.

After several long moments, she found her composure, grabbed some tissue, then saw her eyes in the visor mirror.

If Vida did have sex with my husband, she deserves to be dead.

Lisa's eyes widened, and she gasped.

No, I didn't mean that. No!

Suddenly Lisa was pulled back to that day...

Coming home from Tiffany's birthday party in the back seat of Stacey's car...her dad drinking from a can and driving, playing the radio loud... Stacey playing with her...pushing the button... "Don't push the button, Stacey!"... But Stacey won't stop... She pushes the button that releases Lisa's seat belt... Lisa buckles it again, then pushes Stacey's button, the seat belt whipping free when her father curses...brakes screeching...metal and glass exploding... Stacey rocketing from the car, a rag doll...plastered to the grille of the big truck...

Another car had run a red light and Stacey's dad was drinking, they said, but Lisa knew she was the one who'd released Stacey's seat belt... It was her fault...

Now Lisa slammed her palms on the wheel as if trying to break out of her nightmare. All around her, dark clouds were swallowing the sun.

A storm was coming.

85

Sabrina Martinez resumed studying summaries, photos and video footage she'd wrangled from the detectives who'd arrested Jeff Taylor.

Earlier, a paralegal had read much of the information to her over the phone as she drove back from court in Tampa to her home in Miami, wishing she'd flown. She didn't have time to take on Taylor as a client, but after her brother, then Lisa Taylor, had called, she'd agreed.

At her home in Aventura she changed from her shirt and shorts into a dark pantsuit with a white top and pulled her hair back into a taut ponytail. She slid on her gold-framed glasses and headed straight to the Miami-Dade police complex.

They'd placed her in a small room to consult with her client. It afforded privacy. While waiting, she continued examining everything investigators had reluctantly shared. The crime-scene and autopsy photos in Vida Warren's homicide, and those of other women across the country, gave her pause as the enormity of the case settled on her.

Still, the brief information police had given her didn't tell the whole story. Nothing was rock-solid against her client. *Not yet*, she thought, making notes when the door opened and Jeff Taylor was escorted to the table.

He was handcuffed. The uniformed officer secured his cuffs to the metal loop in the table.

"Just knock on the door when you're done," the officer said, then left.

Martinez thanked him, then stood, reached over the table. The chain jingled when she shook Jeff's hand.

"Thank you for coming," he said, assessing her, putting her in her late thirties. "Nick told me you graduated from Yale, that you handle serious criminal cases and you never lose."

"*Almost* never," she focused on her papers and laptop. "Jeff, our immediate goal is to get you released."

"Aren't you going to ask me if I'm guilty?" He indicated all the material on the table. "If I did it?"

"No. That's for a prosecutor to prove. You are not guilty until a court says you are."

Jeff looked at her, and she met his gaze, removing her glasses, her sharp, intelligent eyes reading him carefully.

"Jeff, I am ethically and legally bound to provide all clients with an aggressive defense. That includes those who are likely to be found guilty by the court and those who are innocent."

Jeff nodded with satisfaction.

"All right," she turned to her notes on her yellow legal pad. "I've reviewed everything I've been provided, and quite frankly, at this stage, it looks like a lot of circumstance strung together."

"What do you mean, *at this stage*?"

"For starters, you have not been formally charged with anything."

"Then, why are they holding me?"

"Because they can. In this state, they can hold you for a long time before charging you. It's up to the State Attorney to charge you. It's possible they don't think they have all the evidence yet. Or they're waiting on more evidence."

Jeff nodded.

"Remember," Martinez said, "investigators are legally allowed to employ all kinds of strategies. They can lie to you during questioning, they can bring you in, jam you up, try to fish for a confession, anything that strengthens their case against you."

Jeff swallowed.

"Now, the way I see it," Martinez said, "they've got a boatload of circumstance against you. It's not pretty—it looks bad for you—but it's not that strong. I'm confident I will be able to secure your release soon. You just hang in there."

"Okay."

"Good. Now, we need to go over a few things. First, is there anything you think I should know?"

For a long, tense moment, Jeff considered her question. "I did steal her work."

"You did?"

"She was on her way out of the company. I was

desperate to make my star shine and figured there was no harm… Well…that's what set everything in motion."

"I see."

"But that is all I did. *I swear, that is all.*"

Martinez took some time to absorb his admission.

"Will that hurt my case?"

"What you did was unethical. Even a little shitty. But it's not a crime."

Martinez returned to her notes and the material. For nearly an hour, they discussed dates, places, timelines and facts that could and could not be proved. They went over Jeff's background, his solid career and the fact he had no criminal record. When they'd finished, Martinez got up and knocked on the door. A different officer entered, and Jeff thanked her before he was taken away.

Left alone, Martinez gathered her work, hesitating. Once again, she reviewed the footage of Jeff's angered, rough treatment of Vida Warren at the café, then Vida's text.

I know what you are, and I know what you did in Cleveland.

Was that in reference to Jeff stealing her work, or something else?

Then she looked quickly at the photos, the smiling faces of the other women and the grisly crime-scene photos of their murders.

Martinez cursed under her breath. She looked

at the empty plastic chair where, seconds ago, Jeff Taylor had sat conversing with her intelligently, calmly. He was a smart, successful, professional man with a baby on the way, looking as normal as you would expect any normal man to look.

Martinez was not certain of his innocence or his guilt.

However, there was one thing she was absolutely sure of. One thing she'd learned in all her years as a criminal defense attorney.

Everyone, guilty or innocent, has a dark side.

86

All right, here we go.

Melinda Daxon, a fingerprint specialist with the FBI's Integrated Automated Fingerprint Identification System, was alerted by her colleagues with Miami-Dade by a chime on her computer.

Opening the file, she sat straighter at her desk in the Bureau's Criminal Justice Information Services, housed in a sprawling three-story modular complex in Clarksburg, West Virginia, about two hundred and fifty miles west of Washington, DC.

Daxon's workstation was near a window, and the sun was setting. She'd been waiting to receive Florida's latest set of processed latents in a case involving unsolved homicides and attacks in eight states.

Like the FBI agents and the state and local analysts who had worked on the case over the years, Daxon's objective was to compare the Florida prints with the one partial print recovered in Kentucky and known to belong to The Collector, the elusive suspect in all the killings.

But the quality of the partial fingerprint had been challenging for examiners. They'd been unable to find another similar to it on record because there just was so little there to work with. Consequently, every opportunity was taken to compare every new processed latent connected to the case with the partial.

But Daxon, a court-certified expert who'd testified in multiple homicide cases, had taken things a step further. While waiting for the Florida latents, she worked on the partial. Using the latest technology, she took it through a new round of cleaning, removing residual dirt and digital noise from the image.

It gave her an enhanced, much stronger latent. In fact, she'd determined that the partial was a right thumb, which on a standard ten-card is referred to as *number one*. She had already coded its characteristics and cued up the sample on her oversize monitor.

Now she began cuing up the Florida prints on her second large monitor, which stood beside the first. She set out reviewing the new batch of candidates, looking for right thumbs, one of the most common prints recovered at crime scenes.

After careful examination, she had isolated three different right thumbprints. These were among the prints collected from the knife that had overlapped. Miami-Dade's hard work at separating them had paid off.

They did a stellar job—the quality is super, Daxon thought, as she displayed the first one and set out to make a visual point-by-point comparison with the partial. She zeroed in on the critical minutiae points, like the trail of ridges near the tip. In some jurisdictions, the courts required ten to fifteen clear point matches. From the get-go, she had two that soon climbed to three when she hit on a series of dissimilarities. All it took was one divergent point to instantly eliminate a print.

Okay, let's move on to number two.

With the second print, Daxon studied the loops, whorls and arches, analyzing and comparing them against the partial. She soon had three point matches, and when it climbed to eight, she grew hopeful until she found significant divergent points, eliminating number two.

Daxon rubbed the back of her stiff neck, surprised at how much time had passed. Darkness had fallen over the surrounding green woods by the time she'd come to the last candidate.

Right off, six minutiae points matched, and her breathing stopped as she enlarged the sample to the point where she could count the number of ridges.

Three more matching points.

She leaned closer to the monitor, narrowing her eyes as she concentrated on cluster details, spots, hooks, bifurcations and tented arches in the Florida print and the partial from Kentucky.

Again, the minutiae points matched, point by point.

The branching of the ridges matched. Daxon's breathing quickened as she began counting up the clear points of comparison where the two samples matched. She had fourteen and was still counting. By the time she'd compared the left-slanting patterns, she was thinking ahead about testifying in court.

Daxon confirmed the identification number of the subject and the name.

She would submit the name in a query to several data banks, including the NCIC, but first she had to make a call. Scrolling through the file, she found the name of the case agent and contact numbers. As her call connected, she thought of the murdered women, their grieving families and, while the darkness deepened outside her window, Daxon felt a new light would emerge.

She glanced at the identification card.

We've got the killer.

87

Thunder rumbled and lightning webbed across the night sky as Lisa stood at her bedroom window, her heart turbid with doubt and fear.

Was Jeff a murderer?

Why would Vida follow them to Cleveland—what was *the real reason*? Why had they *really* moved so quickly to Florida? Jeff admitted to some sort of relationship with Vida, and he had that violent streak, going out all night, saying he would take care of Vida.

Now she was dead. Jeff had been arrested. *And we're having a child together.*

Lisa stifled a sob. She flinched as a jarring crash of thunder rattled the window.

Forcing herself to think of something else and gripping Roland's phone, she went downstairs and turned on the TV so she wouldn't feel so alone. So vulnerable.

She landed on the weather channel.

"...looking at the satellite pictures, we see a severe storm rolling in off the coast...not a hurricane, but we've got heavy rain, frequent lightning, and with winds gusting up to fifty, fifty-five miles per hour, we're getting reports of some downed trees, property damage, power outages…cell-signal outages… Folks, this is a good night to stay indoors…"

The TV didn't help. Footage of the storm catapulted Lisa back into turmoil as she remembered the cut on Jeff's hand.

The TV and lights in the house flickered.

Lisa didn't know if Jeff was going to be released soon. Her calls to Sabrina and Nick Martinez had gone to voice mail. Her calls to Miami-Dade police were futile. Nobody would tell her anything.

She couldn't stem the fear rising in her.

Again, she tried calling her sister in Cleveland, relieved when this time her attempt succeeded, and she poured out her heart to Joy.

"I never wanted to leave Cleveland… Now police they think he's involved in a murder… I'm not sure I know who Jeff is anymore, or if I can ever face him again… I don't know what to do…"

"Lisa, listen to me," Joy said. "You have to hold on. Jeff's not a murderer. You two have been together for nearly ten years. Deep down in your heart, you know he's a good guy. He may not be perfect. Who is? But he didn't kill that woman. And he didn't cheat on you. I know him, too. Listen, you're pregnant, far from home, you miss everybody. And—you—what—" Static crackled on the line, Joy's voice breaking up. "This—what—should do right now—"

The line died in Lisa's hand.

"Hello? Joy, are you there?"

Lisa tried redialing, but it was futile. Thunder hammered and lightning flashed. Oh, how she ached to be back in Ohio. Again and again, her agony pulled her back to Cleveland until suddenly, as a spear of lightning lit the sky, she thought of Maylene Marie Siler.

Lisa remembered Detective Reddick calling them, showing them a photo of Siler, asking if they knew the woman who'd been murdered in Cleveland.

No, Lisa didn't know her, but in this moment she wanted to know more about her. Her fingers moved quickly on the phone, praying she still had an online connection. She went to Cleveland's best news site and searched stories about Siler's murder.

Coming to one with the most information, Lisa learned that Siler's body had been discovered in a shallow grave by a man walking his dog near Tiffin Field. News pictures showed the wooded area sectioned off with yellow tape.

Lisa froze.

Tiffin Field.

Jeff and I used to walk there.

Thunder hammered at the windows, the lights flickered, and the house went completely dark except for the glow of the phone in her hand.

A chime sounded, and a message popped up on the screen.

Lisa, this is Roland and Nell. If you see this, please come to our home now. We need your help. A terrible thing has happened.

88

Jeff Taylor's wallet, keys, tie, belt and shoelaces spilled onto the police counter from the large envelope.

Looking at them while grappling with the magnitude of what he was facing, his pulse sped up. He tried to stay calm.

All of his belongings were returned to him, except his phone.

"Guess your phone's still being kept as evidence," the desk officer said.

It was an inconvenience Jeff could endure because he was going home. He signed for the items, laced his shoes, looped his belt and slid on his jacket.

True to her promise, Sabrina Martinez had quietly secured his release.

Her conversations with the people she knew at the Miami-Dade State Attorney's Office had yielded results. She was not present at the police complex. She didn't need to be. The officers holding Jeff had unlocked his cell, escorted him to the desk and told him that he was free to go.

Now Jeff's problem was getting home.

His car had been seized from the Coral Cloud Tower lot downtown. He couldn't call Lisa. Her phone had been seized, along with her computer. She had Dillard's phone, but with all that was going on, he didn't get the number. The desk officer working at a computer exuded indifference.

Jeff stepped into the public bathroom to get cleaned up. In the mirror he met the bloodshot eyes and mussed hair of someone he didn't know.

Who is this beast?

This was how the others had seen him.

Jeff was certain he was going to lose his job. Asgaard would surely claw back the bonus, which by the time this was done was likely going to go to Sabrina Martinez anyway. And given the way Reddick, Bogan and the others had gone at him, they'd probably leak those photos of him with Vida.

He was finished.

Anger bubbled under his skin.

The worst of it was how cold Lisa had become. He'd caused her so much pain. Would the baby be okay?

His rage erupting, he turned and began slamming the metal stall door repeatedly as if trying to power himself out of the hole he was in.

Over and over he slammed, kicked and punched it.

"Hey!" The desk officer materialized in the

bathroom. "Everything all right in here? You looking to get charged?"

Jeff stopped, ran both hands through his hair.

"I'm sorry. I'm… Can you call a taxi for me? Please?"

The cop eyed him coldly. "If it gets you outta here." He held the bathroom door open. "Get out, sit your ass down and behave. It'll take a while because of the storm."

It was nearly twenty-five minutes before the taxi arrived.

"Wild night, you know," the driver said.

Rain pelted the car's roof. The wipers swiped at top speed in a losing battle. Sitting in the back, Jeff felt moisture on his palm but paid little attention, thinking it was rain. Then, in the ambient light, he saw that his palm was bleeding.

Why won't this damn thing heal?

He must've opened the wound again during his explosion in the bathroom. He pressed his palm to his leg as if trying to bury an accusation and stared into the night.

Palm trees bent in the wind, severed fronds skipped along streets, disappearing into the dark, forcing Jeff to continue examining the horror that had befallen him.

Everything he'd worked for all his life was gone. Because of Vida Warren.

It's sad she's dead, but you reap what you sow.

Lightning lit up the sky with an apocalyptic display.

Jeff could not undo what was done. All he could do now was set Lisa straight with the truth.

It's the only way I can end her pain.

89

Wide, lifeless eyes stared at Agent Morrow.

The faces of Vida Warren, Maylene Marie Siler and the other murdered women filled the screen of her tablet as she worked at home.

Thunder crashed and lightning flashed outside her window.

Morrow came back to the fact that Jeff Taylor had opportunity and motive for Warren and had lived in Cleveland within the time frame Siler vanished. They were going to question him again in the morning. And they needed samples of his handwriting. But it was going to be difficult because now he had an attorney.

Morrow massaged her temples. She'd been working on her notes for hours. Another case-status meeting was set for the morning, and they'd see where things stood with the latest evidence.

I hope we get something out of that before we go at him again, she thought, when her phone rang.

"Agent Morrow, this is Melinda Daxon with

IAFIS in Clarksburg. I'm handling latents in your case. Got results you need to know."

The lights dimmed, then came back.

"All right, go ahead, Melinda."

"We've got a match from the Florida knife and the Kentucky case."

"A match? You're certain?"

"Sixteen clear points of comparison. We have identified your subject. I'm sending you the information now."

"Thank you, Melinda. Thank you very much."

The lights went off and on again as Morrow opened the information and read the identity of The Collector.

She froze.

Oh my God. Right in front of us, all this time.

At the same time Morrow got her call, Miami-Dade detective Jack Bogan was across the city, heading home from dinner at Zelinski's house, where they'd spent much of the time discussing the case. Bogan's wife was driving in the downpour while he was on the phone with Joe Reddick.

"You won't believe what just happened," Bogan said.

"What?" Reddick was home studying his case notes while watching a game.

"They released Jeff Taylor."

"What?" Reddick sat bolt upright. "They're supposed to hold him for us until all those latents are analyzed. What the hell happened?"

"Someone dropped the ball. Taylor got a hot-shot attorney with a channel to the Miami-Dade State Attorney."

Their connection crackled, then beeped.

"Hold on," Reddick said. "I'm getting a call from Cruz."

"And I just got a text from Morrow," Bogan said.

Within seconds, all four investigators were up to speed on the identity of the killer known as The Collector.

"How did we miss this?" Reddick said.

Bogan sent a new text to the other partners.

We need to activate the Special Response Team and set up an arrest in Palm Mirage Creek.

90

The rain came down in torrents.

Rushes of wind punched at Lisa as she reached the Dillards' bungalow.

She pressed the doorbell. It didn't work. Remembering the power was out across the neighborhood, she knocked.

A moment passed without a response.

The text the Dillards had sent continued glowing on the phone.

We need your help. A terrible thing has happened.

She knocked again, hard this time, drawing her face to the door.

"Nell! Roland!"

No response.

She raised her fist to knock even harder but stopped at hearing a faint noise from inside, a mournful moaning growing into a plaintive cry.

Lisa shouted for them. "Roland! Nell!"

She tried the door, surprised to find it unlocked.

Lisa pushed it open, and with the storm lashing at her, she stepped into the waiting darkness.

Jeff's taxi entered Palm Mirage Creek.

Several trees had toppled, and the neighborhood was without power, giving him a feeling of isolation, the rhythm of the wipers pulling him back into his memories.

His dad, on the ground...his eyes imploring, "Why, son?... Why did you...?"

No! No, stop dwelling on him.

Jeff's thoughts of his father gave way to those of his own life, everything he'd experienced, everything he'd achieved, and how he was going to lose it all. He searched the night for answers, but it was futile. He needed to ensure that Lisa knew the truth about him.

I saw it in her eyes. What she thinks of me. I've got to make her understand, if it's the last thing I do before it all ends.

The taxi wended through streets near his home, its headlights raking over the Dillards' house as they passed it.

What was that?

Jeff thought he saw a figure at the Dillards' door, but glimpsing it in the darkness through the taxi's rain-streaked window, he was unsure.

He turned and took a second look but saw nothing there.

A moment later, Jeff was home.

Guided by lightning flashes, he walked past

Lisa's rental in the driveway and used his key to unlock his front door.

"Lisa!" he called into the darkness.

Taking careful steps in the dark, Lisa moved through the Dillards' home.

"Roland! Nell!"

She found nothing but stillness and silence, punctuated by the rumble and flash of the storm. Using the flashlight feature on the phone, she went to the living room.

No one there.

Then the kitchen. Empty again.

"Roland! Nell!"

Fear was coiling in her stomach.

Swallowing hard, she continued through the house to the great room, which opened to the pool and gardens, the palms flailing in the storm. The dining room was empty. Lisa went to Nell's tranquil room, swept her light over the empty rocking chair and massive Bible.

"Nell! Roland!"

Bedroom after bedroom, Lisa found nothing.

It was as if the house had been vacated of life, until she came to the hallway where her light landed on something heaped on the floor.

Nell.

The older woman was unconscious.

"Oh my God, Nell!"

The light reflected in Nell's large eyeglasses. Lisa searched the woman's face. She didn't wear her usual scarf on her head, accentuating her skull.

Her eyes were closed, her skin pallid. Lisa touched her shoulder—she didn't respond.

"Nell, wake up."

Lisa took up Nell's gnarled hand and tapped it.

"Nell, please! Please, wake up!"

Lisa felt her loose skin for a pulse but was unable to find one as the couple's message blazed in her mind.

A terrible thing has happened.

The light veered in Lisa's shaking hand as she raised the phone to dial 9-1-1, but she stopped.

"No! No! Oh God, please, no!"

Roland's anguished voice resounded from a distance. Lisa left Nell to follow it to the far end of the house.

"It's Lisa, Roland! Where are you? I'm coming!"

Roland's cry led her to the fourth bedroom. The one they used as a guest room. The one that was self-contained and self-powered, built for survival— the one with the fortified safe room they always kept locked.

But when Lisa arrived, the steel door with its triple locks was open.

Brilliant light and the murmur of a man's voice spilled from it.

91

A small LED night-light glowed from the electrical outlet in the front hallway of Jeff's home.

He was glad he'd installed several of them. They had chargeable batteries so when the power failed, they became emergency lights. He unplugged it, activating the flashlight feature and began searching for Lisa. Except for the tiny red lights of the smoke detectors and the security cameras, which had automatically switched to backup battery power, the house was enveloped in darkness.

"Lisa!"

He went to every room, probing it with the light, searching for her.

Where is she?

He had no phone, no computer, no way of contacting her. The storm pounded as he recalled the coldness in her eyes the last time she'd looked at him.

Had she left him?

His stomach tightened with anger.

No, no, no.

He went to their bedroom.

Had she gone back to Cleveland? But the car was in the driveway—maybe she took a taxi to the airport... *But are there flights with this storm...?*

He checked the closet. Their luggage was still there. He stood at the bedroom window and caught sight of the Dillards' house. Light flickered inside as if someone was moving through their home.

Jeff's mind rolled back, and it suddenly registered.

The figure he'd seen at the Dillards' door was Lisa.

Thunder cracked, the sky streaked white, making the neighbors' house glow for an instant.

What is she doing there?

92

Inching into the safe room, Lisa found Roland sitting in a swivel chair holding a sheet of paper with handwriting on it.

"Nell's gone." He raised his head to her, his face etched with sadness. "She must've taken pills to end the pain. I never knew the depth of her suffering and what she carried inside her."

He handed it to Lisa, and she read the few, neatly penned words.

Forgive me. I just couldn't go on. Nell.

Lisa lowered herself, placed her hands on the tops of his legs. "Oh, Roland."

He stared into space.

"I'm so sorry," she whispered and let a moment pass. "We should call 9-1-1."

Roland shook his head, indicating he needed time, then he shielded his eyes with his hand, sinking into despair. In that heart-wrenching moment, Lisa took stock of the safe room.

It was larger than she'd expected, with two beds, towers of bottled water, canned food and supplies, but something about it bewildered her as she surveyed the vast console of video monitors with all different streams of footage rolling on them like home movies, panels with banks of buttons and switches.

It looked like a mission control center.

Roland removed his hand from his eyes, looked hard at her, then slowly placed both of his large hands on top of hers, covering them as they rested on his legs.

"It's just us now, Lisa."

His expression transformed from grief to happiness.

Confused, Lisa tried to stand, but he seized her hands, and when he suddenly stood, she saw the handgun in his holster.

"Sit down," he said. His strong hands and powerful arms pulled at her. "Please."

Horror dawning, Lisa tried to flee, but he overpowered her, thrust her into the chair and, in a swift motion, handcuffed her wrists to the armrests.

"Stop! Roland, what're you doing? Stop!"

"Shh, shh. There's no need to worry. Shh. Quiet." He stroked her hair, inhaling her scent. "It's just us now. Nell's gone. Jeff's going to die in prison." He looked into her eyes. "Don't look so surprised."

Lisa's body shook.

"I saw the way you looked at me when we first met," he said. "I was captivated by you, too. I knew we were going to be together. I know it's what you wanted. So I took steps to make it happen. I'll show you."

He went to the console and began adjusting switches.

"All these monitors are linked to surveillance cameras, most of them in your house. But they've been rewired so I could watch and hear you. I set it up when we installed your security system. I also cloned your phones, your computers. I knew every waking moment of your lives. Watch this monitor." He pointed to a near screen. "I made a little montage of scenes I've recorded."

Footage rolled, showing Lisa working and talking with her sister, then Lisa and Jeff eating, arguing, getting dressed, making love.

Lisa swallowed as tears came to her eyes. "This can't be real. I don't understand."

"I'm going to help you understand. I retired from my hobbies not too long ago. But I couldn't stop. I wanted to, but I couldn't. My compulsion takes over. Then you came along. I never met anyone like you, and I knew I wanted to spend the rest of my days with you and enjoy my legacy."

She fought against the handcuffs. "I don't—please—"

On one of the live video screens monitoring her home, one that Roland had not been watching, Lisa thought she saw someone going room to room with a flashlight.

"You told me how troubled you were by Vida Warren," Roland said. "So I came out of retirement to remove her, knowing Jeff's involvement with her would seal his fate. The whole Vida-and-Loften thing was a bonus. It drove you closer to me, threw suspicion on Loften to the point where I could play him against Jeff and cause you to doubt your husband. His violent streak and his sleep-walking episodes didn't hurt my case either. That's all behind us now. The good news is you'll never see Jeff again. He didn't deserve you. I mean, those pictures of him with Vida... I'll show you."

Roland worked on one panel, and a slideshow of images flowed, showing Vida naked with Jeff, who was dressed, on a sofa. One image showed them kissing, in another Jeff's hand was on Vida's breast. Another showed Jeff with his pants un-zipped, then came one with Vida's head in Jeff's exposed groin.

"See?" Roland said. "You should be glad he's out of the way. But that's not all I did for us. I helped Nell by expediting the inevitable, adjust-ing her medication. Don't worry, it'll all be fine. I know exactly how these things are investigated. This note will help us. Besides, we won't be here."

Lisa struggled against her handcuffs as tears rolled down her face.

"There'll be a huge insurance payout for Nell. I'll have it sent to us. You and I will move to South America to be safe, either Ecuador or Bolivia be-cause both countries have been known to refuse extradition requests. I've been arranging things, creating the documents we need. We'll leave tomorrow on a private medical charter to Belize. You'll be sedated, of course."

Lisa sobbed.

"Don't cry. I know it's a lot to take in right now, and there's a little bit of cleaning up to take care of, but don't be sad. I need you, and you need me."

Blinking through her tears, hair falling in front of her face, she struggled in vain to comprehend her soul-boiling nightmare.

"You have to see the best part." Roland adjusted the controls. "Watch."

New footage showed Lisa and Jeff's bedroom at night. They were sleeping.

"Remember the night you came over here for dinner and felt a little ill? Well, that was me. I had to make sure you'd be amenable to what I needed to do, *what I know you wanted me to do*."

The footage showed Roland emerging from the darkness in Lisa and Jeff's bedroom, removing his clothes and approaching Lisa's side of the bed. She didn't move as he began caressing her, then pulled away the sheets.

"Oh God!" Lisa's face contorted when she saw Roland mount her. "God, no! No!"

The footage then cut to Lisa in her bathroom taking a home pregnancy test, then Lisa on the phone with her doctor.

Then it ended.

"I've known and savored every inch of you." Roland stroked her hair. "I've known every move you've made. I've watched over you, given you everything Jeff couldn't. You *and our child* belong to me now. We can start our new life together. It's our destiny, Lisa."

She screamed.

93

With its wipers working against the rain, the equipment truck used by the Miami-Dade Police Special Response Team rolled into the parking lot of the park three blocks from the Dillards' bungalow.

It eased to a stop next to the RV that Miami-Dade used as the mobile command post. Inside, huddled around a small table, the team commander and SRT squad leaders studied a map of the community and sketched a strategy for an extraction from the target building.

Unseen for several blocks beyond the Dillards' home, marked units established an outer perimeter. Officers choked off traffic at all access points in what was considered the hot zone. Others went door-to-door, quietly evacuating neighbors from houses deemed to be in the line of fire.

Without making a sound, SRT squad members, wearing helmets with night-vision goggles and headset walkie-talkies, and equipped with rifles, shields and other gear, took up strategic positions at key points of the Dillards' house.

A knock rattled the door of the mobile command post. Reddick and Cruz, rain-soaked in ball caps and raid jackets, crowded into the unit. They nodded to Bogan and Morrow.

"So this is it." Reddick wiped his wet face. "Dillard's been our guy all this time."

Morrow nodded. Lightning flashed, and she recalled the images of all the women Dillard had murdered, praying that tonight justice would be done. She turned to the squad commander, who was waiting for the last of his squad to get into position before giving the order for a tactical entry.

94

In the moments before the Special Response Team converged on the Dillards' house, Jeff had stepped into their home.

"Roland? Nell?"

No response.

"Lisa?"

He listened and heard nothing.

Unknowingly, he followed Lisa's path, using his flashlight to inspect the living room, finding nothing but an eerie stillness as the storm roared.

He moved toward the bedrooms, his light poking into every darkened corner, when he was stopped dead by a fearful, hysterical scream. It was his wife.

"Lisa!" he yelled.

Her cry had come from the far side of the house—the safe room.

Jeff ran as fast as he could.

Hearing Jeff's shouting, Dillard flew to the console. Examining the controls, he switched the cameras to thermal imaging.

"Jeff!" Lisa screamed.

Dillard studied the video monitor and saw Jeff approaching.

He pulled on night-vision goggles, unholstered his gun and left the room, disappearing into the darkness.

"Jeff!" Lisa screamed. *"Roland's coming! He has a gun!"*

From his cover position among shrubs near the floor-to-ceiling windows leading to the pool, Sergeant Andy Valdez saw muzzle flashes and heard several rounds of gunfire.

"Shots fired! Inside!" Valdez reported on his radio.

The commander's response came back for the team.

"Green light! Go! Go!"

Windows of the house shattered as flash grenades shot through them with deafening, disorienting fiery explosions and smoke. Heavily armed SRT members rushed into the house, the beams of their red lasers raking the billowing clouds.

"Police!"

Scouring every inch of the residence, they first came upon a man facedown on the floor. A cluster of laser dots danced on his back.

"Put your hands on your head now!"

They saw a handgun near him and removed it from his reach. They came to a second man, facedown, bleeding profusely. He was not moving, but they handcuffed him as a precaution.

As the smoke dissipated, team members came upon a woman, sitting on the floor, her back against the blood-smeared wall. She was bleeding from a gunshot wound in her chest. The handgun on the floor next to her was removed.

The woman was conscious and speaking softly as they handcuffed her. "I told him, I knew. I said, 'It ends here, Roland.'"

Moving farther inside the house, the team came to the safe room, where they found a second woman, handcuffed to a chair.

She was in shock, hysterical and sobbing.

"Please help… He's a monster… Please help us…"

Awed by the sight, team members surveyed the console, control panels and the banks of video cameras. Radios crackled, the house was cleared, and within minutes, Morrow and Cruz arrived to comfort the woman as bolt cutters were brought in to free her.

"It's going to be all right, Lisa," Cruz said.

Morrow studied the monitors, and her breathing quickened. Some of the older recorded images playing on one of them were familiar, featuring faces of women she recognized. As she stepped closer, she felt the rising, sickening realization that The Collector had made videos of all his killings.

To enjoy over and over. This is his trophy room.

Morrow shut her eyes tight before opening them again.

She looked at Lisa trembling, then toward the doorway, knowing the carnage that was a few feet away and that for years, the outside of this pretty suburban home had never betrayed the lies and the evil that dwelled inside.

Morrow lowered herself and took Lisa's face in her hands.

"It's over now."

Epilogue

"This will sting."

A quarter-sized piece of skin was missing from Jeff's left shoulder, exposing flesh where Roland Dillard's bullet had grazed him.

Using tweezers, the doctor picked out threads of charred fabric that had been embedded into his wound. After cleaning it, she applied antibiotic cream, then put on a bandage.

"It's not deep. There's no serious damage, but we'll need to guard against infection." Turning to Lisa, who'd entered the hospital treatment room, the doctor said, "I'll leave you both alone."

Lisa had been examined by medical staff in the adjoining room. The scrapes on her wrists from the handcuffs had been bandaged.

The trauma had not harmed the baby. They took some comfort in that.

She sat next to Jeff. Still in shock, she took Jeff's hand and cried softly as they grappled with the facts. They'd already given statements to the investigators. Lisa's shouted warning had impelled Jeff to dive to the floor, saving his life. Jeff's search for Lisa in the house had led to saving hers.

They were alive. But there were truths that ran to their marrow.

Lisa followed Jeff's alarmed glance to her stomach.

Dillard had left his mark on both of them.

Adrenaline rippling through them, they waited in silence for the crisis counselors.

On another floor of the hospital, in a cramped but private staff room with a corkboard feathered with memos, vacation schedules and notices selling used textbooks, investigators continued their work.

The preliminary investigation indicated that Roland Dillard was firing his handgun at Jeff Taylor when Nell Dillard emerged, opened fire with a handgun on her husband, the two exchanging fire and suffering gunshot wounds.

Roland Dillard had been pronounced dead at the scene.

Nell Dillard had survived her wounds, was still conscious and was making statements, recorded first by an SRT member while at the scene and then recorded by FBI agent Terri Morrow in the ambulance and hospital, up until she was taken to surgery nearly two hours ago.

From talking with Nell, Lisa and doctors, Morrow had pieced together a timeline of events. It appeared that Dillard had altered Nell's medication with the aim of killing her. After she'd consumed it, she'd remained conscious, then discovered him in his room. She'd reached for her phone to call police before Dillard struck her and she collapsed. According to the doctors, Dillard's blow to Nell's head and the altered medication had slowed her vital signs. But the medication failed to take full effect, allowing her to regain consciousness and intervene with a gun.

Now Morrow, Bogan, Reddick and Cruz sat at a table straining to comprehend some of Nell Dillard's recorded statement.

"...for years...I felt...something maybe not right... I saw him...computer, looking at missing-person cases...cities he visited... Taylors moved in...obsessed with the girl, Lisa...obsessed with murder at airport...that room...he was always locked in that room...tonight it was open... He thought I had passed out from my medication but I went in... I saw and I knew...didn't want to believe...but it was true...all those women, their driver's licenses... On his screens...their faces looking at me... I was married to the devil... I knew what he did and I knew what he was going to do... I had to stop him...no more...no more..."

The recording ended.

Reddick shook his head, cursing under his breath.

"This just tears me up," he said. "Dillard was one of us. We worked with him for years. I had dozens of coffees with the guy, discussed cases with him. Dammit. How the hell did he get by us?"

"They always do, Joe," Morrow said. "There's a photo of serial killer John Wayne Gacy shaking hands with the First Lady. Many of these guys are arrested for something small without anyone knowing who they are. Then they're let go and kill again. The smart ones blend in."

A knock, then a weary doctor in scrubs opened the door.

"I wanted to inform you there were complications in surgery. The patient expired minutes ago."

A moment passed.

Morrow nodded and thanked the doctor.

The investigators exchanged looks, then Bogan tapped Morrow's phone.

"This is Nell Dillard's dying declaration now."

The Collector case became national news for weeks.

Jeff and Lisa Taylor declined all interview requests by major news outlets. Journalists sought out people who knew the Dillards, former coworkers, friends, neighbors, anyone with a connection, to shed light on the chilling crimes and how the story unfolded.

In that time, a task force of investigators confirmed through the evidence they'd found that former New York detective Roland Dillard was responsible for Vida Warren's murder and all the known homicides in The Collector case.

In an investigative profile, the *New York Times* reported that Roland Dillard had had a history of psychological issues that had fallen through the cracks because he was a master at hiding his demons. The *Times* revealed that new information had surfaced tying Dillard to two cold-case homicides in New York City and two on Long Island, committed during the time Dillard was a cop.

In a matter related to Vida Warren, police forensic analysis of her photos and interviews with one of Vida's Cleveland friends confirmed the truth of what Jeff wanted Lisa to know: the photos incriminating him were staged by Warren as a drunken prank. But later, desperate to gain custody of her son, Warren had attempted to use them to extort Jeff, with Clete Loften's help. Jeff had never had any physical relationship with Warren.

For his part, Loften still faced the original charges arising from his burglary and attack on Lisa. He also faced new charges, those related to his escape, identity theft, driving without a license, and several related to his conspiring with Warren to attack and rob Jeff and Lisa.

Wanting to put Jeff on edge, Warren had directed Loften to invade the Taylors' home and scare them any way he chose. Investigators believed that Loften had fully intended to sexually assault Lisa before Jeff stopped him. Investigators were also looking at Loften's past activities and the possibility of additional charges in other jurisdictions.

Jeff and Lisa Taylor had committed no crimes, were not guilty of any criminal wrongdoing. They were victims. These facts were presented by detectives to Leland Slaughter and Foster Shore, much to their relief.

Still, Jeff blamed himself for the whole tragedy. The experience had shaken him to his core. His entire value system had undergone a tectonic shift. He'd spent days and nights reevaluating his career, his achievements—everything he'd thought held meaning.

He examined his life until it became crystalline that he'd been wrong about what really mattered to him. Dead wrong. He'd come so close to losing Lisa and realized how her love, the baby, Lisa's honesty and compassion trumped everything. He knew what he had to do, and he was prepared to accept the consequences because, as long as he had Lisa, he had all that he needed in this world.

Jeff went to Shore and Slaughter and admitted to claiming Vida's idea as his own. He returned the bonus money and submitted Vida's original draft and his resignation, as he concluded that it was only right that he be terminated.

The corporation examined the matter and consulted the legal department. Asgaard found that all ideas conceived by employees are the intellectual property of the company, and given that Jeff had infused Vida's concept with significant additional elements, it rejected his resignation. Asgaard returned half of the bonus to Jeff and determined that Vida Warren's estate would receive the other half and that she would be posthumously credited for her contribution. Asgaard then helped establish a trust fund for Warren's son.

Jeff returned to his job. His standing with Asgaard was bruised but offset by what he and Lisa had endured. The firm's South American project was well underway and, after Shore spoke with the London office, Jeff's European assignment was pushed back three months.

"Right now, the priority is to take the time you need to recover," Shore had told him.

Forensic police in white jumpsuits dug meticulously in the Dillards' property, sifting for possible human remains, while news helicopters hovered overhead.

In the days and weeks after the case broke, Lisa watched them from her bedroom window, touching her belly, numb with disbelief. Joy had wanted to fly to Miami to help Lisa heal. Lisa's parents were preparing to join them in Florida, but she rejected her family's offers. She just wasn't ready to see anyone yet.

During his counseling sessions, Jeff fought to come to terms with what Dillard had done.

He told his therapist how one day after the incident, overcome with wrath, he'd ripped out the security system Dillard had installed. Jeff then had a new security company sweep the house for any hidden devices before installing a new system.

The therapist recognized Jeff's action as a way to compensate for his feelings of guilt, loss and helplessness, much like what he'd endured his entire life after his father's tragedy. The counselor then persuaded Jeff to reveal and confront what he'd kept on the flash drive that he'd labeled *Pain*.

It was a journal of his most secret, private thoughts he'd never shared.

Earlier, he had feared that Vida or Loften had stolen it.

He'd only hinted to Lisa what he'd written, only given her a vague idea of what he'd kept secret.

After reading it, Jeff's therapist guided him back to that fall day when he was eleven years old and hunting in the Wisconsin woods with his dad and Charlie. As Jeff sat in his therapist's office, staring at nothing, he remembered it all.

"The coral sky, the smell of the earth, how Dad took a duck and stepped from our cover to get it. He told me to wait. But I was so excited I couldn't stand it. I was going to explode, I wanted to see so badly. I started running with my gun, my heart racing. Charlie called me back. Dad turned, told me to stop running with the gun—something you never do—but I was just thrilled. I—I tripped on deadfall. There was a fiery flash, a bang *from my gun*… Dad folded to the ground before I hit my head and dropped my gun. When I came to, I went to him. I was kneeling over him, my tears falling on him. There was so much blood, and he was gasping his last words, 'Why, son? Why did you run? I told you never to run.' Then I saw the life flow out of him. His death destroyed my mother— ultimately it killed her. I can never fix what I did. I can never forgive myself."

But no one knew that Jeff had fired the shot that killed his dad because, to protect the boy, Charlie had convinced the police it was him. The investigation ruled it an accident. Charlie died of a heart attack the next year, leaving Jeff to live with the truth and a lifetime of guilt.

The therapist told Jeff to recognize his age, his emotions and the context of that morning. "You never intended to hurt your father," she said. "This was an accident, a terrible tragedy. Charlie's attempt to help you was heartfelt but misguided. You have to accommodate the pain, but don't let it control your life. You have to realize that now you have a chance to start over. You have a baby coming—you need to heal for your child."

The therapist acknowledged that Jeff was facing more immediate, profound forces, and she urged him to address them.

He did—he explained how guilty he felt for not protecting Lisa. How sick he felt that he couldn't undo what had been done to her. And how afraid he was of what might be growing inside her.

Dillard was standing naked in the corner of their bedroom.

Step by step, he approached Lisa's side of the bed.

Slowly he peeled back the sheets, reaching for her—

Until she woke. Screaming.

"The nightmares come almost every night," Lisa told her therapist. "Sometimes…sometimes—" Lisa sobbed "—I can feel him inside me."

In her sessions, Lisa bared the truth: that she

feared that she had inadvertently sent Roland Dillard the wrong signal.

"I'm to blame because I set it all in motion. It's my fault," Lisa said. "I think of those other women he killed and wonder why I survived when they didn't. But then I realize my punishment is the evil thing he did to me."

The therapist discussed the randomness of life's tragedies, that Lisa's survivor guilt and self-directed blame were natural responses, much like what she'd grappled with after surviving the childhood tragedy that claimed the life of her friend.

"You could never have known what intentions were writhing inside Roland Dillard," the therapist said. "He deceived everyone, even his wife. He lived behind a mask, covering the fact that he was extremely disturbed and depraved."

The therapist advised Lisa to accept that she was not to blame.

"But on a more immediate level," the therapist began, "you must come to a decision before you get too far along in your pregnancy."

Niki Tanaka had agreed to conduct the prenatal paternity test and booked an appointment for Jeff and Lisa.

During the drive, Lisa held Jeff's hand.

"We won't decide anything until we know the results, okay?" he said.

She nodded, tears welling in her eyes.

The visit was short; all that was required was a

blood sample drawn from Lisa's arm and a mouth swab from Jeff.

"We'll send the samples to the lab," Dr. Tanaka said. "We'll have the results after three days."

Lisa wrestled with a million fears while they waited.

She had insisted they get rid of their bed and replace it with a new one. Jeff agreed, no question.

Then Lisa insisted they had to sell their home and move back to Cleveland. "How can we stay here?"

"Lisa, we have to give this time," Jeff said. "We don't have all the information we need yet to decide anything. Remember?"

Jeff then showed her an article posted on the website for Palm Mirage Creek community news. The story said that the community association was pressing local and state officials to take ownership of the Dillards' home, tear it down and replace it with a park.

"See?" Jeff said. "We can't let this defeat us. You're a fighter, I'm a fighter, and a lot of people here are in our corner."

"I don't know, Jeff," she said. "I just don't know."

Jeff had a plan.

On the third day, while they were still awaiting results, he suggested they rise early and drive to Key West.

"We need to get away, to think of what's ahead."

The drive along the Keys was calming. They

dropped the windows and welcomed the warm breezes. As they drove over Seven Mile Bridge, the sun was glorious on the crystalline turquoise water. While Lisa was anxious about what was coming, the trip was soothing.

They had lunch in Key West, took a walking tour and browsed some of the shops. They grew increasingly nervous as the day passed into late afternoon without word from Lisa's doctor.

As the sun dropped, they made their way to Mallory Square to watch it set on the Gulf of Mexico, fortunate to find a secluded spot away from the celebration. As the blazing sun sank and began kissing the horizon, Lisa's phone rang.

The display showed that it was Dr. Tanaka.

Lisa froze, swallowed, then answered.

"Hi, Lisa. Niki Tanaka. I have the results."

"Wait. I'm going to put you on speaker so Jeff can hear, okay?" Lisa pressed the key.

"I'm really sorry…" Dr. Tanaka began.

Lisa's heart stopped.

"…that it took so long for me to get back to you. Jeff, are you there?"

"I'm here."

"Congratulations, Dad!"

Lisa's hands were shaking, and she fumbled her phone but Jeff caught it.

"Seriously?" he said.

"Absolutely, one hundred percent, you are the father."

Tears streamed down Lisa's face, gleaming in the amber light.

"Do you want to know if it's a boy or a girl?" Tanaka asked.

Lisa was shaking her head.

"We'll wait," Jeff said, his voice breaking. "Thank you, Doctor!"

Jeff took Lisa in his arms as the sun slipped farther below the horizon.

"You were right," Lisa said.

"I was?"

"We're going to survive."

* * * * *

Acknowledgments and a Personal Note

In creating *The Lying House*, I took immense creative license with police procedure, jurisdiction, the law, technology and geography. Still, I hope that, overall, aspects of the novel ring true for readers who know Florida and Ohio better than I do. But please understand that most of the places mentioned in *The Lying House* exist only in my imagination.

Again, creative license.

The Lying House was largely written in Ottawa, but I also worked on it while I was on trains, in airports, on planes, and in hotels in Toronto, Montreal, New York City and St. Petersburg, Florida.

In bringing the story to you, I benefited from the hard work, generosity and support of a lot of people.

As always, my thanks to my wife, Barbara, and to Wendy Dudley for their invaluable help improving the tale.

Very special thanks to Laura and Michael.

My thanks to the super brilliant Amy Moore-Benson and Meridian Artists, the ever-talented Emily Ohanjanians and the incredible editorial, marketing, sales and PR teams at Harlequin, MIRA Books and HarperCollins.

This brings me to what I hold to be the most critical part of the entire enterprise: you, the reader. This aspect has become something of a credo for me, one that bears repeating with each book.

Thank you for your time, for without you, a book remains an untold tale. Thank you for setting your life on pause and taking the journey. I deeply appreciate my audience around the world and those who've been with me since the beginning who keep in touch. Thank you all for your kind words. I hope you enjoyed the ride and will check out my earlier books while watching for my next one.

Feel free to send me a note. I enjoy hearing from you.

Rick Mofina

http://www.Facebook.com/RickMofina
http://Twitter.com/RickMofina
www.RickMofina.com